# THE SEARCH OF KORAK THE KILLER:

Korak, as he had led the march, led the charge. The warriors were struck with horror and dismay at the sight of this white-skinned youth leading a pack of hideous baboons. For an instant they held their ground, hurling their spears once at the advancing multitude; but before they could fit arrows to their bows, they wavered, gave, and turned in terrified rout. Into their ranks, upon their backs, sinking strong fangs into their necks, sprang the baboons. First among them, most blood-thirsty, was Korak the Killer, son of Tarzan, Lord of Greystoke.

Korak left the villagers to the tender mercies of his allies and turned himself eagerly toward the hut in which Meriem had been a prisoner. It was empty. One after another filthy interior revealed the same disheartening fact—Meriem was in none of them. . . .

By Edgar Rice Burroughs
*Published by Ballantine Books:*

*THE TARZAN SERIES*
Tarzan of the Apes (#1)
The Return of Tarzan (#2)
The Beasts of Tarzan (#3)
The Son of Tarzan (#4)
Tarzan and the Jewels of Opar (#5)
Jungle Tales of Tarzan (#6)
Tarzan the Untamed (#7)
Tarzan the Terrible (#8)
Tarzan and the Golden Lion (#9)
Tarzan and the Ant Men (#10)
Tarzan, Lord of the Jungle (#11)
Tarzan and the Lost Empire (#12)
Tarzan at the Earth's Core (#13)
Tarzan the Invincible (#14)
Tarzan Triumphant (#15)
Tarzan and the City of Gold (#16)
Tarzan and the Lion Man (#17)
Tarzan and the Leopard Men (#18)
Tarzan's Quest (#19)
Tarzan and the Forbidden City (#20)
Tarzan the Magnificent (#21)
Tarzan and the Foreign Legion (#22)
Tarzan and the Madman (#23)
Tarzan and the Castaways (#24)

COMPLETE AND UNABRIDGED!

And be sure to look for all 11 books of the *Mars* series and all 6 books of the *Pellucidar* series, also published by Ballantine!

# THE SON OF TARZAN

## Edgar Rice Burroughs

A Del Rey Book
Ballantine Books • New York

TO
HULBERT BURROUGHS

# 1

THE LONG BOAT of the *Marjorie W.* was floating down the broad Ugambi with ebb tide and current. Her crew were lazily enjoying this respite from the arduous labor of rowing up stream. Three miles below them lay the *Marjorie W.* herself, quite ready to sail so soon as they should have clambered aboard and swung the long boat to its davits. Presently the attention of every man was drawn from his dreaming or his gossiping to the northern bank of the river. There, screaming at them in a cracked falsetto and with skinny arms outstretched, stood a strange apparition of a man.

"Wot the 'ell?" ejaculated one of the crew.

"A white man!" muttered the mate, and then: "Man the oars, boys, and we'll just pull over an' see what he wants."

When they came close to the shore they saw an emaciated creature with scant white locks tangled and matted. The thin, bent body was naked but for a loin cloth. Tears were rolling down the sunken pock-marked cheeks. The man jabbered at them in a strange tongue.

"Rooshun," hazarded the mate. "Savvy English?" he called to the man.

He did, and in that tongue, brokenly and haltingly, as though it had been many years since he had used it, he begged them to take him with them away from this awful country. Once on board the *Marjorie W.* the stranger told his rescuers a pitiful tale of privation, hardships, and torture, extending over a period of ten years. How he happened to have come to Africa he did not tell them, leaving them to assume he had forgotten the incidents of his life prior to the frightful ordeals that had wrecked him mentally and physically. He did not even tell them his true name, and so they knew him only as Michael Sabrov, nor was there any resemblance between this sorry wreck and the virile, though unprincipled, Alexis Paulvitch of old.

It had been ten years since the Russian had escaped the fate of his friend, the arch-fiend Rokoff, and not once, but many times during those ten years had Paulvitch cursed the fate that had given to Nicholas Rokoff death and immunity from suffering while it had meted to him the hideous terrors of an existence infinitely worse than the death that persistently refused to claim him.

Paulvitch had taken to the jungle when he had seen the beasts of Tarzan and their savage lord swarm the deck of the *Kincaid*, and in his terror lest Tarzan pursue and capture him he had stumbled on deep into the jungle, only to fall at last into the hands of one of the savage cannibal tribes that had felt the weight of Rokoff's evil temper and cruel brutality. Some strange whim of the chief of this tribe saved Paulvitch from death only to plunge him into a life of misery and torture. For ten years he had been the butt of the village, beaten and stoned by the women and children, cut and slashed and disfigured by the warriors; a victim of often recurring fevers of the most malignant variety. Yet he did not die. Smallpox laid its hideous clutches upon him, leaving him unspeakably branded with its repulsive marks. Between it and the attentions of the tribe the countenance of Alexis Paulvitch was so altered that his own mother could not have recognized in the pitiful mask he called his face a single familiar feature. A few scraggly, yellow-white locks had supplanted the thick, dark hair that had covered his head. His limbs were bent and twisted, he walked with a shuffling, unsteady gait, his body doubled forward. His teeth were gone—knocked out by his savage masters. Even his mentality was but a sorry mockery of what it once had been.

They took him aboard the *Marjorie W.*, and there they fed and nursed him. He gained a little in strength; but his appearance never altered for the better—a human derelict, battered and wrecked, they had found him; a human derelict, battered and wrecked, he would remain until death claimed him. Though still in his thirties, Alexis Paulvitch could easily have passed for eighty. Inscrutable Nature had demanded of the accomplice a greater penalty than his principal had paid.

In the mind of Alexis Paulvitch there lingered no thoughts of revenge—only a dull hatred of the man whom he and Rokoff had tried to break, and failed. There was hatred, too, of the memory of Rokoff, for Rokoff had led him into the horrors he had undergone. There was hatred of the police of a score of cities from which he had had to flee. There was hatred of law, hatred of order, hatred of everything. Every moment of the man's waking life was filled with morbid thought of hatred—he had become mentally as he was physically in outward appearance, the personification of the blighting emotion of Hate. He had little or nothing to do with the men who had rescued him. He was too weak to work and too morose for company, and so they quickly left him alone to his own devices.

The *Marjorie W.* had been chartered by a syndicate of wealthy manufacturers, equipped with a laboratory and a staff of scientists, and sent out to search for some natural product which the manufacturers who footed the bills had been importing from South America at an enormous cost. What the product was none on board the *Marjorie W.* knew except the scientists, nor is it of any moment to us, other than that it led the ship to a certain island off the coast of Africa after Alexis Paulvitch had been taken aboard.

The ship lay at anchor off the coast for several weeks. The monotony of life aboard her became trying for the crew. They went often ashore, and finally Paulvitch asked to accompany them—he too was tiring of the blighting sameness of existence upon the ship.

The island was heavily timbered. Dense jungle ran down almost to the beach. The scientists were far inland, prosecuting their search for the valuable commodity that native rumor upon the mainland had led them to believe might be found here in marketable quantity. The ship's company fished, hunted, and explored. Paulvitch shuffled up and down the beach, or lay in the shade of the great trees that skirted it. One day, as the men were gathered at a little distance inspecting the body of a panther that had fallen to the gun of one of them who had been hunting inland, Paulvitch lay sleeping beneath his tree. He was awakened by the touch of a hand upon his shoulder. With a start he sat up to see a huge, anthropoid ape squatting at his side, inspecting him intently. The Russian was thoroughly frightened. He glanced toward the sailors—they were a couple of hundred yards away. Again the ape plucked at his shoulder, jabbering plaintively. Paulvitch saw no menace in the inquiring gaze, or in the attitude of the beast. He got slowly to his feet. The ape rose at his side.

Half doubled, the man shuffled cautiously away toward the sailors. The ape moved with him, taking one of his arms. They had come almost to the little knot of men before they were seen, and by this time Paulvitch had become assured that the beast meant no harm. The animal evidently was accustomed to the association of human beings. It occurred to the Russian that the ape represented a certain considerable money value, and before they reached the sailors he had decided he should be the one to profit by it.

When the men looked up and saw the oddly paired couple shuffling toward them they were filled with amazement, and started on a run toward the two. The ape showed no sign of fear. Instead he grasped each sailor by the shoulder and peered long and earnestly into his face. Having inspected them all he returned to Paulvitch's side, disappointment written strongly upon his countenance and in his carriage.

The men were delighted with him. They gathered about, asking Paulvitch many questions, and examining his companion. The Russian told them that the ape was his—nothing further would he offer—but kept harping continually upon the same theme, "The ape is mine. The ape is mine." Tiring of Paulvitch, one of the men essayed a pleasantry. Circling about behind the ape he prodded the anthropoid in the back with a pin. Like a flash the beast wheeled upon its tormentor, and, in the brief instant of turning, the placid, friendly animal was metamorphosed to a frenzied demon of rage. The broad grin that had sat upon the sailor's face as he perpetrated his little joke froze to an expression of terror. He attempted to dodge the long arms that reached for him; but, failing, drew a long knife that hung at his belt. With a single wrench the ape tore the weapon from the man's grasp and flung it to one side, then his yellow fangs were buried in the sailor's shoulder.

With sticks and knives the man's companions fell upon the beast, while Paulvitch danced around the cursing snarling pack mumbling and screaming pleas and threats. He saw his visions of wealth rapidly dissipating before the weapons of the sailors.

The ape, however, proved no easy victim to the superior numbers that seemed fated to overwhelm him. Rising from the sailor who had precipitated the battle he shook his giant shoulders, freeing himself from two of the men that were clinging to his back, and with mighty blows of his open palms felled one after another of his attackers, leaping hither and thither with the agility of a small monkey.

The fight had been witnessed by the captain and mate who were just landing from the *Marjorie W.*, and Paulvitch saw these two now running forward with drawn revolvers while the two sailors who had brought them ashore trailed at their heels. The ape stood looking about him at the havoc he had wrought, but whether he was awaiting a renewal of the attack or was deliberating which of his foes he should exterminate first Paulvitch could not guess. What he could guess, however, was that the moment the two officers came within firing distance of the beast they would put an end to him in short order unless something were done and done quickly to prevent. The ape had made no move to attack the Russian but even so the man was none too sure of what might happen were he to interfere with the savage beast, now thoroughly aroused to bestial rage, and with the smell of new spilled blood fresh in its nostrils. For an instant he hesitated, and then again there rose before him the dreams of affluence which this great anthropoid would doubtless turn to realities once Paulvitch had landed him safely in some great metropolis like London.

The captain was shouting to him now to stand aside that he might have a shot at the animal; but instead Paulvitch shuffled to the ape's side, and though the man's hair quivered at its roots he mastered his fear and laid hold of the ape's arm.

"Come!" he commanded, and tugged to pull the beast from among the sailors, many of whom were now sitting up in wide eyed fright or crawling away from their conqueror upon hands and knees.

Slowly the ape permitted itself to be led to one side, nor did it show the slightest indication of a desire to harm the Russian. The captain came to a halt a few paces from the odd pair.

"Get aside, Sabrov!" he commanded. "I'll put that brute where he won't chew up any more able seamen."

"It wasn't his fault, captain," pleaded Paulvitch. "Please don't shoot him. The men started it—they attacked him first. You see, he's perfectly gentle—and he's mine—he's mine—he's mine! I won't let you kill him," he concluded, as his half-wrecked mentality pictured anew the pleasure that money would buy in London—money that he could not hope to possess without some such windfall as the ape represented.

The captain lowered his weapon. "The men started it, did they?" he repeated. "How about that?" and he turned toward the sailors who had by this time picked themselves from the ground, none of them much the worse for his experience except the fellow who had been the cause of it, and who would doubtless nurse a sore shoulder for a week or so.

"Simpson done it," said one of the men. "He stuck a pin into the monk from behind, and the monk got him—which served him bloomin' well right—an' he got the rest of us, too, for which I can't blame him, since we all jumped him to once."

The captain looked at Simpson, who sheepishly admitted the truth of the allegation, then he stepped over to the ape as though to discover for himself the sort of temper the beast possessed, but it was noticeable that he kept his revolver cocked and leveled as he did so. However, he spoke soothingly to the animal who squatted at the Russian's side looking first at one and then another of the sailors. As the captain approached him the ape half rose and waddled forward to meet him. Upon his countenance was the same strange, searching expression that had marked his scrutiny of each of the sailors he had first encountered. He came quite close to the officer and laid a paw upon one of the man's shoulders, studying his face intently for a long moment, then came the expression of disappointment accompanied by what was almost a human sigh, as he turned away to peer in the same curious fashion into the faces of the mate and the two sailors who had arrived with the officers. In each instance he sighed and passed on, returning at length to Paulvitch's side, where he squatted down once more; thereafter evincing little or no interest in any of the other men, and apparently forgetful of his recent battle with them.

When the party returned aboard the *Marjorie W.*, Paulvitch was accompanied by the ape, who seemed anxious to follow him. The captain interposed no obstacles to the arrangement, and so the great anthropoid was tacitly admitted to membership in the ship's company. Once aboard he examined each new face minutely, evincing the same disappointment in each instance that had marked his scrutiny of the others. The officers and scientists aboard often discussed the beast, but they were unable to account satisfactorily for the strange ceremony with which he greeted each new face. Had he been discovered upon the mainland, or any other place than the almost unknown island that had been his home, they would have concluded that he had formerly been a pet of man; but that theory was not tenable in the face of the isolation of his uninhabited island. He seemed continually to be searching for someone, and during the first days of the return voyage from the island he was often discovered nosing about in various parts of the ship; but after he had seen and examined each face of the ship's company, and explored every corner of the vessel he lapsed into utter indifference of all about him. Even the Russian elicited only casual interest when he brought him food. At other times the ape appeared merely to tolerate him. He never showed affection for him, or for anyone else upon the *Marjorie W.*, nor did he at any time evince any indication of the savage temper that had marked his resentment of the attack of the sailors upon him at the time that he had come among them.

Most of his time was spent in the eye of the ship scanning the horizon ahead, as though he were endowed with sufficient reason to know that the vessel was bound for some port where there would be other human beings to undergo his searching scrutiny. All in all, Ajax, as he had been dubbed, was considered the most remarkable and intelligent ape that any one aboard the *Marjorie W.* ever had seen. Nor was his intelligence the only remarkable attribute he owned. His stature and physique were, for an ape, awe inspiring. That he was old was quite evident, but if his age had impaired his physical or mental powers in the slightest it was not apparent.

And so at length the *Marjorie W.* came to England, and there the officers and the scientists, filled with compassion for the pitiful wreck of a man they had rescued from the jungles, furnished Paulvitch with funds and bid him and his Ajax God-speed.

Upon the dock and all through the journey to London the Russian had his hands full with Ajax. Each new face of the thousands that came within the anthropoid's ken must be carefully scrutinized, much to the horror of many of his victims; but at last, failing, apparently, to discover whom he sought, the great ape relapsed into morbid indifference, only occasionally evincing interest in a passing face.

In London, Paulvitch went directly with his prize to a certain famous animal trainer. This man was much impressed with Ajax with the result that he agreed to train him for a lion's share of the profits of exhibiting him, and in the meantime to provide for the keep of both the ape and his owner.

And so came Ajax to London, and there was forged another link in the chain of strange circumstances that were to affect the lives of many people.

# 2

MR. HAROLD MOORE was a bilious-countenanced, studious young man. He took himself very seriously, and life, and his work, which latter was the tutoring of the young son of a British nobleman. He felt that his charge was not making the progress that his parents had a right to expect, and he was now conscientiously explaining this fact to the boy's mother.

"It's not that he isn't bright," he was saying; "if that were true I should have hopes of succeeding, for then I might bring to bear all my energies in overcoming his obtuseness; but the trouble is that he is exceptionally intelligent, and learns so quickly that I can find no fault in the matter of the preparation of his lessons. What concerns me, however, is that fact that he evidently takes no interest whatever in the subjects we are studying. He merely accomplishes each lesson as a task to be rid of as quickly as possible and I am sure that no lesson ever again enters his mind until the hours of study and recitation once more arrive. His sole interests seem to be feats of physical prowess and the reading of everything that he can get hold of relative to savage beasts and the lives and customs of uncivilized peoples; but particularly do stories of animals appeal to him. He will sit for hours together poring over the work of some African explorer, and upon two occasions I have found him setting up in bed at night reading Carl Hagenbeck's book on men and beasts."

The boy's mother tapped her foot nervously upon the hearth rug.

"You discourage this, of course?" she ventured.

Mr. Moore shuffled embarrassedly.

"I—ah—essayed to take the book from him," he replied, a slight flush mounting his sallow cheek; "but—ah—your son is quite muscular for one so young."

8

"He wouldn't let you take it?" asked the mother.

"He would not," confessed the tutor. "He was perfectly good natured about it; but he insisted upon pretending that he was a gorilla and that I was a chimpanzee attempting to steal food from him. He leaped upon me with the most savage growls I ever heard, lifted me completely above his head, hurled me upon his bed, and after going through a pantomime indicative of choking me to death he stood upon my prostrate form and gave voice to a most fearsome shriek, which he explained was the victory cry of a bull ape. Then he carried me to the door, shoved me out into the hall and locked me from his room."

For several minutes neither spoke again. It was the boy's mother who finally broke the silence.

"It is very necessary, Mr. Moore," she said, "that you do everything in your power to discourage this tendency in Jack, he—"; but she got no further. A loud "Whoop!" from the direction of the window brought them both to their feet. The room was upon the second floor of the house, and opposite the window to which their attention had been attracted was a large tree, a branch of which spread to within a few feet of the sill. Upon this branch now they both discovered the subject of their recent conversation, a tall, well-built boy, balancing with ease upon the bending limb and uttering loud shouts of glee as he noted the terrified expressions upon the faces of his audience.

The mother and tutor both rushed toward the window but before they had crossed half the room the boy had leaped nimbly to the sill and entered the apartment with them.

" 'The wild man from Borneo has just come to town,' " he sang, dancing a species of war dance about his terrified mother and scandalized tutor, and ending by throwing his arms about the former's neck and kissing her upon either cheek.

"Oh, Mother," he cried, "there's a wonderful, educated ape being shown at one of the music halls. Willie Grimsby saw it last night. He says it can do everything but talk. It rides a bicycle, eats with knife and fork, counts up to ten, and ever so many other wonderful things, and can I go and see it too? Oh, please, Mother—please let me."

Patting the boy's cheek affectionately, the mother shook her head negatively. "No, Jack," she said; "you know I do not approve of such exhibitions."

"I don't see why not, Mother," replied the boy. "All the other fellows go and they go to the Zoo, too, and you'll never let me do even that. Anybody'd think I was a girl or—or a mollycoddle. Oh, Father," he exclaimed, as the door opened to admit a tall gray-eyed man. "Oh, Father, can't I go?"

"Go where, my son?" asked the newcomer.

"He wants to go to a music hall to see a trained ape," said the mother, looking warningly at her husband.

"Who, Ajax?" questioned the man.

The boy nodded.

"Well, I don't know that I blame you, my son," said the father, "I wouldn't mind seeing him myself. They say he is very wonderful, and that for an anthropoid he is unusually large. Let's all go, Jane—what do you say?" And he turned toward his wife, but that lady only shook her head in a most positive manner, and turning to Mr. Moore asked him if it was not time that he and Jack were in the study for the morning recitations. When the two had left she turned toward her husband.

"John," she said, "something must be done to discourage Jack's tendency toward anything that may excite the cravings for the savage life which I fear he has inherited from you. You know from your own experience how strong is the call of the wild at times. You know that often it has necessitated a stern struggle on your part to resist the almost insane desire which occasionally overwhelms you to plunge once again into the jungle life that claimed you for so many years, and at the same time you know, better than any other, how frightful a fate it would be for Jack, were the trail to the savage jungle made either alluring or easy to him."

"I doubt if there is any danger of his inheriting a taste for jungle life from me," replied the man, "for I cannot conceive that such a thing may be transmitted from father to son. And sometimes, Jane, I think that in your solicitude for his future you go a bit too far in your restrictive measures. His love for animals—his desire, for example, to see this trained ape—is only natural in a healthy, normal boy of his age. Just because he wants to see Ajax is no indication that he would wish to marry an ape, and even should he, far be it from you Jane to have the right to cry 'shame!' " and John Clayton, Lord Greystoke, put an arm about his wife, laughing good-naturedly down into her upturned face before he bent his head and kissed her. Then, more seriously, he continued: "You have never told Jack anything concerning my early life, nor have you permitted me to, and in this I think that you have made a mistake. Had I been able to tell him of the experiences of Tarzan of the Apes I could doubtless have taken much of the glamour and romance from jungle life that naturally surrounds it in the minds of those who have had no experience of it. He might then have profited by my experience, but now, should the jungle lust ever claim him, he will have nothing to guide him but his own impulses, and I know how powerful these may be in the wrong direction at times.''

But Lady Greystoke only shook her head as she had a hundred other times when the subject had claimed her attention in the past.

"No, John," she insisted, "I shall never give my consent to the implanting in Jack's mind of any suggestion of the savage life which we both wish to preserve him from."

It was evening before the subject was again referred to and then it was raised by Jack himself. He had been sitting, curled in a large chair, reading, when he suddenly looked up and addressed his father.

"Why," he asked, coming directly to the point, "can't I go and see Ajax?"

"Your mother does not approve," replied his father.

"Do you?"

"That is not the question," evaded Lord Greystoke. "It is enough that your mother objects."

"I am going to see him," announced the boy, after a few moments of thoughtful silence. "I am not different from Willie Grimsby, or any other of the fellows who have been to see him. It did not harm them and it will not harm me. I could go without telling you; but I would not do that. So I tell you now, beforehand, that I am going to see Ajax."

There was nothing disrespectful or defiant in the boy's tone or manner. His was merely a dispassionate statement of facts. His father could scarce repress either a smile or a show of the admiration he felt for the manly course his son had pursued.

"I admire your candor, Jack," he said. "Permit me to be candid, as well. If you go to see Ajax without permission, I shall punish you. I have never inflicted corporal punishment upon you, but I warn you that should you disobey your mother's wishes in this instance, I shall."

"Yes, sir," replied the boy; and then: "I shall tell you, sir, when I have been to see Ajax."

Mr. Moore's room was next to that of his youthful charge, and it was the tutor's custom to have a look into the boy's each evening as the former was about to retire. This evening he was particularly careful not to neglect his duty, for he had just come from a conference with the boy's father and mother in which it had been impressed upon him that he must exercise the greatest care to prevent Jack visiting the music hall where Ajax was being shown. So, when he opened the boy's door at about half after nine, he was greatly excited, though not entirely surprised to find the future Lord Greystoke fully dressed for the street and about to crawl from his open bed room window.

Mr. Moore made a rapid sprint across the apartment; but the waste of energy was unnecessary, for when the boy heard him within the chamber and realized that he had been discovered he turned back as though to relinquish his planned adventure.

"Where were you going?" panted the excited Mr. Moore.

"I am going to see Ajax," replied the boy, quietly.

"I am astonished," cried Mr. Moore; but a moment later he was infinitely more astonished, for the boy, approaching close to him, suddenly seized him about the waist, lifted him from his feet and threw him face downward upon the bed, shoving his face deep into a soft pillow.

"Be quiet," admonished the victor, "or I'll choke you."

Mr. Moore struggled; but his efforts were in vain. Whatever else Tarzan of the Apes may or may not have handed down to his son he had at least bequeathed him almost as marvelous a physique as he himself had possessed at the same age. The tutor was as putty in the boy's hands. Kneeling upon him, Jack tore strips from a sheet and bound the man's hands behind his back. Then he rolled him over and stuffed a gag of the same material between his teeth, securing it with a strip wound about the back of his victim's head. All the while he talked in a low, conversational tone.

"I am Waja, chief of the Waji," he explained, "and you are Mohammed Dubn, the Arab sheik, who would murder my people and steal my ivory," and he dexterously trussed Mr. Moore's hobbled ankles up behind to meet his hobbled wrists. "Ah—ha! Villain! I have you in me power at last. I go; but I shall return!" And the son of Tarzan skipped across the room, slipped through the open window, and slid to liberty by way of the down spout from an eaves trough.

Mr. Moore wriggled and struggled about the bed. He was sure that he should suffocate unless aid came quickly. In his frenzy of terror he managed to roll off the bed. The pain and shock of the fall jolted him back to something like sane consideration of his plight. Where before he had been unable to think intelligently because of the hysterical fear that had claimed him he now lay quietly searching for some means of escape from his dilemma. It finally occurred to him that the room in which Lord and Lady Greystoke had been sitting when he left them was directly beneath that in which he lay upon the floor. He knew that some time had elapsed since he had come up stairs and that they might be gone by this time, for it seemed to him that he had struggled about the bed, in his efforts to free himself, for an eternity. But the best that he could do was to attempt to attract attention from below, and so, after many failures, he managed to work himself into a position in which he could tap the toe of his boot against the floor. This he proceeded to do at short intervals, until, after what seemed a very long time, he was rewarded by hearing footsteps ascending the stairs, and presently a knock upon the door. Mr. Moore tapped vigorously with his toe—he could not reply in any other way. The knock was repeated after a moment's silence. Again Mr. Moore tapped. Would they never open the door! Laboriously he rolled in the direction of succor. If he could get his back against the door he could then tap upon its base, when surely he must be heard. The knocking was repeated a little louder, and finally a voice called: "Mr. Jack!"

It was one of the house men—Mr. Moore recognized the fellow's voice. He came near to bursting a blood vessel in an endeavor to scream "come in" through the stifling gag. After a moment the man knocked again, quite loudly and again called the boy's name. Receiving no reply he turned the knob, and at the same instant a sudden recollection filled the tutor anew with numbing terror—he had, himself, locked the door behind him when he had entered the room.

He heard the servant try the door several times and then depart. Upon which Mr. Moore swooned.

In the meantime Jack was enjoying to the full the stolen pleasures of the music hall. He had reached the temple of mirth just as Alex's act was commencing, and having purchased a box seat was now leaning breathlessly over the rail watching every move of the great ape, his eyes wide in wonder. The trainer was not slow to note the boy's handsome, eager face, and as one of Ajax's biggest hits consisted in an entry to one or more boxes during his performance, ostensibly in search of a long-lost relative, as the trainer explained, the man realized the effectiveness of sending him into the box with the handsome boy, who, doubtless, would be terror stricken by proximity to the shaggy, powerful beast.

When the time came, therefore, for the ape to return from the wings in reply to an encore the trainer directed its attention to the boy who chanced to be the sole occupant of the box in which he sat. With a spring the huge anthropoid leaped from the stage to the boy's side; but if the trainer had looked for a laughable scene of fright he was mistaken. A broad smile lighted the boy's features as he laid his hand upon the shaggy arm of his visitor. The ape, grasping the boy by either shoulder, peered long and earnestly into his face, while the latter stroked his head and talked to him in a low voice.

Never had Ajax devoted so long a time to an examination of another as he did in this instance. He seemed troubled and not a little excited, jabbering and mumbling to the boy, and now caressing him, as the trainer had never seen him caress a human being before. Presently he clambered over into the box with him and snuggled down close to the boy's side. The audience was delighted; but they were still more delighted when the trainer, the period of his act having elapsed, attempted to persuade Ajax to leave the box. The ape would not budge. The manager, becoming excited at the delay, urged the trainer to greater haste, but when the latter entered the box to drag away the reluctant Ajax he was met by bared fangs and menacing growls.

The audience was delirious with joy. They cheered the ape. They cheered the boy, and they hooted and jeered at the trainer and the manager, which luckless individual had inadvertently shown himself and attempted to assist the trainer.

Finally, reduced to desperation and realizing that this show of mutiny upon the part of his valuable possession might render the animal worthless for exhibition purposes in the future if not immediately subdued, the trainer had hastened to his dressing room and procured a heavy whip. With this he now returned to the box; but when he had threatened Ajax with it but once he found himself facing two infuriated enemies instead of one, for the boy had leaped to his feet, and seizing a chair was standing ready at the ape's side to defend his new found friend. There was no longer a smile upon his handsome face. In his gray eyes was an expression which gave the trainer pause, and beside him stood the giant anthropoid growling and ready.

What might have happened, but for a timely interruption, may only be surmised; but that the trainer would have received a severe mauling, if nothing more, was clearly indicated by the attitudes of the two who faced him.

\* \* \*

It was a pale-faced man who rushed into the Greystoke library to announce that he had found Jack's door locked and had been able to abtain no response to his repeated knocking and calling other than a strange tapping and the sound of what might have been a body moving about upon the floor.

Four steps at a time John Clayton took the stairs that led to the floor above. His wife and the servant hurried after him. Once he called his son's name in a loud voice; but receiving no reply he launched his great weight, backed by all the undiminished power of his giant muscles, against the heavy door. With a snapping of iron butts and a splintering of wood the obstacle burst inward.

At its foot lay the body of the unconscious Mr. Moore, across whom it fell with a resounding thud. Through the opening leaped Tarzan, and a moment later the room was flooded with light from a dozen electric bulbs.

It was several minutes before the tutor was discovered, so completely had the door covered him; but finally he was dragged forth, his gag and bonds cut away, and a liberal application of cold water had hastened returning consciousness.

"Where is Jack?" was John Clayton's first question, and then; "Who did this?" as the memory of Rokoff and the fear of a second abduction seized him.

Slowly Mr. Moore staggered to his feet. His gaze wandered about the room. Gradually he collected his scattered wits. The details of his recent harrowing experience returned to him.

"I tender my resignation, sir, to take effect at once," were his first words. "You do not need a tutor for your son—what he needs is a wild animal trainer."

"But where is he?" cried Lady Greystoke.

"He has gone to see Ajax."

It was with difficulty that Tarzan restrained a smile, and after satisfying himself that the tutor was more scared than injured, he ordered his closed car around and departed in the direction of a certain well-known music hall.

# 3

A S THE TRAINER, with raised lash, hesitated an instant at the entrance to the box where the boy and the ape confronted him, a tall broad-shouldered man pushed past him and entered. As his eyes fell upon the newcomer a slight flush mounted the boy's cheeks.

"Father!" he exclaimed.

The ape gave one look at the English lord, and then leaped toward him, calling out in excited jabbering. The man, his eyes going wide in astonishment, stopped as though turned to stone.

"Akut!" he cried.

The boy looked, bewildered, from the ape to his father, and from his father to the ape. The trainer's jaw dropped as he listened to what followed, for from the lips of the Englishman flowed the gutterals of an ape that were answered in kind by the huge anthropoid that now clung to him.

And from the wings a hideously bent and disfigured old man watched the tableau in the box, his pock-marked features working spasmodically in varying expressions that might have marked every sensation in the gamut from pleasure to terror.

"Long have I looked for you, Tarzan," said Akut. "Now that I have found you I shall come to your jungle and live there always."

The man stroked the beast's head. Through his mind there was running rapidly a train of recollection that carried him far into the depths of the primeval African forest where this huge, man-like beast had fought shoulder to shoulder with him years before. He saw the black Mugambi wielding his deadly knobstick, and beside them, with bared fangs and bristling whiskers, Sheeta the terrible; and pressing close behind savage and the savage panther, the hideous apes of Akut. The man sighed.

Strong within him surged the jungle lust that he had thought dead. Ah! if he could go back even for a brief month of it, to feel again the brush of leafy branches against his naked hide; to smell the musty rot of dead vegetation—frankincense and myrrh to the jungle born; to sense the noiseless coming of the great carnivora upon his trail; to hunt and to be hunted; to kill! The picture was alluring. And then came another picture—a sweet-faced woman, still young and beautiful; friends; a home; a son. He shrugged his giant shoulders.

"It cannot be, Akut," he said; "but if you would return, I shall see that it is done. You could not be happy here—I may not be happy there."

The trainer stepped forward. The ape bared his fangs, growling.

"Go with him, Akut," said Tarzan of the Apes. "I will come and see you tomorrow."

The beast moved sullenly to the trainer's side. The latter, at John Clayton's request, told where they might be found. Tarzan turned toward his son.

"Come!" he said, and the two left the theater. Neither spoke for several minutes after they had entered the limousine. It was the boy who broke the silence.

"The ape knew you," he said, "and you spoke together in the ape's tongue. How did the ape know you, and how did you learn his language?"

And then, briefly and for the first time, Tarzan of the Apes told his son of his early life—of the birth in the jungle, of the death of his parents, and of how Kala, the great she ape had suckled and raised him from infancy almost to manhood. He told him, too, of the dangers and the horrors of the jungle; of the great beasts that stalked one by day and by night; of the periods of drought, and of the cataclysmic rains; of hunger; of cold; of intense heat; of nakedness and fear and suffering. He told him of all those things that seem most horrible to the creature of civilization in the hope that the knowledge of them might expunge from the lad's mind any inherent desire for the jungle. Yet they were the very things that made the memory of the jungle what it was to Tarzan—that made up the composite jungle life he loved. And in the telling he forgot one thing—the principal thing—that the boy at his side, listening with eager ears, was the son of Tarzan of the Apes.

After the boy had been tucked away in bed—and without the threatened punishment—John Clayton told his wife of the events of the evening, and that he had at last acquainted the boy with the facts of his jungle life. The mother, who had long foreseen that her son must some time know of those frightful years during which his father had roamed the jungle, a naked, savage beast of prey, only shook her head, hoping against hope that the lure she knew was still strong in the father's breast had not been transmitted to his son.

Tarzan visited Akut the following day, but though Jack begged to be allowed to accompany him he was refused. This time Tarzan saw the pock-marked old owner of the ape, whom he did not recognize as the wily Paulvitch of former days. Tarzan, influenced by Akut's pleadings, broached the question of the ape's purchase; but Paulvitch would not name any price, saying that he would consider the matter.

When Tarzan returned home Jack was all excitement to hear the details of his visit, and finally suggested that his father buy the ape and bring it home. Lady Greystoke was horrified at the suggestion. The boy was insistent. Tarzan explained that he had wished to purchase Akut and return him to his jungle home, and to this the mother assented. Jack asked to be allowed to visit the ape, but again he was met with flat refusal. He had the address, however, which the trainer had given his father, and two days later he found the opportunity to elude his new tutor—who had replaced the terrified Mr. Moore—and after a considerable search through a section of London which he had never before visited, he found the smelly little quarters of the pock-marked old man. The old fellow himself replied to his knocking, and when he stated that he had come to see Ajax, opened the door and admitted him to the little room which he and the great ape occupied. In former years Paulvitch had been a fastidious scoundrel; but ten years of hideous life among the cannibals of Africa had eradicated the last vestige of niceness from his habits. His apparel was wrinkled and soiled. His hands were unwashed, his few straggling locks uncombed. His room was a jumble of filthy disorder. As the boy entered he saw the great ape squatting upon the bed, the coverlets of which were a tangled wad of filthy blankets and ill-smelling quilts. At sight of the youth the ape leaped to the floor and shuffled forward. The man, not recognizing his visitor and fearing that the ape meant mischief, stepped between them, ordering the ape back to the bed.

"He will not hurt me," cried the boy. "We are friends, and before, he was my father's friend. They knew one another in the jungle. My father is Lord Greystoke. He does not know that I have come here. My mother forbid my coming; but I wished to see Ajax, and I will pay you if you will let me come here often and see him.''

At the mention of the boy's identity Paulvitch's eyes narrowed. Since he had first seen Tarzan again from the wings of the theater there had been forming in his deadened brain the beginnings of a desire for revenge. It is a characteristic of the weak and criminal to attribute to others the misfortunes that are the result of their own wickedness, and so now it was that Alexis Paulvitch was slowly recalling the events of his past life and as he did so laying at the door of the man whom he and Rokoff had so assiduously attempted to ruin and murder all the misfortunes that had befallen him in the failure of their various schemes against their intended victim.

He saw at first no way in which he could, with safety to himself, wreak vengeance upon Tarzan through the medium of Tarzan's son; but that great possibilities for revenge lay in the boy was apparent to him, and so he determined to cultivate the lad in the hope that fate would play into his hands in some way in the future. He told the boy all that he knew of his father's past life in the jungle and when he found that the boy had been kept in ignorance of all these things for so many years, and that he had been forbidden visiting the zoological gardens; that he had had to bind and gag his tutor to find an opportunity to come to the music hall and see Ajax, he guessed immediately the nature of the great fear that lay in the hearts of the boy's parents—that he might crave the jungle as his father had craved it.

And so Paulvitch encouraged the boy to come and see him often, and always he played upon the lad's craving for tales of the savage world with which Paulvitch was all too familiar. He left him alone with Akut much, and it was not long until he was surprised to learn that the boy could make the great beast understand him—that he had actually learned many of the words of the primitive language of the anthropoids.

During this period Tarzan came several times to visit Paulvitch. He seemed anxious to purchase Ajax, and at last he told the man frankly that he was prompted not only by a desire upon his part to return the beast to the liberty of his native jungle; but also because his wife feared that in some way her son might learn the whereabouts of the ape and through his attachment for the beast become imbued with the roving instinct which, as Tarzan explained to Paulvitch, had so influenced his own life.

The Russian could scarce repress a smile as he listened to

Lord Greystoke's words, since scarce a half hour had passed since the future Lord Greystoke had been sitting upon the disordered bed jabbering away to Ajax with all the fluency of a born ape.

It was during this interview that a plan occurred to Paulvitch, and as a result of it he agreed to accept a certain fabulous sum for the ape, and upon receipt of the money to deliver the beast to a vessel that was sailing south from Dover for Africa two days later. He had a double purpose in accepting Clayton's offer. Primarily, the money consideration influenced him strongly, as the ape was no longer a source of revenue to him, having consistently refused to perform upon the stage after having discovered Tarzan. It was as though the beast had suffered himself to be brought from his jungle home and exhibited before thousands of curious spectators for the sole purpose of searching out his long lost friend and master, and, having found him, considered further mingling with the common herd of humans unnecessary. However that may be, the fact remained that no amount of persuasion could influence him even to show himself upon the music hall stage, and upon the single occasion that the trainer attempted force the results were such that the unfortunate man considered himself lucky to have escaped with his life. All that saved him was the accidental presence of Jack Clayton, who had been permitted to visit the animal in the dressing room reserved for him at the music hall, and had immediately interfered when he saw that the savage beast meant serious mischief.

And after the money consideration, strong in the heart of the Russian was the desire for revenge, which had been growing with constant brooding over the failures and miseries of his life, which he attributed to Tarzan; the latest, and by no means the least, of which was Ajax's refusal to longer earn money for him. The ape's refusal he traced directly to Tarzan, finally convincing himself that the ape man had instructed the great anthropoid to refuse to go upon the stage.

Paulvitch's naturally malign disposition was aggravated by the weakening and warping of his mental and physical faculties through torture and privation. From cold, calculating, highly intelligent perversity it had deteriorated into the indiscriminating, dangerous menace of the mentally defective. His plan, however, was sufficiently cunning to at least cast a doubt upon the assertion that his mentality was wandering. It assured him first of the competence which Lord Greystoke had promised to pay him for the deportation of the ape, and then of revenge upon his benefactor through the son he idolized. That part of his scheme was crude and brutal—it lacked the refinement of torture that had marked the master strokes of the Paulvitch of old, when he had worked with that virtuoso of villainy, Nickolas Rokoff—but it at least assured Paulvitch of immunity from responsibility, placing that upon the ape, who would thus also be punished for his refusal longer to support the Russian.

Everything played with fiendish unanimity into Paulvitch's hands. As chance would have it, Tarzan's son overheard his father relating to the boy's mother the steps he was taking to return Akut safely to his jungle home, and having overheard he begged them to bring the ape home that he might have him for a play-fellow. Tarzan would not have been averse to this plan; but Lady Greystoke was horrified at the very thought of it. Jack pleaded with his mother; but all unavailingly. She was obdurate, and at last the lad appeared to acquiesce in his mother's decision that the ape must be returned to Africa and the boy to school, from which he had been absent on vacation.

He did not attempt to visit Paulvitch's room again that day, but instead busied himself in other ways. He had always been well supplied with money, so that when necessity demanded he had no difficulty in collecting several hundred pounds. Some of this money he invested in various strange purchases which he managed to smuggle into the house, undetected, when he returned late in the afternoon.

The next morning, after giving his father time to precede him and conclude his business with Paulvitch, the lad hastened to the Russian's room. Knowing nothing of the man's true character the boy dared not take him fully into his confidence for fear that the old fellow would not only refuse to aid him, but would report the whole affair to his father. Instead, he simply asked permission to take Ajax to Dover. He explained that it would relieve the old man of a tiresome journey, as well as placing a number of pounds in his pocket, for the lad purposed playing the Russian well.

"You see," he went on, "there will be no danger of detection since I am supposed to be leaving on an afternoon train for school. Instead I will come here after they have left me on board the train. Then I can take Ajax to Dover, you see, and arrive at school only a day late. No one will be the wiser, no harm will be done, and I shall have had an extra day with Ajax before I lose him forever."

The plan fitted perfectly with that which Paulvitch had in

mind. Had he known what further the boy contemplated he would doubtless have entirely abandoned his own scheme of revenge and aided the boy whole heartedly in the consummation of the lad's, which would have been better for Paulvitch, could he have but read the future but a few short hours ahead.

That afternoon Lord and Lady Greystoke bid their son good-bye and saw him safely settled in a first-class compartment of the railway carriage that would set him down at school in a few hours. No sooner had they left him, however, than he gathered his bags together, descended from the compartment and sought a cab stand outside the station. Here he engaged a cabby to take him to the Russian's address. It was dusk when he arrived. He found Paulvitch awaiting him. The man was pacing the floor nervously. The ape was tied with a stout cord to the bed. It was the first time that Jack had ever seen Ajax thus secured. He looked questioningly at Paulvitch. The man, mumbling, explained that he believed the animal had guessed that he was to be sent away and he feared he would attempt to escape.

Paulvitch carried another piece of cord in his hand. There was a noose in one end of it which he was continually playing with. He walked back and forth, up and down the room. His pock-marked features were working horribly as he talked silent to himself. The boy had never seen him thus—it made him uneasy. At last Paulvitch stopped on the opposite side of the room, far from the ape.

"Come here," he said to the lad. "I will show you how to secure the ape should he show signs of rebellion during the trip."

The lad laughed. "It will not be necessary," he replied. "Ajax will do whatever I tell him to do."

The old man stamped his foot angrily. "Come here, as I tell you," he repeated. "If you do not do as I say you shall not accompany the ape to Dover—I will take no chances upon his escaping."

Still smiling, the lad crossed the room and stood before the Russ.

"Turn around, with your back toward me," directed the latter, "that I may show you how to bind him quickly."

The boy did as he was bid, placing his hands behind him when Paulvitch told him to do so. Instantly the old man slipped the running noose over one of the lad's wrists, took a couple of half hitches about his other wrist, and knotted the cord.

The moment that the boy was secured the attitude of the man

changed. With an angry oath he wheeled his prisoner about, tripped him and hurled him violently to the floor, leaping upon his breast as he fell. From the bed the ape growled and struggled with his bonds. The boy did not cry out—a trait inherited from his savage sire whom long years in the jungle following the death of his foster mother, Kala the great ape, had taught that there was none to come to the succor of the fallen.

Paulvitch's fingers sought the lad's throat. He grinned down horribly into the face of his victim.

"Your father ruined me," he mumbled. "This will pay him. He will think that the ape did it. I will tell him that the ape did it. That I left him alone for a few minutes, and that you sneaked in and the ape killed you. I will throw your body upon the bed after I have choked the life from you, and when I bring your father he will see the ape squatting over it," and the twisted fiend cackled in gloating laughter. His fingers closed upon the boy's throat.

Behind them the growling of the maddened beast reverberated against the walls of the little room. The boy paled, but no other sign of fear or panic showed upon his countenance. He was the son of Tarzan. The fingers tightened their grip upon his throat. It was with difficulty that he breathed, gaspingly. The ape lunged against the stout cord that held him. Turning, he wrapped the cord about his hands, as a man might have done, and surged heavily backward. The great muscles stood out beneath his shaggy hide. There was a rending as of splintered wood—the cord held, but a portion of the footboard of the bed came away.

At the sound Paulvitch looked up. His hideous face went white with terror—the ape was free.

With a single bound the creature was upon him. The man shrieked. The brute wrenched him from the body of the boy. Great fingers sunk into the man's flesh. Yellow fangs gaped close to his throat—he struggled, futilely—and when they closed, the soul of Alexis Paulvitch passed into the keeping of the demons who had long been awaiting it.

The boy struggled to his feet, assisted by Akut. For two hours under the instructions of the former the ape worked upon the knots that secured his friend's wrists. Finally they gave up their secret, and the boy was free. Then he opened one of his bags and drew forth some garments. His plans had been well made. He did not consult the beast, which did all that he directed. Together they slunk from the house, but no casual observer might have noted that one of them was an ape.

# 4

THE KILLING OF the friendless old Russian, Michael Sabrov, by his great trained ape, was a matter for newspaper comment for a few days. Lord Greystoke read of it, and while taking special precautions not to permit his name to become connected with the affair, kept himself well posted as to the police search for the anthropoid.

As was true of the general public, his chief interest in the matter centered about the mysterious disappearance of the slayer. Or at least this was true until he learned, several days subsequent to the tragedy, that his son Jack had not reported at the public school en route for which they had seen him safely ensconced in a railway carriage. Even then the father did not connect the disappearance of his son with the mystery surrounding the whereabouts of the ape. Nor was it until a month later that careful investigation revealed the fact that the boy had left the train before it pulled out of the station at London, and the cab driver had been found who had driven him to the address of the old Russian, that Tarzan of the Apes realized that Akut had in some way been connected with the disappearance of the boy.

Beyond the moment that the cab driver had deposited his fare beside the curb in front of the house in which the Russian had been quartered there was no clue. No one had seen either the boy or the ape from that instant—at least no one who still lived. The proprietor of the house identified the picture of the lad as that of one who had been a frequent visitor in the room of the old man. Aside from this he knew nothing. And there, at the door of a grimy, old building in the slums of London, the searchers came to a blank wall—baffled.

The day following the death of Alexis Paulvitch a youth accompanying his invalid grandmother, boarded a steamer at

Dover. The old lady was heavily veiled, and so weakened by age and sickness that she had to be wheeled aboard the vessel in an invalid chair.

The boy would permit none but himself to wheel her, and with his own hands assisted her from the chair to the interior of their stateroom—and that was the last that was seen of the old lady by the ship's company until the pair disembarked. The boy even insisted upon doing the work of their cabin steward, since, as he explained, his grandmother was suffering from a nervous disposition that made the presence of strangers extremely distasteful to her.

Outside the cabin—and none there was aboard who knew what he did in the cabin—the lad was just as any other healthy, normal English boy might have been. He mingled with his fellow passengers, became a prime favorite with the officers, and struck up numerous friendships among the common sailors. He was generous and unaffected, yet carried an air of dignity and strength of character that inspired his many new friends with admiration as well as affection for him.

Among the passengers there was an American named Condon, a noted blackleg and crook who was "wanted" in a half dozen of the larger cities of the United States. He had paid little attention to the boy until on one occasion he had seen him accidentally display a roll of bank notes. From then on Condon cultivated the youthful Briton. He learned, easily, that the boy was traveling alone with his invalid grandmother, and that their destination was a small port on the west coast of Africa, a little below the equator; that their name was Billings, and that they had no friends in the little settlement for which they were bound. Upon the point of their purpose in visiting the place Condon found the boy reticent, and so he did not push the matter—he had learned all that he cared to know as it was.

Several times Condon attempted to draw the lad into a card game; but his victim was not interested, and the black looks of several of the other men passengers decided the American to find other means of transferring the boy's bank roll to his own pocket.

At last came the day that the steamer dropped anchor in the lee of a wooded promontory where a score or more of sheet-iron shacks making an unsightly blot upon the fair face of nature proclaimed the fact that civilization had set its heel. Straggling upon the outskirts were the thatched huts of natives, picturesque in their primeval savagery, harmonizing with the background of tropical jungle and accentuating the squalid hideousness of the white man's pioneer architecture.

The boy, leaning over the rail, was looking far beyond the man-made town deep into the God-made jungle. A little shiver of anticipation tingled his spine, and then, quite without volition, he found himself gazing into the loving eyes of his mother and the strong face of the father which mirrored, beneath its masculine strength, a love no less than the mother's eyes proclaimed. He felt himself weakening in his resolve. Nearby one of the ship's officers was shouting orders to a flotilla of native boats that was approaching to lighter the consignment of the steamer's cargo destined for this tiny post.

"When does the next steamer for England touch here?" the boy asked.

"The *Emanuel* ought to be along most any time now," replied the officer. "I figgered we'd find her here," and he went on with his bellowing remarks to the dusky horde drawing close to the steamer's side.

The task of lowering the boy's grandmother over the side to a waiting canoe was rather difficult. The lad insisted on being always at her side, and when at last she was safely ensconced in the bottom of the craft that was to bear them shoreward her grandson dropped catlike after her. So interested was he in seeing her comfortably disposed that he failed to notice the little package that had worked from his pocket as he assisted in lowering the sling that contained the old woman over the steamer's side, nor did he notice it even as it slipped out entirely and dropped into the sea.

Scarcely had the boat containing the boy and the old woman started for the shore than Condon hailed a canoe upon the other side of the ship, and after bargaining with its owner finally lowered his baggage and himself aboard. Once ashore he kept out of sight of the two-story atrocity that bore the legend "Hotel" to lure unsuspecting wayfarers to its multitudinous discomforts. It was quite dark before he ventured to enter and arrange for accommodations.

In a back room upon the second floor the lad was explaining, not without considerable difficulty, to his grandmother that he had decided to return to England upon the next steamer. He was endeavoring to make it plain to the old lady that she might remain in Africa if she wished but that for his part his conscience demanded that he return to his father and mother, who doubtless were even now suffering untold sorrow because of his absence;

from which it may be assumed that his parents had not been acquainted with the plans that he and the old lady had made for their adventure into African wilds.

Having come to a decision the lad felt a sense of relief from the worry that had haunted him for many sleepless nights. When he closed his eyes in sleep it was to dream of a happy reunion with those at home. And as he dreamed, Fate, cruel and inexorable, crept stealthily upon him through the dark corridor of the squalid building in which he slept—Fate in the form of the American crook, Condon.

Cautiously the man approached the door of the lad's room. There he crouched listening until assured by the regular breathing of those within that both slept. Quietly he inserted a slim, skeleton key in the lock of the door. With deft fingers, long accustomed to the silent manipulation of the bars and bolts that guarded other men's property, Condon turned the key and the knob simultaneously. Gentle pressure upon the door swung it slowly inward upon its hinges. The man entered the room, closing the door behind him. The moon was temporarily overcast by heavy clouds. The interior of the apartment was shrouded in gloom. Condon groped his way toward the bed. In the far corner of the room something moved—moved with a silent stealthiness which transcended even the trained silence of the burglar. Condon heard nothing. His attention was riveted upon the bed in which he thought to find a young boy and his helpless, invalid grandmother.

The American sought only the bank roll. If he could possess himself of this without detection, well and good; but were he to meet resistance he was prepared for that too. The lad's clothes lay across a chair beside the bed. The American's fingers felt swiftly through them—the pockets contained no roll of crisp, new notes. Doubtless they were beneath the pillows of the bed. He stepped closer toward the sleeper; his hand was already half way beneath the pillow when the thick cloud that had obscured the moon rolled aside and the room was flooded with light. At the same instant the boy opened his eyes and looked straight into those of Condon. The man was suddenly conscious that the boy was alone in the bed. Then he clutched for his victim's throat. As the lad rose to meet him Condon heard a low growl at his back, then he felt his wrists seized by the boy, and realized that beneath those tapering, white fingers played muscles of steel.

He felt other hands at his throat, rough hairy hands that reached over his shoulders from behind. He cast a terrified glance backward, and the hairs of his head stiffened at the sight his eyes revealed, for grasping him from the rear was a huge, man-like ape. The bared fighting fangs of the anthropoid were close to his throat. The lad pinioned his wrists. Neither uttered a sound. Where was the grandmother? Condon's eyes swept the room in a single all-inclusive glance. His eyes bulged in horror at the realization of the truth which that glance revealed. In the power of what creatures of hideous mystery had he placed himself! Frantically he fought to beat off the lad that he might turn upon the fearsome thing at his back. Freeing one hand he struck a savage blow at the lad's face. His act seemed to unlose a thousand devils in the hairy creature clinging to his throat. Condon heard a low and savage snarl. It was the last thing that the American ever heard in this life. Then he was dragged backward upon the floor, a heavy body fell upon him, powerful teeth fastened themselves in his jugular, his head whirled in the sudden blackness which rims eternity—a moment later the ape rose from his prostrate form; but Condon did not know—he was quite dead.

The lad, horrified, sprang from the bed to lean over the body of the man. He knew that Akut had killed in his defense, as he had killed Michael Sabrov; but here, in savage Africa, far from home and friends what would they do to him and his faithful ape? The lad knew that the penalty of murder was death. He even knew that an accomplice might suffer the death penalty with the principal. Who was there here who would plead for them? All would be against them. It was little more than a half-civilized community, and the chances were that they would drag Akut and him forth in the morning and hang them both to the nearest tree—he had read of such things being done in America, and Africa was worse even and wilder than the great West of his mother's native land. Yes, they would both be hanged in the morning!

Was there no escape? He thought in silence for a few moments, and then, with an exclamation of relief, he struck his palms together and turned toward his clothing upon the chair. Money would do anything! Money would save him and Akut! He felt for the bank roll in the pocket in which he had been accustomed to carry it. It was not there! Slowly at first and at last frantically he searched through the remaining pockets of his clothing. Then he dropped upon his hands and knees and examined the floor. Lighting the lamp he moved the bed to one side and, inch by inch, felt over the entire floor. Beside the body of Condon he hesitated, but at last he nerved himself to touch it. Rolling it over he sought beneath it for the money. Nor was it there. He guessed that Condon had entered their room to rob; but he did not believe that the man had had time to possess himself of the money; however, as it was nowhere else, it must be upon the body of the dead man. Again and again he went over the room, only to return each time to the corpse; but no where could he find the money.

He was half-frantic with despair. What were they to do? In the morning they would be discovered and killed. For all his inherited size and strength he was, after all, only a little boy— a frightened, homesick little boy—reasoning faultily from the meager experience of childhood. He could think of but a single glaring fact—they had killed a fellow man, and they were among savage strangers, thirsting for the blood of the first victim whom fate cast into their clutches. This much he had gleaned from penny-dreadfuls.

And they must have money!

Again he approached the corpse. This time resolutely. The ape squatted in a corner watching his young companion. The youth commenced to remove the American's clothing piece by piece, and, piece by piece, he examined each garment minutely. Even to the shoes he searched with painstaking care, and when the last article had been removed and scrutinized he dropped back upon the bed with dilated eyes that saw nothing in the present—only a grim tableau of the future in which two forms swung silently from the limb of a great tree.

How long he sat thus he did not know; but finally he was aroused by a noise coming from the floor below. Springing quickly to his feet he blew out the lamp, and crossing the floor silently locked the door. Then he turned toward the ape, his mind made up.

Last evening he had been determined to start for home at the first opportunity, to beg the forgiveness of his parents for this mad adventure. Now he knew that he might never return to them. The blood of a fellow man was upon his hands—in his morbid reflections he had long since ceased to attribute the death of Condon to the ape. The hysteria of panic had fastened the guilt upon himself. With money he might have bought justice; but penniless!—ah, what hope could there be for strangers without money here?

But what had become of the money? He tried to recall when last he had seen it. He could not, nor, could he, would he have been able to account for its disappearance, for he had been entirely unconscious of the falling of the little package from his pocket into the sea as he clambered over the ship's side into the waiting canoe that bore him to shore.

Now he turned toward Akut. "Come!" he said, in the language of the great apes. Forgetful of the fact that he wore only a thin pajama suit he led the way to the open window. Thrusting his head out he listened attentively. A single tree grew a few feet from the window. Nimbly the lad sprang to its bole, clinging cat-like for an instant before he clambered quietly to the ground below. Close behind him came the great ape. Two hundred yards away a spur of the jungle ran close to the straggling town. Toward this the lad led the way. None saw them, and a moment later the jungle swallowed them, and John Clayton, future Lord Greystoke, passed from the eyes and the knowledge of men.

It was late the following morning that a native houseman knocked upon the door of the room that had been assigned to Mrs. Billings and her grandson. Receiving no response he inserted his pass key in the lock, only to discover that another key was already there, but from the inside. He reported the fact to Herr Skopf, the proprietor, who at once made his way to the second floor where he, too, pounded vigorously upon the door. Receiving no reply he bent to the key hole in an attempt to look through into the room beyond. In so doing, being portly, he lost his balance, which necessitated putting a palm to the floor to maintain his equilibrium. As he did so he felt something soft and thick and wet beneath his fingers. He raised his open palm before his eyes and peered at it in the dim light of the corridor and peered at it. Then he gave a little shudder, for even in the semi-darkness he saw a dark red stain upon his hand. Leaping to his feet he hurled his shoulder against the door. Herr Skopf is a heavy man—or at least he was then—I have not seen him for several years. The frail door collapsed beneath his weight, and Herr Skopf stumbled precipitately into the room beyond.

Before him lay the greatest mystery of his life. Upon the floor at his feet was the dead body of a strange man. The neck was broken and the jugular severed as by the fangs of a wild beast. The body was entirely naked, the clothing being strewn about the corpse. The old lady and her grandson were gone. The window was open. They must have disappeared through the window for the door had been locked from the inside.

But how could the boy have carried his invalid grandmother from a second story window to the ground? It was preposterous. Again Herr Skopf searched the small room. He noticed that the bed was pulled well away from the wall—why? He looked beneath it again for the third or fourth time. The two were gone, and yet his judgment told him that the old lady could not have gone without porters to carry her down as they had carried her up the previous day.

Further search deepened the mystery. All the clothing of the two was still in the room—if they had gone then they must have gone naked or in their night clothes. Herr Skopf shook his head; then he scratched it. He was baffled. He had never heard of Sherlock Holmes or he would have lost no time in invoking the aid of that celebrated sleuth, for here was a real mystery: An old woman—an invalid who had to be carried from the ship to her room in the hotel—and a handsome lad, her grandson, had entered a room on the second floor of his hostelry the day before. They had had their evening meal served in their room— that was the last that had been seen of them. At nine the following morning the corpse of a strange man had been the sole occupant of that room. No boat had left the harbor in the meantime—there was not a railroad within hundreds of miles—there was no other white settlement that the two could reach under several day of arduous marching accompanied by a well-equipped *safari*. They had simply vanished into thin air, for the native he had sent to inspect the ground beneath the open window had just returned to report that there was no sign of a footstep there, and what sort of creatures were they who could have dropped that distance to the soft turf without leaving spoor? Herr Skopf shuddered. Yes, it was a great mystery—there was something uncanny about the whole thing—he hated to think about it, and he dreaded the coming of night.

It was a great mystery to Herr Skopf—and, doubtless, still is.

# 5

CAPTAIN ARMAND JACOT of the Foreign Legion sat upon an outspread saddle blanket at the foot of a stunted palm tree. His broad shoulders and his close-cropped head rested in luxurious ease against the rough bole of the palm. His long legs were stretched straight before him overlapping the meager blanket, his spurs buried in the sandy soil of the little desert oasis. The captain was taking his ease after a long day of weary riding across the shifting sands of the desert.

Lazily he puffed upon his cigarette and watched his orderly who was preparing his evening meal. Captain Armand Jacot was well satisfied with himself and the world. A little to his right rose the noisy activity of his troop of sun-tanned veterans, released for the time from the irksome trammels of discipline, relaxing tired muscles, laughing, joking, and smoking as they, too, prepared to eat after a twelve hour fast. Among them, silent and taciturn, squatted five white-robed Arabs, securely bound and under heavy guard.

It was the sight of these that filled Captain Armand Jacot with the pleasurable satisfaction of a duty well-performed. For a long, hot, gaunt month he and his little troop had scoured the places of the desert waste in search of a band of marauders to the sin-stained account of which were charged innumerable thefts of camels, horses, and goats, as well as murders enough to have sent the whole unsavory gang to the guillotine several times over.

A week before, he had come upon them. In the ensuing battle he had lost two of his own men, but the punishment inflicted upon the marauders had been severe almost to extinction. A half dozen, perhaps, had escaped; but the balance, with the exception of the five prisoners, had expiated their crimes before the nickel jacketed bullets of the legionaries. And, best of all, the ring leader, Achmet ben Houdin, was among the prisoners.

From the prisoners Captain Jacot permitted his mind to traverse the remaining miles of sand to the little garrison post where, upon the morrow, he should find awaiting him with eager welcome his wife and little daughter. His eyes softened to the memory of them, as they always did. Even now he could see the beauty of the mother reflected in the childish lines of little Jeanne's face, and both those faces would be smiling up into his as he swung from his tired mount late the following afternoon. Already he could feel a soft cheek pressed close to each of his—velvet against leather.

His reverie was broken in upon by the voice of a sentry summoning a non-commissioned officer. Captain Jacot raised his eyes. The sun had not yet set: but the shadows of the few trees huddled about the water hole and of his men and their horses stretched far away into the east across the now golden sand. The sentry was pointing in this direction, and the corporal, through narrowed lids, was searching the distance. Captain Jacot rose to his feet. He was not a man content to see through the eyes of others. He must see for himself. Usually he saw things long before others were aware that there was anything to see—a trait that had won for him the sobriquet of Hawk. Now he saw, just beyond the long shadows, a dozen specks rising and falling among the sands. They disappeared and reappeared, but always they grew larger. Jacot recognized them immediately. They were horsemen—horsemen of the desert. Already a sergeant was running toward him. The entire camp was straining its eyes into the distance. Jacot gave a few terse orders to the sergeant who saluted, turned upon his heel and returned to the men. Here he gathered a dozen who saddled their horses, mounted and rode out to meet the strangers. The remaining men disposed themselves in readiness for instant action. It was not entirely beyond the range of possibilities that the horsemen riding thus swiftly toward the camp might be friends of the prisoners bent upon the release of their kinsmen by a sudden attack. Jacot doubted this, however, since the strangers were evidently making no attempt to conceal their presence. They were galloping rapidly toward the camp in plain view of all. There might be treachery lurking beneath their fair appearance; but none who knew The Hawk would be so gullible as to hope to trap him thus.

The sergeant with his detail met the Arabs two hundred yards from the camp. Jacot could see him in conversation with a tall, white-robed figure—evidently the leader of the band. Presently the sergeant and this Arab rode side by side toward camp. Jacot awaited them. The two reined in and dismounted before him.

"Sheik Amor ben Khatour," announced the sergeant by way of introduction.

Captain Jacot eyed the newcomer. He was acquainted with nearly every principal Arab within a radius of several hundred miles. This man he never had seen. He was a tall, weather beaten, sour looking man of sixty or more. His eyes were narrow and evil. Captain Jacot did not relish his appearance.

"Well?" he asked, tentatively.

The Arab came directly to the point.

"Achmet ben Houdin is my sister's son," he said. "If you will give him into my keeping I will see that he sins no more against the laws of the French."

Jacot shook his head. "That cannot be," he replied. "I must take him back with me. He will be properly and fairly tried by a civil court. If he is innocent he will be released."

"And if he is not innocent?" asked the Arab.

"He is charged with many murders. For any one of these, if he is proved guilty, he will have to die."

The Arab's left hand was hidden beneath his burnous. Now he withdrew it disclosing a large goatskin purse, bulging and heavy with coins. He opened the mouth of the purse and let a handful of the contents trickle into the palm of his right hand—all were pieces of good French gold. From the size of the purse and its bulging proportions Captain Jacot concluded that it must contain a small fortune. Sheik Amor ben Khatour dropped the spilled gold pieces one by one back into the purse. Jacot was eyeing him narrowly. They were alone. The sergeant, having introduced the visitor, had withdrawn to some little distance—his back was toward them. Now the sheik, having returned all the gold pieces, held the bulging purse outward upon his open palm toward Captain Jacot.

"Achmet ben Houdin, my sister's son, *might* escape tonight," he said. "Eh?"

Captain Armand Jacot flushed to the roots of his close-cropped hair. Then he went very white and took a half-step toward the Arab. His fists were clenched. Suddenly he thought better of whatever impulse was moving him.

"Sergeant!" he called. The non-commissioned officer hurried toward him, saluting as his heels clicked together before his superior.

"Take this black dog back to his people," he ordered. "See that they leave at once. Shoot the first man who comes within range of camp tonight."

Sheik Amor ben Khatour drew himself up to his full height. His evil eyes narrowed. He raised the bag of gold level with the eyes of the French officer.

"You will pay more than this for the life of Achmet ben Houdin, my sister's son," he said. "And as much again for the name that you have called me and a hundred fold in sorrow in the bargain."

"Get out of here!" growled Captain Armand Jacot, "before I kick you out."

All of this happened some three years before the opening of this tale. The trail of Achmet ben Houdin and his accomplices is a matter of record—you may verify it if you care to. He met the death he deserved, and he met it with the stoicism of the Arab.

A month later little Jeanne Jacot, the seven-year-old daughter of Captain Armand Jacot, mysteriously disappeared. Neither the wealth of her father and mother, or all the powerful resources of the great republic were able to wrest the secret of her whereabouts from the inscrutable desert that had swallowed her and her abductor.

A reward of such enormous proportions was offered that many adventurers were attracted to the hunt. This was no case for the modern detective of civilization, yet several of these threw themselves into the search—the bones of some are already bleaching beneath the African sun upon the silent sands of the Sahara.

Two Swedes, Carl Jenssen and Sven Malbihn, after three years of following false leads at last gave up the search far to the south of the Sahara to turn their attention to the more profitable business of ivory poaching. In a great district they were already known for their relentless cruelty and their greed for ivory. The natives feared and hated them. The European governments in whose possessions they worked had long sought them; but, working their way slowly out of the north they had learned many things in the no-man's-land south of the Sahara which gave them immunity from capture through easy avenues of escape that were unknown to those who pursued them. Their raids were sudden and swift. They seized ivory and retreated into the trackless wastes of the north before the guardians of the territory raped could be made aware of their presence. Relentlessly they slaughtered elephants themselves as well as stealing ivory from the natives. Their following consisted of a hundred or more

renegade Arabs and Negro slaves—a fierce, relentless band of
cut-throats. Remember them—Carl Jenssen and Sven Malbihn,
yellow-bearded, Swedish giants—for you will meet them later.

In the heart of the jungle, hidden away upon the banks of a
small unexplored tributary of a large river that empties into the
Atlantic not so far from the equator, lay a small, heavily pali-
saded village. Twenty palm-thatched, beehive huts sheltered its
black population, while a half-dozen goat skin tents in the center
of the clearing housed the score of Arabs who found shelter here
while, by trading and raiding, they collected the cargoes which
their ships of the desert bore northward twice each year to the
market of Timbuktu.

Playing before one of the Arab tents was a little girl of ten—
a black-haired, black-eyed little girl who, with her nut-brown
skin and graceful carriage looked every inch a daughter of the
desert. Her little fingers were busily engaged in fashioning a
skirt of grasses for a much-disheveled doll which a kindly disposed slave had made for her a year or two before. The head of
the doll was rudely chipped from ivory, while the body was a
rat skin stuffed with grass. The arms and legs were bits of wood,
perforated at one end and sewn to the rat skin torso. The doll
was quite hideous and altogether disreputable and soiled, but
Meriem thought it the most beautiful and adorable thing in the
whole world, which is not so strange in view of the fact that it
was the only object within that world upon which she might
bestow her confidence and her love.

Everyone else with whom Meriem came in contact was, almost without exception, either indifferent to her or cruel. There
was, for example, the old black hag who looked after her, Mabunu—toothless, filthy and ill tempered. She lost no opportunity
to cuff the little girl, or even inflict minor tortures upon her,
such as pinching, or, as she had twice done, searing the tender
flesh with hot coals. And there was The Sheik, her father. She
feared him more than she did Mabunu. He often scolded her for
nothing, quite habitually terminating his tirades by cruelly beating her, until her little body was black and blue.

But when she was alone she was happy, playing with Geeka,
or decking her hair with wild flowers, or making ropes of
grasses. She was always busy and always singing—when they
left her alone. No amount of cruelty appeared sufficient to crush
the innate happiness and sweetness from her full little heart.
Only when The Sheik was near was she quiet and subdued. Him

she feared with a fear that was at times almost hysterical terror. She feared the gloomy jungle too—the cruel jungle that surrounded the little village with chattering monkeys and screaming birds by day and the roaring and coughing and moaning of the carnivora by night. Yes, she feared the jungle; but so much more did she fear The Sheik that many times it was in her childish head to run away, out into the terrible jungle forever rather than longer to face the ever present terror of her father.

As she sat there this day before The Sheik's goatskin tent, fashioning a skirt of grasses for Geeka, The Sheik appeared suddenly approaching. Instantly the look of happiness faded from the child's face. She shrunk aside in an attempt to scramble from the path of the leathern-faced old Arab; but she was not quick enough. With a brutal kick the man sent her sprawling upon her face, where she lay quite still, tearless but trembling. Then, with an oath at her, the man passed into the tent. The old, black hag shook with appreciative laughter, disclosing an occasional and lonesome yellow fang.

When she was sure The Sheik had gone, the little girl crawled to the shady side of the tent, where she lay quite still, hugging Geeka close to her breast, her little form racked at long intervals with choking sobs. She dared not cry aloud, since that would have brought The Sheik upon her again. The anguish in her little heart was not alone the anguish of physical pain; but that infinitely more pathetic anguish—of love denied a childish heart that yearns for love.

Little Meriem could scarce recall any other existence than that of the stern cruelty of The Sheik and Mabunu. Dimly, in the back of her childish memory there lurked a blurred recollection of a gentle mother; but Meriem was not sure but that even this was but a dream picture induced by her own desire for the caresses she never received, but which she lavished upon the much loved Geeka. Never was such a spoiled child as Geeka. Its little mother, far from fashioning her own conduct after the example set her by her father and nurse, went to the extreme of indulgence. Geeka was kissed a thousand times a day. There was play in which Geeka was naughty; but the little mother never punished. Instead, she caressed and fondled; her attitude influenced solely by her own pathetic desire for love.

Now, as she pressed Geeka close to her, her sobs lessened gradually, until she was able to control her voice, and pour out her misery into the ivory ear of her only confidante.

"Geeka loves Meriem," she whispered. "Why does The

Sheik, my father, not love me, too? Am I so naughty? I try to be good; but I never know why he strikes me, so I cannot tell what I have done which displeases him. Just now he kicked me and hurt me so, Geeka; but I was only sitting before the tent making a skirt for you. That must be wicked, or he would not have kicked me for it. But why is it wicked, Geeka? Oh dear! I do not know, I do not know. I wish, Geeka, that I were dead. Yesterday the hunters brought in the body of *el adrea*. *El adrea* was quite dead. No more will he slink silently upon his unsuspecting prey. No more will his great head and his maned shoulders strike terror to the hearts of the grass eaters at the drinking ford by night. No more will his thundering roar shake the ground. *El adrea* is dead. They beat his body terribly when it was brought into the village; but *el adrea* did not mind. He did not feel the blows, for he was dead. When I am dead, Geeka, neither shall I feel the blows of Mabunu, or the kicks of The Sheik, my father. Then shall I be happy. Oh, Geeka, how I wish that I were dead!''

If Geeka contemplated a remonstrance it was cut short by sounds of altercation beyond the village gates. Meriem listened. With the curiosity of childhood she would have liked to have run down there and learn what it was that caused the men to talk so loudly. Others of the village were already trooping in the direction of the noise. But Meriem did not dare. The Sheik would be there, doubtless, and if he saw her it would be but another opportunity to abuse her, so Meriem lay still and listened.

Presently she heard the crowd moving up the street toward The Sheik's tent. Cautiously she stuck her little head around the edge of the tent. She could not resist the temptation, for the sameness of the village life was monotonous, and she craved diversion. What she saw was two strangers—white men. They were alone, but as they approached she learned from the talk of the natives that surrounded them that they possessed a considerable following that was camped outside the village. They were coming to palaver with The Sheik.

The old Arab met them at the entrance to his tent. His eyes narrowed wickedly when they had appraised the newcomers. They stopped before him, exchanging greetings. They had come to trade for ivory they said. The Sheik grunted. He had no ivory. Meriem gasped. She knew that in a near-by hut the great tusks were piled almost to the roof. She poked her little head further forward to get a better view of the strangers. How white their skins! How yellow their great beards!

Suddenly one of them turned his eyes in her direction. She

tried to dodge back out of sight, for she feared all men; but he saw her. Meriem noticed the look of almost shocked surprise that crossed his face. The Sheik saw it too, and guessed the cause of it.

"I have no ivory," he repeated. "I do not wish to trade. Go away. Go now."

He stepped from his tent and almost pushed the strangers about in the direction of the gates. They demurred, and then The Sheik threatened. It would have been suicide to have disobeyed, so the two men turned and left the village, making their way immediately to their own camp.

The Sheik returned to his tent; but he did not enter it. Instead he walked to the side where little Meriem lay close to the goat skin wall, very frightened. The Sheik stooped and clutched her by the arm. Viciously he jerked her to her feet, dragged her to the entrance of the tent, and shoved her viciously within. Following her he again seized her, beating her ruthlessly.

"Stay within!" he growled. "Never let the strangers see thy face. Next time you show yourself to strangers I shall kill you!"

With a final vicious cuff he knocked the child into a far corner of the tent, where she lay stifling her moans, while The Sheik paced to and fro muttering to himself. At the entrance sat Mabunu, muttering and chuckling.

In the camp of the strangers one was speaking rapidly to the other.

"There is no doubt of it, Malbihn," he was saying. "Not the slightest; but why the old scoundrel hasn't claimed the reward long since is what puzzles me."

"There are some things dearer to an Arab, Jenssen, than money," returned the first speaker—"revenge is one of them."

"Anyhow it will not harm to try the power of gold," replied Jenssen.

Malbihn shrugged.

"Not on The Sheik," he said. "We might try it on one of his people; but The Sheik will not part with his revenge for gold. To offer it to him would only confirm his suspicions that we must have awakened when we were talking to him before his tent. If we got away with our lives, then, we should be fortunate."

"Well, try bribery, then," assented Jenssen.

But bribery failed—grewsomely. The tool they selected after a stay of several days in their camp outside the village was a tall, old headman of The Sheik's native contingent. He fell to the lure of the shining metal, for he had lived upon the coast and knew the power of gold. He promised to bring them what they craved, late that night.

Immediately after dark the two white men commenced to make arrangements to break camp. By midnight all was prepared. The porters lay beside their loads, ready to swing them aloft at a moment's notice. The armed *askaris* loitered between the balance of the *safari* and the Arab village, ready to form a rear guard for the retreat that was to begin the moment that the head man brought that which the white masters awaited.

Presently there came the sound of footsteps along the path from the village. Instantly the *askaris* and the whites were on the alert. More than a single man was approaching. Jenssen stepped forward and challenged the newcomers in a low whisper.

"Who comes?" he queried.

"Mbeeda," came the reply.

Mbeeda was the name of the traitorous head man. Jenssen was satisfied, though he wondered why Mbeeda had brought others with him. Presently he understood. The thing they fetched lay upon a litter borne by two men. Jenssen cursed beneath his breath. Could the fool be bringing them a corpse? They had paid for a living prize!

The bearers came to a halt before the white men.

"This has your gold purchased," said one of the two. They set the litter down, turned and vanished into the darkness toward the village. Malbihn looked at Jenssen, a crooked smile twisting his lips. The thing upon the litter was covered with a piece of cloth.

"Well?" queried the latter. "Raise the covering and see what you have bought. Much money shall we realize on a corpse—especially after the six months beneath the burning sun that will be consumed in carrying it to its destination!"

"The fool should have known that we desired her alive," grumbled Malbihn, grasping a corner of the cloth and jerking the cover from the thing that lay upon the litter.

At sight of what lay beneath both men stepped back—involuntary oaths upon their lips—for there before them lay the dead body of Mbeeda, the faithless head man.

Five minutes later the *safari* of Jenssen and Malbihn was forcing its way rapidly toward the west, nervous *askaris* guarding the rear from the attack they momentarily expected.

# 6

H IS FIRST NIGHT in the jungle was one which the son of Tarzan held longest in his memory. No savage carnivora menaced him. There was never a sign of hideous barbarian. Or, if there were, the boy's troubled mind took no cognizance of them. His conscience was harassed by the thought of his mother's suffering. Self-blame plunged him into the depths of misery. The killing of the American caused him little or no remorse. The fellow had earned his fate. Jack's regret on this score was due mainly to the effect which the death of Condon had had upon his own plans. Now he could not return directly to his parents as he had planned. Fear of the primitive, borderland law, of which he had read highly colored, imaginary tales, had thrust him into the jungle a fugitive. He dared not return to the coast at this point—not that he was so greatly influenced through personal fear as from a desire to shield his father and mother from further sorrow and from the shame of having their honored name dragged through the sordid degradation of a murder trial.

With returning day the boy's spirits rose. With the rising sun rose new hope within his breast. He would return to civilization by another way. None would guess that he had been connected with the killing of the stranger in the little out-of-the-way trading post upon a remote shore.

Crouched close to the great ape in the crotch of a tree the boy had shivered through an almost sleepless night. His light pajamas had been but little protection from the chill dampness of the jungle, and only that side of him which was pressed against the warm body of his shaggy companion approximated to comfort. And so he welcomed the rising sun with its promise of warmth as well as light—the blessed sun, dispeller of physical and mental ills.

41

He shook Akut into wakefulness.

"Come," he said. "I am cold and hungry. We will search for food, out there in the sunlight," and he pointed to an open plain, dotted with stunted trees and strewn with jagged rock.

The boy slid to the ground as he spoke, but the ape first looked carefully about, sniffing the morning air. Then, satisfied that no danger lurked near, he descended slowly to the ground beside the boy.

"Numa, and Sabor his mate, feast upon those who descend first and look afterward, while those who look first and descend afterward live to feast themselves." Thus the old ape imparted to the son of Tarzan the boy's first lesson in jungle lore. Side by side they set off across the rough plain, for the boy wished first to be warm. The ape showed him the best places to dig for rodents and worms; but the lad only gagged at the thought of devouring the repulsive things. Some eggs they found, and these he sucked raw, as also he ate roots and tubers which Akut unearthed. Beyond the plain and across a low bluff they came upon water—brackish, ill-smelling stuff in a shallow water hole, the sides and bottom of which were trampled by the feet of many beasts. A herd of zebra galloped away as they approached.

The lad was too thirsty by now to cavil at anything even remotely resembling water, so he drank his fill while Akut stood with raised head, alert for any danger. Before the ape drank he cautioned the boy to be watchful; but as he drank he raised his head from time to time to cast a quick glance toward a clump of bushes a hundred yards away upon the opposite side of the water hole. When he had done he rose and spoke to the boy, in the language that was their common heritage—the tongue of the great apes.

"There is no danger near?" he asked.

"None," replied the boy. "I saw nothing move while you drank."

"Your eyes will help you but little in the jungle," said the ape.

"Here, if you would live, you must depend upon your ears and your nose but most upon your nose. When we came down to drink I knew that no danger lurked near upon this side of the water hole, for else the zebras would have discovered it and fled before we came; but upon the other side toward which the wind blows danger might lie concealed. We could not smell it for its scent is being blown in the other direction, and so I bent my ears and eyes down wind where my nose cannot travel."

"And you found—nothing?" asked the lad, with a laugh.

"I found Numa crouching in that clump of bushes where the tall grasses grow," and Akut pointed.

"A lion?" exclaimed the boy. "How do you know? I can see nothing."

"Numa is there, though," replied the great ape. "First I heard him sigh. To you the sigh of Numa may sound no different from the other noises which the wind makes among the grasses and the trees; but later you must learn to know the sigh of Numa. Then I watched and at last I saw the tall grasses moving at one point to a force other than the force of the wind. See, they are spread there upon either side of Numa's great body, and as he breathes—you see? You see the little motion at either side that is not caused by the wind—the motion that none of the other grasses have?"

The boy strained his eyes—better eyes than the ordinary boy inherits—and at last he gave a little exclamation of discovery.

"Yes," he said, "I see. He lies there," and he pointed. "His head is toward us. Is he watching us?"

"Numa is watching us," replied Akut, "but we are in little danger, unless we approach too close, for he is lying upon his kill. His belly is almost full, or we should hear him crunching the bones. He is watching us in silence merely from curiosity. Presently he will resume his feeding or he will rise and come down to the water for a drink. As he neither fears or desires us he will not try to hide his presence from us; but now is an excellent time to learn to know Numa, for you must learn to know him well if you would live long in the jungle. Where the great apes are many Numa leaves us alone. Our fangs are long and strong, and we can fight; but when we are alone and he is hungry we are no match for him. Come, we will circle him and catch his scent. The sooner you learn to know it the better; but keep close to the trees, as we go around him, for Numa often does that which he is least expected to do. And keep your ears and your eyes and your nose open. Remember always that there may be an enemy behind every bush, in every tree and amongst every clump of jungle grass. While you are avoiding Numa do not run into the jaws of Sabor, his mate. Follow me," and Akut set off in a wide circle about the water hole and the crouching lion.

The boy followed close upon his heels, his every sense upon the alert, his nerves keyed to the highest pitch of excitement. This was life! For the instant he forgot his resolutions of a few

minutes past to hasten to the coast at some other point than that
at which he had landed and make his way immediately back to
London. He thought now only of the savage joy of living, and
of pitting one's wits and prowess against the wiles and might of
the savage jungle brood which haunted the broad plains and the
gloomy forest aisles of the great, untamed continent. He knew
no fear. His father had had none to transmit to him; but honor
and conscience he did have and these were to trouble him many
times as they battled with his inherent love of freedom for possession of his soul.

They had passed but a short distance to the rear of Numa
when the boy caught the unpleasant odor of the carnivore. His
face lighted with a smile. Something told him that he would
have known that scent among a myriad of others even if Akut
had not told him that a lion lay near. There was a strange familiarity—a weird familiarity in it that made the short hairs rise
at the nape of his neck, and brought his upper lip into an involuntary snarl that bared his fighting fangs. There was a sense of
stretching of the skin about his ears, for all the world as though
those members were flattening back against his skull in preparation for deadly combat. His skin tingled. He was aglow with
a pleasurable sensation that he never before had known. He was,
upon the instant, another creature—wary, alert, ready. Thus did
the scent of Numa, the lion, transform the boy into a beast.

He had never seen a lion—his mother had gone to great pains
to prevent it. But he had devoured countless pictures of them,
and now he was ravenous to feast his eyes upon the king of
beasts in the flesh. As he trailed Akut he kept an eye cocked
over one shoulder, rearward, in the hope that Numa might rise
from his kill and reveal himself. Thus it happened that he
dropped some little way behind Akut, and the next he knew he
was recalled suddenly to a contemplation of other matters than
the hidden Numa by a shrill scream of warning from the Ape.
Turning his eyes quickly in the direction of his companion, the
boy saw that, standing in the path directly before him, which
sent tremors of excitement racing along every nerve of his body.
With body half-merging from a clump of bushes in which she
must have lain hidden stood a sleek and beautiful lioness. Her
yellow-green eyes were round and staring, boring straight into
the eyes of the boy. Not ten paces separated them. Twenty paces
behind the lioness stood the great ape, bellowing instructions to
the boy and hurling taunts at the lioness in an evident effort to

attract her attention from the lad while he gained the shelter of a near-by tree.

But Sabor was not to be diverted. She had her eyes upon the lad. He stood between her and her mate, between her and the kill. It was suspicious. Probably he had ulterior designs upon her lord and master or upon the fruits of their hunting. A lioness is short tempered. Akut's bellowing annoyed her. She uttered a little rumbling growl, taking a step toward the boy.

"The tree!" screamed Akut.

The boy turned and fled, and at the same instant the lioness charged. The tree was but a few paces away. A limb hung ten feet from the ground, and as the boy leaped for it the lioness leaped for him. Like a monkey he pulled himself up and to one side. A great forepaw caught him a glancing blow at the hips—just grazing him. One curved talon hooked itself into the waist band of his pajama trousers, ripping them from him as the lioness sped by. Half-naked the lad drew himself to safety as the beast turned and leaped for him once more.

Akut, from a near-by tree, jabbered and scolded, calling the lioness all manner of foul names. The boy, patterning his conduct after that of his preceptor, unstoppered the vials of his invective upon the head of the enemy, until in realization of the futility of words as weapons he bethought himself of something heavier to hurl. There was nothing but dead twigs and branches at hand, but these he flung at the upturned, snarling face of Sabor just as his father had before him twenty years ago, when as a boy he too had taunted and tantalized the great cats of the jungle.

The lioness fretted about the bole of the tree for a short time; but finally, either realizing the uselessness of her vigil, or prompted by the pangs of hunger, she stalked majestically away and disappeared in the brush that hid her lord, who had not once shown himself during the altercation.

Freed from their retreats Akut and the boy came to the ground, to take up their interrupted journey once more. The old ape scolded the lad for his carelessness.

"Had you not been so intent upon the lion behind you you might have discovered the lioness much sooner than you did," he said.

"But you passed right by her without seeing her," retorted the boy.

Akut was chagrined.

"It is thus," he said, "that jungle folk die. We go cautiously for a lifetime, and then, just for an instant, we forget, and—'' he ground his teeth in mimicry of the crunching of great jaws in flesh. "It is a lesson," he resumed. "You have learned that you may not for too long keep your eyes and your ears and your nose all bent in the same direction.''

That night the son of Tarzan was colder than he ever had been in all his life. The pajama trousers had not been heavy; but they had been much heavier than nothing. And the next day he roasted in the hot sun, for again their way led much across wide and treeless plains.

It was still in the boy's mind to travel to the south, and circle back to the coast in search of another outpost of civilization. He had said nothing of this plan to Akut, for he knew that the old ape would look with displeasure upon any suggestion that savored of separation.

For a month the two wandered on, the boy learning rapidly the laws of the jungle; his muscles adapting themselves to the new mode of life that had been thrust upon them. The thews of the sire had been transmitted to the son—it needed only the hardening of use to develop them. The lad found that it came quite naturally to him to swing through the trees. Even at great heights he never felt the slightest dizziness, and when he had caught the knack of the swing and the release, he could hurl himself through space from branch to branch with even greater agility than the heavier Akut.

And with exposure came a toughening and hardening of his smooth, white skin, browning now beneath the sun and wind. He had removed his pajama jacket one day to bathe in a little stream that was too small to harbor crocodiles, and while he and Akut had been disporting themselves in the cool waters a monkey had dropped down from the over hanging trees, snatched up the boy's single remaining article of civilized garmenture, and scampered away with it.

For a time Jack was angry; but when he had been without the jacket for a short while he began to realize that being half-clothed is infinitely more uncomfortable than being entirely naked. Soon he did not miss his clothing in the least, and from that he came to revel in the freedom of his unhampered state. Occasionally a smile would cross his face as he tried to imagine the surprise of his schoolmates could they but see him now. They would envy him. Yes, how they would envy him. He felt sorry for them at such times, and again as he thought of them amid luxuries and comforts of their English homes, happy with their fathers and mothers, a most uncomfortable lump would arise into the boy's throat, and he would see a vision of his mother's face through a blur of mist that came unbidden to his eyes. Then it was that he urged Akut onward, for now they were headed westward toward the coast. The old ape thought that they were searching for a tribe of his own kind, nor did the boy disabuse his mind of this belief. It would do to tell Akut of his real plans when they had come within sight of civilization.

One day as they were moving slowly along beside a river they came unexpectedly upon a native village. Some children were playing beside the water. The boy's heart leaped within his breast at sight of them—for over a month he had seen no human being. What if these were naked savages? What if their skins were black? Were they not creatures fashioned in the mold of their Maker, as was he? They were his brothers and sisters! He started toward them. With a low warning Akut laid a hand upon his arm to hold him back. The boy shook himself free, and with a shout of greeting ran forward toward the ebon players.

The sound of his voice brought every head erect. Wide eyes viewed him for an instant, and then, with screams of terror, the children turned and fled toward the village. At their heels ran their mothers, and from the village gate, in response to the alarm, came a score of warriors, hastily snatched spears and shields ready in their hands.

At sight of the consternation he had wrought the boy halted. The glad smile faded from his face as with wild shouts and menacing gestures the warriors ran toward him. Akut was calling to him from behind to turn and flee, telling him that the blacks would kill him. For a moment he stood watching them coming, then he raised his hand with the palm toward them in signal for them to halt, calling out at the same time that he came as a friend—that he had only wanted to play with their children. Of course they did not understand a word that he addressed to them, and their answer was what any naked creature who had run suddenly out of the jungle upon their women and children might have expected—a shower of spears. The missiles struck all about the boy, but none touched him. Again his spine tingled and the short hairs lifted at the nape of his neck and along the top of his scalp. His eyes narrowed. Sudden hatred flared in them to wither the expression of glad friendliness that had lighted them but an instant before. With a low snarl, quite similar to that of a baffled beast, he turned and ran into the jungle. There was Akut awaiting him in a tree. The ape urged him to hasten in flight, for the wise old anthropoid knew that they two, naked and unarmed, were no match for the sinewy black warriors who would doubtless make some sort of search for them through the jungle.

But a new power moved the son of Tarzan. He had come with a boy's glad and open heart to offer his friendship to these people who were human beings like himself. He had been met with suspicion and spears. They had not even listened to him. Rage and hatred consumed him. When Akut urged speed he held back. He wanted to fight, yet his reason made it all too plain that it would be but a foolish sacrifice of his life to meet these armed men with his naked hands and his teeth—already the boy thought of his teeth, of his fighting fangs, when possibility of combat loomed close.

Moving slowly through the trees he kept his eyes over his shoulder, though he no longer neglected the possibilities of other dangers which might lurk on either hand or ahead—his experience with the lioness did not need a repetition to insure the permanency of the lesson it had taught. Behind he could hear the savages advancing with shouts and cries. He lagged further behind until the pursuers were in sight. They did not see him, for they were not looking among the branches of the trees for human quarry. The lad kept just ahead of them. For a mile perhaps they continued the search, and then they turned back toward the village. Here was the boy's opportunity, that for which he had been waiting, while the hot blood of revenge coursed through his veins until he saw his pursuers through a scarlet haze.

When they turned back he turned and followed them. Akut was no longer in sight. Thinking that the boy followed he had gone on further ahead. He had no wish to tempt fate within range of those deadly spears. Slinking silently from tree to tree the boy dogged the footsteps of the returning warriors. At last one dropped behind his fellows as they followed a narrow path toward the village. A grim smile lit the lad's face. Swiftly he hurried forward until he moved almost above the unconscious black—stalking him as Sheeta, the panther, stalked his prey, as the boy had seen Sheeta do on many occasions.

Suddenly and silently he leaped forward and downward upon the broad shoulders of his prey. In the instant of contact his fingers sought and found the man's throat. The weight of the boy's body hurled the black heavily to the ground, the knees in his back knocking the breath from him as he struck. Then a set of strong, white teeth fastened themselves in his neck, and muscular fingers closed tighter upon his wind-pipe. For a time the warrior struggled frantically, throwing himself about in an effort to dislodge his antagonist; but all the while he was weakening and all the while the grim and silent thing he could not see clung tenaciously to him, and dragged him slowly into the bush to one side of the trail.

Hidden there at last, safe from the prying eyes of searchers, should they miss their fellow and return for him, the lad choked the life from the body of his victim. At last he knew by the sudden struggle, followed by limp relaxation, that the warrior was dead. Then a strange desire seized him. His whole being quivered and thrilled. Involuntarily he leaped to his feet and placed one foot upon the body of his kill. His chest expanded. He raised his face toward the heavens and opened his mouth to voice a strange, weird cry that seemed screaming within him for outward expression, but no sound passed his lips—he just stood there for a full minute, his face turned toward the sky, his breast heaving to the pent emotion, like an animate statue of vengeance.

The silence which marked the first great kill of the son of Tarzan was to typify all his future kills, just as the hideous victory cry of the bull ape had marked the kills of his mighty sire.

# 7

A KUT, DISCOVERING THAT the boy was not close behind him, turned back to search for him. He had gone but a short distance in return when he was brought to a sudden and startled halt by sight of a strange figure moving through the trees toward him. It was the boy, yet could it be? In his hand was a long spear, down his back hung an oblong shield such as the black warriors who had attacked them had worn, and upon ankle and arm were bands of iron and brass, while a loin cloth was twisted about the youth's middle. A knife was thrust through its folds.

When the boy saw the ape he hastened forward to exhibit his trophies. Proudly he called attention to each of his newly won possessions. Boastfully he recounted the details of his exploit.

"With my bare hands and my teeth I killed him," he said. "I would have made friends with them but they chose to be my enemies. And now that I have a spear I shall show Numa, too, what it means to have me for a foe. Only the white men and the great apes, Akut, are our friends. Them we shall seek, all others must we avoid or kill. This have I learned of the jungle."

They made a detour about the hostile village, and resumed their journey toward the coast. The boy took much pride in his new weapons and ornaments. He practiced continually with the spear, throwing it at some object ahead hour by hour as they traveled their loitering way, until he gained a proficiency such as only youthful muscles may attain to speedily. All the while his training went on under the guidance of Akut. No longer was there a single jungle spoor but was an open book to the keen eyes of the lad, and those other indefinite spoor that elude the senses of civilized man and are only partially appreciable to his savage cousin came to be familiar friends of the eager boy. He could differentiate the innumerable species of the herbivora by

50

scent, and he could tell, too, whether an animal was approaching or departing merely by the waxing or waning strength of its effluvium. Nor did he need the evidence of his eyes to tell him whether there were two lions or four up wind,—a hundred yards away or half a mile.

Much of this had Akut taught him, but far more was instinctive knowledge—a species of strange intuition inherited from his father. He had come to love the jungle life. The constant battle of wits and senses against the many deadly foes that lurked by day and by night along the pathway of the wary and the unwary appealed to the spirit of adventure which breathes strong in the heart of every red-blooded son of primordial Adam. Yet, though he loved it, he had not let his selfish desires outweigh the sense of duty that had brought him to a realization of the moral wrong which lay beneath the adventurous escapade that had brought him to Africa. His love of father and mother was strong within him, too strong to permit unalloyed happiness which was undoubtedly causing them days of sorrow. And so he held tight to his determination to find a port upon the coast where he might communicate with them and receive funds for his return to London. There he felt sure that he could now persuade his parents to let him spend at least a portion of his time upon those African estates which from little careless remarks dropped at home he knew his father possessed. That would be something, better at least than a lifetime of the cramped and cloying restrictions of civilization.

And so he was rather contented than otherwise as he made his way in the direction of the coast, for while he enjoyed the liberty and the savage pleasures of the wild his conscience was at the same time clear, for he knew that he was doing all that lay in his power to return to his parents. He rather looked forward, too, to meeting white men again—creatures of his own kind—for there had been many occasions upon which he had longed for other companionship than that of the old ape. The affair with the blacks still rankled in his heart. He had approached them in such innocent good fellowship and with such childlike assurance of a hospitable welcome that the reception which had been accorded him had proved a shock to his boyish ideals. He no longer looked upon the black man as his brother; but rather as only another of the innumerable foes of the bloodthirsty jungle—a beast of prey which walked upon two feet instead of four.

But if the blacks were his enemies there were those in the world who were not. There were those who always would welcome him with open arms; who would accept him as a friend and brother, and with whom he might find sanctuary from every enemy. Yes, there were always white men. Somewhere along the coast or even in the depths of the jungle itself there were white men. To them he would be a welcome visitor. They would befriend him. And there were also the great apes—the friends of his father and of Akut. How glad they would be to receive the son of Tarzan of the Apes! He hoped that he could come upon them before he found a trading post upon the coast. He wanted to be able to tell his father that he had known his old friends of the jungle, that he had hunted with them, that he had joined with them in their savage life, and their fierce, primeval ceremonies—the strange ceremonies of which Akut had tried to tell him. It cheered him immensely to dwell upon these happy meetings. Often he rehearsed the long speech which he would make to the apes, in which he would tell them of the life of their former king since he had left them.

At other times he would play at meeting with white men. Then he would enjoy their consternation at sight of a naked white boy trapped in the war togs of a black warrior and roaming the jungle with only a great ape as his companion.

And so the days passed, and with the traveling and the hunting and the climbing the boy's muscles developed and his agility increased until even phlegmatic Akut marvelled at the prowess of his pupil. And the boy, realizing his great strength and revelling in it, became careless. He strode through the jungle, his proud head erect, defying danger. Where Akut took to the trees at the first scent of Numa, the lad laughed in the face of the king of beasts and walked boldly past him. Good fortune was with him for a long time. The lions he met were well-fed, perhaps, or the very boldness of the strange creature which invaded their domain so filled them with surprise that thoughts of attack were banished from their minds as they stood, round-eyed, watching his approach and his departure. Whatever the cause, however, the fact remains that on many occasions the boy passed within a few paces of some great lion without arousing more than a warning growl.

But no two lions are necessarily alike in character or temper. They differ as greatly as do individuals of the human family. Because ten lions act similarly under similar conditions one cannot say that the eleventh lion will do likewise—the chances are that he will not. The lion is a creature of high nervous development. He thinks, therefore he reasons. Having a nervous system and brains he is the possessor of temperament, which is affected variously by extraneous causes. One day the boy met the eleventh lion. The former was walking across a small plain upon which grew little clumps of bushes. Akut was a few yards to the left of the lad who was the first to discover the presence of Numa.

"Run, Akut," called the boy, laughing. "Numa lies hid in the bushes to my right. Take to the trees. Akut! I, the son of Tarzan, will protect you," and the boy, laughing, kept straight along his way which led close beside the brush in which Numa lay concealed.

The ape shouted to him to come away, but the lad only flourished his spear and executed an improvised war dance to show his contempt for the king of beasts. Closer and closer to the dread destroyer he came, until, with a sudden, angry growl, the lion rose from his bed not ten paces from the youth. A huge fellow he was, this lord of the jungle and the desert. A shaggy mane clothed his shoulders. Cruel fangs armed his great jaws. His yellow-green eyes blazed with hatred and challenge.

The boy, with his pitifully inadequate spear ready in his hand, realized quickly that this lion was different from the others he had met; but he had gone too far now to retreat. The nearest tree lay several yards to his left—the lion could be upon him before he had covered half the distance, and that the beast intended to charge none could doubt who looked upon him now. Beyond the lion was a thorn tree—only a few feet beyond him. It was the nearest sanctuary but Numa stood between it and his prey.

The feel of the long spear shaft in his hand and the sight of the tree beyond the lion gave the lad an idea—a preposterous idea—a ridiculous, forlorn hope of an idea; but there was no time now to weigh chances—there was but a single chance, and that was the thorn tree. If the lion charged it would be too late— the lad must charge first, and to the astonishment of Akut and none the less of Numa, the boy leaped swiftly toward the beast. Just for a second was the lion motionless with surprise and in that second Jack Clayton put to the crucial test an accomplishment which he had practiced at school.

Straight for the savage brute he ran, his spear held butt foremost across his body. Akut shrieked in terror and amazement. The lion stood with wide, round eyes awaiting the attack, ready to rear upon his hind feet and receive this rash creature with blows that could crush the skull of a buffalo.

Just in front of the lion the boy placed the butt of his spear upon the ground, gave a mighty spring, and, before the bewildered beast could guess the trick that had been played upon him, sailed over the lion's head into the rending embrace of the thorn tree—safe but lacerated.

Akut had never before seen a pole-vault. Now he leaped up and down within the safety of his own tree, screaming taunts and boasts at the discomfited Numa, while the boy, torn and bleeding, sought some position in his thorny retreat in which he might find the least agony. He had saved his life; but at considerable cost in suffering. It seemed to him that the lion would never leave, and it was a full hour before the angry brute gave up his vigil and strode majestically away across the plain. When he was at a safe distance the boy extricated himself from the thorn tree; but not without inflicting new wounds upon his already tortured flesh.

It was many days before the outward evidence of the lesson he had learned had left him; while the impression upon his mind was one that was to remain with him for life. Never again did he uselessly tempt fate.

He took long chances often in his after life; but only when the taking of chances might further the attainment of some cherished end—and, always thereafter, he practiced pole-vaulting.

For several days the boy and the ape lay up while the former recovered from the painful wounds inflicted by the sharp thorns. The great anthropoid licked the wounds of his human friend, nor, aside from this, did they receive other treatment, but they soon healed, for healthy flesh quickly replaces itself.

When the lad felt fit again the two continued their journey toward the coast, and once more the boy's mind was filled with pleasurable anticipation.

And at last the much dreamed of moment came. They were passing through a tangled forest when the boy's sharp eyes discovered from the lower branches through which he was traveling an old but well-marked spoor—a spoor that set his heart to leaping—the spoor of man, of white men, for among the prints of naked feet were the well defined outlines of European made boots. The trail, which marked the passage of a good-sized company, pointed north at right angles to the course the boy and the ape were taking toward the coast.

Doubtless these white men knew the nearest coast settlement. They might even be headed for it now. At any rate it would be worth while overtaking them if even only for the pleasure of meeting again creatures of his own kind. The lad was all excitement; palpitant with eagerness to be off in pursuit. Akut demurred. He wanted nothing of men. To him the lad was a fellow ape, for he was the son of the king of apes. He tried to dissuade the boy, telling him that soon they should come upon a tribe of their own folk where some day when he was older the boy should be king as his father had before him. But Jack was obdurate. He insisted that he wanted to see white men again. He wanted to send a message to his parents. Akut listened and as he listened the intuition of the beast suggested the truth to him—the boy was planning to return to his own kind.

The thought filled the old ape with sorrow. He loved the boy as he had loved the father, with the loyalty and faithfulness of a hound for its master. In his ape brain and his ape heart he had nursed the hope that he and the lad would never be separated. He saw all his fondly cherished plans fading away, and yet he remained loyal to the lad and to his wishes. Though disconsolate he gave in to the boy's determination to pursue the *safari* of the white men, accompanying him upon what he believed would be their last journey together.

The spoor was but a couple of days old when the two discovered it, which meant that the slow-moving caravan was but a few hours distant from them whose trained and agile muscles could carry their bodies swiftly through the branches above the tangled undergrowth which had impeded the progress of the laden carriers of the white men.

The boy was in the lead, excitement and anticipation carrying him ahead of his companion to whom the attainment of their goal meant only sorrow. And it was the boy who first saw the rear guard of the caravan and the white men he had been so anxious to overtake.

Stumbling along the tangled trail of those ahead a dozen heavily laden blacks who, from fatigue or sickness, had dropped behind were being prodded by the black soldiers of the rear guard, kicked when they fell, and then roughly jerked to their feet and hustled onward. On either side walked a giant white man, heavy blonde beards almost obliterating their countenances. The boy's lips formed a glad cry of salutation as his eyes first discovered the whites—a cry that was never uttered, for almost immediately he witnessed that which turned his happiness to anger as he saw that both the white men were wielding heavy whips brutally upon the naked backs of the poor devils staggering along beneath loads that would have overtaxed the strength and endurance of strong men at the beginning of a new day.

Every now and then the rear guard and the white men cast apprehensive glances rearward as though momentarily expecting the materialization of some long expected danger from that quarter. The boy had paused after his first sight of the caravan, and now was following slowly in the wake of the sordid, brutal spectacle. Presently Akut came up with him. To the beast there was less of horror in the sight than to the lad, yet even the great ape growled beneath his breath at useless torture being inflicted upon the helpless slaves. He looked at the boy. Now that he had caught up with the creatures of his own kind, why was it that he did not rush forward and greet them? He put the question to his companion.

"They are fiends," muttered the boy. "I would not travel with such as they, for if I did I should set upon them and kill them the first time they beat their people as they are beating them now; but," he added, after a moment's thought, "I can ask them the whereabouts of the nearest port, and then, Akut, we can leave them."

The ape made no reply, and the boy swung to the ground and started at a brisk walk toward the *safari*. He was a hundred yards away, perhaps, when one of the whites caught sight of him. The man gave a shout of alarm, instantly levelling his rifle upon the boy and firing. The bullet struck just in front of its mark, scattering turf and fallen leaves against the lad's legs. A second later the other white and the black soldiers of the rear guard were firing hysterically at the boy.

Jack leaped behind a tree, unhit. Days of panic ridden flight through the jungle had filled Carl Jenssen and Sven Malbihn with jangling nerves and their native boys with unreasoning terror. Every new note from behind sounded to their frightened ears the coming of The Sheik and his bloodthirsty entourage. They were in a blue funk, and the sight of the naked white warrior stepping silently out of the jungle through which they had just passed had been sufficient shock to let loose in action all the pent nerve energy of Malbihn, who had been the first to see the strange apparition. And Malbihn's shout and shot had set the others going.

When their nervous energy had spent itself and they came to take stock of what they had been fighting it developed that Malbihn alone had seen anything clearly. Several of the blacks averred that they too had obtained a good view of the creature but their descriptions of it varied so greatly that Jenssen, who had seen nothing himself, was inclined to be a trifle skeptical. One of the blacks insisted that the thing had been eleven feet tall, with a man's body and the head of an elephant. Another had seen *three* immense Arabs with huge, black beards; but when, after conquering their nervousness, the rear guard advanced upon the enemy's position to investigate they found nothing, for Akut and the boy had retreated out of range of the unfriendly guns.

Jack was disheartened and sad. He had not entirely recovered from the depressing effect of the unfriendly reception he had received at the hands of the blacks, and now he had found an even more hostile one accorded him by men of his own color.

"The lesser beasts flee from me in terror," he murmured, half to himself, "the greater beasts are ready to tear me to pieces at sight. Black men would kill me with their spears or arrows. And now white men, men of my own kind, have fired upon me and driven me away. Are all the creatures of the world my enemies? Has the son of Tarzan no friend other than Akut?"

The old ape drew closer to the boy.

"There are the great apes," he said. "They only will be the friends of Akut's friend. Only the great apes will welcome the son of Tarzan. You have seen that men want nothing of you. Let us go now and continue our search for the great apes—our people."

The language of the great apes is a combination of monosyllabic gutturals, amplified by gestures and signs. It may not be literally translated into human speech; but as near as may be this is what Akut said to the boy.

The two proceeded in silence for some time after Akut had spoken. The boy was immersed in deep thought—bitter thoughts in which hatred and revenge predominated. Finally he spoke: "Very well, Akut," he said, "we will find our friends, the great apes."

The anthropoid was overjoyed; but he gave no outward demonstration of his pleasure. A low grunt was his only response, and a moment later he had limped nimbly upon a small and unwary rodent that had been surprised at a fatal distance from its burrow. Tearing the unhappy creature in two Akut handed the lion's share to the lad.

# 8

A YEAR HAD passed since the two Swedes had been driven in terror from the savage country where The Sheik held sway. Little Meriem still played with Geeka, lavishing all her childish love upon the now almost hopeless ruin of what had never, even in its palmiest days, possessed even a slight degree of loveliness. But to Meriem, Geeka was all that was sweet and adorable. She carried to the deaf ears of the battered ivory head all her sorrows all her hopes and all her ambitions, for even in the face of hopelessness, in the clutches of the dread authority from which there was no escape, little Meriem yet cherished hopes and ambitions. It is true that her ambitions were rather nebulous in form, consisting chiefly of a desire to escape with Geeka to some remote and unknown spot where there were no Sheiks, no Mabunus—where *el adrea* could find no entrance, and where she might play all day surrounded only by flowers and birds and the harmless little monkeys playing in the tree tops.

The Sheik had been away for a long time, conducting a caravan of ivory, skins, and rubber far into the north. The interim had been one of great peace for Meriem. It is true that Mabunu had still been with her, to pinch or beat her as the mood seized the villainous old hag; but Mabunu was only one. When The Sheik was there also there were two of them, and The Sheik was stronger and more brutal even than Mabunu. Little Meriem often wondered why the grim old man hated her so. It is true that he was cruel and unjust to all with whom he came in contact, but to Meriem he reserved his greatest cruelties, his most studied injustices.

Today Meriem was squatting at the foot of a large tree which grew inside the palisade close to the edge of the village. She was fashioning a tent of leaves for Geeka. Before the tent were

58

some pieces of wood and small leaves and a few stones. These were the household utensils. Geeka was cooking dinner. As the little girl played she prattled continuously to her companion, propped in a sitting position with a couple of twigs. She was totally absorbed in the domestic duties of Geeka—so much so that she did not note the gentle swaying of the branches of the tree above her as they bent to the body of the creature that had entered them stealthily from the jungle.

In happy ignorance the little girl played on, while from above two steady eyes looked down upon her—unblinking, unwavering. There was none other than the little girl in this part of the village, which had been almost deserted since The Sheik had left long months before upon his journey toward the north.

And out in the jungle, an hour's march from the village, The Sheik was leading his returning caravan homeward.

A year had passed since the white men had fired upon the lad and driven him back into the jungle to take up his search for the only remaining creatures to whom he might look for companionship—the great apes. For months the two had wandered eastward, deeper and deeper into the jungle. The year had done much for the boy—turning his already mighty muscles to thews of steel, developing his woodcraft to a point where it verged upon the uncanny, perfecting his arboreal instincts, and training him in the use of both natural and artificial weapons.

He had become at last a creature of marvelous physical powers and mental cunning. He was still but a boy, yet so great was his strength that the powerful anthropoid with which he often engaged in mimic battle was no match for him. Akut had taught him to fight as the bull ape fights, nor ever was there a teacher better fitted to instruct in the savage warfare of primordial man, or a pupil better equipped to profit by the lessons of a master.

As the two searched for a band of the almost extinct species of ape to which Akut belonged they lived upon the best the jungle afforded. Antelope and zebra fell to the boy's spear, or were dragged down by the two powerful beasts of prey who leaped upon them from some overhanging limb or from the ambush of the undergrowth beside the trail to the water hole or the ford.

The pelt of a leopard covered the nakedness of the youth; but the wearing of it had not been dictated by any prompting of modesty. With the rifle shots of the white men showering about him he had reverted to the savagery of the beast that is inherent in each of us, but that flamed more strongly in this boy whose father had been raised a beast of prey. He wore his leopard skin at first in response to a desire to parade a trophy of his prowess, for he had slain the leopard with his knife in a hand-to-hand combat. He saw that the skin was beautiful, which appealed to his barbaric sense of ornamentation, and when it stiffened and later commenced to decompose because of his having no knowledge of how to cure or tan it was with sorrow and regret that he discarded it. Later, when he chanced upon a lone, black warrior wearing the counterpart of it, soft and clinging and beautiful from proper curing, it required but an instant to leap from above upon the shoulders of the unsuspecting black, sink a keen blade into his heart and possess the rightly preserved hide.

There were no after-qualms of conscience. In the jungle might is right, nor does it take long to inculcate this axiom in the mind of a jungle dweller, regardless of what his past training may have been. That the black would have killed him had he had the chance the boy knew full well. Neither he nor the black were any more sacred than the lion, or the buffalo, the zebra or the deer, or any other of the countless creatures who roamed, or slunk, or flew, or wriggled through the dark mazes of the forest. Each had but a single life, which was sought by many. The greater number of enemies slain the better chance to prolong that life. So the boy smiled and donned the finery of the vanquished, and went his way with Akut, searching, always searching for the elusive anthropoids who were to welcome them with open arms. And at last they found them. Deep in the jungle, buried far from sight of man, they came upon such another little natural arena as had witnessed the wild ceremony of the Dum-Dum in which the boy's father had taken part long years before.

First, at a great distance, they heard the beating of the drum of the great apes. They were sleeping in the safety of a huge tree when the booming sound smote upon their ears. Both awoke at once. Akut was the first to interpret the strange cadence.

"The great apes!" he growled. "They dance the Dum-Dum. Come, Korak, son of Tarzan, let us go to our people."

Months before Akut had given the boy a name of his own choosing, since he could not master the mangiven name of Jack. Korak is as near as it may be interpreted into human speech. In the language of the apes it means Killer. Now the Killer rose upon the branch of the great tree where he had been sleeping with his back braced against the stem. He stretched his lithe young muscles, the moonlight filtering through the foliage from above dappling his brown skin with little patches of light.

The ape, too, stood up, half squatting after the manner of his kind. Low growls rumbled from the bottom of his deep chest—growls of excited anticipation. The boy growled in harmony with the ape. Then the anthropoid slid softly to the ground. Close by, in the direction of the booming drum, lay a clearing which they must cross. The moon flooded it with silvery light. Half-erect, the great ape shuffled into the full glare of the moon. At his side, swinging gracefully along in marked contrast to the awkwardness of his companion, strode the boy, the dark, shaggy coat of the one brushing against the smooth, clear hide of the other. The lad was humming now, a music hall air that had found its way to the forms of the great English public school that was to see him no more. He was happy and expectant. The moment he had looked forward to for so long was about to be realized. He was coming into his own. He was coming home. As the months had dragged or flown along, retarded or spurred on as privation or adventure predominated, thoughts of his own home, while oft recurring, had become less vivid. The old life had grown to seem more like a dream than a reality, and the balking of his determination to reach the coast and return to London had finally thrown the hope of realization so remotely into the future that it too now seemed little more than a pleasant but hopeless dream.

Now all thoughts of London and civilization were crowded so far into the background of his brain that they might as well have been non-existent. Except for form and mental development he was as much an ape as the great, fierce creature at his side.

In the exuberance of his joy he slapped his companion roughly on the side of the head. Half in anger, half in play the anthropoid turned upon him, his fangs bared and glistening. Long, hairy arms reached out to seize him, and, as they had done a thousand times before, the two clinched in mimic battle, rolling upon the sward, striking, growling and biting, though never closing their teeth in more than a rough pinch. It was wondrous practice for them both. The boy brought into play wrestling tricks that he had learned at school, and many of these Akut learned to use and to foil. And from the ape the boy learned the methods that had been handed down to Akut from some common ancestor of them both, who had roamed the teeming earth when ferns were trees and crocodiles were birds.

But there was one art the boy possessed which Akut could not master, though he did achieve fair proficiency in it for an ape—boxing. To have his bull-like charges stopped and crumpled with a suddenly planted fist upon the end of his snout, or a painful jolt in the short ribs, always surprised Akut. It angered him too, and at such times his mighty jaws came nearer to closing in the soft flesh of his friend than at any other, for he was still an ape, with an ape's short temper and brutal instincts; but the difficulty was in catching his tormentor while his rage lasted, for when he lost his head and rushed madly into close quarters with the boy he discovered that the stinging hail of blows released upon him always found their mark and effectually stopped him—effectually and painfully. Then he would withdraw growling viciously, backing away with grinning jaws distended, to sulk for an hour or so.

Tonight they did not box. Just for a moment or two they wrestled playfully, until the scent of Sheeta, the panther, brought them to their feet, alert and wary. The great cat was passing through the jungle in front of them. For a moment it paused, listening. The boy and the ape growled menacingly in chorus and the carnivore moved on.

Then the two took up their journey toward the sound of the Dum-Dum. Louder and louder came the beating of the drum. Now, at last, they could hear the growling of the dancing apes, and strong to their nostrils came the scent of their kind. The lad trembled with excitement. The hair down Akut's spine stiffened—the symptoms of happiness and anger are often similar.

Silently they crept through the jungle as they neared the meeting place of the apes. Now they were in the trees, worming their way forward, alert for sentinels. Presently through a break in the foliage the scene burst upon the eager eyes of the boy. To Akut it was a familiar one; but to Korak it was all new. His nerves tingled at the savage sight. The great bulls were dancing in the moonlight, leaping in an irregular circle about the flat-topped earthen drum about which three old females sat beating its resounding top with sticks worn smooth by long years of use.

Akut, knowing the temper and customs of his kind, was too wise to make their presence known until the frenzy of the dance had passed. After the drum was quiet and the bellies of the tribe well-filled he would hail them. Then would come a parley, after which he and Korak would be accepted into membership by the community. There might be those who would object; but such could be overcome by brute force, of which he and the lad had an ample surplus. For weeks, possibly months, their presence might cause ever decreasing suspicion among others of the tribe; but eventually they would become as born brothers to these strange apes.

He hoped that they had been among those who had known Tarzan, for that would help in the introduction of the lad and in the consummation of Akut's dearest wish, that Korak should become king of the apes. It was with difficulty, however, that Akut kept the boy from rushing into the midst of the dancing anthropoids—an act that would have meant the instant extermination of them both, since the hysterical frenzy into which the great apes work themselves during the performance of their strange rites is of such a nature that even the most ferocious of the carnivora give them a wide berth at such times.

As the moon declined slowly toward the lofty, foliaged horizon of the amphitheater the booming of the drum decreased and lessened were the exertions of the dancers, until, at last, the final note was struck and the huge beasts turned to fall upon the feast they had dragged hither for the orgy.

From what he had seen and heard Akut was able to explain to Korak that the rites proclaimed the choosing of a new king, and he pointed out to the boy the massive figure of the shaggy monarch, come into his kingship, no doubt, as many human rulers have come into theirs—by the murder of his predecessor.

When the apes had filled their bellies and many of them had sought the bases of the trees to curl up in sleep Akut plucked Korak by the arm.

"Come," he whispered. "Come slowly. Follow me. Do as Akut does."

Then he advanced slowly through the trees until he stood upon a bough overhanging one side of the amphitheater. Here he stood in silence for a moment. Then he uttered a low growl. Instantly a score of apes leaped to their feet. Their savage little eyes sped quickly around the periphery of the clearing. The king ape was the first to see the two figures upon the branch. He gave voice to an ominous growl. Then he took a few lumbering steps in the direction of the intruders. His hair was bristling. His legs were stiff, imparting a halting, jerky motion to his gait. Behind him pressed a number of bulls.

He stopped just a little before he came beneath the two—just far enough to be beyond their spring. Wary king! Here he stood rocking himself to and fro upon his short legs, baring his fangs in hideous grinnings, rumbling out an ever increasing volume of growls, which were slowly but steadily increasing to the proportions of roars. Akut knew that he was an attack upon them. The old ape did not wish to fight. He had come with the boy to cast his lot with the tribe.

"I am Akut," he said. "This is Korak. Korak is the son of Tarzan who was king of the apes. I, too, was king of the apes who dwelt in the midst of the great waters. We have come to hunt with you, to fight with you. We are great hunters. We are mighty fighters. Let us come in peace."

The king ceased his rocking. He eyed the pair from beneath his beetling brows. His bloodshot eyes were savage and crafty. His kingship was very new and he was jealous of it. He feared the encroachments of two strange apes. The sleek, brown, hairless body of the lad spelled "man," and man he feared and hated.

"Go away!" he growled. "Go away, or I will kill you."

The eager lad, standing behind the great Akut, had been pulsing with anticipation and happiness. He wanted to leap down among these hairy monsters and show them that he was their friend, that he was one of them. He had expected that they would receive him with open arms, and now the words of the king ape filled him with indignation and sorrow. The blacks had set upon him and driven him away. Then he had turned to the white men—to those of his own kind—only to hear the ping of bullets where he had expected words of cordial welcome. The great apes had remained his final hope. To them he looked for the companionship man had denied him. Suddenly rage overwhelmed him.

The king ape was almost directly beneath him. The others were formed in a half circle several yards behind the king. They were watching events interestedly. Before Akut could guess his intention, or prevent, the boy leaped to the ground directly in the path of the king, who had now succeeded in stimulating himself to a frenzy of fury.

"I am Korak!" shouted the boy. "I am the Killer. I came to live among you as a friend. You want to drive me away. Very well, then, I shall go; but before I go I shall show you that the son of Tarzan is your master, as his father was before him—that he is not afraid of your king or you."

For an instant the king ape had stood motionless with surprise. He had expected no such rash action upon the part of either of the intruders. Akut was equally surprised. Now he shouted excitedly for Korak to come back, for he knew that in the sacred arena the other bulls might be expected to come to the assistance of their king against an outsider, though there was small likelihood that the king would need assistance. Once those mighty jaws closed upon the boy's soft neck the end would come quickly. To leap to his rescue would mean death for Akut, too; but the brave old ape never hesitated. Bristling and growling, he dropped to the sward just as the king ape charged.

The beast's hands clutched for their hold as the animal sprang upon the lad. The fierce jaws were wide distended to bury the yellow fangs deeply in the brown hide. Korak, too, leaped forward to meet the attack; but leaped crouching, beneath the outstretched arms. At the instant of contact the lad pivoted on one foot, and with all the weight of his body and the strength of his trained muscles drove a clenched fist into the bull's stomach. With a gasping shriek the king ape collapsed, clutching futilely for the agile, naked creature nimbly sidestepping from his grasp.

Howls of rage and dismay broke from the bull apes behind the fallen king, as with murder in their savage little hearts they rushed forward upon Korak and Akut; but the old ape was too wise to court any such unequal encounter. To have counseled the boy to retreat now would have been futile, and Akut knew it. To delay even a second in argument would have sealed the death warrants of them both. There was but a single hope and Akut seized it. Grasping the lad around the waist he lifted him bodily from the ground, and turning ran swiftly toward another tree which swung low branches above the arena. Close upon their heels swarmed the hideous mob; but Akut, old though he was and burdened by the weight of the struggling Korak, was still fleeter than his pursuers.

With a bound he grasped a low limb, and with the agility of a little monkey swung himself and the boy to temporary safety. Nor did he hesitate even here; but raced on through the jungle night, bearing his burden to safety. For a time the bulls pursued; but presently, as the swifter outdistanced the slower and found themselves separated from their fellows they abandoned the chase, standing roaring and screaming until the jungle reverberated to their hideous noises. Then they turned and retraced their way to the amphitheater.

When Akut felt assured that they were no longer pursued he stopped and released Korak. The boy was furious.

"Why did you drag me away?" he cried. "I would have taught them! I would have taught them all! Now they will think that I am afraid of them."

"What they think cannot harm you," said Akut. "You are alive. If I had not brought you away you would be dead now and so would I. Do you not know that even Numa slinks from the path of the great apes when there are many of them and they are mad?"

# 9

I T WAS AN unhappy Korak who wandered aimlessly through the jungle the day following his inhospitable reception by the great apes. His heart was heavy from disappointment. Unsatisfied vengeance smoldered in his breast. He looked with hatred upon the denizens of his jungle world, bearing his fighting fangs and growling at those that came within radius of his senses. The mark of his father's early life was strong upon him and enhanced by months of association with beasts, from whom the imitative faculty of youth had absorbed a countless number of little mannerisms of the predatory creatures of the wild.

He bared his fangs now as naturally and upon as slight provocation as Sheeta, the panther, bared his. He growled as ferociously as Akut himself. When he came suddenly upon another beast his quick crouch bore a strange resemblance to the arching of a cat's back. Korak, the killer, was looking for trouble. In his heart of hearts he hoped to meet the king ape who had driven him from the amphitheater. To this end he insisted upon remaining in the vicinity; but the exigencies of the perpetual search for food led them several miles further away during day.

They were moving slowly down wind, and warily because the advantage was with whatever beast might chance to be hunting ahead of them, where their scent-spoor was being borne by the light breeze. Suddenly the two halted simultaneously. Two heads were cocked upon one side. Like creatures hewn from solid rock they stood immovable, listening. Not a muscle quivered. For several seconds they remained thus, then Korak advanced cautiously a few yards and leaped nimbly into a tree. Akut followed close upon his heels. Neither had made a noise that would have been appreciable to human ears at a dozen paces.

Stopping often to listen they crept forward through the trees.

That both were greatly puzzled was apparent from the questioning looks they cast at one another from time to time. Finally the lad caught a glimpse of a palisade a hundred yards ahead, and beyond it the tops of some goatskin tents and a number of thatched huts. His lip upcurled in a savage snarl. Blacks! How he hated them. He signed to Akut to remain where he was while he advanced to reconnoiter.

Woe betide the unfortunate villager whom The Killer came upon now. Slinking through the lower branches of the trees, leaping lightly from one jungle giant to its neighbor where the distance was not too great, or swinging from one hand hold to another Korak came silently toward the village. He heard a voice beyond the palisade and toward that he made his way. A great tree overhung the enclosure at the very point from which the voice came. Into this Korak crept. His spear was ready in his hand. His ears told him of the proximity of a human being. All that his eyes required was a single glance to show him his target. Then, lightning like, the missile would fly to its goal. With raised spear he crept among the branches of the tree glaring narrowly downward in search of the owner of the voice which rose to him from below.

At last he saw a human back. The spear hand flew to the limit of the throwing position to gather the force that would send the iron shod missile completely through the body of the unconscious victim. And then The Killer paused. He leaned forward a little to get a better view of the target. Was it to insure more perfect aim, or had there been that in the graceful lines and the childish curves of the little body below him that had held in check the spirit of murder running riot in his veins?

He lowered his spear cautiously that it might make no noise by scraping against foliage or branches. Quietly he crouched in a comfortable position along a great limb and there he lay with wide eyes looking down in wonder upon the creature he had crept upon to kill—looking down upon a little girl, a little nut brown maiden. The snarl had gone from his lip. His only expression was one of interested attention—he was trying to discover what the girl was doing. Suddenly a broad grin overspread his face, for a turn of the girl's body had revealed Geeka of the ivory head and the rat skin torso—Geeka of the splinter limbs and the disreputable appearance. The little girl raised the marred face to hers and rocking herself backward and forward crooned a plaintive Arab lullaby to the doll. A softer light entered the eyes of The Killer. For a long hour that passed very quickly to

him Korak lay with gaze riveted upon the playing child. Not
once had he had a view of the girl's full face. For the most part
he saw only a mass of wavy, black hair, one brown little shoulder exposed upon the side where her single robe was caught
beneath her arm, and a shapely knee protruding from beneath
her garment as she sat cross legged upon the ground. A tilt of
the head as she emphasized some maternal admonition to the
passive Geeka revealed occasionally a rounded cheek or a pi-
quant little chin. Now she was shaking a slim finger at Geeka,
reprovingly, and again she crushed to her heart this only object
upon which she might lavish the untold wealth of her childish
affections.

Korak, momentarily forgetful of his bloody mission, permitted the fingers of his spear hand to relax a little their grasp upon
the shaft of his formidable weapon. It slipped, almost falling;
but the occurrence recalled The Killer to himself. It reminded
him of his purpose in slinking stealthily upon the owner of the
voice that had attracted his vengeful attention. He glanced at the
spear, with its well-worn grip and cruel, barbed head. Then he
let his eyes wander again to the dainty form below him. In imagination he saw the heavy weapon shooting downward. He saw
it pierce the tender flesh, driving its way deep into the yielding
body. He saw the ridiculous doll drop from its owner's arms to
lie sprawled and pathetic beside the quivering body of the little
girl. The Killer shuddered, scowling at the inanimate iron and
wood of the spear as though they constituted a sentient being
endowed with a malignant mind.

Korak wondered what the girl would do were he to drop suddenly from the tree to her side. Most likely she would scream
and run away. Then would come the men of the village with
spears and guns and set upon him. They would either kill him
or drive him away. A lump rose in the boy's throat. He craved
the companionship of his own kind, though he scarce realized
how greatly. He would have liked to slip down beside the little
girl and talk with her, though he knew from the words he had
overheard that she spoke a language with which he was unfamiliar. They could have talked by signs a little. That would have
been better than nothing. Too, he would have been glad to see
her face. What he had glimpsed assured him that she was pretty;
but her strongest appeal to him lay in the affectionate nature
revealed by her gentle mothering of the grotesque doll.

At last he hit upon a plan. He would attract her attention, and
reassure her by a smiling greeting from a greater distance. Si-

lently he wormed his way back into the tree. It was his intention to hail her from beyond the palisade, giving her the feeling of security which he imagined the stout barricade would afford.

He had scarcely left his position in the tree when his attention was attracted by a considerable noise upon the opposite side of the village. By moving a little he could see the gate at the far end of the main street. A number of men, women and children were running toward it. It swung open, revealing the head of a caravan upon the opposite side. In trooped the motley organization—black slaves and dark hued Arabs of the northern deserts; cursing camel drivers urging on their vicious charges; overburdened donkeys, waving sadly pendulous ears while they endured with stoic patience the brutalities of their masters; goats, sheep and horses. Into the village they all trooped behind a tall, sour, old man, who rode without greetings to those who shrunk from his path directly to a large goatskin tent in the center of the village. Here he spoke to a wrinkled hag.

Korak, from his vantage spot, could see it all. He saw the old man asking questions of the black woman, and then he saw the latter point toward a secluded corner of the village which was hidden from the main street by the tents of the Arabs and the huts of the natives in the direction of the tree beneath which the little girl played. This was doubtless her father, thought Korak. He had been away and his first thought upon returning was of his little daughter. How glad she would be to see him! How she would run and throw herself into his arms, to be crushed to his breast and covered with his kisses. Korak sighed. He thought of his own father and mother far away in London.

He returned to his place in the tree above the girl. If he couldn't have happiness of this sort himself he wanted to enjoy the happiness of others. Possibly if he made himself known to the old man he might be permitted to come to the village occasionally as a friend. It would be worth trying. He would wait until the old Arab had greeted his daughter, then he would make his presence known with signs of peace.

The Arab was striding softly toward the girl. In a moment he would be beside her, and then how surprised and delighted she would be! Korak's eyes sparkled in anticipation—and now the old man stood behind the little girl. His stern old face was still unrelaxed. The child was yet unconscious of his presence. She prattled on to the unresponsive Geeka. Then the old man coughed. With a start the child glanced quickly up over her shoulder. Korak could see her full face now. It was very beautiful in its sweet and innocent childishness—all soft and lovely curves. He could see her great, dark eyes. He looked for the happy love light that would follow recognition; but it did not come. Instead, terror, stark, paralyzing terror, was mirrored in her eyes, in the expression of her mouth, in the tense, cowering attitude of her body. A grim smile curved the thin, cruel lip of the Arab. The child essayed to crawl away; but before she could get out of his reach the old man kicked her brutally, sending her sprawling upon the grass. Then he followed her up to seize and strike her as was his custom.

Above them, in the tree, a beast crouched where a moment before had been a boy—a beast with dilating nostrils and bared fangs—a beast that trembled with rage.

The Shiek was stooping to reach for the girl when The Killer dropped to the ground at his side. His spear was still in his left hand but he had forgotten it. Instead his right fist was clenched and as The Sheik took a backward step, astonished by the sudden materialization of this strange apparition apparently out of clear air, the heavy fist landed full upon his mouth backed by the weight of the young giant and the terrific power of his more than human muscles.

Bleeding and senseless The Sheik sank to earth. Korak turned toward the child. She had regained her feet and stood wide eyed and frightened, looking first into his face and then, horror struck, at the recumbent figure of The Sheik. In an involuntary gesture of protection The Killer threw an arm about the girl's shoulders and stood waiting for the Arab to regain consciousness. For a moment they remained thus, when the girl spoke.

"When he regains his senses he will kill me," she said, in Arabic.

Korak could not understand her. He shook his head, speaking to her first in English and then in the language of the great apes; but neither of these was intelligible to her. She leaned forward and touched the hilt of the long knife that the Arab wore. Then she raised her clasped hand above her head and drove an imaginary blade into her breast above her heart. Korak understood. The old man would kill her. The girl came to his side again and stood there trembling. She did not fear him. Why should she? He had saved her from a terrible beating at the hands of The Sheik. Never, in her memory, had another so befriended her. She looked up into his face. It was a boyish, handsome face, nut-brown like her own. She admired the spotted leopard skin that circled his lithe body from one shoulder to his knees. The metal anklets and armlets adorning him aroused her envy. Always had she coveted something of the kind; but never had The Sheik permitted her more than the single cotton garment that barely sufficed to cover her nakedness. No furs or silks or jewelry had there ever been for little Meriem.

And Korak looked at the girl. He had always held girls in a species of contempt. Boys who associated with them were, in his estimation, mollycoddles. He wondered what he should do. Could he leave her here to be abused, possibly murdered, by the villainous old Arab? No! But, on the other hand, could he take her into the jungle with him? What could he accomplish burdened by a weak and frightened girl? She would scream at her own shadow when the moon came out upon the jungle night and the great beasts roamed, moaning and roaring, through the darkness.

He stood for several minutes buried in thought. The girl watched his face, wondering what was passing in his mind. She, too, was thinking of the future. She feared to remain and suffer the vengeance of The Sheik. There was no one in all the world to whom she might turn, other than this half-naked stranger who had dropped miraculously from the clouds to save her from one of The Sheik's accustomed beatings. Would her new friend leave her now? Wistfully she gazed at his intent face. She moved a little closer to him, laying a slim, brown hand upon his arm. The contact awakened the lad from his absorption. He looked down at her, and then his arm went about her shoulder once more, for he saw tears upon her lashes.

"Come," he said. "The jungle is kinder than man. You shall live in the jungle and Korak and Akut will protect you."

She did not understand his words, but the pressure of his arm drawing her away from the prostrate Arab and the tents was quite intelligible. One little arm crept about his waist and together they walked toward the palisade. Beneath the great tree that had harbored Korak while he watched the girl at play he lifted her in his arms and throwing her lightly across his shoulder leaped nimbly into the lower branches. Her arms were about his neck and from one little hand Geeka dangled down his straight young back.

And so Meriem entered the jungle with Korak, trusting, in her childish innocence, the stranger who had befriended her, and perhaps influenced in her belief in him by that strange intuitive power possessed by woman. She had no conception of what the future might hold. She did not know, nor could she have guessed the manner of life led by her protector. Possibly she pictured a distant village similar to that of The Sheik in which lived other white men like the stranger. That she was to be taken into the savage, primeval life of a jungle beast could not have occurred to her. Had it, her little heart would have palpitated with fear. Often had she wished to run away from the cruelties of The Sheik and Mabunu; but the dangers of the jungle always had deterred her.

The two had gone but a short distance from the village when the girl spied the huge proportions of the great Akut. With a half-stifled scream she clung more closely to Korak, and pointed fearfully toward the ape.

Akut, thinking that The Killer was returning with a prisoner, came growling toward them—a little girl aroused no more sympathy in the beast's heart than would a full-grown bull ape. She was a stranger and therefore to be killed. He bared his yellow fangs as he approached, and to his surprise The Killer bared his likewise, but he bared them at Akut, and snarled menacingly.

"Ah," thought Akut, "The Killer has taken a mate," and so, obedient to the tribal laws of his kind, he left them alone, becoming suddenly absorbed in a fuzzy caterpillar of peculiarly succulent appearance. The larva disposed of, he glanced from the corner of an eye at Korak. The youth had deposited his burden upon a large limb, where she clung desperately to keep from falling.

"She will accompany us," said Korak to Akut, jerking a thumb in the direction of the girl. "Do not harm her. We will protect her."

Akut shrugged. To be burdened by the young of man was in no way to his liking. He could see from her evident fright at her position on the branch, and from the terrified glances she cast in his direction that she was hopelessly unfit. By all the ethics of Akut's training and inheritance the unfit should be eliminated; but if The Killer wished this there was nothing to be done about it but to tolerate her. Akut certainly didn't want her—of that he was quite positive. Her skin was too smooth and hairless. Quite snake-like, in fact, and her face was most unattractive. Not at all like that of a certain lovely she he had particularly noticed among the apes in the amphitheater the previous night. Ah, there was true feminine beauty for one!—a great, generous mouth; lovely, yellow fangs, and the cutest, softest side whiskers! Akut sighed. Then he rose, expanded his great chest and strutted back and forth along a substantial branch, for even a puny thing like this she of Korak's might admire his fine coat and his graceful carriage.

But poor little Meriem only shrank closer to Korak and almost wished that she were back in the village of The Sheik where the terrors of existence were of human origin, and so more or less familiar. The hideous ape frightened her. He was so large and so ferocious in appearance. His actions she could only interpret as a menace, for how could she guess that he was parading to excite admiration? Nor could she know of the bond of fellowship which existed between this great brute and the godlike youth who had rescued her from the Sheik.

Meriem spent an evening and a night of unmitigated terror. Korak and Akut led her along dizzy ways as they searched for food. Once they hid her in the branches of a tree while they stalked a near-by buck. Even her natural terror of being left alone in the awful jungle was submerged in a greater horror as she saw the man and the beast spring simultaneously upon their prey and drag it down, as she saw the handsome face of her preserver contorted in a bestial snarl; as she saw his strong, white teeth buried in the soft flesh of the kill.

When he came back to her blood smeared his face and hands and breast and she shrank from him as he offered her a huge hunk of hot, raw meat. He was evidently much disturbed by her refusal to eat, and when, a moment later, he scampered away into the forest to return with fruit for her she was once more forced to alter her estimation of him. This time she did not shrink, but acknowledged his gift with a smile that, had she known it, was more than ample payment to the affection starved boy.

The sleeping problem vexed Korak. He knew that the girl could not balance herself in safety in a tree crotch while she slept, nor would it be safe to permit her to sleep upon the ground open to the attacks of prowling beasts of prey. There was but a single solution that presented itself—he must hold her in his arms all night. And that he did, with Akut braced upon one side of her and he upon the other, so that she was warmed by the bodies of them both.

She did not sleep much until the night was half spent; but at last Nature overcame her terrors of the black abyss beneath and the hairy body of the wild beast at her side, and she fell into a deep slumber which outlasted the darkness. When she opened her eyes the sun was well up. At first she could not believe in the reality of her position. Her head had rolled from Korak's shoulder so that her eyes were directed upon the hairy back of the ape. At sight of it she shrank away. Then she realized that someone was holding her, and turning her head she saw the smiling eyes of the youth regarding her. When he smiled she could not fear him, and now she shrank closer against him in natural revulsion toward the rough coat of the brute upon her other side.

Korak spoke to her in the language of the apes; but she shook her head, and spoke to him in the language of the Arab, which was an unintelligible to him as was ape speech to her. Akut sat up and looked at them. He could understand what Korak said but the girl made only foolish noises that were entirely unintelligible and ridiculous. Akut could not understand what Korak saw in her to attract him. He looked at her long and steadily, appraising her carefully, then he scratched his head, rose and shook himself.

His movement gave the girl a little start—she had forgotten Akut for the moment. Again she shrank from him. The beast saw that she feared him, and being a brute enjoyed the evidence of the terror his brutishness inspired. Crouching, he extended his huge hand stealthily toward her, as though to seize her. She shrank still further away. Akut's eyes were busy drinking in the humor of the situation—he did not see the narrowing eyes of the boy upon him, nor the shortening neck as the broad shoulders rose in a characteristic attitude of preparation for attack. As the ape's fingers were about to close upon the girl's arm the youth rose suddenly with a short, vicious growl. A clenched fist flew before Meriem's eyes to land full upon the snout of the astonished Akut. With an explosive bellow the anthropoid reeled backward and tumbled from the tree.

Korak stood glaring down upon him when a sudden swish in the bushes close by attracted his attention. The girl too was looking down; but she saw nothing but the angry ape scrambling to his feet. Then, like a bolt from a cross bow, a mass of spotted, yellow fur shot into view straight for Akut's back. It was Sheeta, the leopard.

# 10

As the leopard leaped for the great ape Meriem gasped in surprise and horror—not for the impending fate of the anthropoid, but at the act of the youth who but an instant before had angrily struck his strange companion; for scarce had the carnivore burst into view than with drawn knife the youth had leaped far out above him, so that as Sheeta was almost in the act of sinking fangs and talons in Akut's broad back The Killer landed full upon the leopard's shoulders.

The cat halted in mid air, missed the ape by but a hair's breadth, and with horrid snarlings rolled over upon its back, clutching and clawing in an effort to reach and dislodge the antagonist biting at its neck and knifing it in the side.

Akut, startled by the sudden rush from his rear, and following hoary instinct, was in the tree beside the girl with an agility little short of marvelous in so heavy a beast. But the moment that he turned to see what was going on below him brought him as quickly to the ground again. Personal differences were quickly forgotten in the danger which menaced his human companion, nor was he a whit less eager to jeopardize his own safety in the service of his friend than Korak had been to succor him.

The result was that Sheeta presently found two ferocious creatures tearing him to ribbons. Shrieking, snarling and growling, the three rolled hither and thither among the underbrush, while with staring eyes the sole spectator of the battle royal crouched trembling in the tree above them hugging Geeka frantically to her breast.

It was the boy's knife which eventually decided the battle, and as the fierce feline shuddered convulsively and rolled over upon its side the youth and the ape rose and faced one another across the prostrate carcass. Korak jerked his head in the direction of the little girl in the tree.

"Leave her alone," he said; "she is mine."

Akut grunted, blinked his blood-shot eyes, and turned toward the body of Sheeta. Standing erect upon it he threw out his great chest, raised his face toward the heavens and gave voice to so horrid a scream that once again the little girl shuddered and shrank. It was the victory cry of the bull ape that has made a kill. The boy only looked on for a moment in silence; then he leaped into the tree again to the girl's side. Akut presently rejoined them. For a few minutes he busied himself licking his wounds, then he wandered off to hunt his breakfast.

For many months the strange life of the three went on unmarked by any unusual occurrences. At least without any occurrences that seemed unusual to the youth or the ape; but to the little girl it was a constant nightmare of horrors for days and weeks, until she too became accustomed to gazing into the eyeless sockets of death and to the feel of the icy wind of his shroud-like mantle. Slowly she learned the rudiments of the only common medium of thought exchange which her companions possessed—the language of the great apes. More quickly she perfected herself in jungle craft, so that the time soon came when she was an important factor in the chase, watching while the others slept, or helping them to trace the spoor of whatever prey they might be stalking. Akut accepted her on a footing which bordered upon equality when it was necessary for them to come into close contact; but for the most part he avoided her. The youth always was kind to her, and if there were many occasions upon which he felt the burden of her presence he hid it from her. Finding that the night damp and chill caused her discomfort and even suffering, Korak constructed a tight little shelter high among the swaying branches of a giant tree. Here little Meriem slept in comparative warmth and safety, while The Killer and the ape perched upon near-by branches, the former always before the entrance to the lofty domicile, where he best could guard its inmate from the dangers of arboreal enemies. They were too high to feel much fear of Sheeta; but there was always Histah, the snake, to strike terror to one's soul, and the great baboons who lived near-by, and who, while never attacking always bared their fangs and barked at any of the trio when they passed near them.

After the construction of the shelter the activities of the three became localized. They ranged less widely, for there was always the necessity of returning to their own tree at nightfall. A river flowed near by. Game and fruit were plentiful, as were fish also. Existence had settled down to the daily humdrum of the wild—the search for food and the sleeping upon full bellies. They looked no further ahead than today. If the youth thought of his past and of those who longed for him in the distant metropolis it was in a detached and impersonal sort of way as though that other life belonged to another creature than himself. He had given up hope of returning to civilization, for since his various rebuffs at the hands of those to whom he had looked for friendship he had wandered so far inland as to realize that he was completely lost in the mazes of the jungle.

Then, too, since the coming of Meriem he had found in her that one thing which he had most missed before in his savage, jungle life—human companionship. In his friendship for her there was appreciable no trace of sex influence of which he was cognizant. They were friends—companions—that was all. Both might have been boys, except for the half tender and always masterful manifestation of the protective instinct which was apparent in Korak's attitude.

The little girl idolized him as she might have idolized an indulgent brother had she had one. Love was a thing unknown to either; but as the youth neared manhood it was inevitable that it should come to him as it did to every other savage, jungle male.

As Meriem became proficient in their common language the pleasures of their companionship grew correspondingly, for now they could converse and aided by the mental powers of their human heritage they amplified the restricted vocabulary of the apes until talking was transformed from a task into an enjoyable pastime. When Korak hunted, Meriem usually accompanied him, for she had learned the fine art of silence, when silence was desirable. She could pass through the branches of the great trees now with all the agility and stealth of The Killer himself. Great heights no longer appalled her. She swung from limb to limb, or she raced through the mighty branches, surefooted, lithe, and fearless. Korak was very proud of her, and even old Akut grunted in approval where before he had growled in contempt.

A distant village of blacks had furnished her with a mantle of fur and feathers, with copper ornaments, and weapons, for Korak would not permit her to go unarmed, or unversed in the use of the weapons he stole for her. A leather thong over one shoulder supported the ever present Geeka who was still the recipient of her most sacred confidences. A light spear and a long knife were her weapons of offense or defense. Her body, rounding into the fulness of an early maturity, followed the lines of a Greek goddess; but there the similarity ceased, for her face was beautiful.

As she grew more accustomed to the jungle and the ways of its wild denizens fear left her. As time wore on she even hunted alone when Korak and Akut were prowling at a great distance, as they were sometimes forced to do when game was scarce in their immediate vicinity. Upon these occasions she usually confined her endeavors to the smaller animals though sometimes she brought down a deer, and once even Horta, the boar—a great tusker that even Sheeta might have thought twice before attacking.

In their stamping grounds in the jungle the three were familiar figures. The little monkeys knew them well, often coming close to chatter and frolic about them. When Akut was by, the small folk kept their distance, but with Korak they were less shy and when both the males were gone they would come close to Meriem, tugging at her ornaments or playing with Geeka, who was a never ending source of amusement to them. The girl played with them and fed them, and when she was alone they helped her to pass the long hours until Korak's return.

Nor were they worthless as friends. In the hunt they helped her locate her quarry. Often they would come racing through the trees to her side to announce the near presence of antelope or giraffe, or with excited warnings of the proximity of Sheeta or Numa. Luscious, sun-kissed fruits which hung far out upon the frail bough of the jungle's waving crest were brought to her by these tiny, nimble allies. Sometimes they played tricks upon her; but she was always kind and gentle with them and in their wild, half-human way they were kind to her and affectionate. Their language being similar to that of the great apes Meriem could converse with them though the poverty of their vocabulary rendered these exchanges anything but feasts of reason. For familiar objects they had names, as well as for those conditions which induced pain or pleasure, joy, sorrow, or rage. These root words were so similar to those in use among the great anthropoids as to suggest that the language of the Manus was the mother tongue. Dreams, aspirations, hopes, the past, the sordid exchange. Dreams, aspirations, hopes, the past, the future held no place in the conversation of Manu, the monkey. All was of the present—particularly of filling his belly and catching lice.

Poor food was this to nourish the mental appetite of a girl just upon the brink of womanhood. And so, finding Manu only amusing as an occasional playfellow or pet, Meriem poured out her sweetest soul thoughts into the deaf ears of Geeka's ivory head. To Geeka she spoke in Arabic, knowing that Geeka, being but a doll, could not understand the language of Korak and Akut, and that the language of Korak and Akut being that of male apes contained nothing of interest to an Arab doll.

Geeka had undergone a transformation since her little mother had left the village of The Sheik. Her garmenture now reflected in miniature that of Meriem. A tiny bit of leopard skin covered her ratskin torso from shoulder to splinter knee. A band of braided grasses about her brow held in place a few gaudy feathers from the parakeet, while other bits of grass were fashioned into imitations of arm and leg ornaments of metal. Geeka was a perfect little savage; but at heart she was unchanged, being the same omnivorous listener as of yore. An excellent trait in Geeka was that she never interrupted in order to talk about herself. Today was no exception. She had been listening attentively to Meriem for an hour, propped against the bole of a tree while her lithe, young mistress stretched catlike and luxurious along a swaying branch before her.

"Little Geeka," said Meriem, "our Korak has been gone for a long time today. We miss him, little Geeka, do we not? It is dull and lonesome in the great jungle when our Korak is away. What will he bring us this time, eh? Another shining band of metal for Meriem's ankle? Or a soft, doeskin loin cloth from the body of a black she? He tells me that it is harder to get the possessions of the shes, for he will not kill them as he does the males, and they fight savagely when he leaps upon them to wrest their ornaments from them. Then come the males with spears and arrows and Korak takes to the trees. Sometimes he takes the she with him and high among the branches divests her of the things he wishes to bring home to Meriem. He says that the blacks fear him now, and at the first sight of him the women and children run shrieking to their huts; but he follows them within, and it is not often that he returns without arrows for himself and a present for Meriem. Korak is mighty among the jungle people—our Korak, Geeka—no, *my* Korak!"

Meriem's conversation was interrupted by the sudden plunge of an excited little monkey that landed upon her shoulders in a flying leap from a neighboring tree.

"Climb!" he cried. "Climb! The Mangani are coming."

Meriem glanced lazily over her shoulder at the excited disturber of her peace.

"Climb, yourself, little Manu," she said. "The only Mangani in our jungle are Korak and Akut. It is they you have seen returning from the hunt. Some day you will see your own shadow, little Manu, and then you will be frightened to death."

But the monkey only screamed his warning more lustily before he raced upward toward the safety of the high terrace where Mangani, the great ape, could not follow. Presently Meriem heard the sound of approaching bodies swinging through the trees. She listened attentively. There were two and they were great apes—Korak and Akut. To her Korak was an ape—a Mangani, for as such the three always described themselves. Man was an enemy, so they did not think of themselves as belonging any longer to the same genus. Tarmangani, or great white ape, which described the white man in their language, did not fit them all. Gomagani—great black ape, or Negro—described none of them so they called themselves plain Mangani.

Meriem decided that she would feign slumber and play a joke on Korak. So she lay very still with eyes tightly closed. She heard the two approaching closer and closer. They were in the adjoining tree now and must have discovered her, for they had halted. Why were they so quiet? Why did not Korak call out his customary greeting? The quietness was ominous. It was followed presently by a very stealthy sound—one of them was creeping upon her. Was Korak planning a joke upon his own account? Well, she would fool him. Cautiously she opened her eyes the tiniest bit, and as she did so her heart stood still. Creeping silently toward her was a huge bull ape that she never before had seen. Behind him was another like him.

With the agility of a squirrel Meriem was upon her feet and at the same instant the great bull lunged for her. Leaping from limb to limb the girl fled through the jungle while close behind her came the two great apes. Above them raced a bevy of screaming, chattering monkeys, hurling taunts and insults at the Mangani, and encouragement and advice to the girl.

From tree to tree swung Meriem working ever upward toward the smaller branches which would not bear the weight of her pursuers. Faster and faster came the bull apes after her. The clutching fingers of the foremost were almost upon her again and again, but she eluded them by sudden bursts of speed or reckless chances as she threw herself across dizzy spaces.

Slowly she was gaining her way to the greater heights where

safety lay, when, after a particularly daring leap, the swaying branch she grasped bent low beneath her weight, nor whipped upward again as it should have done. Even before the rending sound which followed Meriem knew that she had misjudged the strength of the limb. It gave slowly at first. Then there was a ripping as it parted from the trunk. Releasing her hold Meriem dropped among the foliage beneath, clutching for a new support. She found it a dozen feet below the broken limb. She had fallen thus many times before, so that she had no particular terror of a fall—it was the delay which appalled her most, and rightly, for scarce had she scrambled to a place of safety than the body of the huge ape dropped at her side and a great, hairy arm went about her waist.

Almost at once the other ape reached his companion's side. He made a lunge at Meriem; but her captor swung her to one side, bared his fighting fangs and growled ominously. Meriem struggled to escape. She struck at the hairy breast and bearded cheek. She fastened her strong, white teeth in one shaggy forearm. The ape cuffed her viciously across the face, then he had to turn his attention to his fellow who quite evidently desired the prize for his own.

The captor could not fight to advantage upon the swaying bough, burdened as he was by a squirming, struggling captive, so he dropped quickly to the ground beneath. The other followed him, and here they fought, occasionally abandoning their duel to pursue and recapture the girl who took every advantage of her captors' preoccupation in battle to break away in attempted escape; but always they overtook her, and first one and then the other possessed her as they struggled to tear one another to pieces for the prize.

Often the girl came in for many blows that were intended for a hairy foe, and once she was felled, lying unconscious while the apes, relieved of the distraction of detaining her by force, tore into one another in fierce and terrible combat.

Above them screamed the little monkeys, racing hither and thither in a frenzy of hysterical excitement. Back and forth over the battle field flew countless birds of gorgeous plumage, squawking their hoarse cries of rage and defiance. In the distance a lion roared.

The larger bull was slowly tearing his antagonist to pieces. They rolled upon the ground biting and striking. Again, erect upon their hind legs they pulled and tugged like human wrestlers; but always the giant fangs found their bloody part to play until both combatants and the ground about them were red with gore.

Meriem, through it all, lay still and unconscious upon the ground. At last one found a permanent hold upon the jugular of the other and thus they went down for the last time. For several minutes they lay with scarce a struggle. It was the larger bull who arose alone from the last embrace. He shook himself. A deep growl rumbled from his hairy throat. He waddled back and forth between the body of the girl and that of his vanquished foe. Then he stood upon the latter and gave tongue to his hideous challenge. The little monkeys broke, screaming, in all directions as the terrifying noise broke upon their ears. The gorgeous birds took wing and fled. Once again the lion roared, this time at a greater distance.

The great ape waddled once more to the girl's side. He turned her over upon her back, and stooping commenced to sniff and listen about her face and breast. She lived. The monkeys were returning. They came in swarms, and from above hurled down insults upon the victor.

The ape showed his displeasure by baring his teeth and growling up at them. Then he stooped and lifting the girl to his shoulder waddled off through the jungle. In his wake followed the angry mob.

# 11

KORAK, RETURNING FROM the hunt, heard the jabbering of the excited monkeys. He knew that something was seriously amiss. Histah, the snake, had doubtless coiled his slimy folds about some careless Manu. The youth hastened ahead. The monkeys were Meriem's friends. He would help them if he could. He traveled rapidly along the middle terrace. In the tree by Meriem's shelter he deposited his trophies of the hunt and called aloud to her. There was no answer. He dropped quickly to a lower level. She might be hiding from him.

Upon a great branch where Meriem often swung at indolent ease he saw Geeka propped against the tree's great bole. What could it mean? Meriem had never left Geeka thus alone before. Korak picked up the doll and tucked it in his belt. He called again, more loudly; but no Meriem answered his summons. In the distance the jabbering of the excited Manus was growing less distinct.

Could their excitement be in any way connected with Meriem's disappearance? The bare thought was enough. Without waiting for Akut who was coming slowly along some distance in his rear, Korak swung rapidly in the direction of the chattering mob. But a few minutes sufficed to overtake the rearmost. At sight of him they fell to screaming and pointing downward ahead of them, and a moment later Korak came within sight of the cause of their rage.

The youth's heart stood still in terror as he saw the limp body of the girl across the hairy shoulders of a great ape. That she was dead he did not doubt, and in that instant there arose within him a something which he did not try to interpret nor could have had he tried; but all at once the whole world seemed centered in that tender, graceful body, that frail little body, hanging so pitifully limp and helpless across the bulging shoulders of the brute.

He knew then that little Meriem was his world—his sun, his moon, his stars—with her going had gone all light and warmth and happiness. A groan escaped his lips, and after that a series of hideous roars, more bestial than the beasts', as he dropped plummet-like in mad descent toward the perpetrator of this hideous crime.

The bull ape turned at the first note of this new and menacing voice, and as he turned a new flame was added to the rage and hatred of The Killer, for he saw that the creature before him was none other than the king ape which had driven him away from the great anthropoids to whom he had looked for friendship and asylum.

Dropping the body of the girl to the ground the bull turned to battle anew for possession of his expensive prize; but this time he looked for an easy conquest. He too recognized Korak. Had he not chased him away from the amphitheater without even having to lay a fang or paw upon him? With lowered head and bulging shoulders he rushed headlong for the smooth-skinned creature who was daring to question his right to his prey.

They met head on like two charging bulls, to go down together tearing and striking. Korak forgot his knife. Rage and bloodlust such as his could be satisfied only by the feel of hot flesh between rending fangs, by the gush of new life blood against his bare skin, for, though he did not realize it, Korak, The Killer, was fighting for something more compelling than hate or revenge—he was a great male fighting another male for a she of his own kind.

So impetuous was the attack of the man-ape that he found his hold before the anthropoid could prevent him—a savage hold, with strong jaws closed upon a pulsing jugular, and there he clung, with closed eyes, while his fingers sought another hold upon the shaggy throat.

It was then that Meriem opened her eyes. At the sight before her they went wide.

"Korak!" she cried. "Korak! My Korak! I knew that you would come. Kill him, Korak! Kill him!" And with flashing eyes and heaving bosom the girl, coming to her feet, ran to Korak's side to encourage him. Nearby lay The Killer's spear, where he had flung it as he charged the ape. The girl saw it and snatched it up. No faintness overcame her in the face of this battle primeval at her feet. For her there was no hysterical reaction from the nerve strain of her own personal encounter with the bull. She was excited; but cool and entirely unafraid. Her Korak was battling with another Mangani that would have stolen her; but she did not seek the safety of an overhanging bough there to watch the battle from afar, as would a she Mangani. Instead she placed the point of Korak's spear against the bull ape's side and plunged the sharp point deep into the savage heart. Korak had not needed her aid, for the great bull had been already as good as dead, with the blood gushing from his torn jugular; but Korak rose smiling with a word of approbation for his helper.

How tall and fine she was! Had she changed suddenly within the few hours of his absence, or had his battle with the ape affected his vision? He might have been looking at Meriem through new eyes for the many startling and wonderful surprises his gaze revealed. How long it had been since he had found her in her father's village, a little Arab girl, he did not know, for time is of no import in the jungle and so he had kept no track of the passing days. But he realized, as he looked upon her now, that she was no longer such a little girl as he had first seen playing with Geeka beneath the great tree just within the palisade. The change must have been very gradual to have eluded his notice until now. And what was it that had caused him to realize it so suddenly? His gaze wandered from the girl to the body of the dead bull. For the first time there flashed to his understanding the explanation of the reason for the girl's attempted abduction. Korak's eyes went wide and then they closed to narrow slits of rage as he stood glaring down upon the abysmal brute at his feet. When next his glance rose to Meriem's face a slow flush suffused his own. Now, indeed, was he looking upon her through new eyes—the eyes of a man looking upon a maid.

Akut had come up just as Meriem had speared Korak's antagonist. The exultation of the old ape was keen. He strutted, stifflegged and truculent about the body of the fallen enemy. He growled and upcurved his long, flexible lip. His hair bristled. He was paying no attention to Meriem and Korak. Back in the uttermost recesses of his little brain something was stirring—something which the sight and smell of the great bull had aroused. The outward manifestation of the germinating idea was one of bestial rage; but the inner sensations were pleasurable in the extreme. The scent of the great bull and the sight of his huge and hairy figure had wakened in the heart of Akut a longing for the companionship of his own kind. So Korak was not alone undergoing a change.

And Meriem? She was a woman. It is woman's divine right to love. Always she had loved Korak. He was her big brother. Meriem alone underwent no change. She was still happy in the companionship of her Korak. She still loved him—as a sister loves an indulgent brother—and she was very, very proud of him. In all the jungle there was no other creature so strong, so handsome, or so brave.

Korak came close to her. There was a new light in his eyes as she looked up into them; but she did not understand it. She did not realize how close they were to maturity, nor aught of all the difference in their lives the look in Korak's eyes might mean.

"Meriem," he whispered and his voice was husky as he laid a brown hand upon her bare shoulder. "Meriem!" Suddenly he crushed her to him. She looked up into his face, laughing, and then he bent and kissed her full upon the mouth. Even then she did not understand. She did not recall ever having been kissed before. It was very nice. Meriem liked it. She thought it was Korak's way of showing how glad he was that the great ape had not succeeded in running away with her. She was glad too, so she put her arms about The Killer's neck and kissed him again and again. Then, discovering the doll in his belt she transferred it to her own possession, kissing it as she had kissed Korak.

Korak wanted to say something. He wanted to tell her how he loved her; but the emotion of his love choked him and the vocabulary of the Mangani was limited.

There came a sudden interruption. It was from Akut—a sudden, low growl, no louder than those he had been giving vent to the while he pranced about the dead bull, nor half so loud in fact; but of a timbre that bore straight to the perceptive faculties of the jungle beast ingrained in Korak. It was a warning. Korak looked quickly up from the glorious vision of the sweet face so close to his. Now his other faculties awoke. His ears, his nostrils were on the alert. Something was coming!

The Killer moved to Akut's side. Meriem was just behind them. The three stood like carved statues gazing into the leafy tangle of the jungle. The noise that had attracted their attention increased, and presently a great ape broke through the under-brush a few paces from where they stood. The beast halted at sight of them. He gave a warning grunt back over his shoulder, and a moment later coming cautiously another bull appeared.

He was followed by others—both bulls and females with young, until two score hairy monsters stood glaring at the three. It was the tribe of the dead king ape. Akut was the first to speak. He pointed to the body of the dead bull.

"Korak, mighty fighter, has killed your king," he grunted. "There is none greater in all the jungle than Korak, son of Tarzan. Now Korak is king. What bull is greater than Korak?" It was a challenge to any bull who might care to question Korak's right to the kingship. The apes jabbered and chattered and growled among themselves for a time. At last a young bull came slowly forward rocking upon his short legs, bristling, growling, terrible.

The beast was enormous, and in the full prime of his strength. He belonged to that almost extinct species for which white men have long sought upon the information of the natives of the more inaccessible jungles. Even the natives seldom see these great, hairy, primordial men.

Korak advanced to meet the monster. He, too, was growling. In his mind a plan was revolving. To close with this powerful, untired brute after having just passed through a terrific battle with another of his kind would have been to tempt defeat. He must find an easier way to victory. Crouching, he prepared to meet the charge which he knew would soon come, nor did he have long to wait. His antagonist paused only for sufficient time to permit him to recount for the edification of the audience and the confounding of Korak a brief rèsumè of his former victories, of his prowess, and of what he was about to do to this puny Tarmangani. Then he charged.

With clutching fingers and wide opened jaws he came down upon the waiting Korak with the speed of an express train. Korak did not move until the great arms swung to embrace him, then he dropped low beneath them, swung a terrific right to the side of the beast's jaw as he side-stepped his rushing body, and swinging quickly about stood ready over the fallen ape where he sprawled upon the ground.

It was a surprised anthropoid that attempted to scramble to its feet. Froth flecked its hideous lips. Red were the little eyes. Blood curdling roars tumbled from the deep chest. But it did not reach its feet. The Killer stood waiting above it, and the moment that the hairy chin came upon the proper level another blow that would have felled an ox sent the ape over backward.

Again and again the beast struggled to arise, but each time the mighty Tarmangani stood waiting with ready fist and pile driver blow to bowl him over. Weaker and weaker became the efforts of the bull. Blood smeared his face and breast. A red stream trickled from nose and mouth. The crowd that had cheered him on at first with savage yells, now jeered him—their approbation was for the Tarmangani.

"Kagoda?" inquired Korak, as he sent the bull down once more.

Again the stubborn bull essayed to scramble to his feet. Again The Killer struck him a terrific blow. Again he put the question, *kagoda*—have you had enough?

For a moment the bull lay motionless. Then from between battered lips came the single word: *"Kagoda!"*

"Then rise and go back among your people," said Korak. "I do not wish to be king among people who once drove me from them. Keep your own ways, and we will keep ours. When we meet we may be friends, but we shall not live together."

An old bull came slowly toward The Killer.

"You have killed our king," he said. "You have defeated him who would have been king. You could have killed him had you wished. What shall we do for a king?"

Korak turned toward Akut.

"There is your king," he said. But Akut did not want to be separated from Korak, although he was anxious enough to remain with his own kind. He wanted Korak to remain, too. He said as much.

The youth was thinking of Meriem—of what would be best and safest for her. If Akut went away with the apes there would be but one to watch over and protect her. On the other hand were they to join the tribe he would never feel safe to leave Meriem behind when he went out to hunt, for the passions of the ape-folk are not ever well controlled. Even a female might develop an insane hatred for the slender white girl and kill her during Korak's absence.

"We will live near you," he said, at last. "When you change your hunting ground we will change ours, Meriem and I, and so remain near you; but we shall not dwell among you."

Akut raised objections to this plan. He did not wish to be separated from Korak. At first he refused to leave his human friend for the companionship of his own kind; but when he saw the last of the tribe wandering off into the jungle again and his glance rested upon the lithe figure of the dead king's young mate as she cast admiring glances at her lord's successor the call of blood would not be denied. With a farewell glance toward his

beloved Korak he turned and followed the she ape into the lab-
yrinthine mazes of the wood.

After Korak had left the village of the blacks following his
last thieving expedition, the screams of his victim and those of
the other women and children had brought the warriors in from
the forest and the river. Great was the excitement and hot
was the rage of the men when they learned that the white devil
had again entered their homes, frightened their women and
stolen arrows and ornaments and food.

Even their superstitious fear of this weird creature who hunted
with a huge bull ape was overcome in their desire to wreak
vengeance upon him and rid themselves for good and all of the
menace of his presence in the jungle.

And so it was that a score of the fleetest and most doughty
warriors of the tribe set out in pursuit of Korak and Akut but a
few minutes after they had left the scene of The Killer's many
depredations.

The youth and the ape had traveled slowly and with no precautions against a successful pursuit. Nor was their attitude of
careless indifference to the blacks at all remarkable. So many
similar raids had gone unpunished that the two had come to look
upon the Negroes with contempt. The return journey led them
straight up wind. The result being that the scent of their pursuers
was borne away from them, so they proceeded upon their way
in total ignorance of the fact that tireless trackers but little less
expert in the mysteries of woodcraft than themselves were dog-
ging their trail with savage insistence.

The little party of warriors was led by Kovudoo, the chief; a
middle-aged savage of exceptional cunning and bravery. It was
he who first came within sight of the quarry which they had
followed for hours by the mysterious methods of their almost
uncanny powers of observation, intuition, and even scent.

Kovudoo and his men came upon Korak, Akut and Meriem
after the killing of the king ape, the noise of the combat having
led them at last straight to their quarry. The sight of the slender
white girl had amazed the savage chief and held him gazing at
the trio for a moment before ordering his warriors to rush out
upon their prey. In that moment it was that the great apes came
and again the blacks remained awestruck witnesses to the palaver, and the battle between Korak and the young bull.

But now the apes had gone, and the white youth and the white
maid stood alone in the jungle. One of Kovudoo's men leaned

close to the ear of his chief. "Look!" he whispered, and pointed to something that dangled at the girl's side. "When my brother and I were slaves in the village of The Sheik my brother made that thing for The Sheik's little daughter—she played with it always and called it after my brother, whose name is Geeka. Just before we escaped some one came and struck down The Sheik, stealing his daughter away. If this is she The Sheik will pay you well for her return."

Korak's arm had again gone around the shoulders of Meriem. Love raced hot through his young veins. Civilization was but a half-remembered state—London as remote as ancient Rome. In all the world there were but they two—Korak, The Killer, and Meriem, his mate. Again he drew her close to him and covered her willing lips with his hot kisses. And then from behind him broke a hideous bedlam of savage war cries and a score of shrieking blacks were upon them.

Korak turned to give battle. Meriem with her own light spear stood by his side. An avalanche of barbed missiles flew about them. One pierced Korak's shoulder, another his leg, and he went down.

Meriem was unscathed for the blacks had intentionally spared her. Now they rushed forward to finish Korak and make good the girl's capture; but as they came there came also from another point in the jungle the great Akut and at his heels the huge bulls of his new kingdom.

Snarling and roaring they rushed upon the black warriors when they saw the mischief they had already wrought. Kovudoo, re-alizing the danger of coming to close quarters with these mighty ape-men, seized Meriem and called upon his warriors to retreat. For a time the apes followed them, and several of the blacks were badly mauled and one killed before they succeeded in es-caping. Nor would they have gotten off thus easily had Akut not been more concerned with the condition of the wounded Korak than with the fate of the girl upon whom he had always looked as more or less of an interloper and an unquestioned burden.

Korak lay bleeding and unconscious when Akut reached his side. The great ape tore the heavy spears from his flesh, licked the wounds and then carried his friend to the lofty shelter that Korak had constructed for Meriem. Further than this the brute could do nothing. Nature must accomplish the rest unaided or Korak must die.

He did not die, however. For days he lay helpless with fever, while Akut and the apes hunted close by that they might protect him from such birds and beasts as might reach his lofty retreat. Occasionally Akut brought him juicy fruits which helped to slake his thirst and allay his fever, and little by little his powerful constitution overcame the effects of the spear thrusts. The wounds healed and his strength returned. All during his rational moments as he had lain upon the soft furs which lined Meriem's nest he had suffered more acutely from fears for Meriem than from the pain of his own wounds. For her he must live. For her he must regain his strength that he might set out in search of her. What had the blacks done to her? Did she still live, or had they sacrificed her to their lust for torture and human flesh? Korak almost trembled with terror as the most hideous possibilities of the girl's fate suggested themselves to him out of his knowledge of the customs of Kovudoo's tribe.

The days dragged their weary lengths along, but at last he had sufficiently regained his strength to crawl from the shelter and make his way unaided to the ground. Now he lived more upon raw meat, for which he was entirely dependent on Akut's skill and generosity. With the meat diet his strength returned more rapidly, and at last he felt that he was fit to undertake the journey to the village of the blacks.

# 12

Two tall, bearded white men moved cautiously through the jungle from their camp beside a wide river. They were Carl Jenssen and Sven Malbihn, but little altered in appearance since the day, years before, that they and their *safari* had been so badly frightened by Korak and Akut as the former sought haven with them.

Every year had they come into the jungle to trade with the natives, or to rob them; to hunt and trap; or to guide other white men in the land they knew so well. Always since their experience with The Sheik had they operated at a safe distance from his territory.

Now they were closer to his village than they had been for years, yet safe enough from discovery owing to the uninhabited nature of the intervening jungle and the fear and enmity of Kovudoo's people for The Sheik, who, in time past, had raided and all but exterminated the tribe.

This year they had come to trap live specimens for a European zoological garden, and today they were approaching a trap which they had set in the hope of capturing a specimen of the large baboons that frequented the neighborhood. As they approached the trap they became aware from the noises emanating from its vicinity that their efforts had been crowned with success. The barking and screaming of hundreds of baboons could mean naught else than that one or more of their number had fallen a victim to the allurements of the bait.

The extreme caution of the two men was prompted by former experiences with the intelligent and doglike creatures with which they had to deal. More than one trapper has lost his life in battle with enraged baboons who will hesitate to attack nothing upon one occasion, while upon another a single gun shot will disperse hundreds of them.

Heretofore the Swedes had always watched near-by their trap, for as a rule only the stronger bulls are thus caught, since in their greediness they prevent the weaker from approaching the coveted bait, and when once with the ordinary rude trap woven on the spot of interlaced branches they are able, with the aid of their friends upon the outside, to demolish their prison and escape. But in this instance the trappers had utilized a special steel cage which could withstand all the strength and cunning of a baboon. It was only necessary, therefore, to drive away the herd which they knew were surrounding the prison and wait for their boys who were even now following them to the trap.

As they came within sight of the spot they found conditions precisely as they had expected. A large male was battering frantically against the steel wires of the cage that held him captive. Upon the outside several hundred other baboons were tearing and tugging in his aid, and all were roaring and jabbering and barking at the top of their lungs.

But what neither the Swedes nor the baboons saw was the half-naked figure of a youth hidden in the foliage of a nearby tree. He had come upon the scene at almost the same instant as Jenssen and Malbihn, and was watching the activities of the baboons with every mark of interest.

Korak's relations with the baboons had never been over friendly. A species of armed toleration had marked their occasional meetings. The baboons and Akut had walked stiff legged and growling past one another, while Korak had maintained a bared fang neutrality. So now he was not greatly disturbed by the predicament of their king. Curiosity prompted him to tarry a moment, and in that moment his quick eyes caught the unfamiliar coloration of the clothing of the two Swedes behind a bush not far from him. Now he was all alertness. Who were these interlopers? What was their business in the jungle of the Mangani? Korak slunk noiselessly around them to a point where he might get their scent as well as a better view of them, and scarce had he done so when he recognized them—they were the men who had fired upon him years before. His eyes blazed. He could feel the hairs upon his scalp stiffen at the roots. He watched them with the intentness of a panther about to spring upon its prey.

He saw them rise and, shouting, attempt to frighten away the baboons as they approached the cage. Then one of them raised his rifle and fired into the midst of the surprised and angry herd. For an instant Korak thought that the baboons were about to charge, but two more shots from the rifles of the white men sent them scampering into the trees. Then the two Europeans advanced upon the cage. Korak thought that they were going to kill the king. He cared nothing for the king but he cared less for the two white men. The king had never attempted to kill him— the white men had. The king was a denizen of his own beloved jungle—the white men were aliens. His loyalty therefore was to the baboon against the human. He could speak the language of the baboon—it was identical to that of the great apes. Across the clearing he saw the jabbering horde watching.

Raising his voice he shouted to them. The white men turned at the sound of this new factor behind them. They thought it was another baboon that had circled them; but though they searched the trees with their eyes they saw nothing of the now silent figure hidden by the foliage. Again Korak shouted.

"I am The Killer," he cried. "These men are my enemies and yours. I will help you free your king. Run out upon the strangers when you see me do so, and together we will drive them away and free your king."

And from the baboons came a great chorus: "We will do what you say, Korak."

Dropping from his tree Korak ran toward the two Swedes, and at the same instant three hundred baboons followed his example. At sight of the strange apparition of the half-naked white warrior rushing upon them with uplifted spear Jenssen and Malbihn raised their rifles and fired at Korak; but in the excitement both missed and a moment later the baboons were upon them. Now their only hope of safety lay in escape, and dodging here and there, fighting off the great beasts that leaped upon their backs, they ran into the jungle. Even then they would have died but for the coming of their men whom they met a couple of hundred yards from the cage.

Once the white men had turned in flight Korak gave them no further attention, turning instead to the imprisoned baboon. The fastenings of the door that had eluded the mental powers of the baboons, yielded their secret immediately to the human intelligence of The Killer, and a moment later the king baboon stepped forth to liberty. He wasted no breath in thanks to Korak, nor did the young man expect thanks. He knew that none of the baboons would ever forget his service, though as a matter of fact he did not care if they did. What he had done had been prompted by a desire to be revenged upon the two white men. The baboons could never be of service to him. Now they were racing in the direction of the battle that was being waged between their fellows and the followers of the two Swedes, and as the din of battle subsided in the distance, Korak turned and resumed his journey toward the village of Kovudoo.

On the way he came upon a herd of elephants standing in an open forest glade. Here the trees were too far apart to permit Korak to travel through the branches—a trail he much preferred not only because of its freedom from dense underbrush and the wider field of vision it gave him but from pride in his arboreal ability. It was exhilarating to swing from tree to tree; to test the prowess of his mighty muscles; to reap the pleasurable fruits of his hard won agility. Korak joyed in the thrills of the highflung upper terraces of the great forest, where, unhampered and unhindered, he might laugh down upon the great brutes who must keep forever to the darkness and the gloom of the musty soil.

But here, in this open glade where Tantor flapped his giant ears and swayed his huge bulk from side to side, the ape-man must pass along the surface of the ground—a pygmy amongst giants. A great bull raised his trunk to rattle a low warning as he sensed the coming of an intruder. His weak eyes roved hither and thither but it was his keen scent and acute hearing which first located the ape-man. The herd moved restlessly, prepared for fight, for the old bull had caught the scent of man.

"Peace, Tantor," called The Killer. "It is I, Korak, Tarmangani."

The bull lowered his trunk and the herd resumed their interrupted meditations. Korak passed within a foot of the great bull. A sinuous trunk undulated toward him, touching his brown hide in a half caress. Korak slapped the great shoulder affectionately as he went by. For years he had been upon good terms with Tantor and his people. Of all the jungle folk he loved best the mighty pachyderm—the most peaceful and at the same time the most terrible of them all. The gentle gazelle feared him not, yet Numa, lord of the jungle, gave him a wide berth. Among the younger bulls, the cows and the calves Korak wound his way. Now and then another trunk would run out to touch him, and once a playful calf grasped his legs and upset him.

The afternoon was almost spent when Korak arrived at the village of Kovudoo. There were many natives lolling in shady spots beside the conical huts or beneath the branches of the several trees which had been left standing within the enclosure.

Warriors were in evidence upon hand. It was not a good time for a lone enemy to prosecute a search through the village. Korak determined to await the coming of darkness. He was a match for many warriors; but he could not, unaided, overcome an entire tribe—not even for his beloved Meriem. While he waited among the branches and foliage of a near-by tree he searched the village constantly with his keen eyes, and twice he circled it, sniffing the vagrant breezes which puffed erratically from first one point of the compass and then another. Among the various stenches peculiar to a native village the ape-man's sensitive nostrils were finally rewarded by cognizance of the delicate aroma which marked the presence of her he sought. Meriem was there—in one of those huts! But which one he could not know without closer investigation, and so he waited, with the dogged patience of a beast of prey, until night had fallen.

The camp fires of the blacks dotted the gloom with little points of light, casting their feeble rays in tiny circles of luminosity that brought into glistening relief the naked bodies of those who lay or squatted about them. It was then that Korak slid silently from the tree that had hidden him and dropped lightly to the ground within the enclosure.

Keeping well in the shadows of the huts he commenced a systematic search of the village—ears, eyes and nose constantly upon the alert for the first intimation of the near presence of Meriem. His progress must of necessity be slow since not even the keen-eared curs of the savages must guess the presence of a stranger within the gates. How close he came to a detection on several occasions The Killer well knew from the restless whining of several of them.

It was not until he reached the back of a hut at the head of the wide village street that Korak caught again, plainly, the scent of Meriem. With nose close to the thatched wall Korak sniffed eagerly about the structure—tense and palpitant as a hunting hound. Toward the front and the door he made his way when once his nose had assured him that Meriem lay within; but as he rounded the side and came within view of the entrance he saw a burly Negro armed with a long spear squatting at the portal of the girl's prison. The fellow's back was toward him, his figure outlined against the glow of cooking fires further down the street. He was alone. The nearest of his fellows were beside a fire sixty or seventy feet beyond. To enter the hut Korak must either silence the sentry or pass him unnoticed. The danger in the accomplishment of the former alternative lay in the practical certainty of alarming the warriors near by and bringing them and the balance of the village down upon him. To achieve the latter appeared practically impossible. To you or me it would have been impossible; but Korak, The Killer, was not as you or I.

There was a good twelve inches of space between the broad back of the black and the frame of the doorway. Could Korak pass through behind the savage warrior without detection? The light that fell upon the glistening ebony of the sentry's black skin fell also upon the light brown of Korak's. Should one of the many further down the street chance to look long in this direction they must surely note the tall, light-colored, moving figure; but Korak depended upon their interest in their own gossip to hold their attention fast where it already lay, and upon the firelight near them to prevent them seeing too plainly at a distance into the darkness at the village end where his work lay.

Flattened against the side of the hut, yet not arousing a single warning rustle from its dried thatching, The Killer came closer and closer to the watcher. Now he was at his shoulder. Now he had wormed his sinuous way behind him. He could feel the heat of the naked body against his knees. He could hear the man breathe. He marveled that the dull-witted creature had not long since been alarmed; but the fellow sat there as ignorant of the presence of another as though that other had not existed.

Korak moved scarcely more than an inch at a time, then he would stand motionless for a moment. Thus was he worming his way behind the guard when the latter straightened up, opened his cavernous mouth in a wide yawn, and stretched his arms above his head. Korak stood rigid as stone. Another step and he would be within the hut. The black lowered his arms and relaxed. Behind him was the frame work of the doorway. Often before had it supported his sleepy head, and now he leaned back to enjoy the forbidden pleasure of a cat nap.

But instead of the door frame his head and shoulders came in contact with the warm flesh of a pair of living legs. The exclamation of surprise that almost burst from his lips was throttled in his throat by steel-thewed fingers that closed about his windpipe with the suddenness of thought. The black struggled to arise—to turn upon the creature that had seized him—to wriggle from its hold; but all to no purpose. As he had been held in a mighty vise of iron he could not move. He could not scream. Those awful fingers at his throat but closed more and more tightly. His eyes bulged from their sockets. His face turned an ashy blue. Presently he relaxed once more—this time in the final dissolution from which there is no quickening. Korak propped the dead body against the door frame. There it sat, lifelike in the gloom. Then the ape-man turned and glided into the Stygian darkness of the hut's interior.

"Meriem!" he whispered.

"Korak! My Korak!" came an answering cry, subdued by fear of alarming her captors, and half stifled by a sob of joyful welcome.

The youth knelt and cut the bonds that held the girl's wrists and ankles. A moment later he had lifted her to her feet, and grasping her by the hand led her towards the entrance. Outside the grim sentinel of death kept his grisly vigil. Sniffing at his dead feet whined a mangy native cur. At sight of the two emerging from the hut the beast gave an ugly snarl and an instant later as it caught the scent of the strange white man it raised a series of excited yelps. Instantly the warriors at the near-by fire were attracted. They turned their heads in the direction of the commotion. It was impossible that they should fail to see the white skins of the fugitives.

Korak slunk quickly into the shadows at the hut's side, drawing Meriem with him; but he was too late. The blacks had seen enough to arouse their suspicions and a dozen of them were now running to investigate. The yapping cur was still at Korak's heels leading the searchers unerringly in pursuit. The youth struck viciously at the brute with his long spear; but, long accustomed to dodging blows, the wily creature made a most uncertain target.

Other blacks had been alarmed by the running and shouting of their companions and now the entire population of the village was swarming up the street to assist in the search. Their first discovery was the dead body of the sentry, and a moment later one of the bravest of them had entered the hut and discovered the absence of the prisoner. These startling announcements filled the blacks with a combination of terror and rage; but, seeing no foe in evidence they were enabled to permit their rage to get the better of their terror, and so the leaders, pushed on by those behind them, ran rapidly around the hut in the direction of the yapping of the mangy cur. Here they found a single white warrior making away with their captive, and recognizing him as the author of numerous raids and indignities and believing that they had him cornered and at a disadvantage, they charged savagely upon him.

Korak, seeing that they were discovered, lifted Meriem to his shoulders and ran for the tree which would give them egress from the village. He was handicapped in his flight by the weight of the girl whose legs would but scarce bear her weight, to say nothing of maintaining her in rapid flight, for the tightly drawn bonds that had been about her ankles for so long had stopped circulation and partially paralyzed her extremities.

Had this not been the case the escape of the two would have been a feat of little moment, since Meriem was scarcely a whit less agile than Korak, and fully as much at home in the trees as he. But with the girl on his shoulder Korak could not both run and fight to advantage, and the result was that before he had covered half the distance to the tree a score of native curs attracted by the yelping of their mate and the yells and shouts of their masters had closed in upon the fleeing white man, snapping at his legs and at last succeeding in tripping him. As he went down the hyena-like brutes were upon him, and as he struggled to his feet the blacks closed in.

A couple of them seized the clawing, biting Meriem, and subdued her—a blow upon the head was sufficient. For the ape-man they found more drastic measures would be necessary. Weighted down as he was by dogs and warriors he still managed to struggle to his feet. To right and left he swung crushing blows to the faces of his human antagonists—to the dogs he paid not the slightest attention other than to seize the more persistent and wring their necks with a single quick movement of the wrist.

A knob stick aimed at him by an ebon Hercule he caught and wrested from his antagonist, and then the blacks experienced to the full the possibilities for punishment that lay within those smooth flowing muscles beneath the velvet brown skin of the strange, white giant. He rushed among them with all the force and ferocity of a bull elephant gone mad. Hither and thither he charged striking down the few who had the temerity to stand against him, and it was evident that unless a chance spear thrust brought him down he would rout the entire village and regain his prize. But old Kovudoo was not to be so easily robbed of the ransom which the girl represented, and seeing that their attack which had up to now resulted in a series of individual combats with the white warrior, he called his tribesmen off, and forming them in a compact body about the girl and the two who watched over her bid them do nothing more than repel the assaults of the ape-man.

Again and again Korak rushed against this human barricade

bristling with spear points. Again and again he was repulsed, often with sever wounds to caution him to greater wariness. From head to foot he was red with his own blood, and at last, weakening from the loss of it, he came to the bitter realization that alone he could do no more to succor his Meriem.

Presently an idea flashed through his brain. He called aloud to the girl. She had regained consciousness now and replied.

"Korak goes," he shouted; "but he will return and take you from the Gomangani. Good-bye, my Meriem. Korak will come for you again."

"Good-bye!" cried the girl. "Meriem will look for you until you come."

Like a flash, and before they could know his intention or prevent him, Korak wheeled, raced across the village and with a single leap disappeared into the foliage of the great tree that was his highroad to the village of Kovudoo. A shower of spears followed him, but their only harvest was a taunting laugh flung back from out the darkness of the jungle.

# 13

MERIEM, AGAIN BOUND and under heavy guard in Kovu-doo's own hut, saw the night pass and the new day come without bringing the momentarily looked for return of Korak. She had no doubt but that he would come back and less still that he would easily free her from her captivity. To her Korak was little short of omnipotent. He embodied for her all that was finest and strongest and best in her savage world. She gloried in his prowess and worshipped him for the tender thoughtfulness that always had marked his treatment of her. No other within the ken of her memory had ever accorded her the love and gentleness that was his daily offering to her. Most of the gentler attributes of his early childhood had long since been forgotten in the fierce battle for existence which the customs of the mysterious jungle had forced upon him. He was more often savage and bloodthirsty than tender and kindly. His other friends of the wild looked for no gentle tokens of his affection. That he would hunt with them and fight for them was sufficient. If he growled and showed his fighting fangs when they trespassed upon his inalienable rights to the fruits of his kills they felt no anger toward him—only greater respect for the efficient and the fit—for him who could not only kill but protect the flesh of his kill.

But toward Meriem he always had shown more of his human side. He killed primarily for her. It was to the feet of Meriem that he brought the fruits of his labors. It was for Meriem more than for himself that he squatted beside his flesh and growled ominously at whosoever dared sniff too closely to it. When he was cold in the dark days of rain, or thirsty in a prolonged drouth, his discomfort engendered first of all thoughts of Meriem's welfare—after she had been made warm, after her thirst had been slaked, then he turned to the affair of ministering to his own wants.

The softest skins fell gracefully from the graceful shoulders of his Meriem. The sweetest-scented grasses lined her bower where other soft, furry pelts made hers the downiest couch in all the jungle.

What wonder then that Meriem loved her Korak? But she loved him as a little sister might love a big brother who was very good to her. As yet she knew naught of the love of a maid for a man.

So now as she lay waiting for him she dreamed of him and of all that he meant to her. She compared him with The Sheik, her father, and at thought of the stern, grizzled, old Arab she shuddered. Even the savage blacks had been less harsh to her than he. Not understanding their tongue she could not guess what purpose they had in keeping her a prisoner. She knew that man ate man, and she had expected to be eaten; but she had been with them for some time now and no harm had befallen her. She did not know that a runner had been dispatched to the distant village of The Sheik to barter with him for a ransom. She did not know, nor did Kovudoo, that the runner had never reached his destination—that he had fallen in with the *safari* of Jenssen and Malbihn and with the talkativeness of a native to other natives had unfolded his whole mission to the black servants of the two Swedes. These had not been long in retailing the matter to their masters, and the result was that when the runner left their camp to continue his journey he had scarce passed from sight before there came the report of a rifle and he rolled lifeless into the underbrush with a bullet in his back.

A few moments later Malbihn strolled back into the encampment, where he went to some pains to let it be known that he had had a shot at a fine buck and missed. The Swedes knew that their men hated them, and that an overt act against Kovudoo would quickly be carried to the chief at the first opportunity. Nor were they sufficiently strong in either guns of loyal followers to risk antagonizing the wily old chief.

Following this episode came the encounter with the baboons and the strange, white savage who had allied himself with the beasts against the humans. Only by dint of masterful maneuvering and the expenditure of much power had the Swedes been able to repulse the infuriated apes, and even for hours afterward their camp was constantly besieged by hundreds of snarling, screaming devils.

The Swedes, rifles in hand, repelled numerous savage charges which lacked only efficient leadership to have rendered them as effective in results as they were terrifying in appearance. Time and time again the two men thought they saw the smooth-skinned body of the wild ape-man moving among the baboons in the forest, and the belief that he might head a charge upon them proved most disquieting. They would have given much for a clean shot at him, for to him they attributed the loss of their specimen and the ugly attitude of the baboons toward them.

"The fellow must be the same we fired on several years ago," said Malbihn. "That time he was accompanied by a gorilla. Did you get a good look at him, Carl?"

"Yes," replied Jenssen. "He was not five paces from me when I fired at him. He appears to be an intelligent looking European—and not much more than a lad. There is nothing of the imbecile or degenerate in his features or expression, as is usually true in similar cases, where some lunatic escapes into the woods and by living in filth and nakedness wins the title of wild man among the peasants of the neighborhood. No, this fellow is of different stuff—and so infinitely more to be feared. As much as I should like a shot at him I hope he stays away. Should he ever deliberately lead a charge against us I wouldn't give much for our chances if we happened to fail to bag him at the first rush."

But the white giant did not appear again to lead the baboons against them, and finally the angry brutes themselves wandered off into the jungle leaving the frightened *safari* in peace.

The next day the Swedes set out for Kovudoo's village bent on securing possession of the person of the white girl whom Kovudoo's runner had told them lay captive in the chief's village. How they were to accomplish their end they did not know. Force was out of the question, though they would not have hesitated to use it had they possessed it. In former years they had marched rough shod over enormous areas, taking toll by brute force even when kindliness or diplomacy would have accomplished more; but now they were in bad straits—so bad that they had shown their true colors scared twice in a year and then only when they came upon an isolated village, weak in numbers and poor in courage.

Kovudoo was not as these, and though his village was in a way remote from the more populous district to the north his power was such that he maintained an acknowledged suzerainty over the thin thread of villages which connected him with the savage lords to the north. To have antagonized him would have spelled ruin for the Swedes. It would have meant that they might never reach civilization by the northern route. To the west, the village of The Sheik lay directly in their path, barring them effectually. To the east the trail was unknown to them, and to the south there was no trail. So the two Swedes approached the village of Kovudoo with friendly words upon their tongues and deep craft in their hearts.

Their plans were well made. There was no mention of the white prisoner—they chose to pretend that they were not aware that Kovudoo had a white prisoner. They exchanged gifts with the old chief, haggling with his plenipotentiaries over the value of what they were to receive for what they gave, as is customary and proper when one has no ulterior motives. Unwarranted generosity would have aroused suspicion.

During the palaver which followed they retailed the gossip of the villages through which they had passed, receiving in exchange such news as Kovudoo possessed. The palaver was long and tiresome, as these native ceremonies always are to Europeans. Kovudoo made no mention of his prisoner and from his generous offers of guides and presents seemed anxious to assure himself of the speedy departure of his guests. It was Malbihn who, quite casually, near the close of their talk, mentioned the fact that The Sheik was dead. Kovudoo evinced interest and surprise.

"You did not know it?" asked Malbihn. "That is strange. It was during the last moon. He fell from his horse when the beast stepped in a hole. The horse fell upon him. When his men came up The Sheik was quite dead."

Kovudoo scratched his head. He was much disappointed. No Sheik meant no ransom for the white girl. Now she was worthless, unless he utilized her for a feast or—a mate. The latter thought aroused him. He spat at a small beetle crawling through the dust before him. He eyed Malbihn appraisingly. These white men were peculiar. They traveled far from their own villages without women. Yet he knew that they cared for women. But how much did they care for them?—that was the question that disturbed Kovudoo.

"I know where there is a white girl," he said, unexpectedly. "If you wish to buy her she may be had cheap."

Malbihn shrugged. "We have troubles enough, Kovudoo," he said, "without burdening ourselves with an old she-hyena, and as for paying for one—'' Malbihn snapped his fingers in derision.

"She is young," said Kovudoo, "and good looking."

The Swedes laughed. "There are no good looking white women in the jungle, Kovudoo," said Jenssen. "You should be ashamed to try to make fun of old friends."

Kovudoo sprang to his feet. "Come," he said, "I will show you that she is all I say."

Malbihn and Jenssen rose to follow him and as they did so their eyes met, and Malbihn slowly drooped one of his lids in a sly wink. Together they followed Kovudoo toward his hut. In the dim interior they discerned the figure of a woman lying bound upon a sleeping mat.

Malbihn took a single glance and turned away. "She must be a thousand years old, Kovudoo," he said, as he left the hut.

"She is young," cried the savage. "It is dark in here. You cannot see. Wait, I will have her brought out into the sunlight," and he commanded the two warriors who watched the girl to cut the bonds from her ankles and lead her forth for inspection.

Malbihn and Jenssen evinced no eagerness, though both were fairly bursting with it—not to see the girl but to obtain possession of her. They cared not if she had the face of a marmoset, or the figure of pot-bellied Kovudoo himself. All that they wished to know was that she was the girl who had been stolen from The Sheik several years before. They thought that they would recognize her for such if she was indeed the same, but even so the testimony of the runner Kovudoo had sent to The Sheik was such as to assure them that the girl was the one they had once before attempted to abduct.

As Meriem was brought forth from the darkness of the hut's interior the two men turned with every appearance of disinterestedness to glance at her. It was with difficulty that Malbihn suppressed an ejaculation of astonishment. The girl's beauty fairly took his breath from him; but instantly he recovered his poise and turned to Kovudoo.

"Well?" he said to the old chief.

"Is she not both young and good looking?" asked Kovudoo.

"She is not old," replied Malbihn; "but even so she will be a burden. We did not come from the north after wives—there are more than enough there for us."

Meriem stood looking straight at the white men. She expected nothing from them—they were to her as much enemies as the black men. She hated and feared them all. Malbihn spoke to her in Arabic.

"We are friends," he said. "Would you like to have us take you away from here?"

Slowly and dimly as though from a great distance recollection of the once familiar tongue returned to her.

"I should like to go free," she said, "and go back to Korak."

"You would like to go with us?" persisted Malbihn.

"No," said Meriem.

Malbihn turned to Kovudoo. "She does not wish to go with us," he said.

"You are men," returned the black. "Can you not take her by force?"

"It would only add to our troubles," replied the Swede. "No, Kovudoo, we do not wish her; though, if you wish to be rid of her, we will take her away because of our friendship for you."

Now Kovudoo knew that he had made a sale. They wanted her. So he commenced to bargain, and in the end the person of Meriem passed from the possession of the black chieftain into that of the two Swedes in consideration of six yards of Amerikan, three empty brass cartridge shells and a shiny, new jack knife from New Jersey. And all but Meriem were more than pleased with the bargain.

Kovudoo stipulated but a single condition and that was that the Europeans were to leave his village and take the girl with them as early the next morning as they could get started. After the sale was consummated he did not hesitate to explain his reasons for this demand. He told them of the strenuous attempt of the girl's savage mate to rescue her, and suggested that the sooner they got her out of the country the more likely they were to retain possession of her.

Meriem was again bound and placed under guard, but this time in the tent of the Swedes. Malbihn talked to her, trying to persuade her to accompany them willingly. He told her that they would return her to her own village; but when he discovered that she would rather die than go back to the old sheik, he assured her that they would not take her there, nor, as a matter of fact, had they had an intention of so doing. As he talked with the girl the Swede feasted his eyes upon the beautiful lines of her face and figure. She had grown tall and straight and slender toward maturity since he had seen her in The Sheik's village on that long gone day. For years she had represented to him a certain fabulous reward. In his thoughts she had been but the personification of the pleasures and luxuries that many francs would purchase. Now as she stood before him pulsing with life and loveliness she suggested other seductive and alluring possibilities. He came closer to her and laid his hand upon her. The girl shrank from him. He seized her and she struck him heavily in the mouth as he sought to kiss her. Then Jenssen entered the tent.

"Malbihn!" he almost shouted. "You fool!"

Sven Malbihn released his hold upon the girl and turned toward his companion. His face was red with mortification.

"What the devil are you trying to do?" growled Jenssen. "Would you throw away every chance for the reward? If we maltreat her we not only couldn't collect a sou, but they'd send us to prison for our pains. I thought you had more sense, Malbihn."

"I'm not a wooden man," growled Malbihn.

"You'd better be," rejoined Jenssen, "at least until we have delivered her over in safety and collected what will be coming to us."

"Oh, hell," cried Malbihn. "What's the use? They'll be glad enough to have her back, and by the time we get there with her she'll be only too glad to keep her mouth shut. Why not?"

"Because I say not," growled Jenssen. "I've always let you boss things, Sven; but here's a case where what I say has got to go—because I'm right and you're wrong, and we both know it."

"You're getting damned virtuous all of a sudden," growled Malbihn. "Perhaps you think I have forgotten about the inn keeper's daughter, and little Celella, and that nigger at—"

"Shut up!" snapped Jenssen. "It's not a matter of virtue and you are as well aware of that as I. I don't want to quarrel with you, but so help me God, Sven, you're not going to harm this girl if I have to kill you to prevent it. I've suffered and slaved and been nearly killed forty times in the last nine or ten years trying to accomplish what luck has thrown at our feet at last, and now I'm not going to be robbed of the fruits of success because you happen to be more of a beast than a man. Again I warn you, Sven—" and he tapped the revolver that swung in its holster at his hip.

Malbihn gave his friend an ugly look, shrugged his shoulders, and left the tent. Jenssen turned to Meriem.

"If he bothers you again, call me," he said. "I shall always be near."

The girl had not understood the conversation that had been

carried on by her two owners, for it had been in Swedish; but what Jenssen had just said to her in Arabic she understood and from it grasped an excellent idea of what had passed between the two. The expressions upon their faces, their gestures, and Jenssen's final tapping of his revolver before Malbihn had left the tent had all been eloquent of the seriousness of their altercation. Now, toward Jenssen she looked for friendship, and with the innocence of youth she threw herself upon his mercy, begging him to set her free, that she might return to Korak and her jungle life; but she was doomed to another disappointment, for the man only laughed at her roughly and told her that if she tried to escape she would be punished by the very thing that he had just saved her from.

All that night she lay listening for a signal from Korak. All about the jungle life moved through the darkness. To her sensitive ears came sounds that the others in the camp could not hear—sounds that she interpreted as we might interpret the speech of a friend, but not once came a single note that reflected the presence of Korak. But she knew that he would come. Nothing short of death itself could prevent her Korak from returning for her. What delayed him though?

When morning came again and the night had brought no succoring Korak, Meriem's faith and loyalty were still unshaken though misgivings began to assail her as to the safety of her friend. It seemed unbelievable that serious mishap could have overtaken her wonderful Korak who daily passed unscathed through all the terrors of the jungle. Yet morning came, the morning meal was eaten, the camp broken and the disreputable *safari* of the Swedes was on the move northward with still no sign of the rescue the girl momentarily expected.

All that day they marched, and the next and the next, nor did Korak even so much as show himself to the patient little waiter moving, silently and stately, beside her hard captors.

Malbihn remained scowling and angry. He replied to Jenssen's friendly advances in curt monosyllables. To Meriem he did not speak, but on several occasions she discovered him glaring at her from beneath half closed lids—greedily. The look sent a shudder through her. She hugged Geeka closer to her breast and doubly regretted the knife that they had taken from her when she was captured by Kovudoo.

It was on the fourth day that Meriem began definitely to give up hope. Something had happened to Korak. She knew it. He would never come now, and these men would take her far away.

Presently they would kill her. She would never see her Korak again.

On this day the Swedes rested, for they had marched rapidly and their men were tired. Malbihn and Jenssen had gone from camp to hunt, taking different directions. They had been gone about an hour when the door of Meriem's tent was lifted and Malbihn entered. The look of a beast was on his face.

# 14

WITH WIDE EYES fixed upon him, like a trapped creature horrified beneath the mesmeric gaze of a great serpent, the girl watched the approach of the man. Her hands were free, the Swedes having secured her with a length of ancient slave chain fastened at one end to an iron collar padlocked about her neck and at the other to a long stake driven deep into the ground.

Slowly Meriem shrank inch by inch toward the opposite end of the tent. Malbihn followed her. His hands were extended and his fingers half-opened—claw-like—to seize her. His lips were parted, and his breath came quickly, pantingly.

The girl recalled Jenssen's instructions to call him should Malbihn molest her; but Jenssen had gone into the jungle to hunt. Malbihn had chosen his time well. Yet she screamed, loud and shrill, once, twice, a third time, before Malbihn could leap across the tent and throttle her alarming cries with his brute fingers. Then she fought him, as any jungle she might fight, with tooth and nail. The man found her no easy prey. In that slender, young body, beneath the rounded curves and the fine, soft skin, lay the muscles of a young lioness. But Malbihn was no weakling. His character and appearance were brutal, nor did they belie his brawn. He was of giant stature and of giant strength. Slowly he forced the girl back upon the ground, striking her in the face when she hurt him badly either with teeth or nails. Meriem struck back, but she was growing weaker from the choking fingers at her throat.

Out in the jungle Jenssen had brought down two bucks. His hunting had not carried him far afield, nor was he prone to permit it to do so. He was suspicious of Malbihn. The very fact that his companion had refused to accompany him and elected instead to hunt alone in another direction would not, under ordinary circumstances, have seemed fraught with sinister suggestion; but Jenssen knew Malbihn well, and so, having secured meat, he turned immediately back toward camp, while his boys brought in his kill.

He had covered about half the return journey when a scream came faintly to his ears from the direction of camp. He halted to listen. It was repeated twice. Then silence. With a muttered curse Jenssen broke into a rapid run. He wondered if he would be too late. What a fool Malbihn was indeed to thus chance jeopardizing a fortune!

Further away from camp than Jenssen and upon the opposite side another heard Meriem's screams—a stranger who was not even aware of the proximity of white men other than himself—a hunter with a handful of sleek, black warriors. He, too, listened intently for a moment. That the voice was that of a woman in distress he could not doubt, and so he also hastened at a run in the direction of the affrighted voice; but he was much further away than Jenssen so that the latter reached the tent first. What the Swede found there roused no pity within his calloused heart, only anger against his fellow scoundrel. Meriem was still fighting off her attacker. Malbihn still was showering blows upon her. Jenssen, streaming foul curses upon his erstwhile friend, burst into the tent. Malbihn, interrupted, dropped his victim and turned to meet Jenssen's infuriated charge. He whipped a revolver from his hip. Jenssen, anticipating the lightning move of the other's hand, drew almost simultaneously, and both men fired at once. Jenssen was still moving toward Malbihn at the time, but at the flash of the explosion he stopped. His revolver dropped from nerveless fingers. For a moment he staggered drunkenly. Deliberately Malbihn put two more bullets into his friend's body at close range. Even in the midst of the excitement and her terror Meriem found herself wondering at the tenacity of life which the hit man displayed. His eyes were closed, his head dropped forward upon his breast, his hands hung limply before him. Yet still he stood there upon his feet, though he reeled horribly. It was not until the third bullet had found its mark within his body that he lunged forward upon his face. Then Malbihn approached him, and with an oath kicked him viciously. Then he returned once more to Meriem. Again he seized her, and at the same instant the flaps of the tent opened silently and a tall white man stood in the aperture. Neither Meriem or Malbihn saw the newcomer. The latter's back was toward him while his body hid the stranger from Meriem's eyes.

He crossed the tent quickly, stepping over Jenssen's body. The first intimation Malbihn had that he was not to carry out his design without further interruption was a heavy hand upon his shoulder. He wheeled to face an utter stranger—a tall, black-haired, gray-eyed stranger clad in khaki and pith helmet. Malbihn reached for his gun again, but another hand had been quicker than his and he saw the weapon tossed to the ground at the side of the tent—out of reach.

"What is the meaning of this?" the stranger addressed his question to Meriem in a tongue she did not understand. She shook her head and spoke in Arabic. Instantly the man changed his question to that language.

"These men are taking me away from Korak," explained the girl. "This one would have harmed me. The other, whom he had just killed, tried to stop him. They were both very bad men; but this one is the worse. If my Korak were here he would kill him. I suppose you are like them, so you will not kill him."

The stranger smiled. "He deserves killing?" he said. "There is no doubt of that. Once I should have killed him; but not now. I will see, though, that he does not bother you any more."

He was holding Malbihn in a grasp the giant Swede could not break, though he struggled to do so, and he was holding him as easily as Malbihn might have held a little child, yet Malbihn was a huge man, mightily thewed. The Swede began to rage and curse. He struck at his captor, only to be twisted about and held at arm's length. Then he shouted to his boys to come and kill the stranger. In response a dozen strange blacks entered the tent. They, too, were powerful, clean-limbed men, not at all like the mangy crew that followed the Swedes.

"We have had enough foolishness," said the stranger to Malbihn. "You deserve death, but I am not the law. I know now who you are. I have heard of you before. You and your friend here bear a most unsavory reputation. We do not want you in our country. I shall let you go this time; but should you ever return I shall take the law into my own hands. You understand?"

Malbihn blustered and threatened, finishing by applying a most uncomplimentary name to his captor. For this he received a shaking that rattled his teeth. Those who know say that the most painful punishment that can be inflicted upon an adult male, short of injuring him, is a good, old fashioned shaking. Malbihn received such a shaking.

"Now get out," said the stranger, "and next time you see me remember who I am," and he spoke a name in the Swede's ear—a name that more effectually subdued the scoundrel than many beatings—then he gave him a push that carried him bodily through the tent doorway to sprawl upon the turf beyond.

"Now," he said, turning toward Meriem, "who has the key to this thing about your neck?"

The girl pointed to Jenssen's body. "He carried it always," she said.

The stranger searched the clothing on the corpse until he came upon the key. A moment more Meriem was free.

"Will you let me go back to my Korak?" she asked.

"I will see that you are returned to your people," he replied. "Who are they and where is their village?"

He had been eyeing her strange, barbaric garmenture wonderingly. From her speech she was evidently an Arab girl; but he had never before seen one thus clothed.

"Who are your people? Who is Korak?" he asked again.

"Korak! Why Korak is an ape. I have no other people. Korak and I live in the jungle alone since A'ht went to be king of the apes." She had always thus pronounced Akut's name, for so it had sounded to her when first she came with Korak and the ape. "Korak could have been king, but he would not."

A questioning expression entered the stranger's eyes. He looked at the girl closely.

"So Korak is an ape?" he said. "And what, pray, are you?"

"I am Meriem. I, also, am an ape."

"M-m," was the stranger's only oral comment upon this startling announcement; but what he thought might have been partially interpreted through the pitying light that entered his eyes. He approached the girl and started to lay his hand upon her forehead. She drew back with a savage little growl. A smile touched his lips.

"You need not fear me," he said. "I shall not harm you. I only wish to discover if you have fever—if you are entirely well. If you are we will set forth in search of Korak."

Meriem looked straight into the keen gray eyes. She must have found there an unquestionable assurance of the honorableness of their owner, for she permitted him to lay his palm upon her forehead and feel her pulse. Apparently she had no fever.

"How long have you been an ape?" asked the man.

"Since I was a little girl, many, many years ago, and Korak came and took me from my father who was beating me. Since then I have lived in the trees with Korak and A'ht."

"Where in the jungle lives Korak?" asked the stranger.

Meriem pointed with a sweep of her hand that took in, generously, half the continent of Africa.

"Could you find your way back to him?"

"I do not know," she replied; "but he will find his way to me."

"Then I have a plan," said the stranger. "I live but a few marches from here. I shall take you home where my wife will look after you and care for you until we can find Korak or Korak finds us. If he could find you here he can find you at my village. Is it not so?"

Meriem thought that it was so; but she did not like the idea of not starting immediately back to meet Korak. On the other hand the man had no intention of permitting this poor, insane child to wander further amidst the dangers of the jungle. From whence she had come, or what she had undergone he could not guess, but that her Korak and their life among the apes was but a figment of a disordered mind he could not doubt. He knew the jungle well, and he knew that men have lived alone and naked among the savage beasts for years; but a frail and slender girl! No, it was not possible.

Together they went outside. Malbihn's boys were striking camp in preparation for a hasty departure. The stranger's blacks were conversing with them. Malbihn stood at a distance, angry and glowering. The stranger approached one of his own men.

"Find out where they got this girl," he commanded.

The Negro thus addressed questioned one of Malbihn's followers. Presently he returned to his master.

"They bought her from old Kovudoo," he said. "That is all that this fellow will tell me. He pretends that he knows nothing more, and I guess that he does not. These two white men were very bad men. They did many things that their boys knew not the meanings of. It would be well Bwana, to kill the other."

"I wish that I might; but a new law is come into this part of the jungle. It is not as it was in the old days, Muviri," replied the master.

The stranger remained until Malbihn and his *safari* had disappeared into the jungle toward the north. Meriem, trustful now, stood at his side, Geeka clutched in one slim, brown hand. They talked together, the man wondering at the faltering Arabic of the girl, but attributing it finally to her defective mentality. Could he have known that years had elapsed since she had used it until she was taken by the Swedes he would not have wondered that she had half forgotten it. There was yet another reason why the language of The Sheik had thus readily eluded her; but of that reason she herself could not have guessed the truth any better than could the man.

He tried to persuade her to return with him to his "village" as he called it, or *douar*, in Arabic; but she was insistent upon searching immediately for Korak. As a last resort he determined to take her with him by force rather than sacrifice her life to the insane hallucination which haunted her; but, being a wise man, he determined to humor her first and then attempt to lead her as he would have her go. So when they took up their march it was in the direction of the south, though his own ranch lay almost due east.

By degrees he turned the direction of their way more and more eastward, and greatly was he pleased to note that the girl failed to discover that any change was being made. Little by little she became more trusting. At first she had had but her intuition to guide her belief that this big Tarmangani meant her no harm, but as the days passed and she saw that his kindness and consideration never faltered she came to compare him with Korak, and to be very fond of him; but never did her loyalty to her apeman flag.

On the fifth day they came suddenly upon a great plain and from the edge of the forest the girl saw in the distance fenced fields and many buildings. At the sight she drew back in astonishment.

"Where are we?" she asked, pointing.

"We could not find Korak," replied the man, "and as our way led near my *douar* I have brought you here to wait and rest with my wife until my men can find your ape, or he finds you. It is better thus, little one. You will be safer with us, and you will be happier."

"I am afraid, Bwana," said the girl. "In thy douar they will beat me as did The Sheik, my father. Let me go back into the jungle. There Korak will find me. He would not think to look for me in the douar of a white man."

"No one will beat you, child," replied the man. "I have not done so, have I? Well, here all belong to me. They will treat you well. Here no one is beaten. My wife will be very good to you, and at last Korak will come, for I shall send men to search for him."

The girl shook her head. "They could not bring him, for he would kill them, as all men have tried to kill him. I am afraid. Let me go, Bwana."

"You do not know the way to your own country. You would be lost. The leopards or the lions would get you the first night, and after all you would not find your Korak. It is better that you stay with us. Did I not save you from the bad man? Do you not owe me something for that? Well, then remain with us for a few weeks at least until we can determine what is best for you. You are only a little girl—it would be wicked to permit you to go alone into the jungle."

Meriem laughed. "The jungle," she said, "is my father and my mother. It has been kinder to me than have men. I am not afraid of the jungle. Nor am I afraid of the leopard or the lion. When my time comes I shall die. It may be that a leopard or a lion shall kill me, or it may be a tiny bug no bigger than the end of my littlest finger. When the lion leaps upon me, or the little bug stings me I shall be afraid—oh, then I shall be terribly afraid, I know; but life would be very miserable indeed were I to spend it in terror of the thing that has not yet happened. If it be the lion my terror shall be short of life; but if it be the little bug I may suffer for days before I die. And so I fear the lion least of all. He is great and noisy. I can hear him, or see him, or smell him in time to escape; but any moment I may place a hand or foot on the little bug, and never know that he is there until I feel his deadly sting. No, I do not fear the jungle. I love it. I should rather die than leave it forever; but your *douar* is close beside the jungle. You have been good to me. I will do as you wish, and remain here for a while to wait the coming of my Korak."

"Good!" said the man, and he led the way down toward the flower-covered bungalow behind which lay the barns and outhouses of a well-ordered African farm.

As they came nearer a dozen dogs ran barking toward them—gaunt wolf hounds, a huge great Dane, a nimble-footed collie and a number of yapping, quarrelsome fox terriors. At first their appearance was savage and unfriendly in the extreme; but once they recognized the foremost black warriors, and the white men behind them their attitude underwent a remarkable change. The collie and the fox terriers became frantic with delirious joy, and while the wolf hounds and the great Dane were not a whit less delighted at the return of their master their greetings were of a more dignified nature. Each in turn sniffed at Meriem who displayed not the slightest fear of any of them.

The wolf hounds bristled and growled at the scent of wild beasts that clung to her garment; but when she layed her hand upon their heads and her soft voice murmured caressingly they half-closed their eyes, lifting their upper lips in contented canine smiles. The man was watching them and he too smiled, for it was seldom that these savage brutes took thus kindly to strangers. It was as though in some subtle way the girl had breathed a message of kindred savagery to their savage hearts.

With her slim fingers grasping the collar of a wolf hound upon either side of her Meriem walked on toward the bungalow upon the porch of which a woman dressed in white waved a welcome to her returning lord. There was more fear in the girl's eyes now than there had been in the presence of strange men or savage beasts. She hesitated, turning an appealing glance toward the man.

"This is my wife," he said. "She will be glad to welcome you."

The woman came down the path to meet them. The man kissed her, and turning toward Meriem introduced them, speaking in the Arab tongue the girl understood.

"This is Meriem, my dear," he said, and he told the story of the jungle waif in so far as he knew it.

Meriem saw that the woman was beautiful. She saw that sweetness and goodness were stamped indelibly upon her countenance. She no longer feared her, and when her brief story had been narrated and the woman came and put her arms about her and kissed her and called her "poor little darling" something snapped in Meriem's little heart. She buried her face on the bosom of this new friend in whose voice was the mother tone that Meriem had not heard for so many years that she had forgotten its very existence. She buried her face on the kindly bosom and wept as she had not wept before in all her life—tears of relief and joy that she could not fathom.

And so came Meriem, the savage little Mangani, out of her beloved jungle into the midst of a home of culture and refinement. Already "Bwana" and "My Dear," as she first heard them called and continued to call them, were as father and mother to her. Once her savage fears allayed, she went to the opposite extreme of trustfulness and love. Now she was willing to wait here until they found Korak, or Korak found her. She did not give up that thought—Korak, her Korak always was first.

# 15

AND OUT IN the jungle, far away, Korak, covered with wounds, stiff with clotted blood, burning with rage and sorrow, swung back upon the trail of the great baboons. He had not found them where he had last seen them, nor in any of their usual haunts; but he sought them along the well-marked spoor they had left behind them, and at last he overtook them. When first he came upon them they were moving slowly but steadily southward in one of those periodic migrations the reasons for which the baboon himself is best able to explain. At sight of the white warrior who came upon them from down wind the herd halted in response to the warning cry of the sentinel that had discovered him. There was much growling and muttering; much stiff-legged circling on the part of the bulls. The mothers, in nervous, high pitched tones, called their young to their sides, and with them moved to safety behind their lords and masters.

Korak called aloud to the king, who, at the familiar voice, advanced slowly, warily, and still stiff-legged. He must have the confirmatory evidence of his nose before venturing to rely too implicitly upon the testimony of his ears and eyes. Korak stood perfectly still. To have advanced then might have precipitated an immediate attack, or, as easily, a panic of flight. Wild beasts are creatures of nerves. It is a relatively simple thing to throw them into a species of hysteria which may induce either a mania for murder, or symptoms of apparent abject cowardice—it is a question, however, if a wild animal ever is actually a coward.

The king baboon approached Korak. He walked around him in an ever decreasing circle—growling, grunting, sniffing. Korak spoke to him.

"I am Korak," he said. "I opened the cage that held you. I

saved you from the Termangani. I am Korak, The Killer. I am your friend."

"Huh," grunted the king. "Yes, you are Korak. My ears told me that you were Korak. My eyes told me that you were Korak. Now my nose tells me that you are Korak. My nose is never wrong. I am your friend. Come, we shall hunt together."

"Korak cannot hunt now," replied the ape-man. "The Gomangani have stolen Meriem. They have tied her in their village. They will not let her go. Korak, alone, was unable to set her free. Korak set you free. Now will you bring your people and set Korak's Meriem free?"

"The Gomangani have many sharp sticks which they throw. They pierce the bodies of my people. They kill us. The Gomangani are bad people. They will kill us all if we enter their village."

"The Tarmangani have sticks that make a loud noise and kill at a great distance," replied Korak. "They had these when Korak set you free from their trap. If Korak had run away from them you would now be a prisoner among the Tarmangani."

The baboon scratched his head. In a rough circle about him and the ape-man squatted the bulls of his herd. They blinked their eyes, shouldered one another about for more advantageous positions, scratched in the rotting vegetation upon the chance of unearthing a toothsome worm, or sat listlessly eyeing their king and the strange Mangani, who called himself thus but who more closely resembled the hated Tarmangani. The king looked at some of the older of his subjects, as though inviting suggestion.

"We are too few," grunted one.

"There are the baboons of the hill country," suggested another. "They are as many as the leaves of the forest. They, too, hate the Gomangani. They love to fight. They are very savage. Let us ask them to accompany us. Then can we kill all the Gomangani in the jungle." He rose and growled horribly, bristling his stiff hair.

"That is the way to talk," cried The Killer, "but we do not need the baboons of the hill country. We are enough. It will take a long time to fetch them. Meriem may be dead and eaten before we could free her. Let us set out at once for the village of the Gomangani. If we travel very fast it will not take long to reach it. Then, all at the same time, we can charge into the village, growling and barking. The Gomangani will be very frightened and will run away. While they are gone we can seize

Meriem and carry her off. We do not have to kill or be killed—all that Korak wishes is his Meriem.''

''We are too few,'' croaked the old ape again.

"Yes, we are too few," echoed others.

Korak could not persuade them. They would help him, gladly; but they must do it in their own way and that meant enlisting the services of their kinsmen and allies of the hill country. So Korak was forced to give in. All he could do for the present was to urge them to haste, and at his suggestion the king baboon with a dozen of his mightiest bulls agreed to go to the hill country with Korak, leaving the balance of the herd behind.

Once enlisted in the adventure the baboons became quite enthusiastic about it. The delegation set off immediately. They traveled swiftly; but the ape-man found no difficulty in keeping up with them. They made a tremendous racket as they passed through the trees in an endeavor to suggest to enemies in their front that a great herd was approaching, for when the baboons travel in large numbers there is no jungle creature who cares to molest them. When the nature of the country required much travel upon the level, and the distance between trees was great, they moved silently, knowing that the lion and the leopard would not be fooled by noise when they could see plainly for themselves that only a handful of baboons were on the trail.

For two days the party raced through the savage country, passing out of the dense jungle into an open plain, and across this to timbered mountain slopes. Here Korak never before had been. It was a new country to him and the change from the monotony of the circumscribed view in the jungle was pleasing. But he had little desire to enjoy the beauties of nature at this time. Meriem, his Meriem was in danger. Until she was freed and returned to him he had little thought for aught else.

Once in the forest that clothed the mountain slopes the baboons advanced more slowly. Constantly they gave tongue to a plaintive note of calling. Then would follow silence while they listened. At last, faintly from the distance straight ahead came an answer.

The baboons continued to travel in the direction of the voices that floated through the forest to them in the intervals of their own silence. Thus, calling and listening, they came closer to their kinsmen, who, it was evident to Korak, were coming to meet them in great numbers; but when, at last, the baboons of the hill country came in view the ape-man was staggered at the reality that broke upon his vision.

What appeared a solid wall of huge baboons rose from the ground through the branches of the trees to the loftiest terrace to which they dared entrust their weight. Slowly they were approaching, voicing their weird, plaintive call, and behind them, as far as Korak's eyes could pierce the verdure, rose solid walls of their fellows treading close upon their heels. There were thousands of them. The ape-man could not but think of the fate of his little party should some untoward incident arouse even momentarily the rage of fear of a single one of all these thousands.

But nothing such befell. The two kings approached one another, as was their custom, with much sniffing and bristling. They satisfied themselves of each other's identity. Then each scratched the other's back. After a moment they spoke together. Korak's friend explained the nature of their visit, and for the first time Korak showed himself. He had been hiding behind a bush. The excitement among the hill baboons was intense at sight of him. For a moment Korak feared that he should be torn to pieces; but his fear was for Meriem. Should he die there would be none to succor her.

The two kings, however, managed to quiet the multitude, and Korak was permitted to approach. Slowly the hill baboons came closer to him. They sniffed at him from every angle. When he spoke to them in their own tongue they were filled with wonder and delight. They talked to him and listened while he spoke. He told them of Meriem, and of their life in the jungle where they were the friends of all the ape folk from little Manu to Mangani, the great ape.

"The Gomangani, who are keeping Meriem from me, are no friends of yours," he said. "They kill you. The baboons of the low country are too few to go against them. They tell me that you are very many and very brave—that your numbers are as the numbers of the grasses upon the plains or the leaves within the forest, and that even Tantor, the elephant, fears you, so brave you are. They told me that you would be happy to accompany us to the village of the Gomangani and punish these bad people while I, Korak, The Killer, carry away my Meriem."

The king ape puffed out his chest and strutted about very stiff-legged indeed. So also did many of the other great bulls of his nation. They were pleased and flattered by the words of the strange Tarmangani, who called himself Mangani and spoke the language of the hairy progenitors of man.

"Yes," said one, "we of the hill country are mighty fighters. Tantor fears us. Numa fears us. Sheeta fears us. The Gomangani of the hill country are glad to pass us by in peace. I, for one, will come with you to the village of the Gomangani of the low places. I am the king's first he-child. Alone can I kill all the Gomangani of the low country,'' and he swelled his chest and strutted proudly back and forth, until the itching back of a comrade commanded his industrious attention.

"I am Goob,'' cried another. "My fighting fangs are long. They are sharp. They are strong. Into the soft flesh of many a Gomangani have they been buried. Alone I slew the sister of Sheeta. Goob will go to the low country with you and kill so many of the Gomangani that there will be none left to count the dead,'' and then he, too, strutted and pranced before the admiring eyes of the shes and the young.

Korak looked at the king, questioningly.

"Your bulls are very brave,'' he said; "but braver than any is the king.''

Thus addressed, the shaggy bull, still in his prime—else he had been no longer king—growled ferociously. The forest echoed to his lusty challenges. The little baboons clutched fearfully at their mother's hairy necks. The bulls, electrified, leaped high in air and took up the roaring challenge of their king. The din was terrific.

Korak came close to the king and shouted in his ear, "Come.'' Then he started off through the forest toward the plain that they must cross on their long journey back to the village of Kovudoo, the Gomangani. The king, still roaring and shrieking, wheeled and followed him. In their wake came the handful of low country baboons and the thousands of the hill clan—savage, wiry, dog-like creatures, athirst for blood.

And so they came, upon the second day, to the village of Kovudoo. It was mid-afternoon. The village was sunk in the quiet of the great equatorial sun-heat. The mighty herd traveled quietly now. Beneath the thousands of padded feet the forest gave forth no greater sound than might have been produced by the increased soughing of a stronger breeze through the leafy branches of the trees.

Korak and the two kings were in the lead. Close beside the village they halted until the stragglers had closed up. Now utter silence reigned. Korak, creeping stealthily, entered the tree that overhung the palisade. He glanced behind him. The pack were close upon his heels. The time had come. He had warned them continuously during the long march that no harm must befall the white she who lay a prisoner within the village. All others were their legitimate prey. Then, raising his face toward the sky, he gave voice to a single cry. It was the signal.

In response three thousand hairy bulls leaped screaming and barking into the village of the terrified blacks. Warriors poured from every hut. Mothers gathered their babies in their arms and fled toward the gates as they saw the horrid horde pouring into the village street. Kovudoo marshaled his fighting men about him and, leaping and yelling to arouse their courage, offered a bristling, spear tipped front to the charging horde.

Korak, as he had led the march, led the charge. The blacks were struck with horror and dismay at the sight of this white-skinned youth at the head of a pack of hideous baboons. For an instant they held their ground, hurling their spears once at the advancing multitude; but before they could fit arrows to their bows they wavered, gave, and turned in terrified rout. Into their ranks, upon their backs, sinking strong fangs into the muscles of their necks sprang the baboons and first among them, most ferocious, most blood-thirsty, most terrible was Korak, The Killer.

At the village gates, through which the blacks poured in panic, Korak left them to the tender mercies of his allies and turned himself eagerly toward the hut in which Meriem had been a prisoner. It was empty. One after another the filthy interiors revealed the same disheartening fact—Meriem was in none of them. That she had not been taken by the blacks in their flight from the village Korak knew for he had watched carefully for a glimpse of her among the fugitives.

To the mind of the ape-man, knowing as he did the proclivities of the savages, there was but a single explanation—Meriem had been killed and eaten. With the conviction that Meriem was dead there surged through Korak's brain a wave of blood red rage against those he believed to be her murderer. In the distance he could hear the snarling of the baboons mixed with the screams of their victims, and towards this he made his way. When he came upon them the baboons had commenced to tire of the sport of battle, and the blacks in a little knot were making a new stand, using their knob sticks effectively upon the few bulls who still persisted in attacking them.

Among these broke Korak from the branches of a tree above them—swift, relentless, terrible, he hurled himself upon the savage warriors of Kovudoo. Blind fury possessed him. Too, it protected him by its very ferocity. Like a wounded lioness he was here, there, everywhere, striking terrific blows with hard fists and with the precision and timeliness of the trained fighter. Again and again he buried his teeth in the flesh of a foeman. He was upon one and gone again to another before an effective blow could be dealt him. Yet, though great was the weight of his execution in determining the result of the combat, it was out-weighed by the terror which he inspired in the simple, supersti-tious minds of his foeman. To them this white warrior, who consorted with the great apes and the fierce baboons, who growled and snarled and snapped like a beast, was not human. He was a demon of the forest—a fearsome god of evil whom they had offended, and who had come out of his lair deep in the jungle to punish them. And because of this belief there were many who offered but little defense, feeling as they did the fu-tility of pitting their puny mortal strength against that of a deity.

Those who could fled, until at last there were no more to pay the penalty for a deed, which, while not beyond them, they were, nevertheless, not guilty of. Panting and bloody, Korak paused for want of further victims. The baboons gathered about him, sated themselves with blood and battle. They lolled upon the ground, fagged.

In the distance Kovudoo was gathering his scattered tribes-men, and taking account of injuries and losses. His people were panic stricken. Nothing could prevail upon them to remain lon-ger in this country. They would not even return to the village for their belongings. Instead they insisted upon continuing their flight until they had put many miles between themselves and the stamping ground of the demon who had so bitterly attacked them. And thus it befell that Korak drove from their homes the only people who might have aided him in a search for Meriem, and cut off the only connecting link between him and her from whomsoever might come in search of him from the *douar* of the kindly Bwana who had befriended his little jungle sweetheart.

It was a sour and savage Korak who bade farewell to his ba-boon allies upon the following morning. They wished him to accompany them; but the ape-man had no heart for the society of any. Jungle life had encouraged taciturnity in him. His sorrow had deepened this to a sullen moroseness that could not brook even the savage companionship of the ill-natured baboons.

Brooding and despondent he took his solitary way into the deepest jungle. He moved along the ground when he knew that Numa was abroad and hungry. He took to the same trees that harbored Sheeta, the panther. He courted death in a hundred ways and a hundred forms. His mind was ever occupied with reminiscences of Meriem and the happy years that they had spent together. He realized now to the full what she had meant to him. The sweet face, the tanned, supple, little body, the bright smile that always had welcomed his return from the hunt haunted him continually.

Inaction soon threatened him with madness. He must be on the go. He must fill his days with labor and excitement that he might forget—that night might find him so exhausted that he should sleep in blessed unconsciousness of his misery until a new day had come.

Had he guessed that by any possibility Meriem might still live he would at least have had hope. His days could have been devoted to searching for her; but he implicitly believed that she was dead.

For a long year he led his solitary, roaming life. Occasionally he fell in with Akut and his tribe, hunting with them for a day or two; or he might travel to the hill country where the baboons had come to accept him as a matter of course; but most of all was he with Tantor, the elephant—the great gray battle ship of the jungle—the super-dreadnaught of his savage world.

The peaceful quiet of the monster bulls, the watchful solicitude of the mother cows, the awkward playfulness of the calves rested, interested, and amused Korak. The life of the huge beasts took his mind, temporarily from his own grief. He came to love them as he loved not even the great apes, and there was one gigantic tusker in particular of which he was very fond—the lord of the herd—a savage beast that was wont to charge a stranger upon the slightest provocation, or upon no provocation whatsoever. And to Korak this mountain of destruction was docile and affectionate as a lap dog.

He came when Korak called. He wound his trunk about the ape-man's body and lifted him to his broad neck in response to a gesture, and there would Korak lie at full length kicking his toes affectionately into the thick hide and brushing the flies from about the tender ears of his colossal chum with a leafy branch torn from a nearby tree by Tantor for the purpose.

And all the while Meriem was scarce a hundred miles away.

# 16

To meriem, in her new home, the days passed quickly. At first she was all anxiety to be off into the jungle searching for her Korak. Bwana, as she insisted upon calling her benefactor, dissuaded her from making the attempt at once by dispatching a head man with a party of blacks to Kovudoo's village with instructions to learn from the old savage how he came into possession of the white girl and as much of her antecedents as might be culled from the black chieftain. Bwana particularly charged his head men with the duty of questioning Kovudoo relative to the strange character whom the girl called Korak, and of searching for the ape-man if he found the slightest evidence upon which to ground a belief in the existence of such an individual. Bwana was more than fully convinced that Korak was a creature of the girl's disordered imagination. He believed that the terrors and hardships she had undergone during captivity among the blacks and her frightful experience with the two Swedes had unbalanced her mind but as the days passed and he became better acquainted with her and able to observe her under the ordinary conditions of the quiet of his African home he was forced to admit that her strange tale puzzled him not a little, for there was no other evidence whatever that Meriem was not in full possession of her normal faculties.

The white man's wife, whom Meriem had christened "My Dear" from having first heard her thus addressed by Bwana, took not only a deep interest in the little jungle waif because of her forlorn and friendless state, but grew to love her as well for her sunny disposition and natural charm of temperament. And Meriem, similarly impressed by little attributes in the gentle, cultured woman, reciprocated the other's regard and affection.

127

And so the days flew by while Meriem waited the return of the head man and his party from the country of Kovudoo. They were short days, for into them were crowded many hours of insidious instruction of the unlettered child by the lonely woman. She commenced at once to teach the girl English without forcing it upon her as a task. She varied the instruction with lessons in sewing and deportment, nor once did she let Meriem guess that it was not all play. Nor was this difficult, since the girl was avid to learn. Then there were pretty dresses to be made to take the place of the single leopard skin and in this she found the child as responsive and enthusiastic as any civilized miss of her acquaintance.

A month passed before the head man returned—a month that had transformed the savage, half-naked little tarmangani into a daintily frocked girl of at least outward civilization. Meriem had progressed rapidly with the intricacies of the English language, for Bwana and My Dear had persistently refused to speak Arabic from the time they had decided that Meriem must learn English, which had been a day or two after her introduction into their home.

The report of the head man plunged Meriem into a period of despondency, for he had found the village of Kovudoo deserted nor, search as he would, could he discover a single native anywhere in the vicinity. For some time he had camped near the village, spending the days in a systematic search of the environs for traces of Meriem's Korak; but in this quest, too, had he failed. He had seen neither apes nor ape-man. Meriem at first insisted upon setting forth herself in search of Korak, but Bwana prevailed upon her to wait. He would go himself, he assured her, as soon as he could find the time; and at last Meriem consented to abide by his wishes; but it was months before she ceased to mourn almost hourly for her Korak.

My Dear grieved with the grieving girl and did her best to comfort and cheer her. She told her that if Korak lived he would find her; but all the time she believed that Korak had never existed beyond the child's dreams. She planned amusements to distract Meriem's attention from her sorrow, and she instituted a well-designed campaign to impress upon the child the desirability of civilized life and customs. Nor was this difficult, as she was soon to learn, for it rapidly became evident that beneath the uncouth savagery of the girl was a bed rock of innate refinement—a nicety of taste and predilection that quite equaled that of her instructor.

My Dear was delighted. She was lonely and childless, and so she lavished upon this little stranger all the mother love that would have gone to her own had she had one. The result was that by the end of the first year none might have guessed that Meriem ever had existed beyond the lap of culture and luxury.

She was sixteen now, though she easily might have passed for nineteen, and she was very good to look upon, with her black hair and her tanned skin and all the freshness and purity of health and innocence. Yet she still nursed her secret sorrow, though she no longer mentioned it to My Dear. Scarce an hour passed that did not bring its recollection of Korak, and its poignant yearning to see him again.

Meriem spoke English fluently now, and read and wrote it as well. One day My Dear spoke jokingly to her in French and to her surprise Meriem replied in the same tongue—slowly, it is true, and haltingly; but none the less in excellent French, such, though, as a little child might use. Thereafter they spoke a little French each day, and My Dear often marveled that the girl learned this language with a facility that was at times almost uncanny. At first Meriem had puckered her narrow, arched, little eye brows as though trying to force recollection of something all but forgotten which the new words suggested, and then, to her own astonishment as well as to that of her teacher she had used other French words than those in the lessons—used them properly and with a pronunciation that the English woman knew was more perfect than her own; but Meriem could neither read nor write what she spoke so well, and as My Dear considered a knowledge of correct English of the first importance, other than conversational French was postponed for a later day.

"You doubtless heard French spoken at times in your father's *douar*," suggested My Dear, as the most reasonable explanation.

Meriem shook her head.

"It may be," she said, "but I do not recall ever having seen a Frenchman in my father's company—he hated them and would have nothing whatever to do with them, and I am quite sure that I never heard any of these words before, yet at the same time I find them all familiar. I cannot understand it."

"Neither can I," agreed My Dear.

It was about this time that a runner brought a letter that, when she learned the contents, filled Meriem with excitement. Visitors were coming! A number of English ladies and gentlemen had accepted My Dear's invitation to spend a month of hunting and exploring with them. Meriem was all expectancy. What would these strangers be like? Would they be as nice to her as had Bwana and My Dear, or would they be like the other white folk she had known—cruel and relentless. My Dear assured her that they all were gentle folk and that she would find them kind, considerate and honorable.

To My Dear's surprise there was none of the shyness of the wild creature in Meriem's anticipation of the visit of strangers.

She looked forward to their coming with curiosity and with a certain pleasurable anticipation when once she was assured that they would not bite her. In fact she appeared no different than would any pretty young miss who had learned of the expected coming of company.

Korak's image was still often in her thoughts, but it aroused now a less well-defined sense of bereavement. A quiet sadness pervaded Meriem when she thought of him; but the poignant grief of her loss when it was young no longer goaded her to desperation. Yet she was still loyal to him. She still hoped that some day he would find her, nor did she doubt for a moment but that he was searching for her if he still lived. It was this last suggestion that caused her the greatest perturbation. Korak might be dead. It scarce seemed possible that one so well-equipped to meet the emergencies of jungle life should have succumbed so young; yet when she had last seen him he had been beset by a horde of armed warriors, and should he have returned to the village again, as she well knew he must have, he may have been killed. Even her Korak could not, single handed, slay an entire tribe.

At last the visitors arrived. There were three men and two women—the wives of the two older men. The youngest member of the party was Hon. Morison Baynes, a young man of considerable wealth who, having exhausted all the possibilities for pleasure offered by the capitals of Europe, had gladly seized upon this opportunity to turn to another continent for excitement and adventure.

He looked upon all things un-European as rather more than less impossible, still he was not at all averse to enjoying the novelty of unaccustomed places, and making the most of strangers indigenous thereto, however unspeakable they might have seemed to him at home. In manner he was suave and courteous to all—if possible a trifle more punctilious toward those he considered of meaner clay than toward the few he mentally admitted to equality.

Nature had favored him with a splendid physique and a handsome face, and also with sufficient good judgment to appreciate that while he might enjoy the contemplation of his superiority to the masses, there was little likelihood of the masses being equally entranced by the same cause. And so he easily maintained the reputation of being a most democratic and likeable fellow, and indeed he was likable. Just a shade of his egotism was occasionally apparent—never sufficient to become a burden to his associates. And this, briefly, was the Hon. Morison Baynes of luxurious European civilization. What would be the Hon. Morison Baynes of central Africa it were difficult to guess.

Meriem, at first, was shy and reserved in the presence of the strangers. Her benefactors had seen fit to ignore mention of her strange past, and so she passed as their ward whose antecedents not having been mentioned were not to be inquired into. The guests found her sweet and unassuming, laughing, vivacious and a never exhausted storehouse of quaint and interesting jungle lore.

She had ridden much during her year with Bwana and My Dear. She knew each favorite clump of concealing reeds along the river that the buffalo loved best. She knew a dozen places where lions laired, and every drinking hole in the drier country twenty-five miles back from the river. With unerring precision that was almost uncanny she could track the largest or the smallest beast to his hiding place. But the thing that baffled them all was her instant consciousness of the presence of carnivora that others, exerting their faculties to the utmost, could neither see nor hear.

The Hon. Morison Baynes found Meriem a most beautiful and charming companion. He was delighted with her from the first. Particularly so, it is possible, because he had not thought to find companionship of this sort upon the African estate of his London friends. They were together a great deal as they were the only unmarried couple in the little company. Meriem, entirely unaccustomed to the companionship of such as Baynes, was fascinated by him. His tales of the great, gay cities with which he was familiar filled her with admiration and with wonder. If the Hon. Morison always shone to advantage in these narratives Meriem saw in that fact but a most natural consequence to his presence upon the scene of his story—wherever Morison might be he must be a hero; so thought the girl.

With the actual presence and companionship of the young Englishman the image of Korak became less real. Where before it had been an actuality to her she now realized that Korak was but a memory. To that memory she still was loyal; but what weight has a memory in the presence of a fascinating reality?

Meriem had never accompanied the men upon a hunt since the arrival of the guests. She never had cared particularly for the sport of killing. The tracking she enjoyed; but the mere killing for the sake of killing she could not find pleasure in—little savage that she had been, and still, to some measure, was. When Bwana had gone forth to shoot for meat she had always been his enthusiastic companion; but with the coming of the London guests the hunting had deteriorated into mere killing. Slaughter the host would not permit; yet the purpose of the hunts were for heads and skins and not for food. So Meriem remained behind and spent her days either with My Dear upon the shaded verandah, or riding her favorite pony across the plains or to the forest edge. Here she would leave him untethered while she took to the trees for the moment's unalloyed pleasures of a return to the wild, free existence of her earlier childhood.

Then would come again visions of Korak, and, tired at last of leaping and swinging through the trees, she would stretch herself comfortably upon a branch and dream. And presently, as today, she found the features of Korak slowly dissolve and merge into those of another, and the figure of a tanned, half-naked tarmangani become a khaki clothed Englishman astride a hunting pony.

And while she dreamed there came to her ears from a distance, faintly, the terrified bleating of a kid. Meriem was instantly alert. You or I, even had we been able to hear the pitiful wail at so great distance, could not have interpreted it; but to Meriem it meant a species of terror that afflicts the ruminant when a carnivore is near and escape impossible.

It had been both a pleasure and a sport of Korak's to rob Numa of his prey whenever possible, and Meriem too had often enjoyed in the thrill of snatching some dainty morsel almost from the very jaws of the king of beasts. Now, at the sound of the kid's bleat, all the well remembered thrills recurred. Instantly she was all excitement to play again the game of hide and seek with death.

Quickly she loosened her riding skirt and tossed it aside—it was a heavy handicap to successful travel in the trees. Her boots and stockings followed the skirt, for the bare sole of the human foot does not slip upon dry or even wet bark as does the hard leather of a boot. She would have liked to discard her riding breeches also, but the motherly admonitions of My Dear had convinced Meriem that it was not good form to go naked through the world.

At her hip hung a hunting knife. Her rifle was still in its boot at her pony's withers. Her revolver she had not brought.

The kid was still bleating as Meriem started rapidly in its direction, which she knew was straight toward a certain water hole which had once been famous as a rendezvous for lions. Of late there had been no evidence of carnivora in the neighborhood of this drinking place; but Meriem was positive that the bleating of the kid was due to the presence of either lion or panther.

But she would soon know, for she was rapidly approaching the terrified animal. She wondered as she hastened onward that the sounds continued to come from the same point. Why did the kid not run away? And then she came in sight of the little animal and knew. The kid was tethered to a stake beside the waterhole.

Meriem paused in the branches of a near-by tree and scanned the surrounding clearing with quick, penetrating eyes. Where was the hunter? Bwana and his people did not hunt thus. Who could have tethered this poor little beast as a lure to Numa? Bwana never countenanced such acts in his country and his word was law among those who hunted within a radius of many miles of his estate.

Some wandering savages, doubtless, thought Meriem; but where were they? Not even her keen eyes could discover them. And where was Numa? Why had he not long since sprung upon this delicious and defenseless morsel? That he was close by was attested by the pitiful crying of the kid. Ah! Now she saw him. He was lying close in a clump of brush a few yards to her right. The kid was down wind from him and getting the full benefit of his terrorizing scent, which did not reach Meriem.

To circle to the opposite side of the clearing where the trees approached closer to the kid. To leap quickly to the little animal's side and cut the tether that held him would be the work of but a moment. In that moment Numa might charge, and then there would be scarce time to regain the safety of the trees, yet it might be done. Meriem had escaped from closer quarters than that many times before.

The doubt that gave her momentary pause was caused by fear of the unseen hunters more than by fear of Numa. If they were stranger blacks the spears that they held in readiness for Numa might as readily be loosed upon whomever dared release their bait as upon the prey they sought thus to trap. Again the kid struggled to be free. Again his piteous wail touched the tender heart strings of the girl. Tossing discretion aside, she commenced to circle the clearing. Only from Numa did she attempt to conceal her presence. At last she reached the opposite trees. An instant she paused to look toward the great lion, and at the same moment she saw the huge beast rise slowly to his full height. A low roar betokened that he was ready.

Meriem loosened her knife and leaped to the ground. A quick run brought her to the side of the kid. Numa saw her. He lashed his tail against his tawny sides. He roared terribly; but, for an instant, he remained where he stood—surprised into inaction, doubtless, by the strange apparition that had sprung so unexpectedly from the jungle.

Other eyes were upon Meriem, too—eyes in which were no less surprise than that reflected in the yellow-green orbs of the carnivore. A white man, hiding in a thorn *boma*, half rose as the young girl leaped into the clearing and dashed toward the kid. He saw Numa hesitate. He raised his rifle and covered the beast's breast. The girl reached the kid's side. Her knife flashed, and the little prisoner was free. With a parting bleat it dashed off into the jungle. Then the girl turned to retreat toward the safety of the tree from which she had dropped so suddenly and unexpectedly into the surprised view of the lion, the kid and the man.

As she turned the girl's face was turned toward the hunter. His eyes went wide as he saw her features. He gave a little gasp of surprise; but now the lion demanded all his attention—the baffled, angry beast was charging. His breast was still covered by the motionless rifle. The man could have fired and stopped the charge at once; but for some reason, since he had seen the girl's face, he hesitated. Could it be that he did not care to save her? Or, did he prefer, if possible, to remain unseen by her? It must have been the latter cause which kept the trigger finger of the steady hand from exerting the little pressure that would have brought the great beast to at least a temporary pause.

Like an eagle the man watched the race for life the girl was making. A second or two measured the time which the whole exciting event consumed from the moment that the lion broke into his charge. Nor once did the rifle sights fail to cover the broad beast or the tawny sire as the lion's course took him a little to the man's left. Once, at the very last moment, when escape seemed impossible, the hunter's finger tightened ever so little upon the trigger, but almost coincidentally the girl leaped for an over hanging branch and seized it. The lion leaped too; but the nimble Meriem had swung herself beyond his reach without a second or an inch to spare.

The man breathed a sigh of relief as he lowered his rifle. He saw the girl fling a grimace at the angry, roaring, maneater beneath her, and then, laughing, speed away into the forest. For an hour the lion remained about the water hole. A hundred times could the hunter have bagged his prey. Why did he fail to do so? Was he afraid that the shot might attract the girl and cause her to return?

At last Numa, still roaring angrily, strode majestically into the jungle. The hunter crawled from his *boma*, and half an hour later was entering a little camp snugly hidden in the forest. A handful of black followers greeted his return with sullen indifference. He was a great bearded man, a huge, yellow-bearded giant, when he entered his tent. Half an hour later he emerged smooth shaven.

His blacks looked at him in astonishment.

"Would you know me?" he asked.

"The hyena that bore you would not know you, Bwana," replied one.

The man aimed a heavy fist at the black's face; but long experience in dodging similar blows saved the presumptuous one.

# 17

MERIEM RETURNED SLOWLY toward the tree in which she had left her skirt, her shoes and her stockings. She was singing blithely; but her song came to a sudden stop when she came within sight of the tree, for there, disporting themselves with glee and pulling and hauling upon her belongings, were a number of baboons. When they saw her they showed no signs of terror. Instead they bared their fangs and growled at her. What was there to fear in a single she-Tarmangani? Nothing, absolutely nothing.

In the open plain beyond the forest the hunters were returning from the day's sport. They were widely separated, hoping to raise a wandering lion on the homeward journey across the plain. The Hon. Morison Baynes rode closest to the forest. As his eyes wandered back and forth across the undulating, shrub sprinkled ground they fell upon the form of a creature close beside the thick jungle where it terminated abruptly at the plain's edge.

He reined his mount in the direction of his discovery. It was yet too far away for his untrained eyes to recognize it; but as he came closer he saw that it was a horse, and was about to resume the original direction of his way when he thought that he discerned a saddle upon the beast's back. He rode a little closer. Yes, the animal was saddled. The Hon. Morison approached yet nearer, and as he did so his eyes expressed a pleasurable emotion of anticipation, for they had now recognized the pony as the special favorite of Meriem.

He galloped to the animal's side. Meriem must be within the wood. The man shuddered a little at the thought of an unprotected girl alone in the jungle that was still, to him, a fearful place of terrors and stealthily stalking death. He dismounted and left his horse beside Meriem's. On foot he entered the jungle.

136

He knew that she was probably safe enough and he wished to surprise her by coming suddenly upon her.

He had gone but a short distance into the wood when he heard a great jabbering in a near-by tree. Coming closer he saw a band of baboons snarling over something. Looking intently he saw that one of them held a woman's riding skirt and that others had boots and stockings. His heart almost ceased to beat as he quite naturally placed the most direful explanation upon the scene. The baboons had killed Meriem and stripped this clothing from her body. Morison shuddered.

He was about to call aloud in the hope that after all the girl still lived when he saw her in a tree close beside that was occupied by the baboons, and now he saw that they were snarling and jabbering at her. To his amazement he saw the girl swing, ape-like, into the tree below the huge beasts. He saw her pause upon a branch a few feet from the nearest baboon. He was about to raise his rifle and put a bullet through the hideous creature that seemed about to leap upon her when he heard the girl speak. He almost dropped his rifle from surprise as a strange jabbering, identical with that of the apes, broke from Meriem's lips.

The baboons stopped their snarling and listened. It was quite evident that they were as much surprised as the Hon. Morison Baynes. Slowly and one by one they approached the girl. She gave not the slightest evidence of fear of them. They quite surrounded her now so that Baynes could not have fired without endangering the girl's life; but he no longer desired to fire. He was consumed with curiosity.

For several minutes the girl carried on what could be nothing less than a conversation with the baboons, and then with seeming alacrity every article of her apparel in their possession was handed over to her. The baboons still crowded eagerly about her as she donned them. They chattered to her and she chattered back. The Hon. Morison Baynes sat down at the foot of a tree and mopped his perspiring brow. Then he rose and made his way back to his mount.

When Meriem emerged from the forest a few minutes later she found him there, and he eyed her with wide eyes in which were both wonder and a sort of terror.

"I saw your horse here," he explained, "and thought that I would wait and ride home with you—you do not mind?"

"Of course not," she replied. "It will be lovely."

As they made their way stirrup to stirrup across the plain the Hon. Morison caught himself many times watching the girl's regular profile and wondering if his eyes had deceived him or if, in truth, he really had seen this lovely creature consorting with grotesque baboons and conversing with them as fluently as she conversed with him. The thing was uncanny—impossible; yet he had seen it with his own eyes.

And as he watched her another thought persisted in obtruding itself into his mind. She was most beautiful and very desirable; but what did he know of her? Was she not altogether impossible? Was the scene that he had but just witnessed not sufficient proof of her impossibility? A woman who climbed trees and conversed with the baboons of the jungle! It was quite horrible!

Again the Hon. Morison mopped his brow. Meriem glanced toward him.

"You are warm," she said. "Now that the sun is setting I find it quite cool. Why do you perspire now?"

He had not intended to let her know that he had seen her with the baboons; but quite suddenly, before he realized what he was saying, he had blurted it out.

"I perspire from emotion," he said. "I went into the jungle when I discovered your pony. I wanted to surprise you; but it was I who was surprised. I saw you in the trees with the baboons."

"Yes?" she said quite unemotionally, as though it was a matter of little moment that a young girl should be upon intimate terms with savage jungle beasts.

"It was horrible!" ejaculated the Hon. Morison.

"Horrible?" repeated Meriem, puckering her brows in bewilderment. "What was horrible about it? They are my friends. Is it horrible to talk with one's friends?"

"You were really talking with them, then?" cried the Hon. Morison. "You understood them and they understood you?"

"Certainly."

"But they are hideous creatures—degraded beasts of a lower order. How could you speak the language of beasts?"

"They are not hideous, and they are not degraded," replied Meriem. "Friends are never that. I lived among them for years before Bwana found me and brought me here. I scarce knew any other tongue than that of the mangani. Should I refuse to know them now simply because I happen, for the present, to live among humans?"

"For the present!" ejaculated the Hon. Morison. "You cannot mean that you expect to return to live among them? Come, come, what foolishness are we talking! The very idea! You are spoofing me, Miss Meriem. You have been kind to these baboons here and they know you and do not molest you; but that you once lived among them—no, that is preposterous.''

"But I did, though," insisted the girl, seeing the real horror that the man felt in the presence of such an idea reflected in his tone and manner, and rather enjoying baiting him still further. "Yes, I lived, almost naked, among the great apes and the lesser apes. I dwelt among the branches of the trees. I pounced upon the smaller prey and devoured it—raw. With Korak and A'ht I hunted the antelope and the boar, and I sat upon a tree limb and made faces at Numa, the lion, and threw sticks at him and annoyed him until he roared so terribly in his rage that the earth shook.

"And Korak built me a lair high among the branches of a mighty tree. He brought me fruits and flesh. He fought for me and was kind to me—until I came to Bwana and My Dear I do not recall that any other than Korak was ever kind to me.'' There was a wistful note in the girl's voice now and she had forgotten that she was bantering the Hon. Morison. She was thinking of Korak. She had not thought of him a great deal of late.

For a time both were silently absorbed in their own reflections as they rode on toward the bungalow of their host. The girl was thinking of a god-like figure, a leopard skin half concealing his smooth, brown hide as he leaped nimbly through the trees to lay an offering of food before her on his return from a successful hunt. Behind him, shaggy and powerful, swung a huge anthropoid ape, while she, Meriem, laughing and shouting her welcome, swung upon a swaying limb before the entrance to her sylvan bower. It was a pretty picture as she recalled it. The other side seldom obtruded itself upon her memory—the long, black nights—the chill, terrible jungle nights—the cold and damp and discomfort of the rainy season—the hideous mouthings of the savage carnivora as they prowled through the Stygian darkness beneath—the constant menace of Sheeta, the panther, and Histah, the snake—the stinging insects—the loathesome vermine. For, in truth, all these had been outweighed by the happiness of the sunny days, the freedom of it all, and, most, the companionship of Korak.

The man's thoughts were rather jumbled. He had suddenly realized that he had come mighty near falling in love with this girl of whom he had known nothing up to the previous moment when she had voluntarily revealed a portion of her past to him. The more he thought upon the matter the more evident it became to him that he had given her his love—that he had been upon the verge of offering her his honorable name. He trembled a little at the narrowness of his escape. Yet, he still loved her. There was no objection to that according to the ethics of the Hon. Morison Baynes and his kind. She was a meaner clay than he. He could no more have taken her in marriage than he could have taken one of her baboon friends, nor would she, of course, expect such an offer from him. To have his love would be sufficient honor for her—his name he would, naturally, bestow upon one in his own elevated social sphere.

A girl who had consorted with apes, who, according to her own admission, had lived almost naked among them, could have no considerable sense of the finer qualities of virtue. The love that he would offer her, then, would, far from offending her, probably cover all that she might desire or expect.

The more the Hon. Morison Baynes thought upon the subject the more fully convinced he became that he was contemplating a most chivalrous and unselfish act. Europeans will better understand his point of view than Americans, poor, benighted provincials, who are denied a true appreciation of caste and of the fact that "the king can do no wrong." He did not even have to argue the point that she would be much happier amidst the luxuries of a London apartment, fortified as she would be by both his love and his bank account, than lawfully wed to such a one as her social position warranted. There was one question however, which he wished to have definitely answered before he committed himself even to the program he was considering.

"Who were Korak and A'ht?" he asked.

"A'ht was a Mangani," replied Meriem, "and Korak a Tarmangani."

"And what, pray, might a Mangani be, and a Tarmangani?" The girl laughed.

"You are a Tarmangani," she replied. "The Mangani are covered with hair—you would call them apes."

"Then Korak was a white man?" he asked.

"Yes."

"And he was—ah—your—er—your—?" He paused, for he found it rather difficult to go on with that line of questioning while the girl's clear, beautiful eyes were looking straight into his.

"My what?" insisted Meriem, far too unsophisticated in her unspoiled innocence to guess what the Hon. Morison was driving at.

"Why—ah—your brother?" he stumbled.

"No, Korak was not my brother," she replied.

"Was he your husband, then?" he finally blurted.

Far from taking offense, Meriem, broke into a merry laugh.

"My husband!" she cried. "Why how old do you think I am?
I am too young to have a husband. I had never thought of such
a thing. Korak was—why—," and now she hesitated, too, for
she never before had attempted to analyse the relationship that
existed between herself and Korak—"why, Korak was just Korak," and again she broke into a gay laugh as she realized the
illuminating quality of her description.

Looking at her and listening to her the man beside her could
not believe that depravity of any sort or degree entered into the
girl's nature, yet he wanted to believe that she had not been
virtuous, for otherwise his task was less a sinecure—the Hon.
Morison was not entirely without conscience.

For several days the Hon. Morison made no appreciable progress toward the consummation of his scheme. Sometimes he
almost abandoned it for he found himself time and again wondering how slight might be the provocation necessary to trick
him into making a bona-fide offer of marriage to Meriem if he
permitted himself to fall more deeply in love with her, and it
was difficult to see her daily and not love her. There was a
quality about her which, all unknown to the Hon. Morison, was
making his task an extremely difficult one—it was that quality
of innate goodness and cleanness which is a good girl's stoutest
bulwark and protection—an impregnable barrier that only de-
generacy has the affrontery to assail. The Hon. Morison Baynes
would never be considered a degenerate.

He was sitting with Meriem upon the verandah one evening
after the others had retired. Earlier they had been playing ten-
nis—a game in which the Hon. Morison shone to advantage, as,
in truth, he did in most all manly sports. He was telling Meriem
stories of London and Paris, of balls and banquets, of the wonderful women and their wonderful gowns, of the pleasures and
pastimes of the rich and powerful. The Hon. Morison was a past
master in the art of insidious boasting. His egotism was never
flagrant or tiresome—he was never crude in it, for crudeness
was a plebeianism that the Hon. Morison studiously avoided,
yet the impression derived by a listener to the Hon. Morison was
one that was not at all calculated to detract from the glory of the
house of Baynes, or from that of its representative.

Meriem was entranced. His tales were like fairy stories to this little jungle maid. The Hon. Morison loomed large and wonderful and magnificent in her mind's eye. He fascinated her, and when he drew closer to her after a short silence and took her hand she thrilled as one might thrill beneath the touch of a deity—a thrill of exaltation not unmixed with fear.

He bent his lips close to her ear.

"Meriem!" he whispered. "My little Meriem! May I hope to have the right to call you 'my little Meriem'?"

The girl turned wide eyes upward to his face; but it was in shadow. She trembled but she did not draw away. The man put an arm about her and drew her closer.

"I love you!" he whispered.

She did not reply. She did not know what to say. She knew nothing of love. She had never given it a thought; but she did know that it was very nice to be loved, whatever it meant. It was nice to have people kind to one. She had known so little of kindness or affection.

"Tell me," he said, "that you return my love."

His lips came steadily closer to hers. They had almost touched when a vision of Korak sprang like a miracle before her eyes. She saw Korak's face close to hers, she felt his lips hot against hers, and then for the first time in her life she guessed what love meant. She drew away.

"I am not sure," she said, "that I love you. Let us wait. There is plenty of time. I am too young to marry yet, and I am not sure that I should be happy in London or Paris—they rather frighten me."

How easily and naturally she had connected his avowal of love with the idea of marriage! The Hon. Morison was perfectly sure that he had not mentioned marriage—he had been particularly careful not to do so. And then she was not sure that she loved him! That, too, came rather in the nature of a shock to his vanity. It seemed incredible that this little barbarian should have any doubts whatever as to the desirability of the Hon. Morison Baynes.

The first flush of passion cooled, the Hon. Morison was enabled to reason more logically. The start had been all wrong. It would be better now to wait and prepare her mind gradually for the only proposition which his exalted estate would permit him to offer her. He would go slow. He glanced down at the girl's profile. It was bathed in the silvery light of the great tropic moon. The Hon. Morison Baynes wondered if it were to be so easy a matter to "go slow." She was most alluring.

Meriem rose. The vision of Korak was still before her.

"Good night," she said. "It is almost too beautiful to leave," she waved her hand in a comprehensive gesture which took in the starry heavens, the great moon, the broad, silvered plain, and the dense shadows in the distance, that marked the jungle. "Oh, how I love it!"

"You would love London more," he said earnestly. "And London would love you. You would be a famous beauty in any capital of Europe. You would have the world at your feet, Meriem."

"Good night!" she repeated, and left him.

The Hon. Morison selected a cigarette from his crested case, lighted it, blew a thin line of blue smoke toward the moon, and smiled.

# 18

M ERIEM AND BWANA were sitting on the verandah together
the following day when a horseman appeared in the distance riding across the plain toward the bungalow. Bwana shaded
his eyes with his hand and gazed out toward the oncoming rider.
He was puzzled. Strangers were few in Central Africa. Even the
blacks for a distance of many miles in every direction were well
known to him. No white man came within a hundred miles that
word of his coming did not reach Bwana long before the stranger.
His every move was reported to the big Bwana—just what animals he killed and how many of each species, how he killed
them, too, for Bwana would not permit the use of prussic acid
or strychnine; and how he treated his "boys."

Several European sportsmen had been turned back to the coast
by the big Englishman's orders because of unwarranted cruelty
to their black followers, and one, whose name had long been
heralded in civilized communities as that of a great sportsman,
was driven from Africa with orders never to return when Bwana
found that his big bag of fourteen lions had been made by the
diligent use of poisoned bait.

The result was that all good sportsmen and all the natives
loved and respected him. His word was law where there had
never been law before. There was scarce a head man from coast
to coast who would not heed the big Bwana's commands in
preference to those of the hunters who employed them, and so
it was easy to turn back any undesirable stranger—Bwana had
simply to threaten to order his boys to desert him.

But there was evidently one who had slipped into the country
unheralded. Bwana could not imagine who the approaching
horseman might be. After the manner of frontier hospitality the
globe round he met the newcomer at the gate, welcoming him

144

even before he had dismounted. He saw a tall, well knit man of thirty or over, blonde of hair and smooth shaven. There was a tantalizing familiarity about him that convinced Bwana that he should be able to call the visitor by name, yet he was unable to do so. The newcomer was evidently of Scandinavian origin—both his appearance and accent denoted that. His manner was rough but open. He made a good impression upon the Englishman, who was wont to accept strangers in this wild and savage country at their own valuation, asking no questions and assuming the best of them until they proved themselves undeserving of his friendship and hospitality.

"It is rather unusual that a white man comes unheralded," he said, as they walked together toward the field into which he had suggested that the traveler might turn his pony. "My friends, the natives, keep us rather well-posted."

"It is probably due to the fact that I came from the south," explained the stranger, "that you did not hear of my coming. I have seen no village for several marches."

"No, there are none to the south of us for many miles," replied Bwana. "Since Kovudoo deserted his country I rather doubt that one could find a native in that direction under two or three hundred miles."

Bwana was wondering how a lone white man could have made his way through the savage, unhospitable miles that lay toward the south. As though guessing what must be passing through the other's mind, the stranger vouchsafed an explanation.

"I came down from the north to do a little trading and hunting," he said, "and got way off the beaten track. My head man, who was the only member of the *safari* who had ever before been in the country, took sick and died. We could find no natives to guide us, and so I simply swung back straight north. We have been living on the fruits of our guns for over a month. Didn't have an idea there was a white man within a thousand miles of us when we camped last night by a water hole at the edge of the plain. This morning I started out to hunt and saw the smoke from your chimney, so I sent my gun bearer back to camp with the good news and rode straight over here myself. Of course I've heard of you—everybody who comes into Central Africa does—and I'd be mighty glad of permission to rest up and hunt around here for a couple of weeks."

"Certainly," replied Bwana. "Move your camp up close to the river below my boys' camp and make yourself at home."

They had reached the verandah now and Bwana was introducing the stranger to Meriem and My Dear, who had just come from the bungalow's interior.

"This is Mr. Hanson," he said, using the name the man had given him. "He is a trader who has lost his way in the jungle to the south."

My Dear and Meriem bowed their acknowledgments of the introduction. The man seemed rather ill at ease in their presence. His host attributed this to the fact that his guest was unaccustomed to the society of cultured women, and so found a pretext to quickly extricate him from his seemingly unpleasant position and lead him away to his study and the brandy and soda which were evidently much less embarrassing to Mr. Hanson.

When the two had left them Meriem turned toward My Dear.

"It is odd," she said, "but I could almost swear that I had known Mr. Hanson in the past. It is odd, but quite impossible," and she gave the matter no further thought.

Hanson did not accept Bwana's invitation to move his camp closer to the bungalow. He said his boys were inclined to be quarrelsome, and so were better off at a distance; and he, himself, was around but little, and then always avoided coming into contact with the ladies. A fact which naturally aroused only laughing comment on the rough trader's bashfulness. He accompanied the men on several hunting trips where they found him perfectly at home and well versed in all the finer points of big game hunting. Of an evening he often spent much time with the white foreman of the big farm, evidently finding in the society of this rougher man more common interests than the cultured guests of Bwana possessed for him. So it came that his was a familiar figure about the premises by night. He came and went as he saw fit, often wandering along in the great flower garden that was the especial pride and joy of My Dear and Meriem. The first time that he had been surprised there he apologized gruffly, explaining that he had always been fond of the good old blooms of northern Europe which My Dear had so successfully transplanted in African soil.

Was it, though, the ever beautiful blossoms of hollyhocks and phlox that drew him to the perfumed air of the garden, or that other infinitely more beautiful flower who wandered often among the blooms beneath the great moon—the black-haired, suntanned Meriem?

For three weeks Hanson had remained. During this time he said that his boys were resting and gaining strength after their terrible ordeals in the untracked jungle to the south; but he had not been as idle as he appeared to have been. He divided his small following into two parties, entrusting the leadership of each to men whom he believed that he could trust. To them he explained his plans and the rich reward that they would win from him if they carried his designs to a successful conclusion. One party he moved very slowly northward along the trail that connects with the great caravan routes entering the Sahara from the south. The other he ordered straight westward with orders to halt and go into permanent camp just beyond the great river which marks the natural boundary of the country that the big Bwana rightfully considers almost his own.

To his host he explained that he was moving his *safari* slowly toward the north—he said nothing of the party moving westward. Then, one day, he announced that half his boys had deserted, for a hunting party from the bungalow had come across his northerly camp and he feared that they might have noticed the reduced numbers of his following.

And thus matters stood when, one hot night, Meriem, unable to sleep, rose and wandered out into the garden. The Hon. Morison had been urging his suit once more that evening, and the girl's mind was in such a turmoil that she had been unable to sleep.

The wide heavens about her seemed to promise a greater freedom from doubt and questioning. Baynes had urged her to tell him that she loved him. A dozen times she thought that she might honestly give him the answer that he demanded. Korak fast was becoming but a memory. That he was dead she had come to believe, since otherwise he would have sought her out. She did not know that he had even better reason to believe her dead, and that it was because of that belief he had made no effort to find her after his raid upon the village of Kovudoo.

Behind a great flowering shrub Hanson lay gazing at the stars and waiting. He had lain thus and there many nights before. For what was he waiting, or for whom? He heard the girl approaching, and half raised himself to his elbow. A dozen paces away, the reins looped over a fence post, stood his pony.

Meriem, walking slowly, approached the bush behind which the waiter lay. Hanson drew a large bandanna handkerchief from his pocket and rose stealthily to his knees. A pony neighed down at the corrals. Far out across the plain a lion roared. Hanson changed his position until he squatted upon both feet, ready to come erect quickly.

Again the pony neighed—this time closer. There was the

sound of his body brushing against shrubbery. Hanson heard and wondered how the animal had gotten from the corral, for it was evident that he was already in the garden. The man turned his head in the direction of the beast. What he saw sent him to the ground, huddled close beneath the shrubbery—a man was coming, leading two ponies.

Meriem heard now and stopped to look and listen. A moment later the Hon. Morison Baynes drew near, the two saddled mounts at his heels.

Meriem looked up at him in surprise. The Hon. Morison grinned sheepishly.

"I couldn't sleep," he explained, "and was going for a bit of a ride when I chanced to see you out here, and I thought you'd like to join me. Ripping good sport, you know, night riding. Come on."

Meriem laughed. The adventure appealed to her.

"All right." she said.

Hanson swore beneath his breath. The two led their horses from the garden to the gate and through it. There they discovered Hanson's mount.

"Why here's the trader's pony," remarked Baynes.

"He's probably down visiting with the foreman," said Meriem.

"Pretty late for him, isn't it?" remarked the Hon. Morison. "I'd hate to have to ride back through that jungle at night to his camp."

As though to give weight to his apprehensions the distant lion roared again. The Hon. Morison shivered and glanced at the girl to note the effect of the uncanny sound upon her. She appeared not to have noticed it.

A moment later the two had mounted and were moving slowly across the moon-bathed plain. The girl turned her pony's head straight toward the jungle. It was in the direction of the roaring of the hungry lion.

"Hadn't we better steer clear of that fellow?" suggested the Hon. Morison. "I guess you didn't hear him."

"Yes, I heard him," laughed Meriem. "Let's ride over and call on him."

The Hon. Morison laughed uneasily. He didn't care to appear at a disadvantage before this girl, nor did he care, either, to approach a hungry lion too closely at night. He carried his rifle in his saddle boot; but moonlight is an uncertain light to shoot by, nor ever had he faced a lion alone—even by day. The thought gave him a distinct nausea. The beast ceased his roaring now. They heard him no more and the Hon. Morison gained courage accordingly. They were riding down wind toward the jungle. The lion lay in a little swale to their right. He was old. For two nights he had not fed, for no longer was his charge as swift or his spring as mighty as in the days of his prime when he spread terror among the creatures of his wild domain. For two nights and days he had gone empty, and for long time before that he had fed only upon carrion. He was old; but he was yet a terrible engine of destruction.

At the edge of the forest the Hon. Morison drew rein. He had no desire to go further. Numa, silent upon his padded feet, crept into the jungle beyond them. The wind, now, was blowing gently between him and his intended prey. He had come a long way in search of man, for even in his youth he had tasted human flesh and while it was poor stuff by comparison with eland and zebra it was less difficult to kill. In Numa's estimation man was a slow-witted, slow-footed creature which commanded no respect unless accompanied by the acrid odor which spelled to the monarch's sensitive nostrils the great noise and the blinding flash of an express rifle.

He caught the dangerous scent tonight; but he was ravenous to madness. He would face a dozen rifles, if necessary, to fill his empty belly. He circled about into the forest that he might again be down wind from his victims, for should they get his scent he could not hope to overtake them. Numa was famished; but he was old and crafty.

Deep in the jungle another caught faintly the scent of man and of Numa both. He raised his head and sniffed. He cocked it upon one side and listened.

"Come on," said Meriem, "let's ride in a way—the forest is wonderful at night. It is open enough to permit us to ride."

The Hon. Morison hesitated. He shrank from revealing his fear in the presence of the girl. A braver man, sure of his own position, would have had the courage to have refused uselessly to expose the girl to danger. He would not have thought of himself at all; but the egotism of the Hon. Morison required that he think always of self first. He had planned the ride to get Meriem away from the bungalow. He wanted to talk to her alone and far enough away so should she take offense at his purposed suggestion he would have time in which to attempt to right himself in her eyes before they reached home. He had little doubt, of course, but that he should succeed; but it is to his credit that he did have some slight doubts.

"You needn't be afraid of the lion," said Meriem, noting his slight hesitancy. "There hasn't been a man eater around here for two years, Bwana says, and the game is so plentiful that there is no necessity to drive Numa to human flesh. Then, he has been so often hunted that he rather keeps out of man's way."

"Oh, I'm not afraid of lions," replied the Hon. Morison. "I was just thinking what a beastly uncomfortable place a forest is to ride in. What with the underbrush and the low branches and all that, you know, it's not exactly cut out for pleasure riding."

"Let's go a-foot then," suggested Meriem, and started to dismount.

"Oh, no," cried the Hon. Morison, aghast at this suggestion. "Let's ride," and he reined his pony into the dark shadows of the wood. Behind him came Meriem and in front, prowling ahead waiting a favorable opportunity, skulked Numa, the lion.

Out upon the plain a lone horseman muttered a low curse as he saw the two disappear from sight. It was Hanson. He had followed them from the bungalow. Their way led in the direction of his camp, so he had a ready and plausible excuse should they discover him; but they had not seen him for they had not turned their eyes behind.

Now he turned directly toward the spot at which they had entered the jungle. He no longer cared whether he was observed or not. There were two reasons for his indifference. The first was that he saw in Baynes' act a counterpart of his own planned abduction of the girl. In some way he might turn the thing to his own purposes. At least he would keep in touch with them and make sure that Baynes did not get her. His other reason was based on his knowledge of an event that had transpired at his camp the previous night—an event which he had not mentioned at the bungalow for fear of drawing undesired attention to his movements and bringing the blacks of the big Bwana into dangerous intercourse with his own boys. He had told at the bungalow that half his men had deserted. That story might be quickly disproved should his boys and Bwana's grow confidential.

The event that he had failed to mention and which now urged him hurriedly after the girl and her escort had occurred during his absence early the preceding evening. His men had been sitting around their camp fire, entirely encircled by a high, thorn *boma*, when, without the slightest warning, a huge lion had leaped amongst them and seized one of their number. It had been solely due to the loyalty and courage of his comrades that his life had been saved, and then only after a battle royal with the hunger-enraged beast had they been able to drive him off with burning brands, spears, and rifles.

From this Hanson knew that a man eater had wandered into the district or been developed by the aging of one of the many lions who ranged the plains and hills by night, or lay up in the cool wood by day. He had heard the roaring of a hungry lion not half an hour before, and there was little doubt in his mind but that the man eater was stalking Meriem and Baynes. He cursed the Englishman for a fool, and spurred rapidly after them.

Meriem and Baynes had drawn up in a small, natural clearing. A hundred yards beyond them Numa lay crouching in the underbrush, his yellow-green eyes fixed upon his prey, the tip of his sinuous tail jerking spasmodically. He was measuring the distance between him and them. He was wondering if he dared venture a charge, or should he wait yet a little longer in the hope that they might ride straight into his jaws. He was very hungry; but also was he very crafty. He could not chance losing his meat by a hasty and ill-considered rush. Had he waited the night before until the blacks slept he would not have been forced to go hungry for another twenty-four hours.

Behind him the other that had caught his scent and that of man together came to a sitting posture upon the branch of a tree in which he had reposed himself for slumber. Beneath him a lumbering gray hulk swayed to and fro in the darkness. The beast in the tree uttered a low guttural and dropped to the back of the gray mass. He whispered a word in one of the great ears and Tantor, the elephant, raised his trunk aloft, swinging it high and low to catch the scent that the word had warned him of. There was another whispered word—was it a command?—and the lumbering beast wheeled into an awkward, yet silent shuffle, in the direction of Numa, the lion, and the stranger Tarmangani his rider had scented.

Onward they went, the scent of the lion and his prey becoming stronger and stronger. Numa was becoming impatient. How much longer must he wait for his meat to come his way? He lashed his tail viciously now. He almost growled. All unconscious of their danger the man and the girl sat talking in the little clearing.

Their horses were pressed side by side. Baynes had found

Meriem's hand and was pressing it as he poured words of love into her ear, and Meriem was listening.

"Come to London with me," urged the Hon. Morison. "I can gather a *safari* and we can be a whole day upon the way to the coast before they guess that we have gone."

"Why must we go that way?" asked the girl. "Bwana and My Dear would not object to our marriage."

"I cannot marry you just yet," explained the Hon. Morison, "there are some formalities to be attended to first—you do not understand. It will be all right. We will go to London. I cannot wait. If you love me you will come. What of the apes you lived with? Did they bother about marriage? They love as we love. Had you stayed among them you would have mated as they mate. It is the law of nature—no man-made law can abrogate the laws of God. What difference does it make if we love one another? What do we care for anyone in the world besides ourselves? I would give my life for you—will you give nothing for me?"

"You love me?" she said. "You will marry me when we have reached London?"

"I swear it," he cried.

"I will go with you," she whispered, "though I do not understand why it is necessary." She leaned toward him and he took her in his arms and bent to press his lips to hers.

At the same instant the head of a huge tusker poked through the trees that fringed the clearing. The Hon. Morison and Meriem, with eyes and ears for one another alone, did not see or hear; but Numa did. The man upon Tantor's broad head saw the girl in the man's arms. It was Korak; but in the trim figure of the neatly garbed girl he did not recognize his Meriem. He only saw a Tarmangani with his she. And then Numa charged.

With a frightful roar, fearful lest Tantor had come to frighten away his prey, the great beast leaped from his hiding place. The earth trembled to his mighty voice. The ponies stood for an instant transfixed with terror. The Hon. Morison Baynes went white and cold. The lion was charging toward them full in the brilliant light of the magnificent moon. The muscles of the Hon. Morison no longer obeyed his will—they flexed to the urge of a greater power—the power of Nature's first law. They drove his spurred heels deep into his pony's flanks, they bore the rein against the brute's neck that wheeled him with an impetuous drive toward the plain and safety.

The girl's pony, squealing in terror, reared and plunged upon the heels of his mate. The lion was close upon him. Only the girl was cool—the girl and the half-naked savage who bestrode the neck of his mighty mount and grinned at the exciting spectacle chance had staked for his enjoyment.

To Korak here were but two strange Tarmangani pursued by Numa, who was empty. It was Numa's right to prey; but one was a she. Korak felt an intuitive urge to rush to her protection. Why, he could not guess. All Tarmangani were enemies now. He had lived too long a beast to feel strongly the humanitarian impulses that were inherent in him—yet feel them he did, for the girl at least.

He urged Tantor forward. He raised his heavy spear and hurled it at the flying target of the lion's body. The girl's pony had reached the trees upon the opposite side of the clearing. Here he would become easy prey to the swiftly moving lion; but Numa, infuriated, preferred the woman upon his back. It was for her he leaped.

Korak gave an exclamation of astonishment and approval as Numa landed upon the pony's rump and at the same instant the girl swung free of her mount to the branches of a tree above her.

Korak's spear struck Numa in the shoulder, knocking him from his precarious hold upon the frantically plunging horse. Freed of the weight of both girl and lion the pony raced ahead toward safety. Numa tore and struck at the missile in his shoulder but could not dislodge it. Then he resumed the chase.

Korak guided Tantor into the seclusion of the jungle. He did not wish to be seen, nor had he.

Hanson had almost reached the wood when he heard the lion's terrific roars, and knew that the charge had come. An instant later the Hon. Morison broke upon his vision, racing like mad for safety. The man lay flat upon his pony's back hugging the animal's neck tightly with both arms and digging the spurs into his sides. An instant later the second pony appeared—riderless.

Hanson groaned as he guessed what had happened out of sight in the jungle. With an oath he spurred on in the hope of driving the lion from his prey—his rifle was ready in his hand. And then the lion came into view behind the girl's pony. Hanson could not understand. He knew that if Numa had succeeded in seizing the girl he would not have continued in pursuit of the others.

He drew in his own mount, took quick aim and fired. The lion stopped in his tracks, turned and bit at his side, then rolled over dead. Hanson rode on into the forest, calling aloud to the girl.

"Here I am," came a quick response from the foliage of the trees just ahead. "Did you hit him?"

"Yes," replied Hanson. "Where are you? You had a mighty narrow escape. It will teach you to keep out of the jungle at night."

Together they returned to the plain where they found the Hon. Morison riding slowly back toward them. He explained that his pony had bolted and that he had had hard work stopping him at all. Hanson grinned, for he recalled the pounding heels that he had seen driving sharp spurs into the flanks of Baynes' mount; but he said nothing of what he had seen. He took Meriem up behind him and the three rode in silence toward the bungalow.

# 19

BEHIND THEM KORAK emerged from the jungle and recovered his spear from Numa's side. He still was smiling. He had enjoyed the spectacle exceedingly. There was one thing that troubled him—the agility with which the she had clambered from her pony's back into the safety of the tree *above* her. That was more like mangani—more like his lost Meriem. He sighed. His lost Meriem! His little, dead Meriem! He wondered if this she stranger resembled his Meriem in other ways. A great longing to see her overwhelmed him. He looked after the three figures moving steadily across the plain. He wondered where might lie their destination. A desire to follow them came over him, but he only stood there watching until they had disappeared in the distance. The sight of the civilized girl and the dapper, khaki clad Englishman had aroused in Korak memories long dormant.

Once he had dreamed of returning to the world of such as these; but with the death of Meriem hope and ambition seemed to have deserted him. He cared now only to pass the remainder of his life in solitude, as far from man as possible. With a sigh he turned slowly back into the jungle.

Tantor, nervous by nature, had been far from reassured by close proximity to the three strange whites, and with the report of Hanson's rifle had turned and ambled away at his long, swinging shuffle. He was nowhere in sight when Korak returned to look for him. The ape-man, however, was little concerned by the absence of his friend. Tantor had a habit of wandering off unexpectedly. For a month they might not see one another, for Korak seldom took the trouble to follow the great pachyderm, nor did he upon this occasion. Instead he found a comfortable perch in a large tree and was soon asleep.

At the bungalow Bwana had met the returning adventurers on

the verandah. In a moment of wakefulness he had heard the report of Hanson's rifle far out across the plain, and wondered what it might mean. Presently it had occurred to him that the man whom he considered in the light of a guest might have met with an accident on his way back to camp, so he had arisen and gone to his foreman's quarters where he had learned that Hanson had been there earlier in the evening but had departed several hours before. Returning from the foreman's quarters Bwana had noticed that the corral gate was open and further investigation revealed the fact that Meriem's pony was gone and also the one most often used by Baynes. Instantly Bwana assumed that the shot had been fired by Hon. Morison, and had again aroused his foreman and was making preparations to set forth in investigation when he had seen the party approaching across the plain.

Explanations on the part of the Englishman met a rather chilly reception from his host. Meriem was silent. She saw that Bwana was angry with her. It was the first time and she was heart broken.

"Go to your room, Meriem," he said; "and Baynes, if you will step into my study, I'd like to have a word with you in a moment."

He stepped toward Hanson as the others turned to obey him. There was something about Bwana even in his gentlest moods that commanded instant obedience.

"How did you happen to be with them, Hanson?" he asked.

"I'd been sitting in the garden," replied the trader, "after leaving Jervis' quarters. I have a habit of doing that as your lady probably knows. Tonight I fell asleep behind a bush, and was awakened by them two spooning. I couldn't hear what they said, but presently Baynes brings two ponies and they ride off. I didn't like to interfere for it wasn't any of my business, but I knew they hadn't ought to be ridin' about that time of night, leastways not the girl—it wasn't right and it wasn't safe. So I follows them and it's just as well I did. Baynes was gettin' away from the lion as fast as he could, leavin' the girl to take care of herself, when I got a lucky shot into the beast's shoulder that fixed him."

Hanson paused. Both men were silent for a time. Presently the trader coughed in an embarrassed manner as though there was something on his mind he felt in duty bound to say, but hated to.

"What is it, Hanson?" asked Bwana. "You were about to say something weren't you?"

"Well, you see it's like this," ventured Hanson. "Bein'

around here evenings a good deal I've seen them two together a lot, and, beggin' your pardon, sir, but I don't think Mr. Baynes means the girl any good. I've overheard enough to make me think he's tryin' to get her to run off with him." Hanson, to fit his own ends, hit nearer the truth than he knew. He was afraid that Baynes would interfere with his own plans, and he had hit upon a scheme to both utilize the young Englishman and get rid of him at the same time.

"And I thought," continued the trader, "that inasmuch as I'm about due to move you might like to suggest to Mr. Baynes that he go with me. I'd be willin' to take him north to the caravan trails as a favor to you, sir."

Bwana stood in deep thought for a moment. Presently he looked up.

"Of course, Hanson, Mr. Baynes is my guest," he said, a grim twinkle in his eye. "Really I cannot accuse him of planning to run away with Meriem on the evidence that we have, and as he is my guest I should hate to be so discourteous as to ask him to leave; but, if I recall his words correctly, it seems to me that he has spoken of returning home, and I am sure that nothing would delight him more than going north with you—you say you start tomorrow? I think Mr. Baynes will accompany you. Drop over in the morning, if you please, and now good night, and thank you for keeping a watchful eye on Meriem."

Hanson hid a grin as he turned and sought his saddle. Bwana stepped from the verandah to his study, where he found the Hon. Morison pacing back and forth, evidently very ill at ease.

"Baynes," said Bwana, coming directly to the point, "Hanson is leaving for the north tomorrow. He has taken a great fancy to you, and just asked me to say to you that he'd be glad to have you accompany him. Good night, Baynes."

At Bwana's suggestion Meriem kept to her room the following morning until after the Hon. Morison Baynes had departed. Hanson had come for him early—in fact he had remained all night with the foreman, Jervis, that they might get an early start.

The farewell exchanges between the Hon. Morison and his host were of the most formal type, and when at last the guest rode away Bwana breathed a sigh of relief. It had been an unpleasant duty and he was glad that it was over; but he did not regret his action. He had not been blind to Baynes' infatuation for Meriem, and knowing the young man's pride in caste he had never for a moment believed that his guest would offer his name to this nameless Arab girl, for, extremely light in color though she was for a full blood Arab, Bwana believed her to be such.

He did not mention the subject again to Meriem, and in this he made a mistake, for the young girl, while realizing the debt of gratitude she owed Bwana and My Dear, was both proud and sensitive, so that Bwana's action in sending Baynes away and giving her no opportunity to explain or defend hurt and mortified her. Also it did much toward making a martyr of Baynes in her eyes and arousing in her breast a keen feeling of loyalty toward him.

What she had half-mistaken for love before, she now wholly mistook for love. Bwana and My Dear might have told her much of the social barriers that they only too well knew Baynes must feel existed between Meriem and himself, but they hesitated to wound her. It would have been better had they inflicted this lesser sorrow, and saved the child the misery that was to follow because of her ignorance.

As Hanson and Baynes rode toward the former's camp the Englishman maintained a morose silence. The other was attempting to formulate an opening that would lead naturally to the proposition he had in mind. He rode a neck behind his companion, grinning as he noted the sullen scowl upon the other's patrician face.

"Rather rough on you, wasn't he?" he ventured at last, jerking his head back in the direction of the bungalow as Baynes turned his eyes upon him at the remark. "He thinks a lot of the girl," continued Hanson, "and don't want nobody to marry her and take her away; but it looks to me as though he was doin' her more harm than good in sendin' you away. She ought to marry some time, and she couldn't do better than a fine young gentleman like you."

Baynes, who had at first felt inclined to take offense at the mention of his private affairs by this common fellow, was mollified by Hanson's final remark, and immediately commenced to see in him a man of fine discrimination.

"He's a darned bounder," grumbled the Hon. Morison; "but I'll get even with him. He may be the whole thing in Central Africa but I'm as big as he is in London, and he'll find it out when he comes home."

"If I was you," said Hanson, "I wouldn't let any man keep me from gettin' the girl I want. Between you and me I ain't got no use for him either, and if I can help you any way just call on me."

"It's mighty good of you, Hanson," replied Baynes, warming up a bit; "but what can a fellow do here in this God-forsaken hole?"

"I know what I'd do," said Hanson. "I'd take the girl along with me. If she loves you she'll go, all right."

"It can't be done," said Baynes. "He bosses this whole blooming country for miles around. He'd be sure to catch us."

"No, he wouldn't, not with me running things," said Hanson. "I've been trading and hunting here for ten years and I know as much about the country as he does. If you want to take the girl along I'll help you, and I'll guarantee that there won't nobody catch up with us before we reach the coast. I'll tell you what, you write her a note and I'll get it to her by my head man. Ask her to meet you to say goodbye—she won't refuse that. In the meantime we can be movin' camp a little further north all the time and you can make arrangements with her to be all ready on a certain night. Tell her I'll meet her then while you wait for us in camp. That'll be better for I know the country well and can cover it quicker than you. You can take care of the *safari* and be movin' along slow toward the north and the girl and I'll catch up to you."

"But suppose she won't come?" suggested Baynes.

"Then make another date for a last good-bye," said Hanson, "and instead of you I'll be there and I'll bring her along anyway. She'll have to come, and after it's all over she won't feel so bad about it—especially after livin' with you for two months while we're makin' the coast."

A shocked and angry protest rose to Baynes' lips; but he did not utter it, for almost simultaneously came the realization that this was practically the same thing he had been planning upon himself. It had sounded brutal and criminal from the lips of the rough trader; but nevertheless the young Englishman saw that with Hanson's help and his knowledge of African travel the possibilities of success would be much greater than as though the Hon. Morison were to attempt the thing single handed. And so he nodded a glum assent.

The balance of the long ride to Hanson's northerly camp was made in silence, for both men were occupied with their own thoughts, most of which were far from being either complimentary or loyal to the other. As they rode through the wood the sounds of their careless passage came to the ears of another jungle wayfarer. The Killer had determined to come back to the place where he had seen the white girl who took to the trees with the ability of long habitude. There was a compelling something in the recollection of her that drew him irresistibly toward her. He wished to see her by the light of day, to see her features, to see the color of her eyes and hair. It seemed to him that she must bear a strong resemblance to his lost Meriem, and yet he knew that the chances were that she did not. The fleeting glimpse that he had had of her in the moonlight as she swung from the back of her plunging pony into the branches of the tree above her had shown him a girl of about the same height as his Meriem; but of a more rounded and developed femininity.

Now he was moving lazily back in the direction of the spot where he had seen the girl when the sounds of the approaching horsemen came to his sharp ears. He moved stealthily through the branches until he came within sight of the riders. The younger man he instantly recognized as the same he had seen with his arms about the girl in the moonlit glade just the instant before Numa charged. The other he did not recognize though there was a familiarity about his carriage and figure that puzzled Korak.

The ape-man decided that to find the girl again he would but have to keep in touch with the young Englishman, and so he fell in behind the pair, following them to Hanson's camp. Here the Hon. Morison penned a brief note, which Hanson gave into the keeping of one of his boys who started off forthwith toward the south.

Korak remained in the vicinity of the camp, keeping a careful watch upon the Englishman. He had half expected to find the girl at the destination of the two riders and had been disappointed when no sign of her materialized about the camp.

Baynes was restless, pacing back and forth beneath the trees when he should have been resting against the forced marches of the coming flight. Hanson lay in his hammock and smoked. They spoke but little. Korak lay stretched upon a branch among the dense foliage above them. Thus passed the balance of the afternoon. Korak became hungry and thirsty. He doubted that either of the men would leave camp now before morning, so he withdrew, but toward the south, for there it seemed most likely the girl still was.

In the garden beside the bungalow Meriem wandered thoughtfully in the moonlight. She still smarted from Bwana's, to her, unjust treatment of the Hon. Morison Baynes. Nothing had been explained to her, for both Bwana and My Dear had wished to spare her the mortification and sorrow of the true explanation of Baynes' proposal. They knew, as Meriem did not, that the man had had no intention of marrying her, else he would have come directly to Bwana, knowing full well that no objection would be interposed if Meriem really cared for him.

Meriem loved them both and was grateful to them for all that they had done for her; but deep in her little heart surged the savage love of liberty that her years of untrammeled freedom in the jungle had made part and parcel of her being. Now, for the first time since she had come to them, Meriem felt like a prisoner in the bungalow of Bwana and My Dear.

Like a caged tigress the girl paced the length of the enclosure. Once she paused near the outer fence, her head upon one side— listening. What was it she had heard? The pad of naked human feet just beyond the garden. She listened for a moment. The sound was not repeated. Then she resumed her restless walking. Down to the opposite end of the garden she passed, turned and retraced her steps toward the upper end. Upon the sward near the bushes that hid the fence, full in the glare of the moonlight, lay a white envelope that had not been there when she had turned almost upon the very spot a moment before.

Meriem stopped short in her tracks, listening again, and sniffing—more than ever the tigress; alert, ready. Beyond the bushes a naked black runner squatted, peering through the foliage. He saw her take a step closer to the letter. She had seen it. He rose quietly and following the shadows of the bushes that ran down to the corral was soon gone from sight.

Meriem's trained ears heard his every move. She made no attempt to seek closer knowledge of his identity. Already she had guessed that he was a messenger from the Hon. Morison. She stooped and picked up the envelope. Tearing it open she easily read the contents by the moon's brilliant light. It was, as she had guessed, from Baynes.

"I cannot go without seeing you again," it read. "Come to the clearing early tomorrow morning and say good-bye to me. Come alone."

There was a little more—words that made her heart beat faster and a happy flush mount her cheek.

# 20

I T WAS STILL dark when the Hon. Morison Baynes set forth for
the trysting place. He insisted upon having a guide, saying
that he was not sure that he could find his way back to the little
clearing. As a matter of fact the thought of that lonely ride
through the darkness before the sun rose had been too much for
his courage, and he craved company. A black, therefore, preceded him on foot. Behind and above him came Korak, whom
the noise in the camp had awakened.

It was nine o'clock before Baynes drew rein in the clearing.
Meriem had not yet arrived. The black lay down to rest. Baynes
lolled in his saddle. Korak stretched himself comfortably upon
a lofty limb, where he could watch those beneath him without
being seen.

An hour passed. Baynes gave evidence of nervousness. Korak
had already guessed that the young Englishman had come here
to meet another, nor was he at all in doubt as to the identity of
that other. The Killer was perfectly satisfied that he was soon
again to see the nimble she who had so forcefully reminded him
of Meriem.

Presently the sound of an approaching horse came to Korak's
ears. She was coming! She had almost reached the clearing
before Baynes became aware of her presence, and then as he
looked up, the foliage parted to the head and shoulders of her
mount and Meriem rode into view. Baynes spurred to meet her.
Korak looked searchingly down upon her, mentally anathema-
tizing the broad-brimmed hat that hid her features from his eyes.
She was abreast the Englishman now. Korak saw the man take
both her hands and draw her close to his breast. He saw the
man's face concealed for a moment beneath the same broad brim
that hid the girl's. He could imagine their lips meeting, and a

162

twinge of sorrow and sweet recollection combined to close his eyes for an instant in that involuntary muscular act with which we attempt to shut out from the mind's eye harrowing reflections.

When he looked again they had drawn apart and were conversing earnestly. Korak could see the man urging something. It was equally evident that the girl was holding back. There were many of her gestures, and the way in which she tossed her head up and to the right, tip-tilting her chin, that reminded Korak still more strongly of Meriem. And then the conversation was over and the man took the girl in his arms again to kiss her goodbye. She turned and rode toward the point from which she had come. The man sat on his horse watching her. At the edge of the jungle she turned to wave him a final farewell.

"Tonight!" she cried, throwing back her head as she called the words to him across the little distance which separated them—throwing back her head and revealing her face for the first time to the eyes of The Killer in the tree above. Korak started as though pierced through the heart with an arrow. He trembled and shook like a leaf. He closed his eyes, pressing his palms across them, and then he opened them again and looked but the girl was gone—only the waving foliage of the jungle's rim marked where she had disappeared. It was impossible! It could not be true! And yet, with his own eyes he had seen his Meriem—older a little, with figure more rounded by nearer maturity, and subtly changed in other ways; more beautiful than ever, yet still his little Meriem. Yes, he had seen the dead alive again; he had seen his Meriem in the flesh. She lived! She had not died! He had seen her—he had seen his Meriem—*in the arms of another man*! And that man sat below him now, within easy reach. Korak, The Killer, fondled his heavy spear. He played with the grass rope dangling from his gee-string. He stroked the hunting knife at his hip. And the man beneath him called to his drowsy guide, bent the rein to his pony's neck and moved off toward the north. Still sat Korak, The Killer, alone among the trees. Now his hands hung idly at his sides. His weapons and what he had intended were forgotten for the moment. Korak was thinking. He had noted that subtle change in Meriem. When last he had seen her she had been his little, half-naked Mangani—wild, savage, and uncouth. She had not seemed uncouth to him then; but now, in the change that had come over her, he knew that such she had been; yet no more uncouth than he, and he was still uncouth.

In her had taken place the change. In her he had just seen a sweet and lovely flower of refinement and civilization, and he shuddered as he recalled the fate that he himself had planned for her—to be the mate of an ape-man, his mate, in the savage jungle. Then he had seen no wrong in it, for he had loved her, and the way he had planned had been the way of the jungle which they two had chosen as their home; but now, after having seen the Meriem of civilized attire, he realized the hideousness of his once cherished plan, and he thanked God that chance and the blacks of Kovudoo had thwarted him.

Yet he still loved her, and jealousy seared his soul as he recalled the sight of her in the arms of the dapper young Englishman. What were his intentions toward her? Did he really love her? How could one not love her? And she loved him, of that Korak had had ample proof. Had she not loved him she would not have accepted his kisses. His Meriem loved another! For a long time he let that awful truth sink deep, and from it he tried to reason out his future plan of action. In his heart was a great desire to follow the man and slay him; but ever there rose in his consciousness the thought: She loves him. Could he slay the creature Meriem loved? Sadly he shook his head. No, he could not. Then came a partial decision to follow Meriem and speak with her. He half started, and then glanced down at his nakedness and was ashamed. He, the son of a British peer, had thus thrown away his life, had thus degraded himself to the level of a beast that he was ashamed to go to the woman he loved and lay his love at her feet. He was ashamed to go to the little Arab maid who had been his jungle playmate, for what had he to offer her?

For years circumstances had prevented a return to his father and mother, and at last pride had stepped in and expunged from his mind the last vestige of any intention to return. In a spirit of boyish adventure he had cast his lot with the jungle ape. The killing of the crook in the coast inn had filled his childish mind with terror of the law, and driven him deeper into the wilds. The rebuffs that he had met at the hands of men, both black and white, had had their effect upon his mind while yet it was in a formative state, and easily influenced.

He had come to believe that the hand of man was against him, and then he had found in Meriem the only human association he required or craved. When she had been snatched from him his sorrow had been so deep that the thought of ever mingling again with human beings grew still more unutterably distasteful.

Finally and for all time, he thought, the die was cast. Of his own volition he had become a beast, a beast he had lived, a beast he would die.

Now that it was too late, he regretted it. For now Meriem, still living, had been revealed to him in a guise of progress and advancement that had carried her completely out of his life. Death itself could not have further removed her from him. In her new world she loved a man of her own kind. And Korak knew that it was right. She was not for him—not for the naked, savage ape. No, she was not for him; but he still was hers. If he could not have her and happiness, he would at least do all that lay in his power to assure happiness to her. He would follow the young Englishman. In the first place he would know that he meant Meriem no harm, and after that, though jealously wrenched his heart, he would watch over the man Meriem loved, for Meriem's sake; but God help that man if he thought to wrong her!

Slowly he aroused himself. He stood erect and stretched his great frame, the muscles of his arms gliding sinuously beneath his tanned skin as he bent his clenched fists behind his head. A movement on the ground beneath caught his eye. An antelope was entering the clearing. Immediately Korak became aware that he was empty—again he was a beast. For a moment love had lifted him to sublime heights of honor and renunciation.

The antelope was crossing the clearing. Korak dropped to the ground upon the opposite side of the tree, and so lightly that not even the sensitive ears of the antelope apprehended his presence. He uncoiled his grass rope—it was the latest addition to his armament, yet he was proficient with it. Often he traveled with nothing more than his knife and his rope—they were light and easy to carry. His spear and bow and arrows were cumbersome and he usually kept one or all of them hidden away in a private cache.

Now he held a single coil of the long rope in his right hand, and the balance in his left. The antelope was but a few paces from him. Silently Korak leaped from his hiding place swinging the rope free from the entangling shrubbery. The antelope sprang away almost instantly; but instantly, too, the coiled rope, with its sliding noose, flew through the air above him. With unerring precision it settled about the creature's neck. There was a quick wrist movement of the thrower, the noose tightened. The Killer braced himself with the rope across his hip, and as the antelope tautened the singing strands in a last frantic bound for liberty he was thrown over upon his back.

Then, instead of approaching the fallen animal as a roper of the western plains might do, Korak dragged his captive to himself, pulling him in hand over hand, and when he was within reach leaping upon him even as Sheeta the panther might have done, and burying his teeth in the animal's neck while he found its heart with the point of his hunting knife. Recoiling his rope, he cut a few generous strips from his kill and took to the trees again, where he ate in peace. Later he swung off in the direction of a nearby water hole, and then he slept.

In his mind, of course, was the suggestion of another meeting between Meriem and the young Englishman that had been borne to him by the girl's parting: "Tonight!"

He had not followed Meriem because he knew from the direction from which she had come and in which she returned that wheresoever she had found an asylum it lay out across the plains and not wishing to be discovered by the girl he had not cared to venture into the open after her. It would do as well to keep in touch with the young man, and that was precisely what he intended doing.

To you or me the possibility of locating the Hon. Morison in the jungle after having permitted him to get such a considerable start might have seemed remote; but to Korak it was not at all so. He guessed that the white man would return to his camp; but should he have done otherwise it would be a simple matter to The Killer to trail a mounted man accompanied by another on foot. Days might pass and still such a spoor would be sufficiently plain to lead Korak unfalteringly to its end; while a matter of a few hours only left it as clear to him as though the makers themselves were still in plain sight.

And so it came that a few minutes after the Hon. Morison Baynes entered the camp to be greeted by Hanson, Korak slipped noiselessly into a near-by tree. There he lay until late afternoon and still the young Englishman made no move to leave camp. Korak wondered if Meriem were coming there. A little later Hanson and one of his black boys rode out of camp. Korak merely noted the fact. He was not particularly interested in what any other member of the company than the young Englishman did.

Darkness came and still the young man remained. He ate his evening meal, afterward smoking numerous cigarettes. Presently he began to pace back and forth before his tent. He kept his boy busy replenishing the fire. A lion coughed and he went into his tent to reappear with an express rifle. Again he admonished the boy to throw more brush upon the fire. Korak saw that he was nervous and afraid, and his lip curled in a sneer of contempt.

Was this the creature who had supplanted him in the heart of his Meriem? Was this a man, who trembled when Numa coughed? How could such as he protect Meriem from the countless dangers of the jungle? Ah, but he would not have to. They would live in the safety of European civilization, where men in uniforms were hired to protect them. What need had a European of prowess to protect his mate? Again the sneer curled Korak's lip.

Hanson and his boy had ridden directly to the clearing. It was already dark when they arrived. Leaving the boy there Hanson rode to the edge of the plain, leading the boy's horse. There he waited. It was nine o'clock before he saw a solitary figure galloping toward him from the direction of the bungalow. A few moments later Meriem drew in her mount beside him. She was nervous and flushed. When she recognized Hanson she drew back, startled.

"Mr. Baynes' horse fell on him and sprained his ankle," Hanson hastened to explain. "He couldn't very well come so he sent me to meet you and bring you to camp."

The girl could not see in the darkness the gloating, triumphant expression on the speaker's face.

"We had better hurry," continued Hanson, "for we'll have to move along pretty fast if we don't want to be overtaken."

"Is he hurt badly?" asked Meriem.

"Only a little sprain," replied Hanson. "He can ride all right; but we both thought he'd better lie up tonight, and rest, for he'll have plenty hard riding in the next few weeks."

"Yes," agreed the girl.

Hanson swung his pony about and Meriem followed him. They rode north along the edge of the jungle for a mile and then turned straight into it toward the west. Meriem, following, payed little attention to directions. She did not know exactly where Hanson's camp lay and so she did not guess that he was not leading her toward it. All night they rode, straight toward the west. When morning came, Hanson permitted a short halt for breakfast, which he had provided in well-filled saddle bags before leaving his camp. Then they pushed on again, nor did they halt a second time until in the heat of the day he stopped and motioned the girl to dismount.

"We will sleep here for a time and let the ponies graze," he said.

"I had no idea the camp was so far away," said Meriem.

"I left orders that they were to move on at day break," explained the trader, "so that we could get a good start. I knew that you and I could easily overtake a laden *safari*. It may not be until tomorrow that we'll catch up with them."

But though they traveled part of the night and all the following day no sign of the *safari* appeared ahead of them. Meriem, an adept in jungle craft, knew that none had passed ahead of them for many days. Occasionally she saw indications of an old spoor, a very old spoor, of many men. For the most part they followed this well-marked trail along elephant paths and through park-like groves. It was an ideal trail for rapid traveling.

Meriem at last became suspicious. Gradually the attitude of the man at her side had begun to change. Often she surprised him devouring her with his eyes. Steadily the former sensation of previous acquaintanceship urged itself upon her. Somewhere, sometime before she had known this man. It was evident that he had not shaved for several days. A blonde stubble had commenced to cover his neck and cheeks and chin, and with it the assurance that he was no stranger continued to grow upon the girl.

It was not until the second day, however, that Meriem rebelled. She drew in her pony at last and voiced her doubts. Hanson assured her that the camp was but a few miles further on.

"We should have overtaken them yesterday," he said. "They must have marched much faster than I had believed possible."

"They have not marched here at all," said Meriem. "The spoor that we have been following is weeks old."

Hanson laughed.

"Oh, that's it, is it?" cried. "Why didn't you say so before? I could have easily explained. We are not coming by the same route; but we'll pick up their trail sometime today, even if we don't overtake them."

Now, at last, Meriem knew the man was lying to her. What a fool he must be to think that anyone could believe such a ridiculous explanation? Who was so stupid as to believe that they could have expected to overtake another party, and he had certainly assured her that momentarily he expected to do so, when that party's route was not to meet theirs for several miles yet?

She kept her own counsel however, planning to escape at the first opportunity when she might have a sufficient start of her captor, as she now considered him, to give her some assurance of outdistancing him. She watched his face continually when she could without being observed. Tantalizingly the placing of his familiar features persisted in eluding her. Where had she known him? Under what conditions had they met before she had seen him about the farm of Bwana? She ran over in her mind all the few white men she ever had known. There were some who had come to her father's *douar* in the jungle. Few it is true, but there had been some. Ah, now she had it! She had seen him there! She almost seized upon his identity and then, in an instant, it had slipped from her again.

It was mid afternoon when they suddenly broke out of the jungle upon the banks of a broad and placid river. Beyond, upon the opposite store, Meriem described a camp surrounded by a high, thorn *boma*.

"Here we are at last," said Hanson. He drew his revolver and fired in the air. Instantly the camp across the river was astir. Black men ran down the river's bank. Hanson hailed them. But there was no sign of the Hon. Morison Baynes.

In accordance with their master's instructions the blacks manned a canoe and rowed across. Hanson placed Meriem in the little craft and entered it himself, leaving two boys to watch the horses, which the canoe was to return for and swim across to the camp side of the river.

Once in the camp Meriem asked for Baynes. For the moment her fears had been allayed by the sight of the camp, which she had come to look upon as more or less a myth. Hanson pointed toward the single tent that stood in the center of the enclosure. "There," he said, and preceded her toward it. At the entrance he held the flap aside and motioned her within. Meriem entered and looked about. The tent was empty. She turned toward Hanson. There was a broad grin on his face.

"Where is Mr. Baynes?" she demanded.

"He ain't here," replied Hanson. "Leastwise I don't see him, do you? But I'm here, and I'm a damned sight better man than that thing ever was. You don't need him no more—you got me," and he laughed uproariously and reached for her.

Meriem struggled to free herself. Hanson encircled her arms and body in his powerful grip and bore her slowly backward toward the pile of blankets at the far end of the tent. His face was bent close to hers. His eyes were narrowed to two slits of heat and passion and desire. Meriem was looking full into his face as she fought for freedom when there came over her a sudden recollection of a similar scene in which she had been a participant and with it full recognition of her assailant. He was the Swede Malbihn who had attacked her once before, who had shot his companion who would have saved her, and from whom she had been rescued by Bwana. His smooth face had deceived her; but now with the growing beard and the similarity of conditions recognition came swift and sure.

But today there would be no Bwana to save her.

# 21

THE BLACK BOY whom Malbihn had left awaiting him in the clearing with instructions to remain until he returned sat crouched at the foot of a tree for an hour when he was suddenly startled by the coughing grunt of a lion behind him. With celerity born of the fear of death the boy clambered into the branches of the tree, and a moment later the king of beasts entered the clearing and approached the carcass of an antelope which, until now, the boy had not seen.

Until daylight the beast fed, while the black clung, sleepless, to his perch, wondering what had become of his master and the two ponies. He had been with Malbihn for a year, and so was fairly conversant with the character of the white. His knowledge presently led him to believe that he had been purposely abandoned. Like the balance of Malbihn's followers, this boy hated his master cordially—fear being the only bond that held him to the white man. His present uncomfortable predicament but added fuel to the fires of his hatred.

As the sun rose the lion withdrew into the jungle and the black descended from his tree and started upon his long journey back to camp. In his primitive brain revolved various fiendish plans for a revenge that he would not have the courage to put into effect when the test came and he stood face to face with one of the dominant race.

A mile from the clearing he came upon the spoor of two ponies crossing his path at right angles. A cunning look entered the black's eyes. He laughed uproariously and slapped his thighs.

Negroes are tireless gossipers, which, of course, is but a roundabout way of saying that they are human. Malbihn's boys had been no exception to the rule and as many of them had been with him at various times during the past ten years there was

171

little about his acts and life in the African wilds that was not know.. directly or by hearsay to them all.

And so, knowing his master and many of his past deeds, knowing, too, a great deal about the plans of Malbihn and Baynes that had been overheard by himself, or other servants; and knowing well from the gossip of the head-men that half of Malbihn's party lay in camp by the great river far to the west, it was not difficult for the boy to put two and two together and arrive at four as the sum—the four being represented by a firm conviction that his master had deceived the other white man and taken the latter's woman to his western camp, leaving the other to suffer capture and punishment at the hands of the Big Bwana whom all feared. Again the boy bared his rows of big, white teeth and laughed aloud. Then he resumed his northward way, traveling at a dogged trot that ate up the miles with marvelous rapidity.

In the Swede's camp the Hon. Morison had spent an almost sleepless night of nervous apprehension and doubts and fears. Toward morning he had slept, utterly exhausted. It was the headman who awoke him shortly after sun rise to remind him that they must at once take up their northward journey. Baynes hung back. He wanted to wait for "Hanson" and Meriem. The headman urged upon him the danger that lay in loitering. The fellow knew his master's plans sufficiently well to understand that he had done something to arouse the ire of the Big Bwana and that it would fare ill with them all if they were overtaken in Big Bwana's country. At the suggestion Baynes took alarm.

What if the Big Bwana, as the head-man called him, had surprised "Hanson" in his nefarious work. Would he not guess the truth and possibly be already on the march to overtake and punish him? Baynes had heard much of his host's summary method of dealing out punishment to male-factors great and small who transgressed the laws or customs of his savage little world which lay beyond the outer ramparts of what men are pleased to call frontiers. In this savage world where there was no law the Big Bwana was law unto himself and all who dwelt about him. It was even rumored that he had extracted the death penalty from a white man who had maltreated a native girl.

Baynes shuddered at the recollection of this piece of gossip as he wondered what his host would exact of the man who had attempted to steal his young, white ward. The thought brought him to his feet.

"Yes," he said, nervously, "we must get away from here at once. Do you know the trail to the north?"

The head-man did, and he lost no time in getting the *safari* upon the march.

It was noon when a tired and sweat-covered runner overtook the trudging little column. The man was greeted with shouts of welcome from his fellows, to whom he imparted all that he knew and guessed of the actions of their master, so that the entire *safari* was aware of matters before Baynes, who marched close to the head of the column, was reached and acquainted with the facts and the imaginings of the black boy whom Malbihn had deserted in the clearing the night before.

When the Hon. Morison had listened to all that the boy had to say and realized that the trader had used him as a tool whereby he himself might get Meriem into his possession, his blood ran hot with rage and he trembled with apprehension for the girl's safety.

That another contemplated no worse a deed than he had contemplated in no way palliated the hideousness of the other's offense. At first it did not occur to him that he would have wronged Meriem no less than he believed "Hanson" contemplated wronging her. Now his rage was more the rage of a man beaten at his own game and robbed of the prize that he had thought already his.

"Do you know where your master has gone?" he asked the black.

"Yes, Bwana," replied the boy. "He has gone to the other camp beside the big *afi* that flows far toward the setting sun."

"Can you take me to him?" demanded Baynes.

The boy nodded affirmatively. Here he saw a method of revenging himself upon his hated Bwana and at the same time of escaping the wrath of the Big Bwana whom all were positive would first follow after the northerly *safari*.

"Can you and I, alone, reach his camp?" asked the Hon. Morison.

"Yes, Bwana," assured the black.

Baynes turned toward the head-man. He was conversant with "Hanson's" plans now. He understood why he had wished to move the northern camp as far as possible toward the northern boundary of the Big Bwana's country—it would give him far more time to make his escape toward the West Coast while the Big Bwana was chasing the northern contingent. Well, he would utilize the man's plans to his own end. He, too, must keep out of the clutches of his host.

"You may take the men north as fast as possible," he said to the head-man. "I shall return and attempt to lead the Big Bwana to the west."

The Negro assented with a grunt. He had no desire to follow this strange white man who was afraid at night; he had less to remain at the tender mercies of the Big Bwana's lusty warriors, between whom and his people there was long-standing blood feud; and he was more than delighted, into the bargain, for a legitimate excuse for deserting his much hated Swede master. He knew a way to the north and his own country that the white men did not know—a short cut across an arid plateau where lay water holes of which the white hunters and explorers that had passed from time to time the fringe of the dry country had never dreamed. He might even elude the Big Bwana should he follow them, and with this thought uppermost in his mind he gathered the remnants of Malbihn's *safari* into a semblance of order and moved off toward the north. And toward the southwest the black boy led the Hon. Morison Baynes into the jungles.

Korak had waited about the camp, watching the Hon. Morison until the *safari* had started north. Then, assured that the young Englishman was going in the wrong direction to meet Meriem he had abandoned him and returned slowly to the point where he had seen the girl, for whom his heart yearned, in the arms of another.

So great had been his happiness at seeing Meriem alive that, for the instant, no thought of jealousy had entered his mind. Later these thoughts had come—dark, bloody thoughts that would have made the flesh of the Hon. Morison creep could he have guessed that they were revolving in the brain of a savage creature creeping stealthily among the branches of the forest giant beneath which he waited the coming of "Hanson" and the girl.

And with passing of the hours had come subdued reflection in which he had weighed himself against the trimly clad English gentleman and—found that he was wanting. What had he to offer her by comparison with that which the other might offer? What was his "mess of pottage" to the birthright that the other had preserved? How could he dare go, naked and unkempt, to that fair thing who had once been his jungle-fellow and propose the thing that had been in his mind when first the realization of his love had swept over him? He shuddered as he thought of the irreparable wrong that his love would have done the innocent child but for the chance that had snatched her from him before it was too late. Doubtless she knew now the horror that had been in his mind. Doubtless she hated and loathed him as he hated and loathed himself when he let his mind dwell upon it. He had lost her. No more surely had she been lost when he thought her dead than she was in reality now that he had seen her living—living in the guise of a refinement that had transfigured and sanctified her.

He had loved her before, now he worshipped her. He knew that he might never possess her now, but at last he might see her. From a distance he might look upon her. Perhaps he might serve her; but never must she guess that he had found her or that he lived.

He wondered if she ever thought of him—if the happy days that they had spent together never recurred to her mind. It seemed unbelievable that such could be the case, and yet, too, it seemed almost equally unbelievable that this beautiful girl was the same disheveled, half naked, little sprite who skipped nimbly among the branches of the trees as they ran and played in the lazy, happy days of the past. It could not be that her memory held more of the past than did her new appearance.

It was a sad Korak who ranged the jungle near the plain's edge waiting for the coming of his Meriem—the Meriem who never came.

But there came another—a tall, broad-shouldered man in khaki at the head of a swarthy crew of ebon warriors. The man's face was set in hard, stern lines and the marks of sorrow were writ deep about his mouth and eyes—so deep that the set expression of rage upon his features could not obliterate them.

Korak saw the man pass beneath him where he hid in the great tree that had harbored him before upon the edge of that fateful little clearing. He saw him come and he set rigid and frozen and suffering above him. He saw him search the ground with his keen eyes, and he only sat there watching with eyes that glazed from the intensity of his gaze. He saw him sign to his men that he had come upon that which he sought and he saw him pass out of sight toward the north, and still Korak sat like a graven image, with a heart that bled in dumb misery. An hour later Korak moved slowly away, back into the jungle toward the west. He went listlessly, with bent head and stooped shoulders, like an old man who bore upon his back the weight of a great sorrow.

Baynes, following his black guide, battled his way through

the dense underbrush, riding stooped low over his horse's neck, or often he dismounted where the low branches swept too close to earth to permit him to remain in the saddle. The black was taking him the shortest way, which was no way at all for a horseman, and after the first day's march the young Englishman was forced to abandon his mount, and follow his nimble guide entirely on foot.

During the long hours of marching the Hon. Morison had much time to devote to thought, and as he pictured the probable fate of Meriem at the hands of the Swede his rage against the man became the greater. But presently there came to him a realization of the fact that his own base plans had led the girl into this terrible predicament, and that even had she escaped "Hanson" she would have found but little better deserts awaiting her with him.

There came too, the realization that Meriem was infinitely more precious to him than he had imagined. For the first time he commenced to compare her with other women of his acquaintance—women of birth and position—and almost to his surprise—he discovered that the young Arab girl suffered less than they by the comparison. And then from hating "Hanson" he came to look upon himself with hate and loathing—to see himself and his perfidious act in all their contemptible hideousness.

Thus, in the crucible of shame amidst the white heat of naked truths, the passion that the man had felt for the girl he had considered his social inferior was transmuted into love. And as he staggered on there burned within him beside his newborn love another great passion—the passion of hate urging him on to the consummation of revenge.

A creature of ease and luxury, he had never been subjected to the hardships and tortures which now were his constant companionship, yet, his clothing torn, his flesh scratched and bleeding, he urged the black to greater speed, though with every dozen steps he himself fell from exhaustion.

It was revenge which kept him going—that and a feeling that in his suffering he was partially expiating the great wrong he had done the girl he loved—for hope of saving her from the fate into which he had trapped her had never existed. "Too late! Too late!" was the dismal accompaniment of thought to which he marched. "Too late! Too late to save; but not too late to avenge!" That kept him up.

Only when it became too dark to see would he permit of a

halt. A dozen times in the afternoon he had threatened the black with instant death when the tired guide insisted upon resting. The fellow was terrified. He could not understand the remarkable change that had so suddenly come over the white man who had been afraid in the dark the night before. He would have deserted this terrifying master had he had the opportunity; but Baynes guessed that some such thought might be in the other's mind, and so gave the fellow none. He kept close to him by day and slept touching him at night in the rude thorn *boma* they constructed as a slight protection against prowling carnivora.

That the Hon. Morison could sleep at all in the midst of the savage jungle was sufficient indication that he had changed considerably in the past twenty-four hours, and that he could lie close beside a none-too-fragrant black man spoke of possibilities for democracy within him yet all undreamed of.

Morning found him stiff and lame and sore, but none the less determined to push on in pursuit of "Hanson" as rapidly as possible. With his rifle he brought down a buck at a ford in a small stream shortly after they broke camp, breakfastless. Begrudgingly he permitted a halt while they cooked and ate, and then on again through the wilderness of trees and vines and underbrush.

And in the meantime Korak wandered slowly westward, coming upon the trail of Tantor, the elephant, whom he overtook browsing in the deep shade of the jungle. The ape-man, lonely and sorrowing, was glad of the companionship of his huge friend. Affectionately the sinuous trunk encircled him, and he was swung to the mighty back where so often before he had lolled and dreamed the long afternoon away.

Far to the north the Big Bwana and his black warriors clung tenaciously to the trail of the fleeing *safari* that was luring them further and further from the girl they sought to save, while back at the bungalow the woman who had loved Meriem as though she had been her own waited impatiently and in sorrow for the return of the rescuing party and the girl she was positive her invincible lord and master would bring back with him.

# 22

As MERIEM STRUGGLED with Malbihn, her hands pinioned to her sides by his brawny grip, hope died within her. She did not utter a sound for she knew that there was none to come to her assistance, and, too, the jungle training of her earlier life had taught her the futility of appeals for succor in the savage world of her up-bringing.

But as she fought to free herself one hand came in contact with the butt of Malbihn's revolver where it rested in the holster at his hip. Slowly he was dragging her toward the blankets, and slowly her fingers encircled the coveted prize and drew it from its resting place.

Then, as Malbihn stood at the edge of the disordered pile of blankets, Meriem suddenly ceased to draw away from him, and as quickly hurled her weight against him with the result that he was thrown backward, his feet stumbled against the bedding and he was hurled to his back. Instinctively his hands flew out to save himself and at the same instant Meriem leveled the revolver at his breast and pulled the trigger.

But the hammer fell futilely upon an empty shell, and Malbihn was again upon his feet clutching at her. For a moment she eluded him, and ran toward the entrance to the tent, but at the very doorway his heavy hand fell upon her shoulder and dragged her back. Wheeling upon him with the fury of a wounded lioness Meriem grasped the long revolver by the barrel, swung it high above her head and crashed it down full in Malbihn's face.

With an oath of pain and rage the man staggered backward, releasing his hold upon her and then sank unconscious to the ground. Without a backward look Meriem turned and fled into the open. Several of the blacks saw her and tried to intercept her flight, but the menace of the empty weapon kept them at a distance. And so she won beyond the encircling *boma* and disappeared into the jungle to the south.

Straight into the branches of a tree she went, true to the arboreal instincts of the little mangani she had been, and here she stripped off her riding skirt, her shoes and her stockings, for she knew that she had before her a journey and a flight which would not brook the burden of these garments. Her riding breeches and jacket would have to serve as protection from cold and thorns, nor would they hamper her over much; but a skirt and shoes were impossible among the trees.

She had not gone far before she commenced to realize how slight were her chances for survival without means of defense or a weapon to bring down meat. Why had she not thought to strip the cartridge belt from Malbihn's waist before she had left his tent! With cartridges for the revolver she might hope to bag small game, and to protect herself from all but the most ferocious of the enemies that would beset her way back to the beloved hearthstone of Bwana and My Dear.

With the thought came determination to return and obtain the coveted ammunition. She realized that she was taking great chances of recapture; but without means of defense and of obtaining meat she felt that she could never hope to reach safety. And so she turned her face back toward the camp from which she had but just escaped.

She thought Malbihn dead, so terrific a blow had she dealt him, and she hoped to find an opportunity after dark to enter the camp and search his tent for the cartridge belt; but scarcely had she found a hiding place in a great tree at the edge of the *boma* where she could watch without danger of being discovered, then she saw the Swede emerge from his tent, wiping blood from his face, and hurling a volley of oaths and questions at his terrified followers.

Shortly after the entire camp set forth in search of her and when Meriem was positive that all were gone she descended from her hiding place and ran quickly across the clearing to Malbihn's tent. A hasty survey of the interior revealed no ammunition; but in one corner was a box in which were packed the Swede's personal belongings that he had sent along by his headman to this westerly camp.

Meriem seized the receptacle as the possible container of extra ammunition. Quickly she loosed the cords that held the canvas covering about the box, and a moment later had raised the lid and was rummaging through the heterogeneous accumulation of odds and ends within. There were letters and papers and cuttings from old newspapers, and among other things the photograph of a little girl upon the back of which was pasted a cutting from a Paris daily—a cutting that she could not read, yellowed and dimmed by age and handling—but something about the photograph of the little girl which was also reproduced in the newspaper cutting held her attention. Where had she seen that picture before? And then, quite suddenly, it came to her that this was a picture of herself as she had been years and years before.

Where had it been taken? How had it come into the possession of this man? Why had it been reproduced in a newspaper? What was the story that the faded type told of it?

Meriem was baffled by the puzzle that her search for ammunition had revealed. She stood gazing at the faded photograph for a time and then bethought herself of the ammunition for which she had come. Turning again to the box she rummaged to the bottom and there in a corner she came upon a little box of cartridges. A single glance assured her that they were intended for the weapon she had thrust inside the band of her riding breeches, and slipping them into her pocket she turned once more for an examination of the baffling likeness of herself that she held in her hand.

As she stood thus in vain endeavor to fathom this inexplicable mystery the sound of voices broke upon her ears. Instantly she was all alert. They were coming closer! A second later she recognized the lurid profanity of the Swede. Malbihn, her persecutor, was returning! Meriem ran quickly to the opening of the tent and looked out. It was too late! She was fairly cornered! The white man and three of his black henchmen were coming straight across the clearing toward the tent. What was she to do? She slipped the photograph into her waist. Quickly she slipped a cartridge into each of the chambers of the revolver. Then she backed toward the end of the tent, keeping the entrance covered by her weapon. The man stopped outside, and Meriem could hear Malbihn profanely issuing instructions. He was a long time about it, and while he talked in his bellowing, brutish voice, the girl sought some avenue of escape. Stooping, she raised the bottom of the canvas and looked beneath and beyond. There was no one in sight upon that side. Throwing herself upon her stomach she wormed beneath the tent wall just as Malbihn, with a final word to his men, entered the tent.

Meriem heard him cross the floor, and then she rose and,

stooping low, ran to a native hut directly behind. Once inside
this she turned and glanced back. There was no one in sight.
She had not been seen. And now from Malbihn's tent she heard
a great cursing. The Swede had discovered the rifling of his box.
He was shouting to his men, and as she heard them reply Meriem darted from the hut and ran toward the edge of the *boma*
furthest from Malbihn's tent. Overhanging the *boma* at this point
was a tree that had been too large, in the eyes of the rest-loving
blacks, to cut down. So they had terminated the *boma* just short
of it. Meriem was thankful for whatever circumstance had resulted in the leaving of that particular tree where it was, since it
gave her the much-needed avenue of escape which she might
not otherwise have had.

From her hiding place she saw Malbihn again enter the jungle,
this time leaving a guard of three of his boys in the camp. He
went toward the south, and after he had disappeared, Meriem
skirted the outside of the enclosure and made her way to the
river. Here lay the canoes that had been used in bringing the
party from the opposite shore. They were unwieldy things for a
lone girl to handle, but there was no other way and she must
cross the river.

The landing place was in full view of the guard at the camp.
To risk the crossing under their eyes would have meant un-
doubted capture. Her only hope lay in waiting until darkness
had fallen, unless some fortuitous circumstance should arise
before. For an hour she lay watching the guard, one of whom
seemed always in a position where he would immediately discover her should she attempt to launch one of the canoes.

Presently Malbihn appeared, coming out of the jungle, hot
and puffing. He ran immediately to the river where the canoes
lay and counted them. It was evident that it had suddenly occurred to him that the girl must cross here if she wished to return
to her protectors. The expression of relief on his face when he
found that none of the canoes was gone was ample evidence of
what was passing in his mind. He turned and spoke hurriedly
to the head man who had followed him out of the jungle and
with whom were several other blacks.

Following Malbihn's instructions they launched all the canoes
but one. Malbihn called to the guards in the camp and a moment
later the entire party had entered the boats and were paddling
up stream.

Meriem watched them until a bend in the river directly above
the camp hid them from her sight. They were gone! She was

alone, and they had left a canoe in which lay a paddle! She could scarce believe the good fortune that had come to her. To delay now would be suicidal to her hopes. Quickly she ran from her hiding place and dropped to the ground. A dozen yards lay between her and the canoe.

Up stream, beyond the bend, Malbihn ordered his canoes in to shore. He landed with his head man and crossed the little point slowly in search of a spot where he might watch the canoe he had left at the landing place. He was smiling in anticipation of the almost certain success of his stratagem—sooner or later the girl would come back and attempt to cross the river in one of their canoes. It might be that the idea would not occur to her for some time. They might have to wait a day, or two days; but that she would come if she lived or was not captured by the men he had scouting the jungle for her Malbihn was sure. That she would come so soon, however, he had not guessed, and so when he topped the point and came again within sight of the river he saw that which drew an angry oath from his lips—his quarry already was half way across the river.

Turning, he ran rapidly back to his boats, the head man at his heels. Throwing themselves in Malbihn urged his paddlers to their most powerful efforts. The canoes shot out into the stream and down with the current toward the fleeing quarry. She had almost completed the crossing when they came in sight of her. At the same instant she saw them, and redoubled her efforts to reach the opposite shore before they should overtake her. Two minutes' start of them was all Meriem cared for. Once in the trees she knew that she could outdistance and elude them. Her hopes were high—they could not overtake her now—she had had too good a start of them.

Malbihn, urging his men onward with a stream of hideous oaths and blows from his fists, realized that the girl was again slipping from his clutches. The leading canoe, in the bow of which he stood, was yet a hundred yards behind the fleeing Meriem when she ran the point of her craft beneath the overhanging trees on the shore of safety.

Malbihn screamed to her to halt. He seemed to have gone mad with rage at the realization that he could not overtake her, and then he threw his rifle to his shoulder, aimed carefully at the slim figure scrambling into the trees, and fired.

Malbihn was an excellent shot. His misses at so short a distance were practically non-existent, nor would he have missed this time but for an accident occurring at the very instant that his finger tightened upon the trigger—an accident to which Meriem owed her life—the providential presence of a water-logged tree trunk, one end of which was embedded in the mud of the river bottom and the other end of which floated just beneath the surface where the prow of Malbihn's canoe ran upon it as he fired. The slight deviation of the boat's direction was sufficient to throw the muzzle of the rifle out of aim. The bullet whizzed harmlessly by Meriem's head and an instant later she had disappeared into the foliage of the tree.

There was a smile on her lips as she dropped to the ground to cross a little clearing where once had stood a native village surrounded by its fields. The ruined huts still stood in crumbling decay. The rank vegetation of the jungle overgrew the cultivated ground. Small trees already had sprung up in what had been the village street; but desolation and loneliness hung like a pall above the scene. To Meriem, however, it presented but a place denuded of large trees which she must cross quickly to regain the jungle upon the opposite side before Malbihn should have landed.

The deserted huts were, to her, all the better because they were deserted—she did not see the keen eyes watching her from a dozen points, from tumbling doorways, from behind tottering granaries. In utter unconsciousness of impending danger she started up the village street because it offered the clearest pathway to the jungle.

A mile away toward the east, fighting his way through the jungle along the trail taken by Malbihn when he had brought Meriem to his camp, a man in torn khaki—filthy, haggard, unkempt—came to a sudden stop at the resort of Malbihn's rifle resounded faintly through the tangled forest. The black man just ahead of him stopped, too.

"We are almost there, Bwana," he said. There was awe and respect in his tone and manner.

The white man nodded and motioned his ebon guide forward once more. It was the Hon. Morison Baynes—the fastidious—the exquisite. His face and hands were scratched and smeared with dried blood from the wounds he had come by in thorn and thicket. His clothes were tatters. But through the blood and the dirt and the rags a new Baynes shone forth—a handsomer Baynes than the dandy and the fop of yore.

In the heart and soul of every son of woman lies the germ of manhood and honor. Remorse for a scurvy act, and an honorable desire to right the wrong he had done the woman he now knew he really loved had excited these germs to rapid growth in Morison Baynes—and the metamorphosis had taken place.

Onward the two stumbled toward the point from which the single rifle shot had come. The black was unarmed—Baynes, fearing his loyalty had not dared trust him even to carry the rifle which the white man would have been glad to be relieved of many times upon the long march; but now that they were approaching their goal, and knowing as he did that hatred of Malbihn burned hot in the black man's brain, Baynes handed him the rifle, for he guessed that there would be fighting—he intended that there should, or he had come to avenge. Himself, an excellent revolver shot, would depend upon the smaller weapon at his side.

As the two forged ahead toward their goal they were startled by a volley of shots ahead of them. Then came a few scattering reports, some savage yells, and silence. Baynes was frantic in his endeavors to advance more rapidly, but there the jungle seemed a thousand times more tangled than before. A dozen times he tripped and fell. Twice the black followed a blind trail and they were forced to retract their steps; but at last they came out into a little clearing near the big *afi*—a clearing that once held a thriving village, but lay somber and desolate in decay and ruin.

In the jungle vegetation that overgrew what had once been the main village street lay the body of a black man, pierced through the heart with a bullet, and still warm. Baynes and his companion looked about in all directions; but no sign of living being could they discover. They stood in silence listening intently.

What was that! Voices and the dip of paddles out upon the river?

Baynes ran across the dead village toward the fringe of jungle upon the river's brim. The black was at his side. Together they forced their way through the screening foliage until they could obtain a view of the river, and there, almost to the other shore, they saw Malbihn's canoes making rapidly for camp. The black recognized his companions immediately.

"How can we cross?" asked Baynes.

The black shook his head. There was no canoe and the crocodiles made it equivalent to suicide to enter the water in an attempt to swim across. Just then the fellow chanced to glance downward. Beneath him, wedged among the branches of a tree, lay the canoe in which Meriem had escaped. The Negro grasped Baynes' arm and pointed toward his find. The Hon. Morison could scarce repress a shout of exultation. Quickly the two slid down the drooping branches into the boat. The black seized the paddle and Baynes shoved them out from beneath the tree. A second later the canoe shot out upon the bosom of the river and headed toward the opposite shore and the camp of the Swede. Baynes squatted in the bow, straining his eyes after the men pulling the other canoes upon the bank across from him. He saw Malbihn step from the bow of the foremost of the little craft. He saw him turn and glance back across the river. He could see his start of surprise as his eyes fell upon the pursuing canoe, and called the attention of his followers to it.

Then he stood waiting, for there was but one canoe and two men—little danger to him and his followers in that. Malbihn was puzzled. Who was this white man? He did not recognize him though Baynes' canoe was now in mid stream and the features of both its occupants plainly discernible to those on shore. One of Malbihn's blacks it was who first recognized his fellow black in the person of Baynes' companion. Then Malbihn guessed who the white man must be, though he could scarce believe his own reasoning. It seemed beyond the pale of wildest conjecture to suppose that the Hon. Morison Baynes had followed him through the jungle with but a single companion—and yet it was true. Beneath the dirt and dishevelment he recognized him at last, and in the necessity of admitting that it was he, Malbihn was forced to recognize the incentive that had driven Baynes, the weakling and coward, through the savage jungle upon his trail.

The man had come to demand an accounting and to avenge. It seemed incredible, and yet there could be no other explanation. Malbihn shrugged. Well, others had sought Malbihn for similar reasons in the course of a long and checkered career. He fingered his rifle, and waited.

Now the canoe was within easy speaking distance of the shore. "What do you want?" yelled Malbihn, raising his weapon threateningly.

The Hon. Morison Baynes leaped to his feet.

"You, damn you!" he shouted, whipping out his revolver and firing almost simultaneously with the Swede.

As the two reports rang out Malbihn dropped his rifle, clutched frantically at his breast, staggered, fell first to his knees and then lunged upon his face. Baynes stiffened. His head flew back spasmodically. For an instant he stood thus, and then crumpled very gently into the bottom of the boat.

The black paddler was at a loss as to what to do. If Malbihn really were dead he could continue on to join his fellows without fear; but should the Swede only be wounded he would be safer upon the far shore. Therefore he hesitated, holding the canoe in mid stream. He had come to have considerable respect for his new master and was not unmoved by his death. As he sat gazing at the crumpled body in the bow of the boat he saw it move. Very feebly the man essayed to turn over. He still lived. The black moved forward and lifted him to a sitting position. He was standing in front of him, his paddle in one hand, asking Baynes where he was hit when there was another shot from shore and the Negro pitched head long overboard, his paddle still clutched in his dead fingers—shot through the forehead.

Baynes turned weakly in the direction of the shore to see Malbihn drawn up upon his elbows levelling his rifle at him. The Englishman slid to the bottom of the canoe as a bullet whizzed above him. Malbihn, sore hit, took longer in aiming, nor was his aim as sure as formerly. With difficulty Baynes turned himself over on his belly and grasping his revolver in his right hand drew himself up until he could look over the edge of the canoe.

Malbihn saw him instantly and fired; but Baynes did not flinch or duck. With painstaking care he aimed at the target upon the shore from which he now was drifting with the current. His finger closed upon the trigger—there was a flash and a report, and Malbihn's giant frame jerked to the impact of another bullet.

But he was not yet dead. Again he aimed and fired, the bullet splintering the gunwale of the canoe close by Baynes face. Baynes fired again as his canoe drifted further down stream and Malbihn answered from the shore where he lay in a pool of his own blood. And thus, doggedly, the two wounded men continued to carry on their weird duel until the winding African river had carried the Hon. Morison Baynes out of sight around a wooded point.

# 23

MERIEM HAD TRAVERSED half the length of the village street when a score of white-robed Negroes and half-castes leaped out upon her from the dark interiors of surrounding huts. She turned to flee, but heavy hands seized her, and when she turned at last to plead with them her eyes fell upon the face of a tall, grim, old man glaring down upon her from beneath the folds of his burnous.

At sight of him she staggered back in shocked and terrified surprise. It was The Sheik!

Instantly all the old fears and terrors of her childhood returned upon her. She stood trembling before this horrible old man, as a murderer before the judge about to pass sentence of death upon him. She knew that The Sheik recognized her. The years and the changed raiment had not altered her so much but what one who had known her features so well in childhood would know her now.

"So you have come back to your people, eh?" snarled The Sheik. "Come back begging for food and protection, eh?"

"Let me go," cried the girl. "I ask nothing of you, but that you let me go back to the Big Bwana."

"The Big Bwana?" almost screamed The Sheik, and then followed a stream of profane, Arabic invective against the white man whom all the transgressors of the jungle feared and hated. "You would go back to the Big Bwana, would you? So that is where you have been since you ran away from me, is it? And who comes now across the river after you—the Big Bwana?"

"The Swede whom you once chased away from your country when he and his companion conspired with Nbeeda to steal me from you," replied Meriem.

The Shiek's eyes blazed, and he called his men to approach

the shore and hide among the bushes that they might ambush and annihilate Malbihn and his party; but Malbihn already had landed and crawling through the fringe of jungle was at that very moment looking with wide and incredulous eyes upon the scene being enacted in the street of the deserted village. He recognized The Sheik the moment his eyes fell upon him. There were two men in the world that Malbihn feared as he feared the devil. One was the Big Bwana and the other The Sheik. A single glance he took at that gaunt, familiar figure and then he turned tail and scurried back to his canoe calling his followers after him. And so it happened that the party was well out in the stream before The Sheik reached the shore, and after a volley and a few parting shots that were returned from the canoes the Arab called his men off and securing his prisoner set off toward the South.

One of the bullets from Malbihn's force had struck a black standing in the village street where he had been left with another to guard Meriem, and his companions had left him where he had fallen, after appropriating his apparel and belongings. His was the body that Baynes had discovered when he had entered the village.

The Sheik and his party had been marching southward along the river when one of them, dropping out of line to fetch water, had seen Meriem paddling desperately from the opposite shore. The fellow had called The Shiek's attention to the strange sight— a white woman alone in Central Africa and the old Arab had hidden his men in the deserted village to capture her when she landed, for thoughts of ransom were always in the mind of The Sheik. More than once before had glittering gold filtered through his fingers from a similar source. It was easy money and The Sheik had none too much easy money since the Big Bwana had so circumscribed the limits of his ancient domain that he dared not even steal ivory from natives within two hundred miles of the Big Bwana's *douar*. And when at last the woman had walked into the trap he had set for her and he had recognized her as the same little girl he had brutalized and mal-treated years before his gratification had been huge. Now he lost no time in establishing the old relations of father and daughter that had existed between them in the past. At the first opportunity he struck her a heavy blow across the face. He forced her to walk when he might have dismounted one of his men instead, or had her carried on a horse's rump. He seemed to revel in the discovery of new methods for torturing or humiliating her, and among all his followers she found no single one to offer her sympathy, or who dared defend her, even had they had the desire to do so.

A two days' march brought them at last to the familiar scenes of her childhood, and the first face upon which she set her eyes as she was driven through the gates into the strong stockade was that of the toothless, hideous Mabunu, her one time nurse. It was as though all the years that had intervened were but a dream. Had it not been for her clothing and the fact that she had grown in stature she might well have believed it so. All was there as she had left it—the new faces which supplanted some of the old were of the same bestial, degraded type. There were a few young Arabs who had joined The Sheik since she had been away. Otherwise all was the same—all but one. Geeka was not there, and she found herself missing Geeka as though the ivory-headed one had been a flesh and blood intimate and friend. She missed her ragged little confidante, into whose deaf ears she had been wont to pour her many miseries and her occasional joys—Geeka, of the splinter limbs and the ratskin torso—Geeka the disreputable—Geeka the beloved.

For a time the inhabitants of The Shiek's village who had not been upon the march with him amused themselves by inspecting the strangely clad white girl, whom some of them had known as a little child. Mabunu pretended great joy at her return, baring her toothless gums in a hideous grimace that was intended to be indicative of rejoicing. But Meriem could but shudder as she recalled the cruelties of this terrible old hag in the years gone by.

Among the Arabs who had come in her absence was a tall young fellow of twenty—a handsome, sinister looking youth—who stared at her in open admiration until The Sheik came and ordered him away, and Abdul Kamak went, scowling.

At last, their curiosity satisfied, Meriem was alone. As of old, she was permitted the freedom of the village, for the stockade was high and strong and the only gates were well-guarded by day and by night; but as of old she cared not for the companionship of the cruel Arabs and the degraded blacks who formed the following of The Sheik, and so, as had been her wont in the sad days of her childhood, she slunk down to an unfrequented corner of the enclosure where she had often played at housekeeping with her beloved Geeka beneath the spreading branches of the great tree that had overhung the palisade; but now the tree was gone, and Meriem guessed the reason. It was from this tree that Korak had descended and struck down The Sheik the day that he had rescued her from the life of misery and torture that had been her lot for so long that she could remember no other.

There were low bushes growing within the stockade, however, and in the shade of these Meriem sat down to think. A little glow of happiness warmed her heart as she recalled her first meeting with Korak and then the long years that he had cared for and protected her with the solicitude and purity of an elder brother. For months Korak had not so occupied her thoughts as he did today. He seemed closer and dearer now than ever he had before, and she wondered that her heart had drifted so far from loyalty to his memory. And then came the image of the Hon. Morison, the exquisite, and Meriem was troubled. Did she really love the flawless young Englishman? She thought of the glories of London, of which he had told her in such glowing language. She tried to picture herself admired and honored in the midst of the gayest society of the great capital. The pictures she drew were the pictures that the Hon. Morison had drawn for her. They were alluring pictures, but through them all the brawny, half-naked figure of the giant Adonis of the jungle persisted in obtruding itself.

Meriem pressed her hand above her heart as she stifled a sigh, and as she did so she felt the hard outlines of the photograph she had hidden there as she slunk from Malbihn's tent. Now she drew it forth and commenced to re-examine it more carefully than she had had time to do before. She was sure that the baby face was hers. She studied every detail of the picture. Half hidden in the lace of the dainty dress rested a chain and locket. Meriem puckered her brows. What tantalizing half-memories it awakened! Could this flower of evident civilization be the little Arab Meriem, daughter of The Sheik? It was impossible, and yet that locket? Meriem knew it. She could not refute the conviction of her memory. She had seen that locket before and it had been hers. What strange mystery lay buried in her past?

As she sat gazing at the picture she suddenly became aware that she was not alone—that someone was standing close behind her—some one who had approached her noiselessly. Guiltily she thrust the picture back into her waist. A hand fell upon her shoulder. She was sure that it was The Sheik and she awaited in dumb terror the blow that she knew would follow.

No blow came and she looked upward over her shoulder—into the eyes of Abdul Kamak, the young Arab.

"I saw," he said, "the picture that you have just hidden. It is you when you were a child—a very young child. May I see it again?''

Meriem drew away from him.

"I will give it back," he said. "I have heard of you and I know that you have no love for The Sheik, your father. Neither have I. I will not betray you. Let me see the picture."

Friendless among cruel enemies, Meriem clutched at the straw that Abdul Kamak held out to her. Perhaps in him she might find the friend she needed. Anyway he had seen the picture and if he was not a friend he could tell The Sheik about it and it would be taken away from her. So she might as well grant his request and hope that he had spoken fairly, and would deal fairly. She drew the photograph from its hiding place and handed it to him.

Abdul Kamak examined it carefully, comparing it, feature by feature with the girl sitting on the ground looking up into his face. Slowly he nodded his head.

"Yes," he said, "it is you, but where was it taken? How does it happen that The Shiek's daughter is clothed in the garments of the unbeliever?"

"I do not know," replied Meriem. "I never saw the picture until a couple of days ago, when I found it in the tent of the Swede, Malbihn."

Abdul Kamak raised his eyebrows. He turned the picture over and as his eyes fell upon the old newspaper cutting they went wide. He could read French, with difficulty, it is true; but he could read it. He had been to Paris. He had spent six months there with a troupe of his desert fellows, upon exhibition, and he had improved his time, learning many of the customs, some of the language, and most of the vices of his conquerors. Now he put his learning to use. Slowly, laboriously he read the yellowed cutting. His eyes were no longer wide. Instead they narrowed to two slits of cunning. When he had done he looked at the girl.

"You have read this?" he asked.

"It is French," she replied, "and I do not read French."

Abdul Kamak stood long in silence looking at the girl. She was very beautiful. He desired her, as had many other men who had seen her. At last he dropped to one knee beside her.

A wonderful idea had sprung to Abdul Kamak's mind. It was an idea that might be furthered if the girl were kept in ignorance of the contents of that newspaper cutting. It would certainly be doomed should she learn its contents.

"Meriem," he whispered, "never until today have my eyes beheld you, yet at once they told my heart that it must ever be your servant. You do not know me, but I ask that you trust me. I can help you. You hate The Sheik—so do I. Let me take you away from him. Come with me, and we will got back to the great desert where my father is a sheik mightier than is yours. Will you come?"

Meriem sat in silence. She hated to wound the only one who had offered her protection and friendship; but she did not want Abdul Kamak's love. Deceived by her silence the man seized her and strained her to him; but Meriem struggled to free herself.

"I do not love you," she cried. "Oh, please do not make me hate you. You are the only one who has shown kindness toward me, and I want to like you, but I cannot love you."

Abdul Kamak drew himself to his full height.

"You will learn to love me," he said, "for I shall take you whether you will or no. You hate The Sheik and so you will not tell him, for if you do I will tell him of the picture. I hate The Sheik, and—"

"You hate The Sheik?" came a grim voice from behind them.

Both turned to see The Sheik standing a few paces from them. Abdul still held the picture in his hand. Now he thrust it within his burnous.

"Yes," he said, "I hate The Sheik," and as he spoke he sprang toward the older man, felled him with a blow and dashed on across the village to the line where his horse was picketed, saddled and ready, for Abdul Kamak had been about to ride forth to hunt when he had seen the stranger girl alone by the bushes.

Leaping into the saddle Abdul Kamak dashed for the village gates. The Sheik, momentarily stunned by the blow that had felled him, now staggered to his feet, shouting lustily to his followers to stop the escaped Arab. A dozen blacks leaped forward to intercept the horseman, only to be ridden down or brushed aside by the muzzle of Abdul Kamak's long musket, which he lashed from side to side about him as he spurred on toward the gate. But here he must surely be intercepted. Already the two blacks stationed there were pushing the unwieldly portals to. Up flew the barrel of the fugitive's weapon. With reins flying loose and his horse at a mad gallop the son of the desert fired once—twice; and both the keepers of the gate dropped in their tracks. With a wild whoop of exultation, twirling his musket high above his head and turning in his saddle to laugh back into the faces of his pursuers Abdul Kamak dashed out of the village of The Sheik and was swallowed up by the jungle.

Foaming with rage The Sheik ordered immediate pursuit, and then strode rapidly back to where Meriem sat huddled by the bushes where he had left her.

"The picture!" he cried. "What picture did the dog speak of? Where is it? Give it to me at once!"

"He took it," replied Meriem, dully.

"What was it?" again demanded The Sheik, seizing the girl roughly by the hair and dragging her to her feet, where he shook her venomously. "What was it a picture of?"

"Of me," said Meriem, "when I was a little girl. I stole it from Malbihn, the Swede—it had printing on the back cut from an old newspaper."

The Sheik went white with rage.

"What said the printing?" he asked in a voice so low that she but barely caught his words.

"I do not know. It was in French and I cannot read French."

The Sheik seemed relieved. He almost smiled, nor did he again strike Meriem before he turned and strode away with the parting admonition that she speak never again to any other than Mabunu and himself. And along the caravan trail galloped Abdul Kamak toward the north.

As his canoe drifted out of sight and range of the wounded Swede the Hon. Morison sank weakly to its bottom where he lay for long hours in partial stupor.

It was night before he fully regained consciousness. And then he lay for a long time looking up at the stars and trying to recollect where he was, what accounted for the gently rocking motion of the thing upon which he lay, and why the position of the stars changed so rapidly and miraculously. For a while he thought he was dreaming, but when he would have moved to shake sleep from him the pain of his wound recalled to him the events that had led up to his present position. Then it was that he realized that he was floating down a great African river in a native canoe—alone, wounded, and lost.

Painfully he dragged himself to a sitting position. He noticed that the wound pained him less than he had imagined it would. He felt of it gingerly—it had ceased to bleed. Possibly it was but a flesh wound after all, and nothing serious. If it totally incapacitated him even for a few days it would mean death, for by that time he would be too weakened by hunger and pain to provide food for himself.

From his own troubles his mind turned to Meriem's. That she had been with the Swede at the time he had attempted to reach the fellow's camp he naturally believed; but he wondered what would become of her now. Even if Hanson died of his wounds would Meriem be any better off? She was in the power of equally villainous men—brutal savages of the lowest order. Baynes buried his face in his hands and rocked back and forth as the hideous picture of her fate burned itself into his consciousness. And it was he who had brought this fate upon her! His wicked desire had snatched a pure and innocent girl from the protection of those who loved her to hurl her into the clutches of the bestial Swede and his outcast following! And not until it had become too late had he realized the magnitude of the crime he himself had planned and contemplated. Not until it had become too late had he realized that greater than his desire, greater than his lust, greater than any passion he had ever felt before was the newborn love that burned within his breast for the girl he would have ruined.

The Hon. Morison Baynes did not fully realize the change that had taken place within him. Had one suggested that he ever had been aught than the soul of honor and chivalry he would have taken umbrage forthwith. He knew that he had done a vile thing when he had plotted to carry Meriem away to London, yet he excused it on the ground of his great passion for the girl having temporarily warped his moral standards by the intensity of its heat. But, as a matter of fact, a new Baynes had been born. Never again could this man be bent to dishonor by the intensity of a desire. His moral fiber had been strengthened by the mental suffering he had endured. His mind and his soul had been purged by sorrow and remorse.

His one thought now was to atone—win to Meriem's side and lay down his life, if necessary, in her protection. His eyes sought the length of the canoe in search of the paddle, for a determination had galvanized him to immediate action despite his weakness and his wound. But the paddle was gone. He turned his eyes toward the shore. Dimly through the darkness of a moonless night he saw the awful blackness of the jungle, yet it touched no responsive chord of terror within him now as it had done in the past. He did not even wonder that he was unafraid, for his mind was entirely occupied with thoughts of another's danger.

Drawing himself to his knees he leaned over the edge of the

canoe and commenced to paddle vigorously with his open palm. Though it tired and hurt him he kept assiduously at his self imposed labor for hours. Little by little the drifting canoe moved nearer and nearer the shore. The Hon. Morison could hear a lion roaring directly opposite him and so close that he felt he must be almost to the shore. He drew his rifle closer to his side; but he did not cease to paddle.

After what seemed to the tired man an eternity of time he felt the brush of branches against the canoe and heard the swirl of the water about them. A moment later he reached out and clutched a leafy limb. Again the lion roared—very near it seemed now, and Baynes wondered if the brute could have been following along the shore waiting for him to land.

He tested the strength of the limb to which he clung. It seemed strong enough to support a dozen men. Then he reached down and lifted his rifle from the bottom of the canoe, slipping the sling over his shoulder. Again he tested the branch, and then reaching upward as far as he could for a safe hold he drew himself painfully and slowly upward until his feet swung clear of the canoe, which, released, floated silently from beneath him to be lost forever in the blackness of the dark shadows down stream.

He had burned his bridges behind him. He must either climb aloft or drop back into the river; but there had been no other way. He struggled to raise one leg over the limb, but found himself scarce equal to the effort, for he was very weak. For a time he hung there feeling his strength ebbing. He knew that he must gain the branch above at once or it would be too late.

Suddenly the lion roared almost in his ear. Baynes glanced up. He saw two spots of flame a short distance from and above him. The lion was standing on the bank of the river glaring at him, and—waiting for him. Well, thought the Hon. Morison, let him wait. Lions can't climb trees, and if I get into this one I shall be safe enough for him.

The young Englishman's feet hung almost to the surface of the water—closer than he knew, for all was pitch dark below as above him. Presently he heard a slight commotion in the river beneath him and something banged against one of his feet, followed almost instantly by a sound that he felt he could not have mistaken—the click of great jaws snapping together.

"By George!" exclaimed the Hon. Morison, aloud. "The beggar nearly got me," and immediately he struggled again to climb higher and to comparative safety; but with that final effort he knew that it was futile. Hope that had survived persistently until now began to wane. He felt his tired, numbed fingers slipping from their hold—he was dropping back into the river—into the jaws of the frightful death that awaited him there.

And then he heard the leaves above him rustle to the movement of a creature among them. The branch to which he clung bent beneath an added weight—and no light weight, from the way it sagged; but still Baynes clung desperately—he would not give up voluntarily either to the death above or the death below.

He felt a soft, warm pad upon the fingers of one of his hands where they circled the branch to which he clung, and then something reached down out of the blackness above and dragged him up among the branches of the tree.

# 24

SOMETIMES LOLLING UPON Tantor's back, sometimes roaming the jungle in solitude, Korak made his way slowly toward the West and South. He made but a few miles a day, for he had a whole lifetime before him and no place in particular to go. Possibly he would have moved more rapidly but for the thought which continually haunted him that each mile he traversed carried him further and further away from Meriem—no longer his Meriem, as of yore, it is true! but still as dear to him as ever.

Thus he came upon the trail of The Sheik's band as it traveled down river from the point where The Sheik had captured Meriem to his own stockaded village. Korak pretty well knew who it was that had passed, for there were few in the great jungle with whom he was not familiar, though it had been years since he had come this far north. He had no particular business, however, with the old Sheik and so he did not propose following him—the further from men he could stay the better pleased he would be—he wished that he might never see a human face again. Men always brought him sorrow and misery.

The river suggested fishing and so he waddled upon its shores, catching fish after a fashion of his own devising and eating them raw. When night came he curled up in a great tree beside the stream—the one from which he had been fishing during the afternoon—and was soon asleep. Numa, roaring beneath him, awoke him. He was about to call out in anger to his noisy neighbor when something else caught his attention. He listened. Was there something in the tree beside himself? Yes, he heard the noise of something below him trying to clamber upward. Presently he heard the click of a crocodile's jaws in the waters beneath, and then, low but distinct: "By George! The beggar nearly got me." The voice was familiar.

Korak glanced downward toward the speaker. Outlined against the faint luminosity of the water he saw the figure of a man clinging to a lower branch of the tree. Silently and swiftly the ape-man clambered downward. He felt a hand beneath his foot. He reached down and clutched the figure beneath him and dragged it up among the branches. It struggled weakly and struck at him; but Korak paid no more attention than Tantor to an ant. He lugged his burden to the higher safety and greater comfort of a broad crotch, and there he propped it in a sitting position against the bole of the tree. Numa still was roaring beneath them, doubtless in anger that he had been robbed of his prey. Korak shouted down at him, calling him, in the language of the great apes, "Old green-eyed eater of carrion," "Brother of Dango," the hyena, and other choice appellations of jungle approbrium.

The Hon. Morison Baynes, listening, felt assured that a gorilla had seized upon him. He felt for his revolver, and as he was drawing it stealthily from its holster a voice asked in perfectly good English. "Who are you?"

Baynes started so that he nearly fell from the branch.

"My God!" he exclaimed. "Are you a man?"

"What did you think I was?" asked Korak.

"A gorilla," replied Baynes, honestly.

Korak laughed.

"Who are you?" he repeated.

"I'm an Englishman by the name of Baynes; but who the devil are you?" asked the Hon. Morison.

"They call me The Killer," replied Korak, giving the English translation of the name that Akut had given him. And then after a pause during which the Hon. Morison attempted to pierce the darkness and catch a glimpse of the features of the strange being into whose hands he had fallen, "You are the same whom I saw kissing the girl at the edge of the great plain to the East, that time that the lion charged you?"

"Yes," replied Baynes.

"What are you doing here?"

"The girl was stolen—I am trying to rescue her."

"Stolen!" The word was shot out like a bullet from a gun. "Who stole her?"

"The Swede trader, Hanson," replied Baynes.

"Where is he?"

Baynes related to Korak all that has transpired since he had come upon Hanson's camp. Before he was done the first gray dawn had relieved the darkness. Korak made the Englishman comfortable in the trees. He filled his canteen from the river and fetched him fruits to eat. Then he bid him good-bye.

"I am going to the Swede's camp," he announced. "I will bring the girl back to you here."

"I shall go, too, then," insisted Baynes. "It is my right and my duty, for she was to have become my wife."

Korak winced. "You are wounded. You could not make the trip," he said. "I can go much faster alone."

"Go, then," replied Baynes; "but I shall follow. It is my right and duty."

"As you will," replied Korak, with a shrug. If the man wanted to be killed it was none of his affair. He wanted to kill him himself, but for Meriem's sake he would not. If she loved him then he must do what he could to preserve him, but he could not prevent his following him, more than to advise him against it, and this he did, earnestly.

And so Korak set out rapidly toward the North, and limping slowly and painfully along, soon far to the rear, came the tired and wounded Baynes. Korak had reached the river bank opposite Malbihn's camp before Baynes had covered two miles. Late in the afternoon the Englishman was still plodding wearily along, forced a stop often for rest when he heard the sound of the galloping feet of a horse behind him. Instinctively he drew into the concealing foliage of the underbrush and a moment later a white-robed Arab dashed by. Baynes did not hail the rider. He had heard of the nature of the Arabs who penetrate thus far to the South, and what he had heard had convinced him that a snake or a panther would as quickly befriend him as one of these villainous renegades from the Northland.

When Abdul Kamak had passed out of sight toward the North Baynes resumed his weary march. A half hour later he was again surprised by the unmistakable sound of galloping horses. This time there were many. Once more he sought a hiding place; but it chanced that he was crossing a clearing which offered little opportunity for concealment. He broke into a slow trot—the best that he could do in his weakened condition; but it did not suffice to carry him to safety and before he reached the opposite side of the clearing a band of white-robed horsemen dashed into view behind him.

At sight of him they shouted in Arabic, which, of course, he could not understand, and then they closed about him, threatening and angry. Their questions were unintelligible to him, and no more could they interpret his English. At last, evidently out of patience, the leader ordered two of his men to seize him, which they lost no time in doing. They disarmed him and ordered him to climb to the rump of one of the horses, and then the two who had been detailed to guard him turned and rode back toward the South, while the others continued their pursuit of Abdul Kamak.

As Korak came out upon the bank of the river across from which he could see the camp of Malbihn he was at a loss as to how he was to cross. He could see men moving about among the huts inside the *boma*—evidently Hanson was still there. Korak did not know the true identity of Meriem's abductor.

How was he to cross. Not even he would dare the perils of the river—almost certain death. For a moment he thought, then wheeled and sped away into the jungle, uttering a peculiar cry, shrill and piercing. Now and again he would halt to listen as though for an answer to his weird call, then on again, deeper and deeper into the wood.

At last his listening ears were rewarded by the sound they craved—the trumpeting of a bull elephant, and a few moments later Korak broke through the trees into the presence of Tantor, standing with upraised trunk, waving his great ears.

"Quick, Tantor!" shouted the ape-man, and the beast swung him to his head. "Hurry!" and the mighty pachyderm lumbered off through the jungle, guided by kicking of naked heels against the sides of his head.

Toward the northwest Korak guided his huge mount, until they came out upon the river a mile or more above the Swede's camp, at a point where Korak knew that there was an elephant ford. Never pausing the ape-man urged the beast into the river, and with trunk held high Tantor forged steadily toward the opposite bank. Once an unwary crocodile attacked him but the sinuous trunk dove beneath the surface and grasping the amphibian about the middle dragged it to light and hurled it a hundred feet down stream. And so, in safety, they made the opposite shore, Korak perched high and dry above the turgid flood.

Then back toward the South Tantor moved, steadily, relentlessly, and with a swinging gait which took no heed of any obstacle other than the larger jungle trees. At times Korak was forced to abandon the broad head and take to the trees above, so close the branches raked the back of the elephant; but at last they came to the edge of the clearing where lay the camp of the renegade Swede, nor even then did they hesitate or halt. The gate lay upon the east side of the camp, facing the river. Tantor and Korak approached from the north. There was no gate there; but what cared Tantor or Korak for gates.

At a word from the ape man and raising his tender trunk high above the thorns Tantor breasted the *boma*, walking through it as though it had not existed. A dozen blacks squatted before their huts looked up at the noise of his approach. With sudden howls of terror and amazement they leaped to their feet and fled for the open gates. Tantor would have pursued. He hated man, and he though that Korak had come to hunt these; but the ape man held him back, guiding him toward a large, canvas tent that rose in the center of the clearing—there should be the girl and her abductor.

Malbihn lay in a hammock beneath canopy before his tent. His wounds were painful and he had lost much blood. He was very weak. He looked up in surprise as he heard the screams of his men and saw them running toward the gate. And then from around the corner of his tent loomed a huge bulk, and Tantor, the great tusker, towered above him. Malbihn's boy, feeling neither affection nor loyalty for his master, broke and ran at the first glimpse of the beast, and Malbihn was left alone and helpless.

The elephant stopped a couple of paces from the wounded man's hammock. Malbihn cowered, moaning. He was too weak to escape. He could only lie there with staring eyes gazing in horror into the blood rimmed, angry little orbs fixed upon him, and await his death.

Then, to his astonishment, a man slid to the ground from the elephant's back. Almost at once Malbihn recognized the strange figure as that of the creature who consorted with apes and baboons—the white warrior of the jungle who had freed the king baboon and led the whole angry horde of hairy devils upon him and Jenssen. Malbihn cowered still lower.

"Where is the girl?" demanded Korak, in English.

"What girl?" asked Malbihn. "There is no girl here—only the women of my boys. Is it one of them you want?"

"The white girl," replied Korak. "Do not lie to me—you lured her from her friends. You have her. Where is she?"

"It was not I," cried Malbihn. "It was an Englishman who hired me to steal her. He wished to take her to London with him. She was willing to go. His name is Baynes. Go to him, if you want to know where the girl is."

"I have just come from him," said Korak. "He sent me to you. The girl is not with him. Now stop your lying and tell me the truth. Where is she?" Korak took a threatening step toward the Swede.

Malbihn shrank from the anger in the other's face.

"I will tell you," he cried. "Do not harm me and I will tell you all that I know. I had the girl here; but it was Baynes who persuaded her to leave her friends—he had promised to marry her. He does not know who she is; but I do, and I know that there is a great reward for whoever takes her back to her people. It was only the reward I wanted. But she escaped and crossed the river in one of my canoes. I followed her, but The Sheik was there, God knows how, and he captured her and attacked me and drove me back. Then came Baynes, angry because he had lost the girl, and shot me. If you want her, go to The Sheik and ask him for her—she has passed as his daughter since childhood."

"She is not The Sheik's daughter?" asked Korak.

"She is not," replied Malbihn.

"Who is she then?" asked Korak.

Here Malbihn saw his chance. Possibly he could make use of his knowledge after all—it might even buy back his life for him. He was not so credulous as to believe that this savage ape-man would have any compunctions about slaying him.

"When you find her I will tell you," he said, "if you will promise to spare my life and divide the reward with me. If you kill me you will never know, for only The Sheik knows and he will never tell. The girl herself is ignorant of her origin."

"If you have told me the truth I will spare you," said Korak. "I shall go now to The Sheik's village and if the girl is not there I shall return and slay you. As for the other information you have, if the girl wants it when we have found her we will find a way to purchase it from you."

The look in The Killer's eyes and his emphasis of the word "purchase" were none too reassuring to Malbihn. Evidently, unless he found means to escape, this devil would have both his secret and his life before he was done with him. He wished he would be gone and take his evil-eyed companion away with him. The swaying bulk towering high above him, and the ugly little eyes of the elephant watching his every move made Malbihn nervous.

Korak stepped into the Swede's tent to assure himself that Meriem was not hid there. As he disappeared from view Tantor, his eyes still fixed upon Malbihn, took a step nearer the man. An elephant's eyesight is none too good; but the great tusker evidently had harbored suspicions of this yellow-bearded white man from the first. Now he advanced his snake-like trunk toward the Swede, who shrank still deeper into his hammock.

The sensitive member felt and smelled back and forth along the body of the terrified Malbihn. Tantor uttered a low, rumbling sound. His little eyes blazed. At last he had recognized the creature who had killed his mate long years before. Tantor, the elephant, never forgets and never forgives. Malbihn saw in the demoniacal visage above him the murderous purpose of the beast. He shrieked aloud to Korak. "Help! Help! The devil is going to kill me!"

Korak ran from the tent just in time to see the enraged elephant's trunk encircle the beast's victim, and then hammock, canopy and man were swung high over Tantor's head. Korak leaped before the animal, commanding him to put down his prey unharmed; but as well might he have ordered the eternal river to reverse its course. Tantor wheeled around like a cat, hurled Malbihn to the earth and kneeled upon him with the quickness of a cat. Then he gored the prostrate thing through and through with his mighty tusks, trumpeting and roaring in his rage, and at last, convinced that no slightest spark of life remained in the crushed and lacerated flesh, he lifted the shapeless clay that had been Sven Malbihn far aloft and hurled the bloody mass, still entangled in canopy and hammock, over the *boma* and out into the jungle.

Korak stood looking sorrowfully on at the tragedy he gladly would have averted. He had no love for the Swede, in fact only hatred; but he would have preserved the man for the sake of the secret he possessed. Now that secret was gone forever unless The Sheik could be made to divulge it; but in that possibility Korak placed little faith.

The ape-man, as unafraid of the mighty Tantor as though he had not just witnessed his shocking murder of a human being, signalled the beast to approach and lift him to its head, and Tantor came as he was bid, docile as a kitten, and hoisted The Killer tenderly aloft.

From the safety of their hiding places in the jungle Malbihn's boys had witnessed the killing of their master, and now, with wide, frightened eyes, they saw the strange white warrior, mounted upon the head of his ferocious charger, disappear into the jungle at the point from which he had emerged upon their terrified vision.

# 25

THE SHEIK GLOWERED at the prisoner which his two men brought back to him from the North. He had sent the party after Abdul Kamak, and he was wroth that instead of his erstwhile lieutenant they had sent back a wounded and useless Englishman. Why had they not dispatched him where they had found him? He was some penniless beggar of a trader who had wandered from his own district and became lost. He was worthless. The Sheik scowled terribly upon him.

"Who are you?" he asked in French.

"I am the Hon. Morison Baynes of London," replied his prisoner.

The title sounded promising, and at once the wily old robber had visions of ransom. His intentions, if not his attitude toward the prisoner underwent a change—he would investigate further.

"What were you doing poaching in my country?" growled he.

"I was not aware that you owned Africa," replied the Hon. Morison. "I was searching for a young woman who had been abducted from the home of a friend. The abductor wounded me and I drifted down river in a canoe—I was on my way back to his camp when your men seized me."

"A young woman?" asked The Sheik. "Is that she?" and he pointed to his left over toward a clump of bushes near the stockade.

Baynes looked in the direction indicated and his eyes went wide, for there, sitting cross-legged upon the ground, her back toward them, was Meriem.

"Meriem!" he shouted, starting toward her; but one of his guards grasped his arm and jerked him back. The girl leaped to her feet and turned toward him as she heard her name.

205

"Morison!" she cried.

"Be still, and stay where you are," snapped The Sheik, and then to Baynes. "So you are the dog of a Christian who stole my daughter from me?"

"Your daughter?" ejaculated Baynes. "She is your daughter?"

"She is my daughter," growled the Arab, "and she is not for any unbeliever. You have earned death, Englishman, but if you can pay for your life I will give it to you."

Baynes eyes were still wide at the unexpected sight of Meriem here in the camp of the Arab when he had thought her in Hanson's power. What had happened? How had she escaped the Swede? Had the Arab taken her by force from him, or had she escaped and come voluntarily back to the protection of the man who called her "daughter"? He would have given much for a word with her. If she was safe here he might only harm her by antagonizing the Arab in an attempt to take her away and return her to her English friends. No longer did the Hon. Morison harbor thoughts of luring the girl to London.

"Well?" asked The Sheik.

"Oh," exclaimed Baynes; "I beg your pardon—I was thinking of something else. Why yes, of course, glad to pay, I'm sure. How much do you think I'm worth?"

The Sheik named a sum that was rather less exorbitant than the Hon. Morison had anticipated. The latter nodded his head in token of his entire willingness to pay. He would have promised a sum far beyond his resources just as readily, for he had no intention of paying anything—his one reason for seemingly to comply with The Sheik's demands was that the wait for the coming of the ransom money would give him the time and the opportunity to free Meriem if he found that she wished to be freed. The Arab's statement that he was her father naturally raised the question in the Hon. Morison's mind as to precisely what the girl's attitude toward escape might be. It seemed, of course, preposterous that this fair and beautiful young woman should prefer to remain in the filthy *douar* of an illiterate old Arab rather than return to the comforts, luxuries, and congenial associations of the hospitable African bungalow from which the Hon. Morison had tricked her. The man flushed at the thought of his duplicity which these recollections aroused—thoughts which were interrupted by The Sheik, who instructed the Hon. Morison to write a letter to the British consul at Algiers, dictating the exact phraseology of it with a fluency that indicated to his captive that this was not the first time the old rascal had had occasion to negotiate with English relatives for the ransom of a kinsman. Baynes demurred when he saw that the letter was addressed to the consul at Algiers, saying that it would require the better part of a year to get the money back to him; but The Sheik would not listen to Baynes' plan to send a messenger directly to the nearest coast town, and from there communicate with the nearest cable state, sending the Hon. Morison's request for funds straight to his own solicitors. No, The Sheik was cautious and wary. He knew his own plan had worked well in the past. In the other were too many untried elements. He was in no hurry for the money—he could wait a year, or two years if necessary; but it should not require over six months. He turned to one of the Arabs who had been standing behind him and gave the fellow instructions in relation to the prisoner.

Baynes could not understand the words, spoken in Arabic, but the jerk of the thumb toward him showed that he was the subject of conversation. The Arab addressed by The Sheik bowed to his master and beckoned Baynes to follow him. The Englishman looked toward The Sheik for confirmation. The latter nodded impatiently, and the Hon. Morison rose and followed his guide toward a native hut which lay close beside one of the outside goatskin tents. In the dark, stifling interior his guard led him, then stepped to the doorway and called to a couple of black boys squatting before their own huts. They came promptly and in accordance with the Arab's instructions bound Baynes' wrists and ankles securely. The Englishman objected strenuously; but as neither the blacks nor the Arab could understand a word he said his pleas were wasted. Having bound him they left the hut. The Hon. Morison lay for a long time contemplating the frightful future which awaited him during the long months which mush intervene before his friends learned of his predicament and could get succor to him. Now he hoped that they would send the ransom—he would gladly pay all that he was worth to be out of this hole. At first it had been his intention to cable his solicitors to send no money but to communicate with the British West African authorities and have an expedition sent to his aid.

His patrician nose wrinkled in disgust as his nostrils were assailed by the awful stench of the hut. The nasty grasses upon which he lay exuded the effluvium of sweaty bodies, of decayed animal matter and of offal. But worse was yet to come. He had lain in the uncomfortable position in which they had thrown him but for a few minutes when he became distinctly conscious of an acute itching sensation upon his hands, his neck and scalp. He wriggled to a sitting posture horrified and disgusted. The itching rapidly extended to other parts of his body—it was torture, and his hands were bound securely at his back!

He tugged and pulled at his bonds until he was exhausted; but not entirely without hope, for he was sure that he was working enough slack out of the knot to eventually permit of his withdrawing one of his hands. Night came. They brought him neither food nor drink. He wondered if they expected him to live on nothing for a year. The bites of the vermin grew less annoying though not less numerous. The Hon. Morison saw a ray of hope in this indication of future immunity through inoculation. He still worked weakly at his bonds, and then the rats came. If the vermin were disgusting the rats were terrifying. They scurried over his body, squealing and fighting. Finally one commenced to chew at one of his ears. With an oath, the Hon. Morison struggled to a sitting posture. The rats retreated. He worked his legs beneath him and came to his knees, and then, by superhuman effort, rose to his feet. There he stood, reeling drunkenly, dripping with cold sweat.

"God!" he muttered, "what have I done to deserve—" He paused. What had he done? He thought of the girl in another tent in that accursed village. He was getting his deserts. He set his jaws firmly with the realization. He would never complain again! At that moment he became aware of voices raised angrily in the goatskin tent close beside the hut in which he lay. One of them was a woman's. Could it be Meriem's? The language was probably Arabic—he could not understand a word of it; but the tones were hers.

He tried to think of some way of attracting her attention to his near presence. If she could remove his bonds they might escape together—if she wished to escape. That thought bothered him. He was not sure of her status in the village. If she were the petted child of the powerful Sheik then she would probably not care to escape. He must know, definitely.

At the bungalow he had often heard Meriem sing God Save the King, as My Dear accompanied her on the piano. Raising his voice he now hummed the tune. Immediately he heard Meriem's voice from the tent. She spoke rapidly.

"Good bye, Morison," she cried. "If God is good I shall be dead before morning, for if I still live I shall be worse than dead after tonight."

Then he heard an angry exclamation in a man's voice, followed by the sounds of a scuffle. Baynes went white with horror. He struggled frantically again with his bonds. They were giving. A moment later one hand was free. It was but the work of an instant then to loose the other. Stooping, he untied the rope from his ankles, then he straighted and started for the hut doorway bent on reaching Meriem's side. As he stepped out into the night the figure of a huge black rose and barred his progress.

When speed was required of him Korak depended upon no other muscles than his own, and so it was that the moment Tantor had landed him safely upon the same side of the river as lay the village of The Sheik, the ape-man deserted his bulky comrade and took to the trees in a rapid race toward the south and the spot where the Swede had told him Meriem might be. It was dark when he came to the palisade, strengthened considerably since the day that he had rescued Meriem from her pitiful life within its cruel confines. No longer did the giant tree spread its branches above the wooden rampart; but ordinary man-made defenses were scarce considered obstacles by Korak. Loosening the rope at his waist he tossed the noose over one of the sharpened posts that composed the palisade. A moment later his eyes were above the level of the obstacle taking in all within their range beyond. There was no one in sight close by, and Korak drew himself to the top and dropped lightly to the ground within the enclosure.

Then he commenced his stealthy search of the village. First toward the Arab tents he made his way, sniffing and listening. He passed behind them searching for some sign of Meriem. Not even the wild Arab curs heard his passage, so silently he went— a shadow passing through shadows. The odor of tobacco told him that the Arabs were smoking before their tents. The sound of laughter fell upon his ears, and then from the opposite side of the village came the notes of a once familiar tune: God Save the King. Korak halted in perplexity. Who might it be—the tones were those of a man. He recalled the young Englishman he had left on the river trail and who had disappeared before he returned. A moment later there came to him a woman's voice in reply—it was Meriem's, and The Killer, quickened into action, slunk rapidly in the direction of these two voices.

The evening meal over Meriem had gone to her pallet in the women's quarters of The Sheik's tent, a little corner screened off in the rear by a couple of priceless Persian rugs to form a partition. In these quarters she had dwelt with Mabunu alone, for The Sheik had no wives. Nor were conditions altered now after the years of her absence—she and Mabunu were alone in the women's quarters.

Presently The Sheik came and parted the rugs. He glared through the dim light of the interior.

"Meriem!" he called. "Come hither."

The girl arose and came into the front of the tent. There the light of a fire illuminated the interior. She saw Ali ben Kadin, The Sheik's half brother, squatted upon a rug, smoking. The Sheik was standing. The Sheik and Ali ben Kadin had had the same father, but Ali ben Kadin's mother had been a slave—a West Coast Negress. Ali ben Kadin was old and hideous and almost black. His nose and part of one cheek were eaten away by disease. He looked up and grinned as Meriem entered.

The Sheik jerked his thumb toward Ali ben Kadin and addressed Meriem.

"I am getting old," he said, "I shall not live much longer. Therefore I have given you to Ali ben Kadin, my brother."

That was all. Ali ben Kadin rose and came toward her. Meriem shrank back, horrified. The man seized her wrist.

"Come!" he commanded, and dragged her from The Sheik's tent and to his own.

After they had gone The Sheik chuckled. "When I send her north in a few months," he soliloquized, "they will know the reward for slaying the son of the sister of Amor ben Khatour."

And in Ali ben Kadin's tent Meriem pleaded and threatened, but all to no avail. The hideous old halfcaste spoke soft words at first, but when Meriem loosed upon him the vials of her horror and loathing he became enraged, and rushing upon her seized her in his arms. Twice she tore away from him, and in one of the intervals during which she managed to elude him she heard Baynes' voice humming the tune that she knew was meant for her ears. At her reply Ali ben Kadin rushed upon her once again. This time he dragged her back into the rear apartment of his tent where three Negresses looked up in stolid indifference to the tragedy being enacted before them.

As the Hon. Morison saw his way blocked by the huge frame of the giant black his disappointment and rage filled him with a bestial fury that transformed him into a savage beast. With an oath he leaped upon the man before him, the momentum of his body hurling the black to the ground. There they fought, the black to draw his knife, the white to choke the life from the black.

Baynes' fingers shut off the cry for help that the other would have been glad to voice; but presently the Negro succeeded in drawing his weapon and an instant later Baynes felt the sharp steel in his shoulder. Again and again the weapon fell. The white man removed one hand from its choking grip upon the black throat. He felt around upon the ground beside him searching for some missile, and at last his fingers touched a stone and closed upon it. Raising it above his antagonist's head the Hon. Morison drove home a terrific blow. Instantly the black relaxed—stunned. Twice more Baynes struck him. Then he leaped to his feet and ran for the goat skin tent from which he had heard the voice of Meriem in distress.

But before him was another. Naked but for his leopard skin and his loin cloth, Korak, The Killer, slunk into the shadows at the back of Ali ben Kadin's tent. The half-caste had just dragged Meriem into the rear chamber as Korak's sharp knife slit a six foot opening in the tent wall, and Korak, tall and mighty, sprang through upon the astonished visions of the inmates.

Meriem saw and recognized him the instant that he entered the apartment. Her heart leaped in pride and joy at the sight of the noble figure for which it had hungered for so long.

"Korak!" she cried.

"Meriem!" He uttered the single word as he hurled himself upon the astonished Ali ben Kadin. The three Negresses leaped from their sleeping mats, screaming. Meriem tried to prevent them from escaping; but before she could succeed the terrified blacks had darted through the hole in the tent wall made by Korak's knife, and were gone screaming through the village.

The Killer's fingers closed once upon the throat of the hideous Ali. Once his knife plunged into the putrid heart—and Ali ben Kadin lay dead upon the floor of his tent. Korak turned toward Meriem and at the same moment a bloody and disheveled apparition leaped into the apartment.

"Morison!" cried the girl.

Korak turned and looked at the new corner. He had been about to take Meriem in his arms, forgetful of all that might have transpired since last he had seen her. Then the coming of the young Englishman recalled the scene he had witnessed in the little clearing, and a wave of misery swept over the ape man.

Already from without came the sounds of the alarm that the three Negresses had started. Men were running toward the tent of Ali ben Kadin. There was no time to be lost.

"Quick!" cried Korak, turning toward Baynes, who had

scarce yet realized whether he was facing a friend or foe. "Take her to the palisade, following the rear of the tents. Here is my rope. With it you can scale the wall and make your escape."

"But you, Korak?" cried Meriem.

"I will remain," replied the ape-man. "I have business with The Sheik."

Meriem would have demurred, but The Killer seized them both by the shoulders and hustled them through the slit wall and out into the shadows beyond.

"Now run for it," he admonished, and turned to meet and hold those who were pouring into the tent from the front.

The ape-man fought well—fought as he had never fought before; but the odds were too great for victory, though he won that which he most craved—time for the Englishman to escape with Meriem. Then he was overwhelmed by numbers, and a few minutes later, bound and guarded, he was carried to The Sheik's tent.

The old men eyed him in silence for a long time. He was trying to fix in his own mind some form of torture that would gratify his rage and hatred toward this creature who twice had been the means of his losing possession of Meriem. The killing of Ali ben Kadin caused him little anger—always had he hated the hideous son of his father's hideous slave. The blow that this naked white warrior had once struck him added fuel to his rage. He could think of nothing adequate to the creature's offense.

And as he sat there looking upon Korak the silence was broken by the trumpeting of an elephant in the jungle beyond the palisade. A half smile touched Korak's lips. He turned his head a trifle in the direction from which the sound had come and then there broke from his lips, a low, weird call. One of the blacks guarding him struck him across the mouth with the haft of his spear; but none there knew the significance of his cry.

In the jungle Tantor cocked his ears as the sound of Korak's voice fell upon them. He approached the palisade and lifting his trunk above it, sniffed. Then he placed his head against the wooden logs and pushed; but the palisade was strong and only gave a little to the pleasure.

In The Sheik's tent The Sheik rose at last, and, pointing toward the bound captive, turned to one of his lieutenants.

"Burn him," he commanded. "At once. The stake is set."

The guard pushed Korak from The Sheik's presence. They dragged him to the open space in the center of the village, where a high stake was set in the ground. It had not been intended for burnings, but offered a convenient place to tie up refractory slaves that they might be beaten—ofttimes until death relieved their agonies.

To this stake they bound Korak. Then they brought brush and piled about him, and The Sheik came and stood by that he might watch the agonies of his victim. But Korak did not wince even after they had fetched a brand and the flames had shot up among the dry tinder.

Once, then, he raised his voice in the low call that he had given in The Sheik's tent, and now, from beyond the palisade, came again the trumpeting of an elephant.

Old Tantor had been pushing at the palisade in vain. The sound of Korak's voice calling him, and the scent of man, his enemy, filled the great beast with rage and resentment against the dumb barrier that held him back. He wheeled and shuffled back a dozen paces, then he turned, lifted his trunk and gave voice to a mighty roaring, trumpet-call of anger, lowered his head and charged like a huge battering ram of flesh and bone and muscle straight for the mighty barrier.

The palisade sagged and splintered to the impact, and through the breach rushed the infuriated bull. Korak heard the sounds that the others heard, and he interpreted them as the others did not. The flames were creeping closer to him when one of the blacks, hearing a noise behind him turned to see the enormous bulk of Tantor lumbering toward them. The man screamed and fled, and then the bull elephant was among them tossing Negroes and Arabs to right and left as he tore through the flames he feared to the side of the comrade he loved.

The Sheik, calling orders to his followers, ran to his tent to get his rifle. Tantor wrapped his trunk about the body of Korak and the stake to which it was bound, and tore it from the ground. The flames were searing his sensitive hide—sensitive for all its thickness—so that in his frenzy to both rescue his friend and escape the hated fire he had all but crushed the life from the ape-man.

Lifting his burden high above his head the giant beast wheeled and raced for the breach that he had just made in the palisade. The Sheik, rifle in hand, rushed from his tent directly into the path of the maddened brute. He raised his weapon and fired once, the bullet missed its mark, and Tantor was upon him, crushing him beneath those gigantic feet as he raced over him as you and I might crush out the life of an ant that chanced to be in our pathway.

And then, bearing his burden carefully, Tantor, the elephant, entered the blackness of the jungle.

# 26

MERIEM, DAZED BY the unexpected sight of Korak whom she had long given up as dead, permitted herself to be led away by Baynes. Among the tents he guided her safely to the palisade, and there, following Korak's instructions, the Englishman pitched a noose over the top of one of the upright logs that formed the barrier. With difficulty he reached the top and then lowered his hand to assist Meriem to his side.

"Come!" he whispered. "We must hurry." And then, as though she had awakened from a sleep, Meriem came to herself. Back there, fighting her enemies, alone, was Korak—her Korak. Her place was by his side, fighting with him and for him. She glanced up at Baynes.

"Go!" she called. "Make your way back to Bwana and bring help. My place is here. You can do no good remaining. Get away while you can and bring the Big Bwana back with you."

Silently the Hon. Morison Baynes slid to the ground inside the palisade to Meriem's side.

"It was only for you that I left him," he said, nodding toward the tents they had just left. "I knew that he could hold them longer than I and give you a chance to escape that I might not be able to have given you. It was I though who should have remained. I heard you call him Korak and so I know now who he is. He befriended you. I would have wronged you. No—don't interrupt. I'm going to tell you the truth now and let you know just what a beast I have been. I planned to take you to London, as you know; but I did not plan to marry you. Yes, shrink from me—I deserve it. I deserve your contempt and loathing; but I didn't know then what love was. Since I have learned that I have learned something else—what a cad and what a coward I have been all my life. I looked down upon those whom I considered

215

my social inferiors. I did not think you good enough to bear my name. Since Hanson tricked me and took you for himself I have been through hell; but it has made a man of me, though too late. Now I can come to you with an offer of honest love, which will realize the honor of having such as you share my name with me.''

For a moment Meriem was silent, buried in thought. Her first question seemed irrelevant.

''How did you happen to be in this village?'' she asked.

He told her all that had transpired since the black had told him of Hanson's duplicity.

''You say that you are a coward,'' she said, ''and yet you have done all this to save me? The courage that it must have taken to tell me the things that you told me but a moment since, while courage of a different sort, proves that you are no moral coward, and the other proves that you are not a physical coward. I could not love a coward.''

''You mean that you love me?'' he gasped in astonishment, taking a step toward her as though to gather her into his arms; but she placed her hand against him and pushed him gently away, as much as to say, not yet. What she did mean she scarcely knew. She thought that she loved him, of that there can be no question; nor did she think that love for this young Englishman was disloyalty to Korak, for her love for Korak was undiminished—the love of a sister for an indulgent brother. As they stood there for the moment of their conversation the sounds of tumult in the village subsided.

''They have killed him,'' whispered Meriem.

The statement brought Baynes to a realization of the cause of their return.

''Wait here,'' he said. ''I will go and see. If he is dead we can do him no good. If he lives I will do my best to free him.''

''We will go together,'' replied Meriem. ''Come!'' And she led the way back toward the tent in which they last had seen Korak. As they went they were often forced to throw themselves to the ground in the shadow of a tent or hut, for people were passing hurriedly to and fro now—the whole village was aroused and moving about. The return to the tent of Ali ben Kadin took much longer than had their swift flight to the palisade. Cautiously they crept to the slit that Korak's knife had made in the rear wall. Meriem peered within—the rear apartment was empty. She crawled through the aperture, Baynes at her heels, and then silently crossed the space to the rugs that partitioned the tent into two rooms. Parting the hangings Meriem looked into the front room. It, too, was deserted. She crossed to the door of the tent and looked out. Then she gave a little gasp of horror. Baynes at her shoulder looked past her to the sight that had startled her, and he, too, exclaimed; but his was an oath of anger.

A hundred feet away they saw Korak bound to a stake—the brush piled about him already alight. The Englishman pushed Meriem to one side and started to run for the doomed man. What he could do in the face of scores of hostile blacks and Arabs he did not stop to consider. At the same instant Tantor broke through the palisade and charged the group. In the face of the maddened beast the crowd turned and fled, carrying Baynes backward with them. In a moment it was all over, and the elephant had disappeared with his prize; but pandemonium reigned throughout the village. Men, women and children ran helter skelter for safety. Curs fled, yelping. The horses and camels and donkeys, terrorized by the trumpeting of the pachyderm, kicked and pulled at their tethers. A dozen or more broke loose, and it was the galloping of these past him that brought a sudden idea into Baynes' head. He turned to search for Meriem only to find her at his elbow.

"The horses!" he cried. "If we can get a couple of them!"

Filled with the idea Meriem led him to the far end of the village.

"Loosen two of them," she said, "and lead them back into the shadows behind those huts. I know where there are saddles. I will bring them and the bridles," and before he could stop her she was gone.

Baynes quickly untied two of the restive animals and led them to the point designated by Meriem. Here he waited impatiently for what seemed an hour; but was, in reality, but a few minutes. Then he saw the girl approaching beneath the burden of two saddles. Quickly they placed these upon the horses. They could see by the light of the torture fire that still burned that the blacks and Arabs were recovering from their panic. Men were running about gathering in the loose stock, and two or three were already leading their captives back to the end of the village where Meriem and Baynes were busy with the trappings of their mounts.

Now the girl flung herself into the saddle.

"Hurry!" she whispered. "We shall have to run for it. Ride through the gap that Tantor made," and as she saw Baynes swing his leg over the back of his horse, she shook the reins free over her mount's neck. With a lunge, the nervous beast leaped forward. The shortest path led straight through the center of the village, and this Meriem took. Baynes was close behind her, their horses running at full speed.

So sudden and impetuous was their dash for escape that it carried them half-way across the village before the surprised inhabitants were aware of what was happening. Then an Arab recognized them, and, with a cry of alarm, raised his rifle and fired. The shot was a signal for a volley, and amid the rattle of musketry Meriem and Baynes leaped their flying mounts through the breach in the palisade and were gone up the well-worn trail toward the north.

And Korak?

Tantor carried him deep into the jungle, nor paused until no sound from the distant village reached his keen ears. Then he laid his burden gently down. Korak struggled to free himself from his bonds, but even his great strength was unable to cope with the many strands of hard-knotted cord that bound him. While he lay there, working and resting by turns, the elephant stood guard above him, nor was there jungle enemy with the hardihood to tempt the sudden death that lay in that mighty bulk.

Dawn came, and still Korak was no nearer freedom than before. He commenced to believe that he should die there of thirst and starvation with plenty all about him, for he knew that Tantor could not unloose the knots that held him.

And while he struggled through the night with his bonds, Baynes and Meriem were riding rapidly northward along the river. The girl had assured Baynes that Korak was safe in the jungle with Tantor. It had not occurred to her that the ape-man might not be able to burst his bonds. Baynes had been wounded by a shot from the rifle of one of the Arabs, and the girl wanted to get him back to Bwana's home, where he could be properly cared for.

"Then," she said, "I shall get Bwana to come with me and search for Korak. He must come and live with us."

All night they rode, and the day was still young when they came suddenly upon a party hurrying southward. It was Bwana himself and his sleek, black warriors. At sight of Baynes the big Englishman's brows contracted in a scowl; but he waited to hear Meriem's story before giving vent to the long anger in his breast. When she had finished he seemed to have forgotten Baynes. His thoughts were occupied with another subject.

"You say that you found Korak?" he asked. "You really saw him?"

"Yes," replied Meriem; "as plainly as I see you, and I want you to come with me, Bwana, and help me find him again."

"Did you see him?" He turned toward the Hon. Morison.

"Yes, sir," replied Baynes; "very plainly."

"What sort of appearing man is he?" continued Bwana. "About how old, should you say?"

"I should say he was an Englishman, about my own age," replied Baynes; "though he might be older. He is remarkably muscled, and exceedingly tanned."

"His eyes and hair, did you notice them?" Bwana spoke rapidly, almost excitedly. It was Meriem who answered him.

"Korak's hair is black and his eyes are gray," she said.

Bwana turned to his headman.

"Take Miss Meriem and Mr. Baynes home," he said. "I am going into the jungle."

"Let me go with you, Bwana," cried Meriem. "You are going to search for Korak. Let me go, too."

Bwana turned sadly but firmly upon the girl.

"Your place," he said, "is beside the man you love."

Then he motioned to his head-man to take his horse and commence the return journey to the farm. Meriem slowly mounted the tired Arab that had brought her from the village of The Sheik. A litter was rigged for the now feverish Baynes, and the little cavalcade was soon slowly winding off along the river trail.

Bwana stood watching them until they were out of sight. Not once had Meriem turned her eyes backward. She rode with bowed head and drooping shoulders. Bwana sighed. He loved the little Arab girl as he might have loved an own daughter. He realized that Baynes had redeemed himself, and so he could interpose no objections now if Meriem really loved the man; but, somehow, some way, Bwana could not convince himself that the Hon. Morison was worthy of his little Meriem. Slowly he turned toward a nearby tree. Leaping upward he caught a lower branch and drew himself up among the branches. His movements were cat-like and agile. High into the tree he made his way and there commenced to divest himself of his clothing. From the game bag slung across one shoulder he drew a long strip of doe-skin, a neatly coiled rope, and a wicked looking knife. The doe-skin, he fashioned into a loin cloth, the rope he looped over one shoulder, and the knife he thrust into the belt formed by his gee string.

When he stood erect, his head thrown back and his great chest expanded a grim smile touched his lips for a moment. His nostrils dilated as he sniffed the jungle odors. His gray eyes narrowed. He crouched and leaped to a lower limb and was away through the trees toward the southeast, bearing away from the river. He moved swiftly, stopping only occasionally to raise his voice in a weird and piercing scream, and to listen for a moment after for a reply.

He had traveled thus for several hours when, ahead of him and a little to his left, he heard, far off in the jungle, a faint response—the cry of a bull ape answering his cry. His nerves tingled and his eyes lighted as the sound fell upon his ears. Again he voiced his hideous call, and sped forward in the new direction.

Korak, finally becoming convinced that he must die if he remained where he was, waiting for the succor that could not come, spoke to Tantor in the strange tongue that the great beast understood. He commanded the elephant to lift him and carry him toward the northeast. There, recently, Korak had seen both white men and black. If he could come upon one of the latter it would be a simple matter to command Tantor to capture the fellow, and then Korak could get him to release him from the stake. It was worth trying at least—better than lying there in the jungle until he died. As Tantor bore him along through the forest Korak called aloud now and then in the hope of attracting Akut's band of anthropoids, whose wanderings often brought them into their neighborhood. Akut, he thought, might possibly be able to negotiate the knots—he had done so upon that other occasion when the Russian had bound Korak years before; and Akut, to the south of him, heard his calls faintly, and came. There was another who heard them, too.

After Bwana had left his party, sending them back toward the farm, Meriem had ridden for a short distance with bowed head. What thoughts passed through that active brain who may say? Presently she seemed to come to a decision. She called the headman to her side.

"I am going back with Bwana," she announced.

The black shook his head. "No!" he announced. "Bwana says I take you home. So I take you home."

"You refuse to let me go?" asked the girl.

The black nodded, and fell to the rear where he might better watch her. Meriem half smiled. Presently her horse passed beneath a low-hanging branch, and the black headman found himself gazing at the girl's empty saddle. He ran forward to the tree into which she had disappeared. He could see nothing of her.

He called; but there was no response, unless it might have been a low, taunting laugh far to the right. He sent his men into the jungle to search for her; but they came back empty handed. After a while he resumed his march toward the farm, for Baynes, by this time, was delirious with fever.

Meriem raced straight back toward the point she imagined Tantor would make for—a point where she knew the elephants often gathered deep in the forest due east of The Sheik's village. She moved silently and swiftly. From her mind she had expunged all thoughts other than that she must reach Korak and bring him back with her. It was her place to do that. Then, too, had come the tantalizing fear that all might not be well with him. She upbraided herself for not thinking of that before—of letting her desire to get the wounded Morison back to the bungalow blind her to the possibilities of Korak's need for her. She had been traveling rapidly for several hours without rest when she heard ahead of her the familiar cry of a great ape calling to his kind.

She did not reply, only increased her speed until she almost flew. Now there came to her sensitive nostrils the scent of Tantor and she knew that she was on the right trail and close to him she sought. She did not call out because she wished to surprise him, and presently she did, breaking into sight of them as the great elephant shuffled ahead balancing the man and the heavy stake upon his head, holding them there with his upcurled trunk.

"Korak!" cried Meriem from the foliage above him.

Instantly the bull swung about, lowered his burden to the ground and, trumpeting savagely, prepared to defend his comrade. The ape-man, recognizing the girl's voice, felt a sudden lump in his throat.

"Meriem!" he called back to her.

Happily the girl clambered to the ground and ran forward to release Korak; but Tantor lowered his head ominously and trumpeted a warning.

"Go back! Go back!" cried Korak. "He will kill you."

Meriem paused. "Tantor!" she called to the huge brute. "Don't you remember me? I am little Meriem. I used to ride on your broad back;" but the bull only rumbled in his throat and shook his tusks in angry defiance. Then Korak tried to placate him. Tried to order him away, that the girl might approach and release him; but Tantor would not go. He saw in every human being other than Korak an enemy. He thought the girl bent upon harming his friend and he would take no chances.

For an hour the girl and the man tried to find some means whereby they might circumvent the beast's ill directed guardianship, but all to no avail; Tantor stood his ground in grim determination to let no one approach Korak.

Presently the man hit upon a scheme. "Pretend to go away," he called to the girl. "Keep down wind from us so that Tantor won't get your scent, then follow us. After a while I'll have him put me down, and find some pretext for sending him away. While he is gone you can slip up and cut my bonds—have you a knife?"

"Yes, I have a knife," she replied. "I'll go now—I think we may be able to fool him; but don't be too sure—Tantor invented cunning."

Korak smiled, for he knew that the girl was right. Presently she had disappeared. The elephant listened, and raised his trunk to catch her scent. Korak commanded him to raise him to his head once more and proceed upon their way. After a moment's hesitation he did as he was bid. It was then that Korak heard the distant call of an ape.

"Akut!" he thought. "Good! Tantor knew Akut well. He would let him approach." Raising his voice Korak replied to the call of the ape; but he let Tantor move off with him through the jungle; it would do no harm to try the other plan. They had come to a clearing and plainly Korak smelled water. Here was a good place and a good excuse. He ordered Tantor to lay him down, and go and fetch him water in his trunk. The big beast deposited him upon the grass in the center of the clearing, then he stood with cocked ears and attentive trunk, searching for the slightest indication of danger—there seemed to be none and he moved away in the direction of the little brook that Korak knew was some two or three hundred yards away. The ape-man could scarce help smiling as he thought how cleverly he had tricked his friend; but well as he knew Tantor he little guessed the guile of his cunning brain. The animal ambled off across the clearing and disappeared in the jungle beyond in the direction of the stream; but scarce had his great bulk been screened by the dense foliage than he wheeled about and came cautiously back to the edge of the clearing where he could see without being seen. Tantor, by nature, is suspicious. Now he still feared the return of the she Tarmangani who had attempted to attack his Korak. He would just stand there for a moment and assure himself that all was well before he continued on toward the water. Ah! It was well that he did! There she was now dropping from the branches of a tree across the clearing and running swiftly toward the ape-man. Tantor waited. He would let her reach Korak before he charged—that would ensure that she had no chance of escape. His little eyes blazed savagely. His tail was elevated stiffly. He could scarce restrain a desire to trumpet forth his rage to the world. Meriem was almost at Korak's side when Tantor saw the long knife in her hand, and then he broke forth from the jungle, bellowing horribly, and charged down upon the frail girl.

# 27

KORAK SCREAMED COMMANDS to his huge protector, in an effort to halt him; but all to no avail. Meriem raced toward the bordering trees with all the speed that lay in her swift, little feet; but Tantor, for all his huge bulk, drove down upon her with the rapidity of an express train.

Korak lay where he could see the whole frightful tragedy. The cold sweat broke out upon his body. His heart seemed to have stopped its beating. Meriem might reach the trees before Tantor overtook her, but even her agility would not carry her beyond the reach of that relentless trunk—she would be dragged down and tossed. Korak could picture the whole frightful scene. Then Tantor would follow her up, goring the frail, little body with his relentless tusks, or trampling it into an unrecognizable mass beneath his ponderous feet.

He was almost upon her now. Korak wanted to close his eyes, but could not. His throat was dry and parched. Never in all his savage existence had he suffered such blighting terror—never before had he known what terror meant. A dozen more strides and the brute would seize her. What was that? Korak's eyes started from their sockets. A strange figure had leaped from the tree the shade of which Meriem already had reached—leaped beyond the girl straight into the path of the charging elephant. It was a naked white giant. Across his shoulder a coil of rope was looped. In the band of his gee string was a hunting knife. Otherwise he was unarmed. With naked hands he faced the maddening Tantor. A sharp command broke from the stranger's lips—the great beast halted in his tracks—and Meriem swung herself upward into the tree to safety. Korak breathed a sigh of relief not unmixed with wonder. He fastened his eyes upon the

224

face of Meriem's deliverer and as recognition slowly filtered into his understanding they went wide in incredulity and surprise.

Tantor, still rumbling angrily, stood swaying to and fro close before the giant white man. Then the latter stepped straight beneath the upraised trunk and spoke a low word of command. The great beast ceased his muttering. The savage light died from his eyes, and as the stranger stepped forward toward Korak, Tantor trailed docilely at his heels.

Meriem was watching, too, and wondering. Suddenly the man turned toward her as though recollecting her presence after a moment of forgetfulness. "Come! Meriem," he called, and then she recognized him with a startled: "Bwana!" Quickly the girl dropped from the tree and ran to his side. Tantor cocked a questioning eye at the white giant, but receiving a warning word let Meriem approach. Together the two walked to where Korak lay, his eyes wide with wonder and filled with a pathetic appeal for forgiveness, and, mayhap, a glad thankfulness for the miracle that had brought these two of all others to his side.

"Jack!" cried the white giant, kneeling at the ape-man's side.

"Father!" came chokingly from The Killer's lips. "Thank God that it was you. No one else in all the jungle could have stopped Tantor."

Quickly the man cut the bonds that held Korak, and as the youth leaped to his feet and threw his arms about his father, the older man turned toward Meriem.

"I thought," he said, sternly, "that I told you to return to the farm."

Korak was looking at them wonderingly. In his heart was a great yearning to take the girl in his arms; but in time he remembered the other—the dapper young English gentleman—and that he was but a savage, uncouth ape-man.

Meriem looked up pleadingly into Bwana's eyes.

"You told me," she said, in a very small voice, "that my place was beside the man I loved," and she turned her eyes toward Korak all filled with the wonderful light that no other man had yet seen in them, and that none other ever would.

The Killer started toward her with outstretched arms; but suddenly he fell upon one knee before her, instead, and lifting her hand to his lips kissed it more reverently than he could have kissed the hand of his country's queen.

A rumble from Tantor brought the three, all jungle bred, to instant alertness. Tantor was looking toward the trees behind them, and as their eyes followed his gaze the head and shoulders of a great ape appeared amidst the foliage. For a moment the creature eyed them, and then from its throat rose a loud scream of recognition and of joy, and a moment later the beast had leaped to the ground, followed by a score of bulls like himself, and was waddling toward them, shouting in the primordial tongue of the anthropoid:

"Tarzan has returned! Tarzan, Lord of the Jungle!"

It was Akut, and instantly he commenced leaping and bounding about the trio, uttering hideous shrieks and mouthings that to any other human beings might have indicated the most ferocious rage; but these three knew that the king of the apes was doing homage to a king greater than himself. In his wake leaped his shaggy bulls, vying with one another as to which could spring the highest and which utter the most uncanny sounds.

Korak laid his hand affectionately upon his father's shoulder. "There is but one Tarzan," he said. "There can never be another."

Two days later the three dropped from the trees on the edge of the plain across which they could see the smoke rising from the bungalow and the cook house chimneys. Tarzan of the Apes had regained his civilized clothing from the tree where he had hidden it, and as Korak refused to enter the presence of his mother in the savage half-raiment that he had worn so long and as Meriem would not leave him, for fear, as she explained, that he would change his mind and run off into the jungle again, the father went on ahead to the bungalow for horses and clothes.

My Dear met him at the gate, her eyes filled with questioning and sorrow, for she saw that Meriem was not with him.

"Where is she?" she asked, her voice trembling. "Muviri told me that she disobeyed your instructions and ran off into the jungle after you had left them. Oh, John, I cannot bear to lose her, too!" And Lady Greystoke broke down and wept, as she pillowed her head upon the broad breast where so often before she had found comfort in the great tragedies of her life.

Lord Greystoke raised her head and looked down into her eyes, his own smiling and filled with the light of happiness.

"What is it, John?" she cried. "You have good news—do not keep me waiting for it."

"I want to be quite sure that you can stand hearing the best news that ever came to either of us," he said.

"Joy never kills," she cried. "You have found—her?" She could not bring herself to hope for the impossible.

"Yes, Jane," he said, and his voice was husky with emotion; "I have found her, and—*him*!"

"Where is he? Where are they?" she demanded.

"Out there at the edge of the jungle. He wouldn't come to you in his savage leopard skin and his nakedness—he sent me to fetch him civilized clothing."

She clapped her hands in ecstasy, and turned to run toward the bungalow. "Wait!" she cried over her shoulder. "I have all his little suits—I have saved them all. I will bring one to you."

Tarzan laughed and called to her to stop.

"The only clothing on the place that will fit him," he said, "is mine—if it isn't too small for him—your little boy has grown, Jane."

She laughed, too; she felt like laughing at everything, or at nothing. The world was all love and happiness and joy once more—the world that had been shrouded in the gloom of her great sorrow for so many years. So great was her joy that for the moment she forgot the sad message that awaited Meriem. She called to Tarzan after he had ridden away to prepare her for it, but he did not hear and rode on without knowing himself what the event was to which his wife referred.

And so, an hour later, Korak, The Killer, rode home to his mother—the mother whose image had never faded in his boyish heart—and found in her arms and her eyes the love and forgiveness that he plead for.

And then the mother turned toward Meriem, an expression of pitying sorrow erasing the happiness from her eyes.

"My little girl," she said, "in the midst of our happiness a great sorrow awaits you—Mr. Baynes did not survive his wound."

The expression of sorrow in Meriem's eyes expressed only what she sincerely felt; but it was not the sorrow of a woman bereft of her best beloved.

"I am sorry," she said, quite simply. "He would have done me a great wrong; but he amply atoned before he died. Once I thought that I loved him. At first it was only fascination for a type that was new to me—then it was respect for a brave man who had the moral courage to admit a sin and the physical courage to face death to right the wrong he had committed. But it was not love. I did not know what love was until I knew that Korak lived," and she turned toward The Killer with a smile.

Lady Greystoke looked quickly up into the eyes of her son—the son who one day would be Lord Greystoke. No thought of the difference in the stations of the girl and her boy entered her mind. To her Meriem was fit for a king. She only wanted to know that Jack loved the little Arab waif. The look in his eyes answered the question in her heart, and she threw her arms about them both and kissed them each a dozen times.

"Now," she cried, "I shall really have a daughter!"

It was several weary marches to the nearest mission; but they only waited at the farm a few days for rest and preparation for the great event before setting out upon the journey, and after the marriage ceremony had been performed they kept on to the coast to take passage for England. Those days were the most wonderful of Meriem's life. She had not dreamed even vaguely of the marvels that civilization held in store for her. The great ocean and the commodious steamship filled her with awe. The noise, and bustle and confusion of the English railway station frightened her.

"If there was a good-sized tree at hand," she confided to Korak, "I know that I should run to the very top of it in terror of my life."

"And make faces and throw twigs at the engine?" he laughed back.

"Poor old Numa," sighed the girl. "What will he do without us?"

"Oh, there are others to tease him, my little Mangani," assured Korak.

The Greystoke town house quite took Meriem's breath away; but when strangers were about none might guess that she had not been to the manner born.

They had been home but a week when Lord Greystoke received a message from his friend of many years, D'Arnot.

It was in the form of a letter of introduction brought by one General Armand Jacot. Lord Greystoke recalled the name, as who familiar with modern French history would not, for Jacot was in reality the Prince de Cadrenet—that intense republican who refused to use, even by courtesy, a title that had belonged to his family for four hundred years.

"There is no place for princes in a republic," he was wont to say.

Lord Greystoke received the hawk-nosed, gray mustached soldier in his library, and after a dozen words the two men had formed a mutual esteem that was to endure through life.

"I have come to you," explained General Jacot, "because

our dear Admiral tells me that there is no one in all the world who is more intimately acquainted with Central Africa than you.

"Let me tell you my story from the beginning. Many years ago my little daughter was stolen, presumably by Arabs, while I was serving with the Foreign Legion in Algeria. We did all that love and money and even government resources could do to discover her; but all to no avail. Her picture was published in the leading papers of every large city in the world, yet never did we find a man or woman who ever had seen her since the day she mysteriously disappeared.

"A week since there came to me in Paris a swarthy Arab, who called himself Abdul Kamak. He said that he had found my daughter and could lead me to her. I took him at once to Admiral d'Arnot, whom I knew had traveled some in Central Africa. The man's story led the Admiral to believe that the place where the white girl the Arab supposed to be my daughter was held in captivity was not far from your African estates, and he advised that I come at once and call upon you—that you would know if such a girl were in your neighborhood."

"What proof did the Arab bring that she was your daughter?" asked Lord Greystoke.

"None," replied the other. "That is why we thought best to consult you before organizing an expedition. The fellow had only an old photograph of her on the back of which was pasted a newspaper cutting describing her and offering a reward. We feared that having found this somewhere it had aroused his cupidity and led him to believe that in some way he could obtain the reward, possibly by foisting upon us a white girl on the chance that so many years had elapsed that we would not be able to recognize an imposter as such."

"Have you the photograph with you?" asked Lord Greystoke.

The General drew an envelope from his pocket, took a yellowed photograph from it and handed it to the Englishman.

Tears dimmed the old warrior's eyes as they fell again upon the pictured features of his lost daughter.

Lord Greystoke examined the photograph for a moment. A queer expression entered his eyes. He touched a bell at his elbow, and an instant later a footman entered.

"Ask my son's wife if she will be so good as to come to the library," he directed.

The two men sat in silence. General Jacot was too well bred to show in any way the chagrin and disappointment he felt in the summary manner in which Lord Greystoke had dismissed the subject of his call. As soon as the young lady had come and he had been presented he would make his departure. A moment later Meriem entered.

Lord Greystoke and General Jacot rose and faced her. The Englishman spoke no word of introduction—he wanted to mark the effect of the first sight of the girl's face on the Frenchman, for he had a theory—a heaven-born theory that had leaped into his mind the moment his eyes had rested on the baby face of Jeanne Jacot.

General Jacot took one look at Meriem, then he turned toward Lord Greystoke.

"How long have you known it?" he asked, a trifle accusingly.

"Since you showed me that photograph a moment ago," replied the Englishman.

"It is she," said Jacot, shaking with suppressed emotion; "but she does not recognize me—of course she could not." Then he turned to Meriem. "My child," he said, "I am your—"

But she interrupted him with a quick, glad cry, as she ran toward him with outstretched arms.

"I know you! I know you!" she cried. "Oh, now I remember," and the old man folded her in his arms.

Jack Clayton and his mother were summoned, and when the story had been told them they were only glad that little Meriem had found a father and a mother.

"And really you didn't marry an Arab waif after all," said Meriem. "Isn't it fine!"

"You are fine," replied The Killer. "I married my little Meriem, and I don't care, for my part, whether she is an Arab, or just a little Tarmangani."

"She is neither, my son," said General Armand Jacot. "She is a princess in her own right."

# A NOTE TO ERB ENTHUSIASTS

For readers interested in learning more about the life and work of Edgar Rice Burroughs, Del Rey includes the following list of ERB fan clubs and their magazines. Write to the address below for information on memberships and subscriptions.

*British Edgar Rice Burroughs Society*
77 Pembroke Road
Seven Kings
Ilford, Essex
IG3 8PQ England

*Burroughs Bibliophiles*
Burroughs Memorial Collection
University of Louisville
Louisville, Kentucky 40292

*Erbania*
8001 Fernview Lane
Tampa, Florida 33615

*ERB Collector*
7315 Livingston Road
Oxon Hill, Maryland 20745

*ERB-Fan*
Eschenweg 5
8070 Ingolstadt
West Germany

*ERB News Dateline*
1990 Pine Grove Drive
Jenison, Michigan 49428

*Tarzine*
914 Country Club Drive
Midland, Texas 79701

# ABOUT
# EDGAR RICE BURROUGHS

Edgar Rice Burroughs is one of the world's most popular authors. With no previous experience as an author, he wrote and sold his first novel—*A Princess of Mars*—in 1912. In the ensuing thirty-eight years, until his death in 1950, Burroughs wrote 91 books and a host of short stories and articles. Although best known as the creator of the classic *Tarzan of the Apes* and *John Carter of Mars*, his restless imagination knew few bounds. Burroughs' prolific pen ranged from the American West to primitive Africa and on to romantic adventure on the moon, the planets, and even beyond the farthest star.

No one knows how many copies of ERB books have been published throughout the world. It is conservative to say, however, that of the translations into 32 known languages, including Braille, the number must run into the hundreds of millions. When one considers the additional world-wide following of the Tarzan newspaper feature, radio programs, comic magazines, motion pictures and television, Burroughs must have been known and loved by literally a thousand million or more.